Double-Cross My Heart

Brandon Hill

PARANORMAL LEGENDS
A Mythical Legends Publishing Imprint

Double-Cross My Heart is a work of fiction. The characters, incidents, and dialogs are products of the author's imagination and are not to be construed as real. Any resemblance to actual events or persons, living or dead, is entirely coincidental.

A Paranormal Legends Printing
Paperback Edition

Double-Cross My Heart

Brandon Hill

BRANDON HILL

Chapter One

"This is hardly meditation," I heard Aiko say. I recognized her voice and her scent. "Hiding in a dark corner, with a bed sheet over your head and your knees folded up to your chest cannot be conducive to clearing your mind."

She began to remove the makeshift canopy from atop my head. Quickly, I grabbed it and pulled it back to its former position. I hadn't exactly been hiding. There was no way I could do that, not in the Lair, at least. This was my family's home. Anyone could have found me with laughable ease; the same as my sensei had. Aiko's presence alone was proof that they knew I was here.

It was then that I realized how I'd reacted when Aiko had removed the sheet. I reddened, chagrined at how childish it must have looked and was struck with a mental image of Derek teasing me. He would perhaps have done this and more, had he seen it, maybe even address me by that infuriating title of "old lady."

Derek . . .

I gave a brief shudder at the thought of him, fingering the diamond encrusted heart shape of my tiny engagement ring. The sensation felt more like the ghost of pain, rather than the joy it was supposed to bring.

I caught Aiko's orange spice scent, heard her light, catlike footsteps, and knew her thoughts long before she'd come into this unused room. Save Father, her mind was the most difficult of my family for me to read, but it had not always been so. Before her trauma, before the Others took her and tormented her, her heart had been quite easy to understand in spite of her natural rigidity and sternness. Now, she was guarded, cold, and for lack of a better word, broken. She had only talked to Father about what happened to her at the hands of Lothos, and only after being faced with the loss of her position as chief thaumaturgist. Still, even after three years of counseling and therapy, she had not fully recovered from those two months in captivity, and probably never would. Even now, she was not exactly dressed for company. Barely in her panties and a white tank top undershirt, I gathered she'd merely used her Jewel to fold space into this room. Her hair was slightly unkempt, and she was without the makeup with which she was usually so fastidious.

My recent experience might have done this to me as well had it not been for Derek. I wanted so badly to speak to her about it, but not here. Perhaps we would at last have common ground; perhaps I would be able to help her with the effects of her trauma. However, there was no way I could do so here, or like this, not while having problems of my own.

"Your sense of humor leaves a lot to be desired, sensei," I told her. Truth be told, she never had much of a sense of humor to begin with, and even less in recent years.

"I wasn't joking," Aiko said flatly.

"Really, now? I murmured with sarcasm sharp between our minds. "I'd never have guessed."

"I know you preferred Roland to come." Aiko sighed as she removed the bed sheet from my head a second time. This time, I did not attempt to put it back on, but rather fussed with my curls, which tended to become unkempt rather easily because of their volume. "But he sent me in here to talk with you first. He thought you'd react better with me."

I opened my mouth to speak, indignant at first. Though I'd evolved a newfound understanding of Aiko's condition, my sensei had all the compassion of a brick! How could Roland have made such an unabashedly stupid decision?

But then I realized something that surprised me. I hadn't understood it at first, but this plan actually made sense. I noticed something unbelievable. For the first time in years, I could touch Aiko's mind. It was actually open! I could see that she very much wanted to talk.

"You're in pain, Eri-chan," Aiko said as she kneeled beside me and used her familiar name for me. She rarely did now.

"So are you," I said, catching the landscape of her mind, with echoes of torment from areas she kept hidden from me. I wanted so badly to commiserate with her, to help her know that she wasn't alone, but instead I only felt ashamed. I felt Aiko's mental frown confirming my gaffe. Why would I put this back on her?

Shit, was the only word that came to mind.

"I've been in pain for a long time," she said in a surprisingly even voice. Even more surprising was how she'd seemed to pay my words no mind. She had accepted her pain. It was now merely a part of her. She'd integrated it into her psyche. She'd even expected me to lash out like I had. "But this is about you, isn't it?"

"Yes, it is," I admitted. I sent my feelings of contrition to Aiko, and felt her acceptance; not a word needed to pass between us for this. Then I took a deep breath, more to steady myself than anything else.

"I learned something . . . disturbing," I said.

"Disturbing, how?" Aiko asked.

"This mission, it . . ." I swallowed, feeling a tremble of terror begin somewhere deep within my nerves. I forced myself to become steady. My ordeal was over. Derek and his clan were safe. I had won. My mission had been accomplished. There was no need to be afraid anymore. If I was lucky, I'd never have to face him again. "It became more . . . complicated than I thought it'd be."

Aiko nodded, her gaze falling to my left hand. "I'm guessing this is part of your . . . complication?" she said as she handled my ring between her thumb and index finger.

"A small part, but not what I wanted to say," I said and decided to no longer mince words. "Lothos got involved. Personally."

Aiko froze. Her eyes seemed to flash a brighter shade of

crimson as they widened. I saw a tremor shoot through her, and I watched as she gritted her teeth against her extending fangs. The flare of rage in her heart was like a jab to my sternum, but she mastered it, calming down only moments after flaring up. The rage was not aimed at me, but at Lothos himself and not solely because of me.

"Did he . . . hurt you?"

Aiko's words were careful; her thoughts again sealed up and guarded, though I felt a residual echo of shame that surrounded the now closed door that was her mind.

"Not physically," I said, then allowed her to see what happened.

I felt the storm of her shock like a peal of thunder. Had it been a true sound, we would have been deafened by its intrusion upon the silence of the room. It took a while for Aiko to steady herself from what I had showed her; it had been a long time since I'd seen her thrown off-balance like this. She muttered some phrase in Japanese that I couldn't catch, swallowed, and breathed in deeply.

"You should go to the Master," she said with a renewed sense of urgency. "He has been wanting to speak with you."

"I know." My voice was small. God, I knew that Father wanted to talk. He'd been waiting for me with patience for three nights. He needed to not only be debriefed, but I had to tell him about what I'd learned. My mind was an open book to him, the same as all of us, his children both by direct siring and through his lieutenants. He probably knew already what had shaken me so. I wanted so badly to speak to him of this, to ease my confusion, for him to dispel the lies and deceit that Lothos had tried to plant into my mind, disguised as truth, and allay my fears. Coward that I am, as soon as I made certain that Derek's people were safe, I left him alone when he probably needed me the most! Now the ring on my finger felt more like a weight of shame: a reminder of a betrayal rather than the promise of my deepest longing fulfilled.

I left Derek alone . . . left him to go hide in an empty

guest room in the very place Father could find me . . . but I was too afraid to go and talk to him!

"I'm a bloody coward," I said. "And still a child."

"Eri-chan, don't you ever say that about yourself again!" Aiko snapped, the force of her words startling me out of my melancholy. She grasped me by my shoulders and made me look straight into her eyes. "No child could ever face Lothos . . . and I saw your memories. You were far stronger than I ever was. You dishonor yourself to think otherwise."

I wiped at the tears that began to pool at the edges of my eyes. Broken as she was, my sensei's convictions were abundantly clear. She saw me as few others did. Of course, she had trained me since the time that I was as much a child in mind as I was -and still am- in body.

I stood and tossed the sheet away from me. If one as torn apart inside as Aiko could see the strength within me where I was unable, then I believed I owed it to her to display that strength as well, whether it was truly there or not. I looked at my sensei as she stood by my side, and swore that I saw her give a faint smile. It was such a small thing, but it gave me hope for her. Someday, I was certain she would recover. Her concern for me was certainly proof of that.

I cast about with my mind for Father and found him: the only mind in the Lair whose gates were always closed except for the unique timbre of his presence. He was in his sitting room, as I expected, most likely waiting for me. "I'm going to see Father," I said.

***

I saw Roland standing outside the door to the sitting room. Aiko, once I had assured her that I would be all right, had gone to her usual haunt at the training grounds. I met him alone in the hallway. At once, I knew that he was why she hadn't followed me. The two of them had had a rather complicated relationship, made only more strained in recent years since Aiko's ordeal. The two of them spent most of the time avoiding each other, and then Roland would suddenly vanish, only for an unlucky few to catch the timbre of their minds somewhere in the Lair as they broadcast their indulgences with each other in a manner that would take any human beyond exhaustion. I came to the conclusion that this was a coping mechanism that Aiko had developed, but I never questioned her about such a private matter. I was, of course, in no position to play psychiatrist to my sensei.

One passing glance at Roland's thoughts was enough for me to know that like Father, he had been waiting for me and was about as worried as any mother for her daughter. Of course, I was, in a way, his daughter as well.

His mirrored shades, which he wore indoors or outdoors were uncharacteristically stowed away in the breast pocket of his gray turtleneck shirt. His eyes, which most people hardly ever saw, were soft, gentle, and strikingly beautiful for a man, but he concealed them with his shades as he tended to keep the company of humans outside our circle of knowledge. He could have easily used his Jewel to disguise their crimson, catlike appearance as his original human blue with round pupils, but instead, he chose to use the shades, explaining, rather pretentiously, that it "added to his mystique."

"Had you been waiting for me this whole time?" I asked as I quickened my pace. My joy at seeing Roland should have drawn his attention instantly, but he had been somewhat distracted, lost in his own thoughts, and so he had never sensed my approach. I saw him turn towards me, a bit startled by my voice, and then break into a wide smile. He lowered himself to my level as I ran into his arms and hugged him.

In the days of my true childhood, Father had been more than generous with his attention and time, but as the leader of our clan, he had many responsibilities. Roland had always been like a second father to me, taking care of me whenever Father's duties took him abroad. He told me bedtime stories, took charge of my schooling, and played with me when no one else had time.

"Poppet! I was right worried about you," he said as I kissed his cheek. "I thought something might've happened to you during the . . . Crikey, but that's new!"

When I noticed that his gaze was set upon my ring, I stifled a laugh. It wasn't as if I never wore jewelry; how could something so small be so conspicuous? I knew of few in our clan aside from Amelia who had the talent of psychometry, so he could not have detected it by Derek's emotions inscribed upon it. But then again, this was Roland. He had an eye for jewelry, as he always had some paramour that he tried to impress.

"So who's the lucky man?" He asked as he turned my offered finger over gently, gazing at the ring's shape and hues of reflected light as the hallway lights struck its tiny stones.

"His name is Derek," I said. "He's the . . . well, they don't really have a leader, but if they did, he'd be it. They trust him."

"Sounds like you're speaking of a Vagabond."

"That's because he is a Vagabond." I supposed Father had kept him in the dark about my particular mission.

Roland fixed me with a curious gaze. "So you're going to marry a . . . wait. How could he afford a ring like this? Those are flawless pink diamonds encrusted in a 24 karat gold frame. Pretty high-class for a bum."

"They're not bums!" I protested. "They're transients by choice."

"Ah. Hobos, then?"

Roland laughed as I fumed, though I knew he was only teasing. Vagabonds were hardly "bums." They could acquire money, and great amounts of it, as easily as any of our clan could, though it sometimes required resorting to less than scrupulous means. Long ago, there had been a devastating schism in both our ranks and those of Lothos. Certain members of our kind, disillusioned by our war, chose to take no sides. Vagabonds were their descendants. Their clan sizes ranged from individuals to close-knit "family" groups of sire and fledglings to small nomadic tribes, all scattered across the world, with no allegiance to anyone but themselves. They generally got along with each other, but shied away from us. Our respective clans, in turn, tended to stay out of their way unless they interfered with us, became a threat to our secrecy, or asked for help. The latter was far more likely these days, as Lothos and his minions occasionally used them for target practice, or hounded them if they took in defectors from his clan. Otherwise, they followed their own rules.

"Well, hobo or not, I know you think the world of him," Roland said, and his face softened. "And of course, he thinks the world of you, considering the ring. All things considered, I hope he makes you happy."

"I know he will," I said, not bothering to hide my feelings. Idly, I played with the ring and smiled, then felt the sting of shame over how I had to leave Derek. It felt forcibly thrust upon me as a reminder to what was soon to come. Roland, however, did not seem to catch that part of my thoughts. Instead, he interjected with both an unexpected and rather inappropriate question.

"So, ah . . . have you two . . . ?"

"That's private!" I snapped. Instantly, I submerged those intimate memories in a well so deep inside my mind that I was certain that Roland would not be able to detect them. "And you asked it in front of Father's sitting room! What the bloody hell?"

"Sorry, sorry," Roland said, making emphatic placating gestures. "I got a bit carried away, is all." But you know the Master will probably look even deeper than that."

I couldn't challenge that; Roland and I both knew Father well enough to know that nothing remained hidden from him if he chose to look into the events of the past. Surprisingly, I was more comfortable with this prospect than I was with Roland doing the same. "I know," was all I could say, but not without some irritation. This, however, was the least of my worries. Father was not overprotective, but he could be intrusive. It was never without reason, but it had the disobliging habit of involving the things you most wanted to remain unseen. And so I sighed, steeling myself for what lay ahead. Father was just inside those doors, and though all I could ever feel from him was that powerful presence, I was certain he knew that I was here.

"He's waiting," I told Roland as I faced the door. "I'll see you after it's done."

"You'll probably want to see Derek first," Roland said. Then he held his hands up defensively at the withering glare I gave in return. "I didn't pry, poppet," he explained in a gentle voice. "That was something you've been thinking about since I saw you. I couldn't help but pick it up."

I frowned, letting go of my emotions. Again, Roland had been right. He was more sensitive to my feelings than most and was always my choice for moral support . . . at least since Aiko's misfortune. I knew that I owed Derek an explanation. I could only imagine how cross he would be with me. My frown slowly gave way to a wan smile, and I hugged Roland's waist.

"Thank you," I said, as I felt his hand stroke the curls atop my head.

"As you said, he's waiting," Roland reminded me.

I nodded, and gave him the mental equivalent of a kiss before knocking on the door.

***

Father's spacious, high-ceilinged sitting room was also his study. Near the entrance door and beside a fireplace set into the nearby wall to the right were several high-backed leather couches that surrounded a coffee table. A rounded cherry wood table surrounded by lacquered wooden chairs sat in the middle of the room and was used for meetings with his chief Lieutenants. Shelves upon shelves of books lined every wall of the elongated, rectangular room, broken only by alcoves where the windows were and the door to his chambers on the opposite side of the wall where the fireplace was built. Standing lamps were set at even intervals beside the shelves. Father had them all switched off at the moment, opting instead for the full moon's light through the open windows for illumination. This was too dim for humans; but for our kind, it was more than adequate.

I sat across from Father at the coffee table. A carafe was set between us, and we each held a wine glass of its former contents. The blood was surprisingly fresh and warm, and almost as satisfying as that which had come from a pure source. Father had obviously made preparations prior to my arrival.

"I hope you don't think I'm angry," Father began. His brow furrowed ever so slightly as he brought the glass to his lips. Its contents left a stain that stood out upon his ivory skin like dye on a snow drift. "I'm just concerned. To say I was surprised that you came home, and then hid from me for the last three nights . . . well, I'm certain you would be confused as well."

"I'm sorry I didn't report to you, Father." Despite the fact that I had not fed in three days, I'd barely taken a sip out of my glass. I was quite hungry, but still too nervous to feed. "Did you send an envoy?"

"I went to the site personally," Father said.

"Personally?" I sat forward in my seat, almost spilling the contents of my glass. Not only had Father rarely done this unless it was a matter of extreme importance, but I couldn't imagine how his arrival would have affected the vagabonds. They'd been distrustful even of me -more so once they learned who I truly was. I had to earn their respect by inches. How did they respond to Father?

"I spoke with Derek most of the time," Father said, answering my thoughts.

I smiled with relief. "Then he's awake?"

Father nodded. "He'd only just woken up when I arrived. I learned about you two quickly enough. His mind is quite well-guarded for a Vagabond, though. I never expected that."

"Was he angry?" I asked after a very uncomfortable silence passed between us. I suspected that he had been waiting for me to ask it.

"Angry that you'd vanished?" Father wasn't being accusatory; nevertheless, I felt as if his words were passing a death sentence. I bit my lower lip, unable to hide my shame, would that I could. I replied only with a vague nod.

"No, I wouldn't say that he was angry," Father said after slipping into a momentary thoughtful state. "But he was confused. I know you left him a letter, but I think he was expecting, or rather, hoping that someone from our clan would come and fill him in on what happened with you." He grinned, and I heard him chuckle. "I just don't think he expected me to show up, of all people."

I couldn't help but laugh at this myself. "So, what did you pry from his mind?"

"Pry?" Father fixed me with a blank stare.

"You didn't interrogate him?" I was surprised, to say the least.

"There was no reason to," Father said. "Derek was very forthcoming. He told me everything he could about what happened during the past month involving your mission . . . and involving you and him. Besides, it would be disrespectful to tear into the mind of my future son-in-law, wouldn't it?" He gestured toward my left hand and smiled in his gentle way: the way that made me love him even more. "That's a beautiful ring he gave you by the way."

"Thank you," I said, feeling my face grow somewhat warm. I wanted to use that comment to derail the conversation, to distract Father somehow, but I knew it would be useless. He was too meticulous for that. And besides, he would immediately know my intent, so I didn't bother. "So he told you everything?"

"Everything he felt comfortable giving," Father replied. "There were some details he held back, but I didn't dig any deeper. He told me that you would be able to fill in the holes . . . that it felt right that you should."

"He would say that," I murmured, turning away from Father. I took a deeper draft from my glass, nearly emptying it. The rush of pleasure from its contents gave me a bit more courage; nevertheless, I swallowed against my annoyingly tenacious remnant of fear. "And he's right. There are . . . things I know that he doesn't. Things . . . that I was told."

"Told by whom?" Father asked.

I could no more hold back my tears than I could hold back my thirst when it would come. I drew in a ragged breath and bit my lower lip until even my retracted fangs threatened to pierce the skin. Though I could not detect even a trace of emotion from his mind, I saw my Father's expression become increasingly less placid as he observed me. He leaned forward and placed his half-full glass upon the coffee table as his hands gripped the arms of his chair.

"Elisa . . . who was it?" I heard him say, even more insistent.

I could bear it no longer.

"Lothos."

Only the senses of my kind can pick up movements made at preternatural speed. I saw Father rise from his chair and move forward, leaping over the coffee table and coming to rest on his knees before me, faster than any human could detect.

"Child, what did he tell you?" He said. God, I had never seen him this way, nor heard him sound so alarmed! Through the blurriness of my tears, I could see how his normally gentle eyes were wide, and his slitted pupils dilated. As Aiko had been when she saw what was in my mind, his fangs were extended, and his face was a mask of pleading and uncertainty. If I hadn't known better, I would have said that he was afraid.

"Father . . ." I said as he took my hands into his own. "Aren't you looking into my mind? Don't you see it?"

"Your thoughts are a jumble," Father said. His face was drawn as he shook his head, "and they're suffused with so much emotion. You, me, Derek, Lothos . . . And I'm afraid that my own emotions are resonating with yours. This makes it difficult to see the whole story."

I had never heard of this happening before. It must have indeed been a very rare situation. I had never known just how deep Father's understanding of my mind went, but this was unmistakable. He had just admitted to being unable to read my mind. Despite my initial amazement, I tried to clear my thoughts, to push away as much of the emotional static as I could, and give Father as vivid a picture as possible. I knew that clearing this path would open him up to everything that I experienced, even things that I held private, but I could not afford to be embarrassed by more private details. I wanted him to know how it all came together, and what had happened between me and Lothos. Perhaps I would regret it, but even I had to know what this meant. I was terrified, but at the same time, I was determined.

"It really started in the beginning, when you sent me on the mission," I said as I closed my eyes and opened myself to Father's unknowable mind. "It's . . . complicated . . . a lot more so than you could believe. I don't want to do this, Father, but I need to show you the whole story."

I felt Father's hands touch my temples and guide me towards him. I leaned forward and felt his forehead gently touch my own. For a moment -the blink of an eye, actually, I was privy to the unfathomable depth of his mind. Ten thousand years of experiences: love, joy, rage, pain, tears, gladness . . . I was breathless with astonishment, despite the woefully ephemeral experience. All the memories flashed by my mind's eye with incalculable brevity. I could hold on to nothing -and then a great door shut upon them. I had become aware only of Father's presence once again and only as one is aware of an unseen person in the same room. He became a completely passive observer as my mind opened the stage of events that began one month ago.

Chapter Two

I had wasted little time after Father gave me the orders. The mission was about as priority one as it could get, but it had surprised me that this involved a tribe of Vagabonds. We'd had dealings with them before, rarely ever pleasant, as some tribes would overstep their bounds and threaten the veil of secrecy- the mutually advantageous, unspoken pact between all our kind that we honored, regardless of clan. Fortunately, this visit was not over an issue of such a breach. There were no sloppy members of our kind who couldn't keep their fangs sheathed or went on a blood-soaked tear, leaving the local human law enforcement officials baffled and burdening our clans with the very grueling and unpleasant task of cleanup. This assignment would be far more pleasant . . . relatively speaking.

I folded space to the coordinates of the vagabonds' encampment, stepping from the quiet and comfort of our Lair and into the unknown. Father had told me that swift communication with the group had been impossible, as they'd gone radio and phone silent after their leader's brief exchange with him. At this point, the clan was cut off from the grid: no cell phones, radios, or Jewels. I was none too comfortable with this. I feared my arrival would be something of a surprise for any group not in the know, but Father assured me that I would be expected by at least the one who requested our aid, a vampire by the name of Derek.

I found myself in a densely wooded area, but the scent of my kind was unmistakable as I carefully moved towards the glow of lights ahead. I had intentionally arrived outside of the encampment as not to frighten them. My movements were also casual and deliberately nonthreatening. I was unsure about how many of the lot would know of my arrival. I did not need to reach out with my thoughts to know how guarded and tense their minds were. The feeling suffused the area just ahead. If Lothos had been harassing them recently, as Father had said, then they indeed had good reason to be on edge.

My concentration on that stress was perhaps the reason why I didn't notice the approach of the two guards. This was rectified when a flashlight from the top of a ridge ahead nearly blinded me.

"You there! Hands where we can see them!" One of the two barked in a gravelly voice. I couldn't see him through the glare of his partner's flashlight, but the posture of his silhouette suggested he was carrying a rifle of some kind. I froze, but not because I was afraid. Though it still hurt to get shot, buckshot wouldn't kill me. I could use my Jewel to deflect it, but I preferred not to start an unnecessary fight.

"Drop the purse and get your hands up!" I heard gravel-voice say. I let my supply satchel slide to the ground -slightly miffed at him having called it a "purse"- and showed my hands with no sudden moves. There was no reason to be aggressive; they were just nervous. Well, at least the one with the flashlight was. Gravel-voice was releasing a rather large amount of hostility along with his fear.

Let them overreact if they must, I thought to myself, forcing calm in spite of the tension I sensed from the two men ahead. Show them you're no threat.

"It's just a kid, Joe!" I heard the one who held the flashlight say to his partner.

"Like hell it is!" Gravel-voice -Joe- thrust his finger my way. "You can't smell her, Wadih? She's one of us!

"Ain't never seen a kid vampire." I could sense genuine surprise mixed with confusion at the sight of me from the one named Wadih as he scratched his head with his free hand. "But you're right about the smell." He then projected his voice my way. "You there! What are you doing here? You one of the mind-readers or shape-shifters?"

Their pithy names for our clans were inadequate to say

the least. It would have been a mistake to assume that all of my clan were "mind readers," just as much as saying that all of Lothos's clan were shape-shifters. Nearly all of my clan was telepathic to some extent, but we did have a few who had honed the opposing talent, usually found in Lothos' clan. It was well-known that Lothos had had a few telepaths in his ranks, but I didn't quibble over details.

"Fa- Talante sent me," I replied to Wadih. I hardly ever needed to refer to my Father by name; it felt somewhat awkward, especially saying it to someone who was pointing a gun at me.

"So you're a mind-reader, then?" Joe asked.

"I can read minds," I said, correcting him.

"Why'd your master send you here?"

"I was invited."

"Bullshit."

"So I wasn't invited?" I sensed he was trying to hide something. I had to keep him talking and make him tip his hand somehow.

"Well, what if we did invite you?"

That did it. I stood in silent consternation. He'd just denied that I had been invited, and now he was lying to me outright. Did he think I was a total idiot?

"You didn't invite me," I said, tapping my forehead as a reminder to him of my abilities, "But somebody did. You're not going to be able to lie to me."

I supposed that this was a proverbial "no-win" situation, since I felt Joe's panic spike to unbelievable levels.

"Get out of my mind!" he screamed, and I heard him cock his rifle.

I guess that was a bad idea, I thought, cringing inside from embarrassment.

"I'm not in your mind," I said, trying, however futilely, to defuse the situation, "but I can read what's on the sur-"

"And you call me a liar, you little midget?" Joe snapped, stepping over my words with panicked fury and a voice that was several octaves higher. "Keep flapping your little baby doll lips now! I dare you!"

His silhouette shifted, and I was certain he would fire if I said the wrong thing. Actually, I surmised that he might fire anyway. His fear had made him irrational. Even I could feel Wadih's helplessness. He was wary, but didn't see me as a threat. This Joe, on the other hand, was itching to shoot something.

A little bit jumpy doesn't even begin to describe them, I thought with chagrin. I was beginning to wonder if Father had made a mistake by selecting me.

"Joe! Wadih! What are you doing?" The voice came from beyond the ridge, and I became aware of another, much calmer and self-assured mind approaching, though it betrayed the youth of the voice I'd heard. It was male, but sounded only a bit more mature than the timbre of my own prepubescent vocal cords. It also contained a slight rasp, as if puberty had not quite caught up with him yet. The flashlight's glare still annoyingly blocked my view, but I could see the silhouette of the other person who appeared at the hilltop. He was significantly shorter than the other two men, though he seemed taller than me. Joe's sudden shift from loud and posturing to deferential, however, told me volumes more than even the new arrival's air of authority.

"Well, is someone gonna say something?" I heard the stranger say. I felt the force of his personality prod against the two men. Their fear and respect were quite evident, though Joe resisted. Wadih remained silent more out of confusion. I suspected that Joe was the one who took initiative, but this felt like an unusual situation. It was, in effect, a battle of wills between Joe and the stranger. Despite his respect for this shorter individual, there emanated a background of carefully hidden anger.

"We caught an intruder," Wadih finally said, taking initiative. This, I gathered from his apprehension, was most likely a rare thing. "Says Talante, the mind-readers' leader, called her here … that someone asked for her."

"It was me," the stranger said almost on top of Wadih's last words. "Let her in."

"Derek, I don't think that's a good idea," Joe had started to say, but the one I now knew was Derek cut him off.

"You guys put me in charge, right?" Derek's thoughts aimed that question at Joe more than Wadih. I could sense Joe's assent but couldn't see whether or not he nodded.

"I thought my putting you in security could put your trigger-happiness to good use," Derek continued, "but it still hasn't stopped you from jumping at shadows, Joe. So, do your damn job and stop worrying about who I invite to our home." I then felt a flash of near-fury from both of them after what came out of his mouth. "You sure as hell didn't care about it before. If you had, we wouldn't be in this mess."

"You're never going to let me live it down, are you, little bro?" Joe retorted, and this made me confused for a brief moment. I felt no resonance between their minds as was what existed between two individuals who were blood-related, but I came to notice that there was a deep familiarity that existed between the two. I supposed they had known each other for a long time. I wished I could see them properly . . . and that was when I found myself really wanting Wadih do get that bloody flashlight out of my face. "And what's up with not telling me about this? If we were waiting for some kind of ambassador, shouldn't I have been the first to know?"

"You would've been," Derek replied, and his silhouette shifted to suggest that he'd glanced at me, "but the harassment by the shape-shifters has only been getting worse. I'm almost certain we have a mole, and the fewer who know about this little China doll's arrival, the better. And as for not letting you live it down . . . take responsibility and then we'll talk."

Live what down? I thought as I saw Derek gesture in the opposite direction. "Take the other side of the encampment," he said to Joe. "Relieve Wilson. Wadih, you have this area. And cut off your light. You can see well enough without it, and you've been shining that thing right into her eyes for the last several minutes."

Wadih blessedly switched off the flashlight. I lowered my arms, surprised at how stiff they were, and rubbed at my eyes where the large blur frustratingly blocked my vision almost as badly as the flashlight had.

"You, down there," I heard Derek call out as I slung my satchel over my shoulder. I squinted in his direction, wishing that I could see him better. "You want to stay there all night?

The ridge rose about ten or eleven feet, a height I could easily jump, and I quickly joined Derek at the top.

"Not a word of this to the others," I heard him say to Joe and Wadih. Both then moved with preternatural speed into the woods to their assigned posts and out of sight. I hadn't gotten a good look at them before they left, and I felt somewhat annoyed by that. At least with Joe, I wanted to know the face of the man I would need to give a wide berth to, or possibly confront.

The area was lit by a series of floodlights, which were the source of the glow that I saw upon my arrival. I stood beside Derek and the blur in my vision had diminished somewhat to where I could at last see him. He was a head and a half taller than I was, but significantly shorter than the adult-height Joe and Wadih. Now I saw why. It was obvious he had been turned at a young age like I had been, but not quite as young as me. Still, as adults went, I was a comparable height to him since I had been well on my way through my first growth spurt when I was turned. Because of this, I was quite a bit taller than most girls who were my physical age at the time.

Derek's most prominent feature was his nose. It was like a slightly curved isosceles triangle set between sad-looking eyes. His hair was a very dark brown that was slicked back save for several wisps that touched his high forehead. There were a few sparse strands of stubble on his strong chin, and I imagined that that was a frustrating position to be in- frozen so close to adulthood with only the beginnings of a beard.

At least I hadn't heard any cracking in his voice in spite of the rasp; I couldn't imagine what it would be like to have been turned in the middle of puberty. As far as I could tell, he seemed to have dodged that bullet, or at least the worst of it.

"Derek, I presume?" I said, extending my hand. "My name is Elisa."

Derek briefly cast a narrow-eyed gaze my way before taking my offered hand. He shook it, but I knew that he did this for cordiality rather than out of friendliness. This troubled me. I knew that Vagabonds didn't trust us, and so I wanted to make a good first impression. This was apparently lost on him.

"So you're the one Talante sent?" Derek asked, gesturing for me to follow as he set off on a makeshift path through the woods. I kept pace beside him as we passed between the rows of floodlights.

"You're the one who asked for our help?" I said in return.

"Not by choice, believe me," Derek said. His voice was an indistinct almost-monotone, affected to perhaps disguise his feelings, but this didn't shield me from his mind. His simmering dislike was fairly obvious and not unexpected, but not exactly aimed at me. Rather, it was a generalized disdain towards all of our kind . . . at least the ones associated with Father's clan and Lothos'. I frowned and wondered how I could reach him. I wanted to put him at ease, to let him know that we weren't the bad guys, but I knew very little about Vagabonds. Many were turned and raised by their respective clans, but others had been members of our fold or part of the Others, and had run away from the war for their own personal reasons. Turning him to our point of view would perhaps be an exercise in futility, but I at least wanted to understand him.

"If this hadn't happened to us, we'd be happy to never see you guys. But at least you're not trying to hunt us down."

"So you supposed the enemy of your enemy would be your friend?" I asked.

"More like the enemy of our enemy would be useful,"

Derek corrected. "Don't be naive, little girl, I-"

"I am not a little girl!" I stopped in my tracks and grabbed the sleeve of Derek's charcoal gray hoodie. He fancied himself something of a leader, and I sensed that had I not done this, he would have been content to ignore me. I needed to make a stronger show of force to let him know that doing such a thing would be a bad idea. I believe I succeeded when I spun him around until he faced me. My strength was enhanced by my Jewel, and I felt him resist at first. It must have been quite a shock to him to see me overpower him so easily.

"How old do you think I am?" I said, keeping a hard gaze into his eyes. They as crimson as my own, though nowhere near as large.

"Well, that's hardly fair," Derek said, still nonplussed at what I'd done. "You know that's impossible to tell. You could be three or three thousand… who knows?"

"Oh, bloody hell," I whispered, keeping no restraint on my exasperation. "Do I look like I'm three?" I was incensed at his having made such an asinine guess. I felt my fangs extend, and I was certain my eyes had flashed. His decision to be either coy or obtuse was a sticking point to this charade. If I were too old, he'd figure trying to play the alpha male would get him a trip to whatever clinic they had to reattach a severed limb; too young and he could figure out a way to get back at me. "Yes, I know we all look whatever age we were when we were turned, unless we were elderly, and then the process reverses the aging to where we look almost thirty. But . . . three?"

I felt Derek's ego finally cave in, and he capitulated. "All right, I'm sorry! Bad call, okay? How old are you, then?"

"I don't know if I should tell you now," I said, trying to avoid the appearance of sulking. "You called my Father, asking for help, and when I arrive, I see that you've obviously made it a point not to like me even though you barely know me from Eve. Why should I be accommodating for you when you're obviously not interested in treating me with the same courtesy?"

Derek's burgeoning anger at my furthering onslaught began to melt away into an uncomfortable shame, which he tried in vain to bury. There was, however, something else, but it was buried out of my immediate detection beneath many veils. Feeling that he should be grateful that private thoughts were sacrosanct to us except in dire situations, out of respect, I didn't pursue what he hid. He sighed deeply as his shoulders sagged and his clenched fists loosened. He beckoned me to follow as he continued down the lit path. When he spoke, I realized that the only thing that had not yet relaxed were his fangs. They were still extended, and slurring his speech almost comically.

"I'm sorry. I really am. I just don't have a lot of good things to say about either your clan or the Others. It's a long boring story that I'd prefer not to get into. But you're right. I did contact your- Wait! Did you say 'Father'?"

I think I froze for several moments because I felt his anger begin to flare again. He must have thought that my omitting that detail was some sort of a betrayal or obfuscation. I cringed inside, cursing myself. I had wanted to keep that secret. I would have enough issues to deal with working with a tribe of Vagabonds, and I didn't want to make them worry more about my pedigree.

"Well?" Derek said in a terse voice, and I could feel his impatience rising geometrically. "Didn't you?"

This time, I was the one who sighed.

"Yes. Talante is my father -adopted father, actually. But he raised me since I was truly a child."

"Holy freaking crap." Derek ran his fingers through his hair as he looked at me with new eyes. His thoughts were confusion as he re-assessed me, not sure what to think now. "So the king brought his princess to come to our rescue?"

"He's not a king," I retorted. "And I'm hardly a princess. I'm his daughter, but I'm no different from anyone else in our clan."

"You're too modest," Derek said. "You're the daughter of the father of your clan and half of our kind. You've gotta be treated with some deference, or at least were spoiled rotten."

I bared my fangs and cast a hard gaze at him, but this time, he did not back down.

"Look, I'm not saying that you are spoiled. I know your father wouldn't have sent someone who wasn't competent, or who doesn't have more than a few tricks up her sleeve for this job. So you and I both know that you're more than just some goodwill ambassador. From the way you talk and carry yourself, I know you're a lot older than you look, and I'll bet you've probably figured that we're alike in at least that way. I think it's fair to say that neither of us were born yesterday. So let's not play verbal footsie anymore. I'm Derek, and I was the one who contacted your father. You'll excuse my abrasiveness from earlier; I haven't had good experiences from either clan."

I believe I smiled at him for the first time then. At last, there was some honesty. I felt free to be more forthcoming with him.

"I'm one hundred seventy-three years old," I said. "I was turned when I was ten."

Derek gave a low whistle. "Guess I was way off, then," he remarked, giving a rather silly-looking smirk. "You're an old lady."

"That's even worse than thinking I was three!" I said with a scowl.

"Geez, you need to lighten up just a bit." Derek's shoulders shook with a silent laugh, and I knew from his thoughts that he meant no disrespect. However, I figured his brand of humor seemed tailor-made to rub me the wrong way. "Besides, compared to you, I'm the 'little kid.' I'm thirty-four; I was fourteen when I was turned."

"Now that is a very peculiar irony if I've ever seen one," I said with genuine intrigue as we entered the encampment. The lit path hadn't been that long, but we had been walking slowly from the slope in the hill. I wasn't quite certain, however, if the pace was in order to allow time for pleasantries or to just establish Derek's original idea of "an understanding."

The encampment was larger than I'd expected: a large clearing filled with several small trailer homes attached to various weathered-looking cars and trucks, about five or six Khyam tents, and a couple of large, Winnebago-type RVs, all arranged in a circle. A fire was set in the center of the clearing, but with no signs or scents of human food -I suspected it was more for ambiance. A few vagabonds, three men and two women, stood around talking; all of them froze when they caught my scent. Their spike in wariness at the sight of me made the very air seem unsettling. I saw one of the females bare her fangs my way, nearly slapping me with intense dislike before she vanished at preternatural speed into the camp's shadows. I'd barely gotten a glimpse of her, but she had straight falls of strikingly black hair that made the rest of her seem downright ghostly. The others simply stared at me. One of them, a very wide-framed man with a rounded, weathered-looking face and thick crown of graying hair, seemed eerily familiar. I believe it was because he had what looked like a parakeet on his shoulder. This made him seem not only familiar, but peculiar as well, since animals did not usually take to us.

"Are there more?" I asked Derek, nodding to the group.

"More than those few?" Derek's voice had lowered to a subvocal level that would be difficult for even our kind to hear from far away. "Yeah, we're about ten in all. Some float in and out. I told them you were a newbie."

"You told them?" I said. At first I was confused, and then it all fell together. "You can read minds? Like me?"

"Yeah." Derek made a vague nod, and I felt nothing from him that resembled pride. "I try not to do it often; it freaks some of the others out. I talked to them just now to tell them your cover story."

"So you're passing me off as a newcomer?" I said.

Derek flexed his shoulders and exhaled. "That's supposed to be the plan, China doll. Your dad and I didn't talk for long, but we agreed to that."

I opened my mouth to protest his newest attempt at sticking me with another nickname, but decided to let it stay as he seemed more comfortable with it than first names. Besides, that one was not too bad. Besides, I was certain that my given name made me sound even more of an "old lady" anyway.

"Oh, by the way," Derek said with abrupt caution, "the one who ran away is Deb. She hasn't been with us long, but she keeps to herself most of the time. For some reason, she doesn't take well to noobs. I'd steer clear of her."

". . . As well as Joe, I guess," I said in a quiet voice.

Derek's mind became troubled at that name, but his thoughts submerged those feelings more quickly than I could sort them out.

"I'll . . . talk with Joe," he said.

"What is he to you?" I asked, prodding some.

"No offense, but that's not your business." Derek spoke tersely, though it sounded as if he was trying not to. I felt his flicker of shame at having spoken that way. His voice was much softer when he spoke again. "It's . . . complicated."

"As you wish," I said without accusation and decided to change the subject. "So where will I be sleeping?"

"With me, it seems," Derek answered. It was then that I noticed that we were headed for the largest of the RVs: one with brown and gold patterns on its chassis. "I cleaned out the living room area for you. The couch is almost the size of a bed. I also installed new sun shutters so you won't fry in the morning."

"How . . . thoughtful," I said, uncertain as to how to take that information. I was sure that Derek didn't mean it, but I wasn't sure if he realized just how morose his assurances had sounded. Did he have any idea how indescribably painful sunlight burns were? And because they destroyed tissue, blood and all, they took much longer to heal than normal wounds.

"Well, the night is early," I said, changing the subject and hoping Derek hadn't picked up my mild discomfort and near-offense at his statement, "so settling in can wait. We ought to get on to plotting a strategy."

"That'll be between you and me," Derek said. "Remember, you're the newbie, and we need to keep that as our story. You'll be put upon enough in the coming nights; but if they knew you were from the mind-readers, they'd eat you alive."

"They don't know me very well," I said.

"They think they know enough," Derek replied, reaching in his pocket for his remote key. We arrived at the RV and he unlocked the side door. Derek entered first and flipped a toggle switch. The lights came on as I followed him up the stair well to the living room.

I was greeted by a spacious, carpeted interior. I had never actually been inside an RV before, and I was impressed, both by its size and its appearance of opulence. I'd never expected Vagabonds to live like this, but then again, I hadn't had many dealings with Vagabonds . . . or rather, none that I preferred to remember. They certainly didn't involve my getting a glimpse into their personal lives.

The sitting area beside the cab was quite nice and well-kept in spite of the pervasive background scent of tobacco mixed with cleaning chemicals. I believe that humans would have not been able to smell it, but very little escaped our kind's olfactory acuity. The furniture was leather and the cabinets in the kitchen area were made of varnished plywood. At the rear end of the vehicle, I glimpsed a very lived-in queen size bed through a crack in the sliding door.

"The sofa converts into a bed," Derek explained, gesturing towards the alcove near the cab, set across from a big screen TV. Even folded up, the sofa seemed twice as big as my bed at the Lair and far larger than my coffin. There was a blanket and pillow situated at one end for me. "The bathroom is next to the bedroom, and I have chilled blood packs in the fridge. You can warm them in the sink . . ." He cast me a brief sideways glance, ". . . or you can go hunting with me whenever there's fresh prey about."

I scowled briefly at the thought of hunting for humans. He knew that our clan found that to be uncouth and dangerous, even though we trained ourselves never to feed until death and to alter memories. Few vampires did it, except for emergencies; Roland was one of the few who still engaged in the activity for the sport of it, and his choice of prey was always young females -small wonder there, considering his notorious sexual proclivities. Father always gave him a hard time about it, and it was only because he was a master at memory alteration that he was given a marginal pass.

"I'll take the blood packs," I said after a groan. I knew that I was consigning myself to meager living for who knew how long. Blood packs, depending on how long the blood had been preserved, were emergency rations in our clan: barely palatable compared to fresh blood from a live host, which we always had available in our villages.

"Sorry, but we don't have humans hanging around us like needy babies," Derek said. "We don't have time to groom and care for them, or keep them as our pets. We stay on the road. Most humans don't take well to that. And most of us haven't exactly mastered our thirst like you."

"You needn't resort to needling me about it," I replied, setting down my satchel next to the sofa. "We understand why you do what you must. We choose a different way."

Derek's face gave a slight twist into a vague scowl as plopped himself into the couch catty-corner to the sofa. "You mean a better way, right?"

"Derek, are you trying to provoke me?" I allowed a certain warning edge to creep into my voice as my fangs extended. I sensed a feeling of chagrin dampen his previous feelings of bitterness, and he seemed to capitulate as he lolled his head back and slouched, legs outward. I felt that same ghost of a sensation rise and then vanish within him before I could fully parse it out.

"No, I'm not trying to provoke you," Derek answered me at the end of an especially long sigh. He was obviously in a less than cordial mood, and I felt him berate himself inwardly. His left hand went to the pocket of his hoodie and removed a box of Swisher Sweets. He sighed as he opened the hinge and drew out a cigarillo, then brought it to his mouth. He then glanced my way, and placed it back into the box, a flutter of something akin to embarrassment touching my mind. I found it almost amusing that he would be so caustic about my clan, but at the same time, feel so self-conscious about smoking around me.

"I've just . . . got issues, is all. And then this crap we're now in. Of all the shitty luck."

"Well, I'm here to hopefully make your luck better," I said, and sat myself in the sofa. I curled up my knees and leaned forward. "And to do that, I'm going to need to know some things beyond what Father told me. So start talking, if you'd be so kind."

Chapter Three

"You know what you're here to protect, right?" Derek asked.

"Father told me that one of you had a baby," I replied. "A little girl, if memory serves? A dhampir?"

"Deb's taking care of her," Derek said with a nod. "And it wasn't one of us. Mother was human. She's dead now; that was a nightmare to cover up. Somewhere along the line, Lothos must've gotten wind of it. Seems like everywhere we go, he's been hounding us. He's been picking us off one by one, every time we make a stop somewhere, probably so she'll have no protectors when he comes for her. We've been keeping on the road for the most part and resting out in the boondocks, so he'll have a harder time finding us. We also shut off all our cell phones for the time being and ditched the road. There used to be twenty-five of us; we sent most of them to other clans or to lay low in different areas around the country. Now there are only the few I told you about. I feel like tonight's the first quiet night we've had in about two weeks."

"Were you able to kill your attackers?" I asked.

"Sometimes yes, sometimes no." I saw him reach for his pack of cigarillos, then place them back in his pocket with a wave of frustration.

"I don't mind if you smoke, you know," I said, betraying a small laugh. "It's not like we can get lung cancer. And besides, it's your home."

"I know," Derek groaned. "It's just . . . well, it's silly, but it's more habit than anything. I don't smoke around kids. I can't bring myself to do it." He held out his hand as I opened my mouth to speak. "And I know you're not a 'kid.' It doesn't matter. You look like one, and my habit kicks in, and it discourages my other habit."

I gave another laugh, and I felt that same ghost of a feeling -quickly suppressed and hidden, erupt in Derek's mind. I longed to probe further, but for some reason, it had such an air of privacy about it that it felt as if doing so would be a violation of some sort.

"I'm sorry," I said, not knowing why I said it. "You were saying that you were able to kill some of the disciples Lothos sent after you?"

"Took out one of them with a crossbow tipped with a phosphorus explosive," Derek explained. "Got him right in the head. Joe's a hell of a sniper; saw the bastard approaching from three miles out. Once he got in range, he was toast. Literally."

"Bet he tasted terrible," I quipped, and this time Derek laughed. I have to admit that I was relieved at that sound. It was the first time I saw him laugh fully and genuinely since we'd met, and until that point, I'd begun to wonder if he was just a wanker by nature. Unfortunately, it was short-lived, and he soon retreated back into his previous melancholy.

"The other two were . . . more difficult. Stealthier. They managed to take us out before we got to them. One almost got to the baby, but Deb's a pyrokinetic. She doesn't do it often, but he sure as hell didn't see it coming. Cost us a trailer, though. After that, they've been coming once every two to three days. Joe and the perimeter guard have been able to take them out, but we knew it was only a matter of time. I suspected they were tracking us somehow; that's why I ordered all our cell phones and computers shut down, save Marie-Laure's. She's our resident hacker."

"I gather Father is the last one you contacted," I said, and Derek nodded.

"As for how I knew his number, I've been 'proselytized' by your clan before. Some weirdo girl who looked more like a ghost than anything else, insisted I have his number. She spoke in riddles like she'd been auguring my future or something."

That piqued my interest. There was only one of our clan who fit that description. I'd heard others describe her this way. "Did she have long, platinum blond hair?" I asked.

"Yeah," Derek nodded. "And she was a-"

"-little bit taller than me," I said, finishing his sentence. "And she was-"

"-blind."

Derek stared at me, mouth agape. "So you know her?"

"Sarah is a prophetess among our clan," I explained, and I saw the image his mind produced. It was Sarah; there was no doubt. The sightless, pale eyes, devoid of crimson, backswept veil, and light blue sash-bound dress were unmistakable. She was only half a foot taller than me, but had been an adult when she was turned, only very petite in stature. Her breast development beneath her dress was plainly apparent while I remained with a chest of a little boy. "She's one of the oldest of our clan, possibly all of our kind, next to Father. There's very little she's said about her past except that she was born in Mesopotamia, and was one of Father's first generation. It's said that she traded her eyesight for the ability to see the future. She keeps to herself most of the time, and only comes out when she has something important to say. She'll seek out the person it involves in order to say it. Otherwise, we often won't see her for months or even years at a time. She must have seen something in your future where you would need to speak with Father. Be grateful that she did."

"I didn't appreciate it at the time," Derek said, "hell, I was about to crumple her paper up and throw it away, but then I figured, 'When a woman who looks like a ghost and seems to see better than you, even though she's blind, tells you to call that number in your darkest hour, and help will be on the way, you'd better give it a second thought.' So I kept the number around."

"Sarah is always a bit unsettling when people first meet her," I assured him. "But at least now I know how you were able to get hold of Father. I thought it odd that a small tribe of Vagabonds would have his number."

"Now you know why," Derek said. "I'm hoping her advice was sound."

"I think it was," I said.

"What makes you think that?"

"Because you're still here," I replied. "That means Lothos hasn't started sending his thaumaturgists."

"You're saying I can't handle some would-be wizards?" I could feel Derek's flash of incredulity.

"I don't know," I said. "How did you fare against them in his clan?"

"How did you -?"

I believe I played my cards well with that little reveal. I'd dug a bit deeper into his mind than perhaps I should have in order to discover that fact, but it was worth the sight and sensation of Derek's momentary unbalance. And I would be lying if I said that the look on his face wasn't just a little amusing. Normally, I would be wary of him, perhaps even hate him, but his mind didn't have the timbre of Lothos' kind. Besides, I pried only deeply enough to know that he hated that monster almost as much as our clan did. That was enough for me. Derek's question died upon his lips with the dawn of understanding. He relaxed and reclined back into his couch from his previous upright position. "I guess nothing gets by you, does it?"

"Oh, there are some things," I said. "But you weren't exactly making that part of your life secret. But I have to ask, is there anything about your past that might make you a target for Lothos?"

"Not really," Derek said. "He sent some troops after me when I left, but they were all grunts. I left their ashes blowing in the wind. It's the same story with just about every runaway from his clan. Those who survive are still alive because he gets bored and considers you a waste of resources, unless you have something he really wants. I know it's the baby he wants in this case. Dhampirs are hard to come by for both of your clans, aren't they?"

"Even harder for Lothos," I said. "It's hard enough for our kind to produce a child with humans. Miscarriages are common; even more so if the mother is human. We only have them more often because we think love is a key factor. The few out of Lothos' clan -the ones we know of- are born by rape."

"No offense . . ." Again, Derek reached for a cigarillo, but this time kept it out of the box and moved it idly about with his fingers, ". . . but that gives me cause to wonder if you don't have the same intentions as Lothos? We don't really have a need for this baby. And she's more trouble than she's worth. Why not take her off our hands?"

"Do you want me to do that?" I asked. "It might make things much easier for you. And you won't have to worry about it."

"We'll keep her, thank you," Derek said with some reluctance. "Her fate isn't my call, as much as I'd like it to be."

"The father's call, then?" I said.

"That's . . . private."

Again, I felt walls go up around Derek's thoughts. I grumbled on the inside, but decided not to pry any deeper. We had digressed quite a bit from the principal subject, though, and so I returned to it.

"All this fuss over a baby. I'm sorry for your losses."

"Tell that to their friends, China doll," Derek said, expressing more of the abrasiveness that had irritated me, despite his not having meant it. The losses of his clan hurt deeply; that was eminently easy to tell, however.

He exhaled and shook his head. "I'm doing it again, aren't I? Why do I want to blame you?"

"It's probably the war," I said with a dismissive wave. "Your people get in the crossfire often enough. I daresay there are a lot of other Vagabond clans who have even more dislike for us. So tell me, what precautions have you taken outside of perimeter guards?"

"Not much more than that," Derek said. "Our resources are limited. We could probably disband, go our separate ways . . . have someone take the baby, but I doubt that'll help."

"That's probably the worst thing you could do," I said with a frown. "Especially if you have a mole, like I overheard you say to your friends."

"Damn, you heard that too?" Derek ran his fingers through his thick hair, and stuffed the cigarillo, now ruined from the motion of his fingers, back into the front pocket of his hoodie.

"I was sent here to help you," I reminded him. "Everything I know about your situation may improve it, so I hope you will lose the secretiveness."

This time, only the ghost of another scowl crossed Derek's handsome features. Though my heart went out to him for the difficulties of his clan, I desired at the same time to peel away at the layers of his psyche and find out the source of his reticence. Perhaps someday I would.

"You're right. I want to trust you, but you have to understand that in my experience, trust is earned. And what I really want to know is, can you help us?"

"I believe I can," I said. "I feel that this was the best time for you to ask for it. Lothos, up until now, has been playing with you. And I believe you're right to be worried about having a mole. Your group is ill-equipped to deal with this."

"Then what do you suggest?" Derek asked after forcing back a wave of incredulity. His face remained expressionless, waiting, but his thoughts rocked between eagerness and almost-desperation.

"First, I'll need you to recall your perimeter guard," I said.

"Excuse me?"

"Recall your perimeter guard." I spoke more slowly and distinctively so that Derek knew that I was not joking.

"Lothos is playing with you. He's been doing it for awhile now, picking you off one by one. He's damaging your morale. You're a tiny flock; he's got an army. It's time for the hunter to be made into the hunted."

"And who will be doing the hunting?" Derek pointed indiscreetly my way.

I nodded at his gesture, suppressing the smug grin that wanted to appear at the edge of my mouth. "That's phase one."

"What's phase two, then?"

"Flush out the mole."

Derek leaned back in his couch and crossed his arms. "The guys I have on guard duty aren't going to like this."

"Tell them I have a plan," I said.

"If it involves you, I can't guarantee they'll do it," Derek replied. "You're an outsider, as far as they're concerned."

"But they trust you."

"I'd rather not push them," Derek said.

"What if I could sway some more to my side?" I asked, an idea coming to mind. Derek was immediately suspicious, and I smiled at his reaction. It always felt inexplicably good when you knew something someone else didn't.

"What do you mean by 'sway'?" Derek asked.

I slid off the couch and stretched my legs. "You ought to find out very shortly," I said, and decided to see if a previous notion I had was true. "Does the name, Cormorant Lyman ring a bell? Nickname of 'Paws'?"

Derek raised an eyebrow and gestured towards the door, and I instantly felt the recognition. The image in Derek's mind was a perfect match. I knew I'd recognized him!

"Paws Lyman? You know him?"

"Quite well," I replied. "He was part of my clan at one time. What do the others in your clan think of him?"

"If you know him, then you ought to know he's invaluable to us," Derek replied. "His dogs took out the last couple of goons Lothos sent our way, though they managed to take one of the two out. Paws took it pretty bad. Fortunately, the one he has left is his best one. I just wish his animals would take to us; he's the only one who can control them."

"Does his opinion hold a lot of weight with your people?"

"Some. He's been here for awhile now . . . since before I came, actually. I was surprised he was so deferential to me when I stepped in as leader. I thought he'd be the one in charge."

I shook my head. "He never fancied himself a leader. But if his opinion carries weight, then he can get the others behind me."

"Maybe some," Derek said with a shrug, "but a few are pretty stubborn. Joe and Deb, especially; good luck with them. But do what you feel you need to do. I can only hope it works out."

Emotions roiled from Derek's mind as he stood: a struggle between worry and curiosity. I stopped and turned to face him as he came to my side.

"You need to trust me," I said. I reached up and touched his cheek reassuringly. Remembering that he could pick up my emotions the same as I could his own, I quickly withdrew my hand, somewhat embarrassed over my temerity. I felt no anger from him. In fact, he smiled. I noticed his hand move as if to go to my hand, but he stopped it. Again, there was that rise and subduing of a thought too frustratingly quick for me to catch.

"There's no need to worry, Derek," I said. "You did the right thing calling for help. Do your part, and let me do mine. Trust me, the same way your people trust you."

***

It was like looking at a ghost.

He was still hovering beside the fire when I returned, reclining in a worn aluminum and vinyl lawn chair. Cormorant "Paws" Lyman was the animal whisperer, famous among our clan in his time. It had been nearly fifty years since I'd last seen him. I'd thought he was dead, or had maybe even defected to Lothos' side after he vanished. But there he was, the same as he ever had been. The others whom I'd seen accompanying him earlier were thankfully gone; this made my business easier, as there would be no eavesdroppers, or at least no one giving me the stink eye. He was alone, save for a dog that lay beside the chair. It was a German shepherd, and a massive specimen of one: three-fourths the size of a motorcycle. Of course, this was to be expected. Its accompanying scent and the ruby color of its eyes were an undeniably telling sign that it had been turned. A large stainless steel dog bowl lay beside it, a quarter the size of a kiddie pool, from which emanated the unmistakable scent of blood. I was somewhat thirsty, but I knew the blood that sustained the animal would not sustain me. Unlike us, beasts that were turned did not require human blood; any kind of blood would do.

"I was wondering when you'd notice me," Lyman said as I approached. I knew I had nothing to fear from his dog. Though I did not possess his knack for controlling them and subduing their thirst-induced madness, animals, turned or otherwise, did not mind my scent. Nevertheless, out of courtesy, I moved in the most nonthreatening manner possible.

His dog awoke from its half-slumber, sniffed the air in front of me, and gave a half-hearted bark before whining and then resting again. I knew I had nothing to fear. Like Lyman, I shared an unusual affinity for animals, but it was not a natural condition. I had none of his talent for training them; still, they did not try to run away or attack when I was near. I crouched beside the dog, catching the scent that told me it was female, and then scratched atop her head.

"She's a beauty," I commented. "I don't recall you having this breed before."

"Got her not too long after I left your dad," Lyman replied. "Name's Grace. She's been pretty good to me ever since."

"You had others," I said. "A whole zoo if memory serves."

"Lothos' cronies got to most of 'em over the years," Lyman replied in a wistful tone. "I had to replenish my stock, but now that I'm running with these bozos, I have to travel light." He gestured towards the run-down trailer behind him. "So Grace keeps me company."

He watched closely as I ran my hand over Grace's thick fur. After being around Lyman all those years ago, animals had started to be less afraid of me: a fact that made most members of my clan more than a little jealous.

"Never ceases to amaze me how animals like you," he remarked as I stood to meet his weathered smile. His eyes, crimson as all of our kind, set under thick eyebrows, were beady, but as intense as I remembered them as they shifted from Grace to me. "Usually being turned makes them even more ornery to company, but you could probably bite her on the face, and she wouldn't care. That's a really rare gift, you know. Seen it in only one other vampire in all my travels."

"So I've been told," I said. "It's good to see you're still alive after all this time. I missed you."

"I hope that doesn't mean that you're going to go telling the Master where I am."

Lyman's thoughts were guarded, but his emotions were quite obvious. He was wary of me, and had been so since he and I first locked eyes. I managed to set his mind somewhat at ease when I shook my head.

"My business here isn't with you," I said. He knew that I couldn't promise him that there would be no more interventions from my clan, but my assurances were limited. I believe he understood this, in spite of his grimace. Clearly, this obviously wasn't the answer he wanted.

"I'm sorry," I said, feeling truly apologetic. "But my clan does have business here that requires our attention."

"Oh, I know," Lyman answered, and sat straighter in his chair. I hadn't noticed it before, but there was a black wooden pipe in his hand. He took a draft from it, blew out a sultry cloud of sweet-smelling smoke, and then dumped its contents into the dirt at his feet. "It's about that baby. Been nothing but trouble since she arrived. I should've known Derek would start looking for help. Didn't know they'd send you, though. But I can't say that it isn't good to see you again. Crusoe was never quite the same since you left."

My memories went back to the silly toucan he kept as a pet. I often kept him on my shoulder for the evening and would visit the dinner spread in the Lair's sitting room, laughing at how merrily he clicked while I fed him grapes and strawberries. Lyman could have turned Crusoe in order to keep him around forever, but turning birds was well known as a catastrophically bad idea. Most bird species lost control far too quickly, even for Lyman's talents to handle, and our condition mutated within them, driving the animal to seek out more of its kind and turn them. Fortunately, these events were rare, and only a few humans had been hurt by these quickly growing bloodthirsty flocks. The only reason they never overran the planet was because their instincts never covered hiding in the day. Come dawn, sunlight incinerated the massive flocks instantly, accomplishing in one fell swoop what would have been an impossible task for us.

"I do miss the little clown," I said. "He's not around anymore, is he?"

"No, he died about forty years ago," Lyman said. "He was a good old bird, though. Kept me company the whole time I was on the lam."

"On the lam?" My voice monotone with surprise from his comment. Lyman, outside of our battles against Lothos, was one of the gentlest of our kind. "Who would want to hunt you down?"

"Your father."

"Wait, why would he have been pursuing you?" I asked, now more confused than before.

Lyman's eyes widened and he gave a sympathetic frown,

matched by a wave of the same emotion. It was a feeling I didn't like, as it was the sympathy one holds for an ignorant child, or someone who was kept out of some important loop that they should have long been a party to.

"You know that your father forbade turning animals, right?" Lyman said.

I nodded.

"They can't be controlled. They go feral for want of blood." Realizing what this entailed, I quickly added, "But you have a rare talent . . . a talent that helped our clan! And you kept your animals under control. I can't remember a single time when any of them went feral, or attacked anyone!"

"Didn't matter to the Master," Lyman said. Despite his having disassociated himself from our clan, he still used the honorific for Father that most everyone used, save perhaps me and Amelia.

"He ordered my animals destroyed. That was like ordering people to kill my best friends. I couldn't have that, of course. So I left. Of course, your father didn't take kindly to troops going AWOL. Dunno why, but I guess he thought I'd become a danger to others, or other animals even though I never let a single one go feral. His soldiers and thaumaturgists tracked me everywhere I went. They didn't hurt me, but they managed to take out some of my pets. I just wanted to be left alone, but I knew that your dad wouldn't stop unless I surrendered, or made a grand enough show of force. Until that time, I'd avoided setting my animals on anyone except for Lothos' people, but when I finally let them loose on my pursuers that gave him the message."

"You killed them?" I asked, dreading the answer, but Lyman set my mind at ease with a shake of his head.

"Mauled some of them is all. Even then, I practiced restraint, God help me. Then I left them with a message."

His mind formed a picture of a crudely scrawled slip of paper that he pressed into an unconscious man's hand. By the look of the black uniform and cloak, I figured it was one of the thaumaturgists whom he'd overpowered.

"I could have set my pets on your people at any time," it read, "but in case you haven't noticed, I showed restraint, even when your soldiers pursued me and killed my friends. Today, you forced my hand. I refuse to lose another one of them to you. You know me, Master. All I want is to be left alone. Stop pursuing me, or I'll be forced to do something we'll both regret."

"I'm surprised Aiko didn't take any solo actions against you for that," I said, shaken by this revelation, but without a defense. I knew that Father could be heavy-handed when he was forced to be, but I'd never seen him go so far as to pursue an otherwise peaceful man to achieve his ends. "She doesn't take well to people making threats against Father."

"It wasn't a threat," Lyman said grimly. "Your dad knows how I am. And he knows what I'm capable of if my friends are threatened. The fact that I didn't kill the ones sent after me was proof that I have a sense of restraint. Maybe Aiko wanted to come after me, and your dad ordered her not to; maybe she didn't. If you don't know, then I don't know either. But I think that's why, after I left that note, I never had any problems from your clan again. I just hated that it had to come to that."

"Even after all that, you still respect him?" I said. I could feel that in his thoughts as he spoke, and I was actually surprised by this, despite Lyman's laid-back attitude in his retelling of those events.

"You don't know how I came to your clan," Lyman said. He shook his head and cast a wry grin my way, making him seem like a wizened old grandfather for a moment. "I don't know who turned me. I woke up in a storm cellar in the middle of nowhere, with the bodies of an entire family at my feet. I was left a babe in the woods. Learned about sunlight quickly enough, and it took me weeks to come to terms with what I was, as much as I didn't want to believe it. If your dad hadn't found me, I don't know what would've happened.

Maybe I'd have just stepped into the daylight and ended it; maybe Lothos' clan would've found me and drafted me . . . maybe I would've just gone batshit crazy; who knows. The Master gave me a home and a sense of purpose. I'm sure it tore him up inside to have to almost make an enemy out of me."

"Animals go feral soon after they're turned," I reminded him, "and Lothos uses them against us all the time. I guess Father might have been worried that he'd somehow get you to use your talents for him. He's broken the minds of more than a few of our clan."

"Yeah, I know," Lyman said, absently reaching down to pet Grace, who whined happily. She seemed to smile, and I could see her fangs, sharpened canines much more vicious-looking than our own, extended below her furry upper lip. "I hope I didn't damage your faith in your dad, little lady."

"I'd be lying if I said it wasn't disconcerting," I admitted, "but Father did have his reasons."

"No doubt about that," Lyman said and closed his mind to that subject. He inhaled and exhaled loudly, and I saw his intense gaze shift from another time back to me. "But you didn't come here just to talk about old times, did you?"

I shook my head. "No. I didn't. I have a favor to ask of you, actually."

Lyman made a noncommittal noise, a sort of grumbling hum. "I might be inclined to help, depending on the request."

"I've come here to help with your clan's situation," I said, "but as I've been told, it may be difficult to gain their trust."

"Yeah, it will be," Lyman said, still stroking the very placid Grace. At least he was still listening.

"I was discussing strategy with Derek and came to a conclusion," I said. "As you fought for our clan before, you've probably guessed the purpose for the attacks."

"They're toying with us," Lyman said, "demoralizing us so they can bring in the big guns."

"Then we're agreed." I betrayed a little smile. "Know it

won't be much longer before we start to see thaumaturgists. Lothos has fewer than we do, but their applications are usually damn effective. They'll do severe damage, perhaps even wipe them out unless we have an effective countermeasure. And all that perimeter guard with conventional weapons will do is give them target practice. So I asked Derek to remove them."

"You've got a Jewel?" He asked, though he and I knew that it was a rhetorical question. I nodded.

"You're proficient with it?"

"I'd been in training for almost a century even when you left," I said. "I'm second only to Aiko in skill."

"Then it's a wise move. But you can bet your tiny ass that some folks are not going to like it," Lyman said. "Lothos took out Killer -he was my other dog. I've only got Grace here now; we've been doing what we can. But if the next attacker's a thaumaturgist, I'm not going to risk her. Besides, she's not been specifically trained for combat, though she does have the instincts. She tore one of the bastards apart about a week ago, but that might've just been beginner's luck. "

"Oh, I wouldn't ask you to use your pets," I said. "I just need you as a fulcrum for a vote of confidence. As far as the rest of this clan is concerned, I'm a newcomer, an outsider. I already know that at least two of them won't like me at all."

"If you're talking about Deb, I wouldn't take her reaction too personally," Lyman said. "She doesn't like anyone, except maybe that baby. She's been taking care of her since Joe arrived with her; she hardly comes out of her trailer unless Derek calls for her."

"So Joe is the father?" I asked, catching the mental image formed by Lyman's memory.

"You didn't know?"

"Derek was unusually . . . guarded about his identity," I said. "Even when I touched on the subject, he shut me out. His mental barriers are unusually strong."

"He comes from Lothos' clan," Lyman said. "I imagine you'd learn to shut others out pretty quickly. I can't even begin to imagine what kinds of sickos he's had to deal with in that nuthouse."

"His defenses were only screens, though," I mused aloud. "I could've broken through them, but it would've been undiplomatic, to say the least."

"Maybe you should give him better training." Lyman was half-joking, but somewhere inside, I figured that this actually wouldn't be a bad idea.

"Perhaps I will," I said and suppressed a chuckle at Lyman's reaction of surprise. "But I digress. What do you think about my proposal?"

"Well, if anyone can help us, I think it's you," Lyman said with very little time for thought. "Even back when I was running with your dad's people, I saw your skill. It really bothered the Master to send you into combat, but you scored a higher body count than most. And even then, you were impressive with the things you could pull with your Jewel. Makes me regret leaving mine behind -not that I was very handy with it. Anyway, I'll do my best to smooth things over with the others. But regardless, I'll bet dollars to donuts you'll have a hell of a time getting some of them on your side."

"No doubt I will," I said as my ears began to pick up a heated conversation in Derek's RV. My gaze drifted in that direction, as did my thoughts. At this distance, however, it came as a jumble of anger.

"That would be about you," Lyman said. I turned back towards him to see him gesture in the same direction I had been looking.

"Is it, now?" I smiled. A scent wafted in on the air, which I recognized as belonging to Joe. I hadn't gotten a good look at him by the ledge, but his smell was unmistakable. I drew upon the power of my Jewel for the first time since I arrived and allowed it to amplify my telepathy by a few degrees just so I could get the timbre of his mind. The anger became more apparent and annoying, like wasps buzzing inside my head, but I felt his thoughts much more clearly than I ever had. I believed it was time to face him.

"Thank you for whatever help you can give," I said to Lyman and took his massive hand into my own.

"Anything for you," he said, and brought my fingers to his lips. In his broad hands, they seemed very much the doll-like appearance from Derek's imagination. A blush came unbidden to my skin, filling me with self-consciousness and a very mild annoyance. Such a reaction was a waste of blood. I would become thirsty more quickly, and have to replenish myself with the packets of near-tasteless blood that Derek kept in his cooler. I took a moment to pat Grace on the head one last time and made my way back to the RV.

Chapter Four

I could hear Joe's gravelly snarl more easily than my nose could catch his scent. His anger was like a high-pressure water hose switched on with no one to control it. Incredulity and outright fury practically suffused the air. I supposed Derek had informed him of the troop withdrawal . . . or he was just always this angry. His quickness to the trigger during our first encounter certainly seemed to justify that guess.

"You're unbelievable; you know that? You expect this little pipsqueak of an outsider to just waltz in here and tell you what to do . . . to tell us what to do, and for me to just be cool with it?" Joe was still blustering as I reached the entrance door. But instead of opening it, I stood quietly and listened on. "We choose this life for a reason: to stay our own people! The mind-readers and shape-shifters fight each other 'til hell freezes over, for all I care. And now that kid wants you to keep us from guarding what's our own? Are you nuts?"

"I have my reasons, Joe." Quite a stark contrast to Joe's anger, Derek's mind was quite calm. He had his doubts; those black spots on his otherwise glowing confidence were painfully obvious, but he was choosing to trust me in spite of my being an outsider and a stranger. I couldn't help but smile at this.

"And I don't feel the need to explain my choice to trust her. Syd left me in charge, and you guys accepted it. So I'm calling the shots around here. So you just need to understand that I do trust her . . . for now, at least."

"Damn mind readers," Joe growled. "She's probably gotten to you. You don't even realize you're trading one tyrant for another, begging for their help."

"And you're an idiot if you think that," Derek retorted. "We're getting our collective asses kicked out there. And

Lothos still hasn't pulled out the heavy-hitters. We need help, Joe; you know it. I know it. Hell, the whole clan, what's left of them, knows it. And you know that if anyone has the resources to help, it's the mind-readers. Besides, Elisa couldn't alter my mind if she wanted to. You know that. "

I wasn't certain of what he meant by that; I could most certainly do some alterations to his mind if I wanted to. Derek had no mental defenses that I was aware of, but I felt the belief in Joe; whether it was founded, or he'd been duped by false information at some earlier point, I didn't know. Nevertheless, I detected the hesitation that Derek's words brought about. Afterwards, he seemed to choose his words more carefully -though maybe not carefully enough.

"You should've just let me pull the trigger on her." Joe's voice had turned cold as a rock submerged in snow. His hard, spiteful dislike for me was like acid in an open wound. He'd meant every word of what he had just said. This pushed me over the edge. Without announcement or pretense, I swung the door open, nearly breaking it as I stalked inside.

"You would never have gotten the chance," I announced as I stepped up the small staircase into the living room. "Had I even thought you were going to pull that trigger, I would have paralyzed you or turned that gun into so many iron filings and sawdust."

I hadn't realized before I crashed the conversation that Joe had still possessed his shotgun, and that it was slung across his back. Joe was naturally taller than Derek, much older-looking, and black-haired. He must have been very dark-skinned in his human days, because despite his vampiric blood, his complexion leaned towards swarthiness. He possessed Mediterranean features similar to but not quite enough like Derek to indicate familial links. His eyes were deep sunk, and his frowning mouth seemed almost too large for his round face. Derek, who stood across from him, became both startled and somewhat frightened by the speed with which things escalated the moment Joe had laid eyes on me.

"Little bitch," Joe murmured as he grasped the shotgun's handle. With preternatural speed, he whirled it over his shoulder in order to aim both barrels directly at me. I felt his intent to fire it, but the thought wrestled momentarily with his common sense, giving pause to his actions -and an opportunity that I took to rob him of the means to do the deed.

Like sand, the gun dissolved into a shower of silver and brown as I drew upon my Jewel and the molecules that composed its matter lost their cohesion. At first, Joe stood stark still, staring at the effect with paralyzing shock. Then, as if believing that he would start to fall apart as well, he dropped the shotgun as the disintegration spread to its handle. What remained of the weapon and its ammo landed, still crumbling, in a pile of its own powdered constituent parts.

That action, however, had the opposite effect from what I expected.

"My gun . . ." Joe quavered as he toppled to his knees into the steel and wood powder that used to be his shotgun. Like a torch flare, I felt his fury rise and boil over, increasing in intensity in waves, until it burned white hot. For a moment, I was concerned, but I relaxed and prepared myself as I allowed my combat training to kick in.

"Elisa, why did you do that?" I heard Derek say as he stepped to my side, his body tense for the fight that he knew would start. I felt a spike of protectiveness as his gaze swept over me and back to Joe. I was amused, but he would soon learn that I was far from in need of protection.

"Just watch," I said to him as I gently nudged him aside. I continued to study Joe while he gave ever further in to his rage. I watched his eyes flash with a fierce light from their crimson irises. His fangs grew, and his animal-like gaze was locked hard on me.

He screamed: a bestial, keening noise, shaking with enraged fury that made me queasy. But I stood my ground. A part of me wanted to goad him somehow, perhaps say something like "Well, what are you going to do about it?" But I cast that thought aside, opting for the moral high ground.

And so I waited. It was something I did not have long to do; Joe let out a snarl like a lion . . . and it was over almost as soon as it began.

Jewels are like a quantum physics version of a Swiss army knife, as Aiko once taught me. The fundamental laws of the universe are all physical expressions of mathematical equations, from the interactions of planets and galaxies, to atoms, molecules, and smaller. Jewels rewrite the equations, balancing them in different ways in order to enhance, subtract, or get around certain rules and paradigms. Jewels are the markers on the whiteboard of the universe, and we can do damn near anything with them that doesn't involve a physical contradiction. But learning to do it with finesse takes decades to centuries. Not even Father knew all the tricks one could pull with them as they seemed to work with slight differences from person to person, and with varying levels of complexity. But what I needed to do with Joe was mere child's play.

He was already too blinded by his rage in order to realize he was telegraphing his moves more easily than I could sense them. Again, I drew upon my Jewel and leaped forward to catch him by the neck as he charged me. With my already prodigious strength enhanced, manipulating his body, even in a full-on charge was laughably easy. I used the momentum of his motions to bring him down to the floor where I redirected kinetic energy to press him down. The entire scene must have looked like a pinwheel felling a charging bull. It left no imprint in the floor, neither did it leave a hole in the RV as Derek had expected. I'd used my Jewel to form an entropy bleed that redirected the waste energy away from its target. Rather than an impact with the floor, Joe's impact was with air, but just as hard as concrete and scalding hot from the entropy bleed.

I looked into his eyes, now much subdued from their former fury, my expression as much of a poker face as I could muster. My fangs extended almost painfully. I believe I caused a small cut in his head with my stunt, as I detected the scent of blood. Nourishing or not, I knew that his blood would have been so easy to take. He was powerless in my grip, and I could have fed from him freely. It would not have killed him, like the bite of any adult-size member of my kind would, but I could have greatly weakened him as a humiliation. Of course, that would have been anything but diplomatic. And as much as he annoyed me, he wasn't quite that annoying.

"Listen, little man. That was only a tiny fraction of what I can do. And there are soldiers for Lothos that can do far worse. If I wanted to, I could already have this camp under my little finger, but I'm not here to rule you. I'm here to protect you. And like it or not, that is what I'll be doing. So I believe we have come to a crossroads. Either you can be part of the solution . . . which means putting your petty paranoia aside and working with Derek and myself in order to ensure your survival, or at least staying the hell out of our way . . . or you can do your own thing. And when Lothos' company starts to play snooker with your eyeballs and man-parts while the rest of you is subjected to torments that would be the stuff of legends in hell, I won't shed a tear for your loss."

I jumped off of his chest, allowing the force of my dismount to wind him slightly. Now I understood why Derek chose to make a show of force to get him to listen, back at the ledge. The timbre of his mind was unmistakable. Joe was a dyed-in-the-wool alpha male who would assert dominance in any situation, given the chance. But his lack of intelligence was his own Achilles' heel. For a moment, I felt just a tinge of regret for my choice of actions. At the same time, I became aware of Derek's chagrin, and I knew why. I didn't need to feed from him; Joe would most likely see this: having been soundly beaten by what he saw as a child, as a humiliation in its own right, and would not be able to live with it. Though Joe's personal feelings were irrelevant to me, this notion filled me with a distinct sense of incredulity. I'd sincerely hoped he would have more sense than that.

Joe glowered at me, his eyes smoldering with a look that could melt diamonds . . . then vanished. I didn't bother to keep track of his preternatural motions, but I knew he'd beaten a hasty retreat as the entrance door, which I'd left open in my haste to enter, swung loosely on its hinges where it hadn't before.

"I'm sorry," I said, following a long and very uncomfortable silence between me and Derek. "Perhaps there was a better way to solve-"

"No, he deserved that," Derek said, much to my surprise. "He was going to shoot you."

"He was conflicted about it," I replied.

"Only about where to shoot you," Derek said. "That's why he hesitated. If he aimed true and shot you at that close range, even your head would've come clean off."

"Only if the buckshot managed to reach me," I said. "I'm second only to Aiko in Jewel mastery. And she's the strongest thaumaturgist in my clan. Do you honestly think a mere bullet could stop me? I have my Jewel set to react to any projectiles headed my way at that speed. My own speed will augment itself and I can either stop them, redirect their kinetic energy, or displace myself from dimensional sync in order to get around them. I was never in any real danger." I afforded a smile at Derek. "But I appreciate the chivalry."

Even Derek could not help but betray a smile of his own at this. Again, I felt him suppress an emotion that still evaded me, and as before, his smile was short-lived as the cares of the day oppressed his thoughts. He sighed and began to pace back and forth, reaching again for the box of cigarillos in his pocket.

"He's always been this way," Derek said, again realizing what he was doing and stuffing the box of cigarillos back into his pocket. "You'd think he'd at least try to be a little bit open, but he acts like such a child-" He paused and glanced my way, "No offense."

"None taken," I said. "I agree with you."

"Well, regardless, you've probably made yourself a dangerous enemy, Elisa." Derek's eyes narrowed as he looked out the window beside the kitchen. "He's gonna be out to get you."

"As long as his actions don't jeopardize this clan, then I can handle some bellend with a Napoleon complex," I said with a shrug. If Joe were to become a thorn in my side, then so be it. But we had bigger worries for now. "You should have told me that he was the father of the child, by the way."

Surprise spiked inside Derek like a spring-loaded blade. His gaze grew hard and penetrating, and I was almost certain he was attempting to look into my mind -"attempting" being the operative word. My defenses would be far more than a match for his own probing.

A look of slight frustration danced across his face, then he exhaled. "Lyman told you, didn't he? Paws?"

"We talked for a bit," I said with a nod, and I almost swore I heard Derek mutter the phrase, "what a loudmouth," subvocally. "I doubt knowing it would have smoothed over relations with Joe, but was there a reason why you didn't want to tell me?"

"Partly for his protection," Derek said. "Partly because he's an irresponsible jackass."

"Didn't want the baby, eh?" I asked.

"It was forced on him," Derek replied. "Joe and I are friends, of a sort, though that term is up for debate at the moment. He and I were hanging out in an old roach motel in Spokane for about a month. Little did Joe know that an old flame of his had been tracking him down. Girl was human, with more money than common sense, and she managed to find him. She showed up at our doorstep with a baby. Her efforts must've reached Lothos somehow, because while Joe confronted her out on the parking lot, leaving me with a squealing dhampir baby in my arms, the gunshot came. Girl was dead, and Joe and I had to do a nasty patch up job to cover our tracks, altering memories, throwing off the cops, and getting the hell out of town. We made it back to our clan, and we've been running ever since. Thank God Deb agreed to care for her, or I'd have been saddled with the baby myself. But Joe wants nothing to do with it. He suggested we just leave it at a police station, the cold bastard. So, more and more every day, I want to break his fangs and force him to take some damn responsibility."

"Well, then," I suppressed the smile that threatened to break out upon the side of my face, "I'm feeling less and less like a bloody heel for rowing with your friend."

"You don't hear me complaining," Derek said, "but as I said, he is vindictive."

I snorted at Derek's worry. "I'll cross that bridge when I come to-"

A knock at the still-open door intruded on our conversation, and another male of thicker build had now appeared upon the entrance stairs. Unlike Joe's crown of curly black hair, he was bald and sported a goatee over a much smaller mouth. Despite his size, his mannerisms suggested a much more amicable and far less dominant personality. In fact, if the timbre of Joe's mind suggested rigidity, this one, just as familiar, seemed downright pliable.

"So you must be Wadih?" I said. My question was immediately received with a wave of skepticism.

"I am," he said, and his voice confirmed what I sensed from him. His thick eyebrows knotted over his worried-looking eyes, and his posture took on a slightly defensive quality.

"You can come in," Derek said. Wadih was less guarded than he had been with me as he stepped inside and closed the door behind him.

"So this is the young lady who made Joe go off on a tear?" Wadih said. He had only given me a passing glance, and now looked directly at Derek, a wall of distrust between himself and me, but one that seemed much more open to being removed than Joe's had been.

"Her name's Elisa," Derek said, "and she's not quite as young as she looks." He gave me a sly grin, letting the words, old lady slip from his mind, much to my consternation. Still, it surprised me that he used his telepathy in this way. Until now, he seemed to have been quite conservative with it.

"Well, then, I have a bone to pick with you," Wadih said to me.

"Not the first; won't be the last," I said in spite of his somber mood. Seeing how both he and Derek found respective seats in the couches across from the sofa, I re-assumed my former perch before speaking again, specifically to Wadih.

"You're hoping I have a damn good reason for recalling you and the other perimeter guards," I said.

"It would be a good thing to know," Wadih answered, a bit taken aback by my having revealed his thoughts so openly. This clan was certainly not used to wanton use of the ability that my clan took for granted.

"I'm surprised you gentlemen haven't considered booby-trapping the area," I said.

Both gentlemen stared at me blankly for a moment. Then Wadih spoke.

"We've never needed to make them before, so none of us know how," he explained. "We looked into it once, but the ones that Marie-Laure's been able to come up with on the net are too complex and expensive to make."

"Besides, we don't stay in one place long enough to make a sophisticated grid of the area," Derek added. "We're looking at too much money, and time we just don't have. Right now, speed and constant movement have been our allies, trying to stay one step ahead of Lothos."

"That hasn't been serving you well thus far," I said.

"We've been doing all we can," Wadih replied, allowing some anger to creep into his words and emotions.

"I never said you weren't," I remarked, shaking my

hand from side to side as if brushing his frustrations from an invisible table. "And come to think of it, you're right. Homemade booby traps that are effective against our kind are prohibitively expensive to make. That's why I came equipped with the high-quality stuff."

"High-quality?" Derek said. He wasn't sure what to make of what I'd just said. Truth be told, he wanted to not believe me for whatever reason, but my words had a way of sounding convincing, even when I was bluffing -which I certainly was not. "You mean like sickspray canisters? UV lamps? That kind of thing?"

When I nodded, Wadih's eyes narrowed. "And where would you be hiding that kind of stuff? When we spotted you, we saw you with only a purse."

"Have you two ever been into tabletop games?" I asked, reaching for my satchel at the opposite end of the couch. "Dungeons & Dragons and the like?"

Both Derek and Wadih shook their heads, and I hefted the satchel into my lap.

"Well, I've been known to play it from time to time. There's a new recruit in our clan named Jesse who turned me on to it. He's neurotic about things like that. He's quite the geek, actually. But I digress. In the game, there's an item called a 'bag of holding,' which is essentially a satchel that is bigger on the inside than the outside."

I unzipped the satchel, reached inside. I smiled at Derek and Wadih's astonishment as I began to pull out a string of all the equipment we needed, attached to a velcro strap that was about fifty feet in length: clearly far more than the bag seemed to be able to hold. Like a magician pulling out a line of tissues from his magic hat, canisters of sickspray, miniature UV lamps, perimeter readers, and much more unwound into an impossibly-sized pile on the floor of the RV, mounted on two velcro straps of equal length.

"As you can see, I came equipped with more than a few tricks," I said, removing the last length of equipment and zipping the mouth of the satchel. "This is one of them. Like a bag of holding, it opens to a dimensional fold and can hold up to a car's mass of equipment with little trouble. It's also encoded to my DNA and brain waves, so it won't open unless I want it to."

"Someone could always steal it," Wadih said, "and then try to ransom it."

I gazed at him curiously, at first puzzled. It was odd for someone to pose such a question out of the blue without ill intent. Still, he did not feel like someone who would do such a thing. But then again, my satchel would perhaps be a valuable commodity to Lothos' clan. I'd never heard of him or his people using anything similar. Fortunately, that wouldn't be possible.

"Would you do it?" I asked Wadih. I allowed my voice to betray a hint of playfulness as well as warning as I spoke.

"What?"

"Would you do it?" I asked again in a much slower cadence.

"Of course not!"

"Then why would you ask?" I said. "Would someone in this clan attempt it?"

"That's enough." Derek spoke with finality in his voice combined with exasperation that exploded from his heart. "Elisa, I'll trust your judgment for our defense for now, but I draw the line at you giving my clan the third degree. Wadih has never stolen anything, and anyone who was guilty of theft in this clan would answer to me. And believe me; that's the last thing anyone wants. So knock it off."

"I never said that Wadih would steal anything," I said, perhaps a bit too innocently. Perhaps that was the reason Derek's tone grew even testier.

"Then why were you so keen on asking him if he would?"

"If you had let me finish," I replied, "I would have explained. If you'll forgive my tendency towards melodrama, I only wanted to give a good lead-in to what I wanted to say.

My satchel, you see, is rigged to give a nasty, continuous shock to any unauthorized handlers. Its voltage increases with each second, making theft more trouble than it's worth."

I then turned to Wadih, smiling with friendliness and contrition. "I do owe you an apology, however. I promise that I never suspected you of having any kind of desire to steal my belongings. As I said, I can sometimes be over-dramatic. Call it a bad habit. Are we forgiven?"

"I think I can forgive that," Wadih said. Though his forgiveness was genuine, he was still somewhat standoffish, not knowing what to truly make of me. I planned to rectify that.

"Now that that's done, back to business," I said, eyeing Derek. "We'll need another in our inner circle. It'll be good for a support structure in case some of your people have misgivings. And if Joe's little outburst is any indication, I'd bet on there being more than a few before this ordeal is over. Would you consider Wadih trustworthy?"

"A lot more than most here," Derek said, and then spoke to Wadih. "She's come to help us with our little problem with the shape-shifters, but we're passing her off as a newbie come to join us, at least for the time being."

Wadih nodded. "Seems logical. We haven't had the best track record of trusting strangers."

"Joe was less than enthusiastic about it," Derek said, and I saw him grin, albeit ruefully, "but you seem to be less . . . aggressive."

"Booby traps are only going to do so much," Wadih said to me, and I smiled at his insight. The timbre of his mind revealed a man who was brighter than he let on. I liked that. "I hope you have a back-up plan."

I gestured towards the considerable pile of equipment on the floor in front of me. "Oh, I'm quite aware that these will only be effective for so long. And afterwards, Lothos' troops will only be more determined to wipe you out. But-" I raised my finger in the air to make an edge to my point. "-that will only be if they'll be able to find you . . . which they won't."

Wadih rubbed at his goatee, and glanced at Derek, who seemed to have a disbelieving look of his own. "Really? And how will you pull that off?"

"By giving you a land of your own," I said.

Chapter Five

For some reason, I thought that my suggestion would have gone over better. I was perhaps being too optimistic. Derek and Wadih had been deliberating it still when I stuffed my equipment back into my satchel, excused myself, and went outside to set the traps.

All was quiet, save the sounds of crickets and nighttime animals that scurried in the tree limbs above. The temperature was cool and comfortable, and a small mist had developed. I hoped it wouldn't become fog. Darkness of night and shrouding mists were our allies, but we did prefer the loveliness of a clear, starry sky and a view of the moon above. Fog was just depressing.

The woods were dense with underbrush, and I poured my concentration into all my senses, becoming alert for the sound or scent of any approaching vampires, particularly the enemy, as I attended to my work. I first sent out a scouting module at the end of the strip that housed the traps. Linked to my Jewel, this device fed a grid of the area into my mind, including the lay of the land and the location of every tree that surrounded the encampment for half a mile. This way, I could direct each trap and its accompanying proximity trigger where I wanted it to go, and fasten it to any tree. It was a tedious process; I had hoped that Derek would have been able to help me, but he and Wadih were currently deadlocked, it appeared, on any decision. A part of me did not understand the reason for such heated debate. The life of a Vagabond was not a good life to raise a child, especially one of such a sought-after bloodline. Lothos' clan saw Vagabonds as trash, unworthy of birthing a dhampir. He would stop at absolutely nothing to claim her unless we could manage to keep her safe long enough for her to come of age and defend herself . . .

when she would be more than a match for any of the Others who would wish her harm.

I drew upon my Jewel to levitate each trap and send it to its respective spot on the map. I designated a section for the sickspray canisters, another for the UV lamps, and buried their proximity triggers in areas where any unwitting attacker would be certain to cross. Each unit had to be positioned one at a time. But it took little thought, as the program automatically calculated each module's best positioning.

The resulting reprieve from the confusion and pressure in the RV gave my mind a chance to wander in a moment of solace. In my first few hours, I had earned tenuous trust with Derek, utterly alienated and quite possibly made an enemy of Joe, had attained the uncertain respect of Wadih, and had re-awakened loyalty -at least to me- in Lyman, while the other members of this clan didn't yet know who I was. And I hadn't even met the baby. Still, all things considered, I supposed things could have turned out far worse.

I mulled over this as I worked, passing the time in my thoughts until my task's eventual end. I finagled the last few sickspray dispensers and UV lamps into position, then prepared to return to the encampment. I was feeling strangely hungry now, and I couldn't understand why. I had fed directly before leaving on my mission, after all. Our kind can go without feeding for at least three days, with effort. Once during special survival training, I had even gone four before my instincts threatened to take over and Justin brought me blood to assuage the beast within. This was distractingly mysterious. The contents of Derek's cooler were available to me, but I grimaced at the thought of drinking from those near-tasteless blood packs.

I caught the scent before I could even turn back towards the direction of the camp. It came on the breeze, sudden, clear and unmistakable. Its savor was so irresistible that my fangs extended until they hurt. I was suddenly a great deal hungrier than I had first felt, and this was just what I needed. Slinging my satchel over my shoulder, I set to follow the scent with the tenacity of a beast to a fresh spoor.

It was male, young, and very close.

Had the lights from the camp attracted the human? I wondered as I moved with all the silence my kind could muster, bounding from tree to tree above the brush line, allowing the scent to draw me further on. I recalled that the map grid had showed a nearby gravel road about half a mile to the east. This confirmed what I'd supposed; the lights from the camp would most likely have been visible from that area. I could not remember the last time I'd needed to hunt a human for food, but to say that it was like riding a bike would not be a proper comparison. Despite how my clan abhorred the act, it felt inexplicably "right" to do this. This wasn't just second nature; this was our nature: atavistic and primal. It was nothing that we needed to learn. As much as we hated to admit it, Lothos, for all his twisted nature, lies, and megalomania, had been right with one thing: We were apex predators, the things that hunted humans. All our powers, our senses, our speed, our titanic strength, our physical beauty -these were inborn tools to locate, attract, and subdue our prey. Father had managed to train himself to use those powers for a higher purpose, one that would benefit humankind. He subdued the bloodlust that rages within us all and chose instead, to thrive alongside humans, rather than be merely facilitators of death. Restraint was an unbelievably difficult choice, as it went against our very core nature. But through it, he learned things that he could never have known had he taken the path of least resistance. One of these discoveries was how the toxins in our saliva actually served a quasi-beneficial purpose in humans. Though they became irrevocably "addicted" to us, humans gained a greatly increased lifespan and near-perfect health, in addition to increased strength, stamina, and speed. Thus, Father shifted the paradigm, changing what would have been a predator-prey relationship into one of mutuality. We obtained a renewable supply of food, and at times, companionship, and our human friends obtained a higher quality of life, paid only in a portion of blood. Many of them, their lives and families joined to our own in that mutual relationship, understood the fact that this war was just as much for their survival as our own, and used the gifts our kiss bestowed upon them to rally to our cause.

But in times where we found ourselves in need, we could still hunt. It was distasteful, but a matter of satiation versus the madness of starvation. Still, there were rules we followed in doing this. First, we were never to drink more than a pint. This was the minimum amount that would sustain us and would leave the host only slightly weak. Second, we were to always erase the memory of the experience from the host, so that he or she would be able to live their lives as normally as possible afterwards.

I was only a few feet from him when I stopped my forest trek. I grasped the trunk of the tree hard, sinking my claws into its firm bark and stopping myself. Despite the fluidity of my movements, I made a tiny rattle in the branches above. The human nearly spotted me as he swept his flashlight beam in my direction. Had I not shifted myself quickly onto the opposite side of the tree, my hunt would perhaps have become messier than intended.

Judging by his uniform, the walkie-talkie at his hip and the tranquilizer gun slung over his back, I deduced that he was a park ranger of some sort. I stayed where I was, keeping watch as his gaze swept suspiciously over the lay of the land. Barely breathing, I waited until doubts began to creep into his heart over what he'd heard.

"Must've been my imagination," I at last heard him mutter. "But I could've sworn I . . . Maybe some kind of mosquito swarm? Nah, guess I was just hearing things."

His words explained it. He must have been attracted by the buzzing noise that the booby trap modules made as they floated to their positions. It had been rather loud, even to a human who would happen to be driving by, but I thought that Derek and his clan had pitched camp far away from civilization? Of course, moving all those RVs and trailers would have still required a nearby road, which I did not see connecting to the camp on the map grid. But hadn't I seen a bunch of felled trees upon my arrival here? True, our kind, if they worked as a team, could have brought trees down and moved them quickly, and without making much noise in the bargain, but a road would still have been needed. It then occurred to me that Derek and his clan must have carved their own pathway into the forest for extra safety. If this was the case, then I was impressed. They possessed more elegance and finesse than I had given them credit for.

I waited patiently, watching the human, feeling the distant agony of my hunger growing with his closeness. I restrained myself as I anticipated the right moment to strike. If he spotted me before the deed, I would frighten him. This I could deal with when I would erase his memory, but perhaps not well enough. Fear was a particularly tenacious emotion, the memory of which being especially difficult to remove. If I left a deep enough memory of that fear, it might evade erasure, and keep him coming back, despite having remembered nothing else. The worse scenario, however, the one I wanted most to avoid, was the possibility that I might be too slow in my subduing him. If that happened, he might have the chance to use his walkie-talkie and alert his colleagues before I could take him. I needed to bring him down swiftly and suddenly in order to avoid that.

My mouth watered at his pervasive scent, and the cornucopia of toxins in my saliva was primed and ready to take him over. I remained still and silent for several moments more, waiting until the exact moment when he would be the least wary. He was alone, and the night, at least to his less sensitive ears, was dead silent. And by measures, his certainty decreased.

At last, it came. Discouraged at last, the ranger turned

away and headed back for his jeep, which lay a few hundred feet down the road. His thoughts broadcasted his belief that he had come out here for nothing, that he'd only been hearing things, and this was my cue. Making barely a deathwatch's click, I rounded the tree, and leaped from its boughs onto the back of my prey.

He gasped only once before I bit him. He had intended to scream, but my toxins drowned his initial feelings in bliss that was as profound as it was unexpected. Humans always expect the first puncture to hurt, but it rarely does. Our toxins erase the pain before the brain has a chance to register it . . . then comes the euphoria, which takes us both.

I felt him try to grab me, to try and struggle in order to throw me off -not that he would have succeeded-, but my toxins quickly sapped him of the will to fight. More out of reflex than fright, his fist pounded uselessly upon my back only once. I felt him grasp the back of my blouse, then felt his grip loosen, and his arm slumping back down to his side. I held on steadfastly as he staggered to his knees; the euphoria flooded through him, and I relished that moment as the full effect of his blood suffused me. I swallowed several delightful gouts, feeling my muscles tighten in reflexive bliss. My eyes rolled back as I licked over the wounds from my fangs, the chemicals in my tongue speeding the healing process of his flesh so that the punctures partially sealed. This stanched the blood to a languorous flow, allowing me to take my time with him. I overlapped my mind to his own, shielding him from any effects of fear, and whispering sweet words as my drink sank him deeper into a mellow, sweet oblivion.

Everything will be all right, my dear. There's nothing to fear. You will not die from my kiss. Be happy and don't fight. You'll wake up in your jeep, having dreamed a sweet dream. There, now . . . just fall asleep. Asleep . . . Asleep . . .

I may not have liked the method it took to feed from him, but I had to admit that his blood was exquisite. I must have sighed aloud several times as I continued to drink, wistfully regretting having to make him forget. National parks were sometimes haunts for Lothos' disciples, and there were too few of my clan to patrol them all, report the vermin, and clean them out. I considered informing Father of this human at a later time, to have him visited for recruitment into our clan for just that purpose, though my intent, admittedly, would not be entirely altruistic. I would have loved to have tasted his blood again. But for now, that plan would have to be shelved for the sake of my mission. He would remember this only as a sweet dream before it faded from his mind.

I drank my fill, which for my size, was somewhat less than a pint, then sealed the wounds completely. Still, I admit that I had overindulged just a bit. An advantage to my size is that under normal circumstances, I am too small to ever be in danger of taking a grown human's life; however, I knew that my drink would give him quite a row with illness as his body purged my toxins throughout the next day or so. This was the downside to taking a human who was not already a host. To that nameless ranger, it would be a mysterious, short-lived bout with nausea and tremors after a very pleasant dream that evaded any attempt to recall. Otherwise, he would be fine. I hefted him onto my shoulders and returned him to his jeep, where I sat him in the driver's seat to wake up none the wiser. I then used my Jewel to erase the path we made in the gravel road, and kissed his cheek before retreating back into the woods and towards the camp, leaving as soundlessly as I came.

***

Derek had been looking for me. I knew it by the urgency and intent in his thoughts. He seemed almost worried, in fact. This was somewhat puzzling, seeing how we had known each other barely three hours. I was confident that I'd at least begun to earn his respect, but thus far, he had been otherwise neutral or cordial at best towards me and distrustful at worst.

Had something happened at the camp? I quickened my pace, returning to the spot where I had set up the traps, following the timbre of his mind to meet up with him.

I arrived at the same time I saw him appear, walking casually, as if he hadn't been urgently seeking me out but moments ago. Even his thoughts, at first focused keenly on me, were now like the flat surface of a lake. It was a fair enough ruse, I decided, since I myself was now feigning quiet and calm, as if I hadn't been hurrying back to meet up with him with just as much alacrity as he'd sought me.

"Hey, China doll," he said. "You finished setting up the traps?"

I nodded and made a sweeping gesture about the forest. "They've been posted all around the camp, creating a one hundred foot perimeter. You needn't worry about your people tripping them, by the way. They've been encoded to scent markers unique to those who have been part of Lothos' clan for awhile. So unless you have any new arrivals from the other side, everyone should be able to take a short-distance stroll in the woods safely."

"And how will we know they work?" Derek asked.

"Oh, believe me. You'll know." I made a vague gesture towards the perimeter just beyond the ridge. "The sickspray traps might not create much of a giveaway if the target has a strong enough constitution, but I've been hit by the stuff before. It was only a mild dose, but I could only barely keep myself from crying."

Derek grimaced. His revulsion, I realized, came from personal experience, but his thoughts were not specific enough for me to determine when or where. "Yeah, sickspray's some vicious stuff, all right. Who knew mixing garlic with a few inert compounds could be so nasty?"

"The UV emitters will get a good scream out of them, though," I said, betraying a sinister grin.

"I'm hoping for that." Derek smiled back with the same wickedness as me. "Payback for all the trouble they've caused us."

I knew he was aware that this would only be a temporary fix. Booby traps would be nothing to a thaumaturgist. This would perhaps dispatch the next few waves of attackers because of their ignorance, possibly even get an unwitting thaumaturgist . . . perhaps two if we were lucky. However, all it would take would be someone surviving the perimeter and reporting what he or she found. Once Lothos got wise to the traps, Derek's troubles would begin anew, perhaps worse than before, because Lothos' people would be out for payback. He had no idea how much I had hoped that he would consider my offer.

"So, how did deliberations go?" I asked, switching unceremoniously to that subject. I'd hoped that some kind of agreement had at least been made with Wadih.

"Wadih's open to it, but he doesn't like how you just barged in and demanded all these changes," Derek replied with a notably sour look. "I don't blame him."

"You were only getting by," I reminded him.

Derek hissed out a frustrated breath. "I know, I know. We're not idiots, but some of this bunch can be stubborn as hell. We've been just fine on our own for centuries, you know. But I know what you're thinking. Some might say that we've just been lucky until now."

"I believe you have been," I said.

"I'm inclined to agree after our last few adventures with the shape-shifters," Derek said, "But your offer is something that I can't just turn one member of my clan on to; I'll have to consult everyone. They all have to be part of this."

I let a long pause hang in the air. I was about to make another suggestion that he wouldn't like, yet would make all the sense in the world, and I believe he knew it. So I said it before he could ask.

"Why tell them right now?"

"Excuse me?"

"You're their leader, are you not?" I said. "So why are

you obligated to clear your decisions with them? This is your entire clan's survival we're talking about, after all. Shouldn't that take precedence?"

"Whoa! Wait a minute! I think you overestimate what it means to be a leader, here!" Derek was gesticulating wildly as if I'd said something so absurd as to be obscene.

"I don't profess to know how you operate, Derek, but from what I've seen, your clan does defer to you," I said, making another observation that I hoped he wouldn't find quite so difficult to take. "It seems you tell them where to go and what to do. Is that true?"

"Well, yes, but they're not obligated to do what I say," Derek said.

"Are you their leader, or not?" I asked again. My question triggered a burst of anger, quickly suppressed, then frustration. Derek opened, then closed his mouth several times before inhaling deeply, struggling to find a place of calm before speaking again.

"We don't like to say we have a 'leader,' he explained making air quotes, "but I guess I fit the bill. I'm the go-to guy for things. They do what I tell them, if it's within reason. I say where we go next, and arrange things like hunting parties, clean-up, buying supplies, protection, et cetera. They trust me. I have no idea why, but they do."

"Why wouldn't they?" I asked. "You seem a capable enough leader."

"Yeah, but I don't look it." Derek gestured across the breadth of his body, only a head and a half taller than me, but still, noticeably more mature: muscles more developed, if his frame beneath the hoodie were any indication, his features still soft, but frozen in the midst of maturing while I was little more than a tiny, slender, round-faced "China doll," as he'd taken to calling me. Nevertheless, no one would have been able to mistake him for an adult. He was far too short, and nowhere near filled out enough.

"This body isn't without its problems. There are places

I can't go, even with adult supervision. Hell, I couldn't go into a bar even if I wanted to. I get harassed by the police wherever I go, especially in places where there's a curfew. I can't even get smokes by myself; Joe has to do that for me! I also can't disguise myself as an adult, because I never learned to shape-shift, even when I was running with Lothos' pack. That little disability put me at peon level with the clan, just to add insult to injury. When I got away and joined this group, Syd and Joe were the only ones who seemed to give two shits about me."

"Syd?" I asked. And as if the night had become darker, a pall of melancholy overlapped Derek's thoughts.

"He was the head guy before me." He looked away as if he'd been ashamed to talk about it. "Lothos' soldiers got him a couple of weeks back. Tell the truth, that really messed us up. He'd been running this pack for about eighty years before. Didn't realize he was grooming me to take his place until he was gone. I didn't even know how old he was, or where he came from. But . . . well, I inherited a clan from him, as you can see."

"Then that means they truly do look up to you."

Slowly, I came to his side and took his hand. Skin-to-skin contact tends to amplify our ability to touch minds, but his mind was surprisingly more guarded than most, even with this type of contact. His skin felt no different from any of our kind: perfect in texture and generally cooler than humans. I was nevertheless surprised at how good it felt just to touch him. I was somehow comfortable with him, even more so than when I hugged Father or Roland. That comfort was short-lived, however, as he jerked his hand away. I felt a spike of incomprehensible emotion just before he did it. There was no malice; rather, it was such a tangle of mixed feelings that it was nearly impossible to tell one from the other. And then, it was snatched up just as quickly as it appeared. The entire experience caught me quite off my guard and left me reeling for just a moment. I gasped at the suddenness and speed of it all.

"I'm sorry." Derek's tone was terse, and he still looked away from me, but I felt that he meant it. "I just . . . I have a thing about being touched. It's nothing personal. What were you saying, now?"

"You don't realize your own power," I said, ignoring his obvious lie. "You are their leader, Derek. I haven't met all of your clan yet, but one thing I have seen from those I've met is that they are at the very least, strongly inclined to trust you. Even Joe. He may hate your current decisions with every fiber of his being, but I've touched his mind deeply enough to know that he won't undermine your authority. I know you don't like my presence, let alone the changes I've suggested, but I think you know that it's the best course of action. I'm not saying that you oughtn't to tell them; I'm only suggesting you postpone it until we're well on our way."

I pleaded with my eyes as Derek at last shifted his gaze to me. "I believe you know that this is your best recourse. My clan has many hiding places. We want to set one aside for you as a temporary refuge. You won't have to give up your ways permanently. It would only be until the baby grows up. We can even help you train her to be an asset to you. Dhampirs are powerful, more so than you realize. They're as strong and fast as any of us; they heal just as quickly, aren't affected by sickspray or sunlight, and they can take either blood or human food. In fact, one of our dhampirs, Nicholas, was supposed to be assigned this mission, but he was needed elsewhere. I was the second choice."

I felt the protest in his mind before he could utter it. So before he could respond, I continued, gesturing sternly to silence him. "But that doesn't make me less knowledgeable. Nicholas is barely older than you are, while I've had nearly two centuries of experience in this war. Also, I speak for Father. You need to lay low in a safe place for a time. I believe it is your best option. You are this clan's leader. I believe I'm offering you the wiser choice, and I'm ready to lead you to safety. However, you must be the leader you need to be. Your clan may not like this, but I'm trying to save them, and I'm trying to save you."

I watched his eyes shift about furtively and felt his uncertainty. He was a leader, but I believe I was correct in my assumptions about his lack of confidence in his own power. I let my words hang in the air as he wrestled with his lingering doubts, despite the fact that he'd just twisted Wadih's arm to capitulate to my plan.

"Are you sure this is our best option?"

Derek spoke as if he loathed asking the very question.

"Unless you have a better idea . . . ?" I remarked, cementing my point.

He scowled, again careful to not direct his emotions at me, but still not liking this predicament at all. On an academic level, I could understand it. I always had been taught that Vagabonds felt the call of the road. They were something like gypsies in that regard. So this was, at its most basic level, a matter of pride. I was asking Derek to give up tradition for much longer than he, or any of his clan, would be comfortable with.

"No, I don't have a better idea," Derek said after a pause so long that I wondered if he would ever respond. "God knows I'd like to have one, though. I know the others won't like it. Some might even want to leave once they do realize it."

"Then you should let them," I said, bearing the sting that my words produced in him across the gulf of our minds. "But I'm almost certain Lothos is keeping tabs on your clan somehow."

"So you're beginning to think there might be a mole too?" Derek asked.

"It's certainly not out of the question." I stood a bit straighter at this. "Any idea who it may be?"

Derek shook his head. "Not a clue."

"Then that is a bridge we'll cross if and when we get to

it," I remarked. "Besides, if you do have a mole, then it's all the more reason for your clan to not know what we're doing."

"We'll go by what you suggested," Derek said after a very loud sigh, "For now. But so you know, if I, or any member of my clan comes up with a better idea, we're going with that instead. No arguments."

"You're the leader," I said with an acquiescent nod.

"You're making me feel less and less like one," Derek remarked sourly.

"I'm sorry."

He was silent for several moments more before he allowed a decidedly unhappy smile to appear at the edge of his mouth.

"I want to like you," he said, "but your suggestions are making it hard to do."

"Oh, I'm not so bad, once you get to know me." I slipped a bit back into my normal puckishness. I was known for being much more lighthearted around my clan, and it felt good to be more myself after such a long night of playing the diplomat out of necessity.

Suddenly Derek paused, sniffed the air, and then his narrow-eyed gaze fell directly upon me. "You smell like a human," he said. "I was so distracted that I didn't notice it until now."

"I . . . caught the scent of one nearby," I admitted, my lighter mood being weighted somewhat with chagrin. "It was a park ranger."

"You fed from him?" Derek said.

"He was nearby, and I was hungry," I explained.

"I thought your clan didn't like hunting humans."

"Normally we don't. A few of us still do it for fun, but the rest of us only do it during emergencies."

"I had blood packs in my RV." Derek raised an eyebrow, and I felt as if I was truly my body's age again, with no experience of feeding or discernment of taste, and Father had caught me raiding the Lair's stock of blood packs.

"Well . . . with all due respect, you should know that blood from packs barely has any taste at all."

Derek said nothing, and I felt my cheeks grow very red as my self-consciousness spiked. Ever more desperately, I felt the need to explain myself, and when I did, my voice was an octave or two higher than normal: a fact that I'm certain Derek found quite amusing -the bastard.

"Your clan hunts humans all the time! And you're suddenly judging me?"

Slowly, Derek smiled, this time with true mirth, and he let loose a guffaw.

"I know, China doll. I know. I could tease you for it; God knows I want to, but I won't. It was just funny to see the look on your face."

I pursed my lips in a pout . . . which was the only expression I could manage. I wanted to punch him square in his man-parts, but I thought better of it. Besides, that injury wasn't as effective with males of our kind; they recovered from it far more quickly than humans did.

"Why do I get the feeling you're going to delight in pissing me off whenever you get the chance?" I said, attempting to distance myself from my anger. I inhaled deeply, and felt it ebbing away, but his next words helped to alleviate it fully.

"And just think, we've barely known each other for one night," Derek said, still unrepentant in his amusement. Perhaps it was because I felt so comfortable in his presence, that despite his hubris, I could not help but laugh myself.

Chapter Six

The next two nights were surprisingly uneventful.

The one exception to this was one very clumsy agent of Lothos who was blinded by one of the sickspray traps, then roasted alive by the UV lamps. It was actually rather disappointing, as it robbed me of the opportunity to interrogate him -not that I believed he would have known anything of any significance. Still, the process would have at least been a change of pace for me, but I couldn't complain. At least we knew the perimeter defenses worked.

We found the victim dead at the outer perimeter of the traps, his charred remains frozen in the middle of a shift, making for a particularly twisted-looking corpse. It seemed as if he had been trying to become a thin, red-headed man, perhaps Wilson, one of the other guards who had been dismissed from his job along with Joe and Wadih. Like Joe, Wilson had been none too happy about his change of position, but was far less vocal about it. Still, like Deb, a willowy, black-haired woman with eyes as thin and cold as Aiko, he avoided me, even when Derek tried to introduce us. In Deb's case, it oddly wasn't distrust or fear I felt from her that day; it was hatred. Derek noticed this as well, but I knew that though he was their de facto leader, there were some things even he had no control over.

Deb's inexplicable feelings towards me aside, our brief encounter at least allowed me to finally see the baby. She was a perfect angel, with wispy brown hair and a cherubic face, but with one blue eye and one red. Heterochromia was a common trait among dhampirs, though most possessed normal human eye color. This, however, was tinged with an ethereal glow that appeared during times of strong emotion, similar to when our own eyes flashed. Her teeth had already grown in; that happened only a week or two after birth, since dhampir babies were just as comfortable drinking blood as they were eating human food. Even vampire's blood could nourish them at least until the age of three. I didn't smell baby food on her, as one would expect, but Deb's breasts were rather large, and as I smelled a great deal of blood upon her skin, there was no need to guess the source of her nutrition.

There were three other men who were regulars in the camp: Randy, Benjamin, and Pablo, who owned a separate truck and were often away on errands when the group would settle in one spot. I met them on the second night of my mission, when they caught up with us in an abandoned field. Randy looked almost like a classic lumberjack with his large frame and flannel shirt, and his hair was just as thick and dark as Derek's, though longer. He held it in a ponytail behind his wide face. Benjamin was Randy's polar opposite with short, blond hair and a willowy frame, and dressed in a simple NFL t-shirt and jeans. Any combination of these was his staple apparel, as I was soon to discover. Pablo was a beanpole, no matter how you looked at him, but he was blindingly fast -the fastest member of the clan, in fact, as I once heard Derek boast. I was hard-pressed to argue that he was right. At preternatural speed, even my eye couldn't keep up with him as he started to unloaded the trucks he and his colleagues had arrived in.

The trio had returned from a supply run with their truck beds filled with boxes of every candy imaginable, as well as cigarettes, pipes, cigars, even jars of shisha for the hookah that I'd seen Wadih smoke once before. As the newest addition to the clan, I was set to work assisting with the distribution and storage of all these luxury items. Despite my delight at the bounty of treats they brought in tow, I was somewhat concerned that I hadn't been told about this group and their extended leave during my arrival, and was more than a little worried that they had been trailed.

Blood is all we need for sustenance, but we can still

eat human food; it just no longer nourishes us. So most of our kind takes to things that humans consider vices, like smoking or excessive sweets since these foods aren't meant to be actual "food," even for humans. With the sweet tooth from our human days quite intact, the taste gives us more pleasure than normal food, and we have the luxury of eating it guilt-free -a fact that our human friends are most decidedly jealous of. Judging by the sheer amount of their parcels, it seemed that these Vagabonds indulged in that part of their lost humanity quite often.

I was paid for my work with boxes of chewing gum in various flavors, Reese's Pieces, small jawbreakers, and a few king-size chocolate bars. I stored them in my satchel once I'd brought it to the RV, then spent my time getting to know these heretofore unknown clan members. They were standoffish, like Wadih, but didn't seem to mind me. In fact, Pablo was quite bemused by my presence. Perhaps this was because it took him the longest among his compatriots to finally accept the fact that I wasn't a child until I could no longer tolerate his talking down to me. But he was contrite and amicable enough after my reprimand. The others, once they became used to my presence, were curious at best, indifferent at worst. But aside from Lyman and Wadih, I surmised that they were the next best prospects for allies.

The rest of the clan who were laying low due to this emergency kept in contact solely through updates given by Marie-Laure, the only other female aside from Deb: dark-skinned and mysterious, and again, none too friendly. Her accent placed her as Haitian in my mind, but I could have been wrong. Her dislike of me came from a sense -a correct sense- that I was not all that I seemed. Still, she didn't seem to outright hate me. She was the "communications specialist," as Derek described her. It was a polite euphemism, but I knew a hacker when I saw one. Of course, she worked with human technology, but her talents were extensive despite the primitive nature of her collection of laptops, tablets and cell phones. I had the privilege of seeing her in action once, keeping tabs on the remaining members of the clan scattered abroad. Derek could give the word, and she would recall them at a moment's notice, if the need arose; for now, they all seemed to be alive and well.

"You're bad juju," Marie-Laure said to me as I stared at one of her collection of computers, specifically, the ones that showed the GPS markers: green dots on a grid laid over a picture of the United States on Google Maps. I felt her presence by my side, her dislike of me disturbing, as if she were breathing down my neck with oven-hot breath, and with a smartly pointed knife at my back. And like a knife, her words were smartly cadenced to convey her threat. "I'll tell you this. If they die, then I'll have a good sharp look at you."

"You worry too much," was all I said, my tone kept safely between overtly hostile and overly kind. Not to be intimidated, I cast a very nonchalant, yet narrow-eyed gaze at her. Responding to my statement, she'd given me a most distasteful, but nonetheless amusing, scowl. "Tell me, is this how your clan greets all their new additions? It's a wonder how any of them stay with you."

"Respect is earned, not given, child." I seethed at that word, "child," but held my tongue for a more opportune time. "I believe you know that, yes? I know things. I can look into files you don't know. Most of us are damn good at erasing ourselves, but I can do the opposite. I can make you the biggest target for local law enforcements. Imagine your face on all the wanted posters in the state . . . in every state we go through. You'd be spending a lot of time in the confines of this caravan. It'd be about the only place you'd be safe. I'd like to see a vampire go stir crazy."

I almost laughed. She didn't know who I was, and I was certain that if she did, she'd stay very far away from me. Her skills were perhaps as good as she boasted, but Reanon, the resident scientist and physician of my clan, had access to Father's technology, which could wipe out just about every system in this trailer with a thought, to say nothing of the most sophisticated government mainframes and servers. I realized that I could have truly angered this woman for her overconfidence, perhaps said something along the lines of, "You're cute," just to goad her into trying whatever she had in mind, but beneath her bravado fueled by dislike, I felt that she really didn't have any such intent. She was simply trying for an "alpha female" assertion. She simply liked feeling like the one in charge . . . the queen of her respective hill. So I countered with something a bit more subtle.

"My dear Marie-Laure, I believe you'll find that I will be of invaluable benefit to your clan," I said with the sweetest smile I could muster. "Also, I feel obligated to remind you that our kind holds their fair share of individual secrets. Please don't provoke me to reveal mine."

I glanced one last time over her collection of hardware before taking my leave. "You do good work, by the way."

She was rightly pissed about the whole affair, but I think my part of the discussion was effective, at least, as she never did quite get up the nerve to come through with her threats. Derek and I had a good laugh about it that night as we walked about the campsite's perimeter. He and I had taken to spending most of our spare time together this way.

It struck me as odd, actually. I'd come to realize that we actually spent quite a bit of time together. I slept in that snug little corner of his RV during the day, yet despite how guarded his thoughts were, as well as his ever-present misgivings about my presence or the defensive situation I'd talked his clan into, we got on fairly well . . . though I wouldn't say that he actually liked me. A more accurate assessment would be that he respected me. It was mutual respect, actually. One would think that being in such close quarters, we would begin to grate on each other's nerves. But instead, I felt comfortable around him, as if I belonged with his clan, or perhaps with him. Of course, I had no intention of joining them; I was content with Father's side and dedicated to our struggle, not to mention that I had friends and family back home. With the exception of Lyman, and perhaps Pablo, no one here seemed to genuinely like me. Derek seemed to only tolerate me at the best of times, and he never did quit calling me "old lady" in his more cantankerous moments. Otherwise, it was often a series of contrasts with him. One moment, we were arguing about tactics for dealing with Lothos' clan; the next, we were satisfying each other's curiosity about our lives. It was both exhilarating and frustrating, but believe it or not, those were the peaceful times.

The caravan had been well on its way to my suggested sanctuary. Thus far, I'd refrained from telling anyone -Derek included- about where it would be. Derek once again gave me grief about this until I explained that it was for his clan's own safety that they not yet know. In the event that one of his clan was captured, even himself, Lothos could get no information this way. He reluctantly agreed, but still fumed about it, as he was wont to do.

The plains that surrounded the abandoned farmhouse were nearly flat, with low hills in the distance, and scraggly trees scattered sparsely about. I'd set the traps underground earlier, wondering if the previous would-be attacker had come with a partner. If he or she did, then Lothos would know, and we would have a much more difficult time the next go-round. But for now, the night was peaceful, and setting the traps here was a much easier task than it had been in the forest. Derek had wanted to help, but I'd finished it before he had a chance to catch up with me after his duties. The vehicles of the caravan surrounded the campfire as always, while Derek and I sat on an old bench outside the farmhouse, the last usable part of an outdoor picnic set, judging from the shapes of the rotting wood across from it.

"I'm a little bit nervous about choosing this campsite," Derek said, glancing warily about. The land was open, and you could see for miles. Visibility was excellent, especially now, as the last vestiges of day reflected off the last remnants of blue in the sky. Sparse clouds in shades of lavender and pink hung at the edge of the horizon. This cast far too little ultraviolet to be harmful to us; in fact, those of us who woke this early, myself especially, found it quite pleasant. It was early autumn and the weather was cool. The sound of distant birds going to roost or beginning their night hunts echoed in the distance amidst the low mooing of cows in some distant pasture that hadn't been left fallow.

"There's good visibility," I said, trying to hide my exasperation at his negativity.

"Yeah, for us and them." Derek sucked on one of his cigarillos, which he had learned to not be so timid of smoking in my presence, and exhaled a sultry plume that released a dense aroma of burning cherries. "It was a place like this where we were first attacked . . . and where Syd bought it."

"I'm sorry," I said.

"Not your fault, China doll. It's an old wound," Derek shook his head with a frown that bordered on pain. It looked more like he was working the kinks out of his muscles than making any kind of negating gesture. "This place just reopens it some. I thought I'd gotten over it. Or maybe it's just my fears come back to haunt me."

"Fears about my instructions?" I said. "You still have misgivings about them?"

"You need me to confirm that?" Derek said. "I thought you could read minds."

"Only what you bring-"

"-to the surface. Yeah, you've told me."

"Your mind is hard for me to read," I said, making another attempt to verbally break through his surprisingly difficult mental wall. I didn't know why I was so eager, or perhaps desperate to do so, but rather than repel as I expected, his privacy vexed and called to me.

"We all have our secrets," Derek said. He carried a subtle yet adamant message in that statement. He certainly had his secrets, and I was not about to learn them today. "Isn't that what you told Marie-Laure?"

"Touché." I giggled with the reminder of that conversation, and he joined me with his own soft laugh, releasing the tension of the moment that I had not realized had previously been there.

"I actually like nights like this," Derek said a few minutes later, breaking the lengthy but not uncomfortable ensuing silence. "I don't normally wake up at times when you can still catch a bit of daylight in the sky."

"Me neither," I said. "And I love it."

"That's a surprise to me," Derek remarked.

"Really?" I said, not knowing whether to be curious or offended. I felt Derek's chagrin. He was blunt, but astute, and I knew that he realized he might have said something wrong.

Derek's words came out with no small amount of trepidation. "Well, correct me if I'm wrong, but didn't you mention yesterday that you only remember being a vampire? I'd have thought that seeing a sunset would be, well, painful."

"Painful how?" I honestly didn't mean to cause Derek distress at this point, but I genuinely didn't understand what he meant.

Derek opened his mouth, closed it, and his expression shifted several times into some variation of confusion or frustration. He started to speak, then stopped, each time becoming more frustrated. And these emotions did come to the surface of his mind. At last, I understood, and rather than reach for his hand, I touched his shoulder, which was covered by the sleeve of his ever-present hoodie. He stopped his pitiful attempts at vocalization and looked at me, his eyes partially pleading.

"Do you remember your last sunset?" I asked. "Your last blue sky?"

"Of course, I do," Derek said. "It's probably one of the things I remember best."

"So when you see this . . ." I swept my hand across the horizon, whose fading light was becoming suffused with the ocean of stars in the encroaching black, ". . . you are struck with fond, wistful, or even painful memories of what you lost of your human days."

He nodded, and I paused for a moment of emphasis.

"Derek, can you think fondly of, or mourn for a limb that you never had?"

"What? I don't understand-"

"It's a simple question," I said, neither angry nor frustrated. "Can you have fond memories of, or mourn for the loss of a limb you never had?"

"Well, no," Derek was still understandably puzzled by my question, "of course not."

"Exactly," I said. "It makes no sense. It's like the blue sky. I have no memory of it. I don't remember being human."

"No memory at all?"

"My first memories are of waking up in the Lair with Justin, Aiko, Father, and Roland," I said, shaking my head. "My first sensation was the thirst for blood. I guess on some instinctual level, I thought something wasn't right . . . that this wasn't the way I was supposed to be, but I didn't know any better. They gave me blood, and I drank it. It ended the thirst. I guess if I remembered being human, I'd have been repulsed by it. I've seen enough newly-turned who react that way, but I've always known myself as I am. Father took me in; He and Roland raised me; Roland and Aiko schooled me; I've only known night. Once, out of curiosity, I burned myself by staying awake until sunrise and opening the sun shutters just a crack. Good thing my coffin was right there and not in the way of the beam of light. The pain of that burn was so bad, I cried myself to sleep. Of course, Father and Roland found out the next day when they saw the wound on my arm that hadn't completely healed. I got a good scolding for that. It ended my curiosity, but that's all I've ever had, Derek. Curiosity. No romantically wistful feelings for what I'd lost, because it's like I never lost it. This life is all I've known. I've never known the sun except as an enemy."

"An enemy?" Derek frowned for only the briefest moment then blew out a gust of air. "Sorry to hear that," he said. "But that's nothing new, or anything. I heard stuff like that when I was running with Lothos. To be honest, you don't know what you're missing."

"I always considered myself lucky to be spared that knowledge," I replied. "It keeps me from silly romantic notions." Quickly I added a qualification. "That's not to say that your thoughts on it are silly."

"No offense taken," Derek gave a wan smile. "I just never thought of it that way. 'Course I've never met another vamp who had never seen the sun before."

"I've never been wistful about it," I remarked, "but as I said, I have been curious. However, Father did invent a device that satisfied that curiosity in ways that allowed me to not be burned. It was only that one time that it happened out of ignorance."

"Device?" Derek breathed, and I felt a sense of interest arouse within him like a woken beast. In fact, it was not unlike the hunger for blood when it rouses within us. There was no secret that despite his misgivings, he found me interesting at the least, but this emotion that my comment evoked went beyond curiosity. Perhaps it was fascination . . . or even lust. For a moment, it actually frightened me.

"I'm sure you know this, but both Father and Lothos have technology that would seem miraculous to people nowadays," I explained, half uncertain that I should do so. "Of course, that's to be expected when you have ten thousand years to pursue your work without the inconvenience of death. One of those technologies is . . . well, it's a room, I guess you could call it. We use it for training mostly, but some of us use it to replicate a sunlit environment without the harmful effects of UV light."

"Like a holodeck or something?"

"You could call it that," I said, and betrayed a brief frown. I hated that word in spite of how well it fit the description of the device; comparing Father's technology to science fiction made it seem pithy to me. "Father doesn't really like us using it for recreation, but not many people share that sentiment, as you can guess. For fledglings, it helps them become more used to life as one of us, and for the rest of us, we can take time for relaxation without ever leaving home. It's become a fairly common household device in my village, but rarer in others."

"Wish we had one here," Derek said, his eyes half-lidded and with a wistful smile on his face. His jealousy was etched into his thoughts like initials on a tree trunk. Despite his feelings about my clan, he certainly wished he'd had some of our creature comforts. Still, I wasn't about to try and convert him to our side. I was here to defend him, not to proselytize our reasons for fighting Lothos.

"You'd need a Jewel first," I said, "several, actually. And you'd have to be taught how to configure them. I couldn't even begin to do that. That being said, that kind of a room is how I'm able to cope without sunlight. I know what it's like, and I appreciate the beauty of it, but I've never experienced true daylight. It just doesn't hold the same meaning for me as it does for you."

"But doesn't it frustrate you?" Derek asked, "even a little?"

"Frustrate me how?"

"Derek's own frustration was thoroughly mixed with confusion as his fingers fumbled for words that his mind sought until at last he found them. Yet for all their conviction, he sounded oddly helpless.

"The fact that such a simple, yet wonderful thing was taken from you . . ." With a loud exhale, Derek flew his hands into the air and dropped them back into his lap. "I guess I just can't fathom having never known true sunlight."

"Your empathy is touching," I said, reaching out to touch his cheek again, realizing that he did not stop me this time.

"Really?" He saw my smile, and a half-smile extended

the crease his thin lips made on the left side of his face.

"It's one of your saving graces."

I wished that he would let me inside his mind of his own free will. Physical contact strengthened the ability of our minds to touch one another's, but the reaction went beyond just enhancing an ability. It created something akin to a need for that intimacy, which became a sort of vague anguish if it was denied. Derek's thoughts as always, shut me out, but I did detect one very clear impression that confirmed my suspicions of earlier. He didn't hate being touched at all. In point of fact, he actually liked it. The emotion was undeniably clear, and intense to the point of being sensual.

He liked it a lot.

It came to my attention that this thought, or rather, this emotion connected to that stray thought, was left to linger. I'd wrapped my mind about it like someone hanging from a cliff, securely grasping the wrist of a rescuer, or a loop of rope. I had not even been aware of how tightly I held on to it, or how naturally the reflex to hold it had come. It was not so different from a baby's grab reflex. Had I desired to clearly read his thoughts so keenly?

It was actually refreshing to be able to read a fragment of his thoughts this clearly. The emotion utterly exposed the lie that Derek had fought so hard to keep from me, and I was caught like a June bug to a porch light about that thread of thought. I was mesmerized and seduced by it, wanting to follow it to its final conclusion . . . a conclusion I knew I'd find at its end . . .

I opened my eyes, still connected to that receding thread of thought so that the world appeared in a dreamlike halo in my field of vision. Something was compelling me forward, in will and action, and as visions and mental impressions cleared in my psychic connection. I became ever more distinctly aware of the sensation of the cool softness of breath upon my lips . . . and then my awareness extended to the sight of Derek's face -and lips- oddly close to mine.

. . . Dangerously close to mine.

At nearly the same time as I let go of the mental connection, Derek became aware of it. The sensation of his rescinding of it was not unlike having duct tape ripped off of my mouth -something I'd had the misfortune of experiencing once before during a mission gone awry. It left me reeling, my eyes watering at the pain of the psychic backlash as Derek shrank back. I felt him force the thread of thought back into that unfathomable jumble and bury it well beneath utterly placid waters, but it was too late. Far too late. Such was the power of that flash of emotion and sensation to which our bodies had responded. I did not have time to suppress my response, and I felt my fangs extend when I broke contact. Quickly, I turned away from him.

"I'm . . . sorry," I whispered, trying as hard as I could to get hold of myself and not speak with that mortifying telltale lisp. "I forgot . . ."

"No, it's okay." I could hear a hint of that damning slur in Derek's consonants as well. Embarrassment shot out from his thoughts in nauseating waves, and I knew that if I touched him, even to reassure him, he would not take it well. Several times, I felt that torrent of unreadable emotion release itself from the depths of his thoughts, and each time, he squelched it. I felt helpless watching him, and even somewhat hurt. He could read minds, the same as I; could he not feel my own confusion? Did he not know that because of what nearly happened, understanding my thoughts were just as important as knowing his own?

Then I remembered that he'd been a scion of Lothos's clan. They did not cultivate our talents, and who knew the kinds of sick, depraved minds he touched while running with that respective pack? My anger faded with the dawn of this realization. For all I knew, he perhaps lacked the etiquette or nuance that my clan possessed. Still, his alarm was deeper than unnerving. I had to say something, but knowing how he was when his decorum was compromised, I was afraid to trigger an anger response.

I opened my mouth, slowly . . . tentatively.

"D- Derek . . . You-"

A blood-chilling howl shook both of us from our present states.

"Grace!" Derek whispered, and stood bolt upright. Like a comfortable jacket, I felt him slip into his leadership mode, pushing everything that we'd experienced into a hole where it would never be found. "Last time I heard her make that sound, there was an attacker."

I heard the sound of rapid footfalls, and from the opposite end of the camp, I saw the German Shepherd's massive form dart off into the darkness. On the next heartbeat, I sensed, and then saw Lyman standing beside us. There was a 12-gauge in his hand, and his thoughts were highly focused. The timbre of his mind told me one abundantly certain thing: danger was near.

"Looks like Grace makes a better alarm than you two lovebirds," Lyman said, his tone straddling the line between amused and sarcastic. I felt Derek's embarrassment deepen at this, but he was quick to compartmentalize that emotion as duty stepped in like a second persona. "Looks like the first one didn't travel alone. And I don't think this one's alone either."

"Lothos must be playing for keeps tonight." Derek glanced at me. "Let's go hunting."

Chapter Seven

The thing about trouble is that it has the most disobliging tendency to come at the worst times.

Of course, one could argue that there's never a good time for trouble, but at least in my own clan we were always ready for it, and far better prepared. Derek and his company, on the other hand, had lived in relative peace for too long, and with little interruption by Lothos's depredations, making this game of survival into something that was most unpleasantly new and unexpected.

But this particular "worst time," had of course, been the odd, exhilarating, and awkward moment that Derek and I had just shared . . . or to be more exact, almost shared. Even now, in the center of this danger, frustration mixed with a plethora of never before experienced emotions that I had no names for. These coursed through me along with the high of adrenaline roused by expectation of a fight. I could not help but long to speak with Derek about what had transpired as we set our thoughts on the present danger. No doubt Derek saw this present situation as a respite from the discomfort of our previous situation, but having to push it aside the way I had . . . that re-prioritizing of plans caused within me a distant, yet aggravating ache.

"I saw movement over the hill to the south," Lyman was saying as he accompanied Derek and me back to the camp. I heard the baby crying in Deb's RV while Wadih came to our side and joined us, rifle in hand. As we pushed further into the twilit night, I saw Wilson, Randy, Benjamin, and Pablo filing from their respective tents and campers, rifles in hand and machetes sheathed in scabbards about their waists. Joe, however, was conspicuously absent. Grace was far ahead of us, pursuing some lone figure I could barely make out in the shadowy distance, lit by the distant stars and pale moonlight. No human could see so clearly in so little light, but these were adequately bright and clear for our kind to see. I paused, knowing where the traps had been laid in that vicinity, and for a moment, figured that it would have been better if we'd just let the devices finish off the intruder. He or she was bound to take a chance and come closer; the sickspray would poison the wretch and the UV lamps would finish him or her off just as surely as it had the other . . .

. . . Unless this one had known what happened to the other.

Feeling a sharp chill at that notion that perhaps we were being unwittingly played for fools I paused and focused my senses about the area, but sensed and scented no one else but the familiar minds and bodies of Derek's clan. Of course, this wasn't surprising; the figure was downwind and too far out of range of my talents for me to catch the timbre of any mind.

As Derek and company quibbled over a plan to go after the intruder, it hit me. While my mind had been mulling over that chain of thought, I noticed an unfamiliar scent . . . an inhuman scent that had not been coming from our intended quarry. Rather, the source lay in the exact opposite direction, its trail wafting in from the northern breeze, back the way Derek and I had come. I felt Derek's hand on my shoulder as my senses focused upon the new scent. He asked me what was wrong, and I explained what I'd smelled. A moment later, he caught the scent. I resolved to go after its source and told him to follow Lyman and the others.

"I can go with you," Derek said, taking hold of my arm. The contact made his thoughts so clear, it was painful. His concern was genuine, focused completely on me, and overflowed in spite of what had happened between us. I wanted him to come with me, wanted it so badly that it frightened me, but I knew better.

"You need to protect your clan," I said, shaking my head, despite my feelings. "And they'll need your guidance."

He fixed me with a puzzled expression for just a second,

then seemed to crane his neck in the direction of that scent. "They're five against one, Elisa," he said. "They'll be fine."

"Derek, please, don't argue with me." I struggled to keep my voice even. "You don't need to be a hero. Remember, I have resources you don't. And besides, you don't know for certain if there's only one in the other direction."

"Yeah, but . . ." Derek's grip faltered, but he did not fully let go. If I had pulled away, I had no doubt he would have tightened it again. "What if it's a thaumaturgist, like you said? Can you handle those alone?"

"Thaumaturgists' Jewels give them a distinctive scent," I said, "this one doesn't smell like one. And very few of them are a match for me. I was trained by the best my Father had to offer." I then gasped as pain pulsed through my wrist at Derek's renewed grip. "Derek, let me go!"

Derek, seemingly oblivious to the strength of his grip until just now, released me. He murmured an apology, and turned distinctively red: something I would have found amusing had the situation not been so dire.

"Derek, your clan needs you," I said, clearly enunciating and with a finality that I knew he could just as much feel as hear. "I'll be fine; I promise. I'll be careful too. They're running a distraction tactic, and besides," I emphatically pointed in the direction of the new scent, "the baby is in that direction!"

My last words seemed to snap together the building blocks of rationality in Derek's head. I still felt the conflict within him, but there was no mistake of what he'd prioritize.

"Be careful," he said, taking both my hands in his own.

"Always." I smiled warmly at him. His concern, however briefly it was felt through our direct contact before he rejoined his clan at preternatural speed, made me feel lightheaded.

When he was gone, I felt more alone than I had in a very long time. Loneliness is a state that is most distasteful, and in tense situations, unnerving to our kind. Still, I kept my constitution and headed in the direction of the scent. I had no idea if this was the work of a slightly smarter grunt that had some sense of strategy, but not enough to keep clear of being scented, or someone higher up the pecking order with a more complex plan, so I made plans of my own. Still in sync with the location of the traps about the encampment through my Jewel, my mind's eye brought up a schematic of the area and led me to one of the closest devices. I could not yet see the intruder and I hoped that he or she could not see me, so I used my Jewel to give a more proper preparation.

I made my way through and away from the trap-laden zone, then moved several more yards into the bare countryside. My senses were on high alert, and I'd come to realize that the scent had become intermittent. One moment, it was as evident as the darkness that surrounded me; the next, it vanished completely. This happened several more times until it set off a vaguely unsettled feeling within me that was dreadfully familiar. That dark familiarity niggled at the back of my mind as I moved further on, its origins frustratingly evasive to my attempts to recall them . . .

Then it struck me. And I knew I was in trouble.

"Shit!" I hissed, and began to back away towards the trap zone. When I exerted my will upon the Jewel, it told me all I needed to know. It was indeed a thaumaturgist, but the specific talent this one possessed did strange things with its scent, eliminating the distinctive quality that marked it as a wielder of a Jewel. Few thaumaturgists on Lothos' side knew how to manipulate dimensions like my clan could, and so to meet one with this talent was rare . . . and very dangerous.

I heard a crack, and I gave a momentary start. I thought I'd stepped on a twig or a particularly crisp leaf from one of the sparse trees, but then I realized where I was. With the exception of a silvery bell-like sound reverberating from an incomprehensible distance, the entire world had become utterly silent, and tinged with a dreamlike bluish hue. It was as if someone had transferred me in an instant to a nearly soundproofed room whose walls had been painted in a perfect imitation of my former surroundings. But I knew this place well -not the location, but rather the world into which the thaumaturgist had brought me. It was actually not a world, but rather, a nonspace, an in-between place, just out of dimensional sync. Anyone with sufficient knowledge of a Jewel could access it, and since two individuals in the same area could access separate dimensional pockets, my clan used this space for solace and privacy. But it could also be deadly. If anyone who was brought to this place could not re-access the real world, he or she could be left forever in this place to die of starvation or thirst . . . or in the case of our immortal bodies, which do not die, even when starved of blood, fall into eternal madness fueled by the desperate need of blood: a fate worse than death in a barren world utterly devoid of life.

Though I did not see the face of my captor, I heard the fiend's mocking laughter, high-pitched and distinctively female. It was a cackle of victory, which already was distorting. And at once, I knew her plan. Her laugh was quickly fading as she crossed the gulf between universes, intent on leaving me here to rot.

Or so she thought.

With preternatural speed, I moved forward in the direction of the last wisp of her scent, estimating the point nearest to where I assumed she would be. I then rendered the same dimensional trick with my Jewel, re-inserting myself into reality, where wind and crickets broke the eerie near-silence. Along with these came the tinkle of mocking laughter from my quarry, originating from the unfamiliar figure who greeted my eyes and senses with a stench that was as distasteful as any from Lothos' clan. Though I had leaped forward in those last few moments where I transitioned into this world, her hearing must have picked up the sudden updraft of air from me, and she turned around in a flurry of voluminous hair that seemed to be at once black and silver in the moonlight. She fixed me with a rounded face with many scars that surrounded dark gray lips and eyes that were tinted a strikingly cold shade of false blue. The surprise I felt from her as it struck my mind was proof that she had not expected me to break free of her trap. This meant that though she was a thaumaturgist, she was merely a rank amateur. She'd already made two deadly mistakes. The first was her overconfidence in trapping me; the second was her not having recognized who I was.

I tackled her, drawing upon my Jewel to enhance my strength in the same way that I had in my brief altercation with Joe. She kicked at me, but did not expect my ability to absorb her blows. My Jewel diffused some of their kinetic energy, slowing, but not stopping my move. She toppled to the ground with a bellow of indignation. I clawed at her face, but she grabbed my wrists, holding them above her, baring gleaming white fangs below her scarred, gray-lipped rictus. Her eyes flashed and the false blue sank away as if it were colored water that had submerged her true crimson. She was now anticipating my augmented strength, and pushed back with the force she would have applied a full grown adult.

My legs straddled her narrow waist, and I squeezed as I pressed forward in our battle of physical power and will. I was not trying to suffocate her, since we didn't really need to breathe except for circulation and keeping cool. I was instead attempting to crush her ribs and succeeding, albeit slowly. The fiend was thrashing with her legs, kicking and twisting, trying desperately to throw me off, but I held on with the tenacity of a bull rider, my mind concentrating deeply, siphoning the well of my Jewel's vast reserves of power, working to overpower and incapacitate her for the killing blow.

This was why I didn't notice the gunshot.

It happened in a blur of sound, sight, and searing pain as the night was pierced by the thunderous crack of the weapon, only a moment after which the force of the bullet sent me flying off of the enemy vampire, a searing pain exploding in my left shoulder. I screamed as I tumbled on the grass; even

I didn't know the exact moment when I stopped, but I was in full control of my faculties when the vampire had landed roughly on top of me. The collar of my blouse was bunched in her tight fist, and she was lifting my limp torso off of the ground.

"Looks like you're not as squishy as the others in that group," she whispered in a high-pitched and catlike voice. I struggled, but the blow from the unseen gun assailant had weakened me, and I knew that I was bleeding out. I could feel the screaming agony of the as of yet unhealed entrance and exit wounds. The pain was causing my concentration to become like slime, pouring out the more I tried to contain and focus it into any kind of shape.

"You don't smell like them either," the fiend continued, "and best of all, you're an adept, like me! That means you're a spy for the weak ones." She threw back her head and burst out a dry, rasping cackle, wild and almost orgasmic, as if the sound of her own voice were a lover driving her to the pinnacle of ecstasy. "My lord and master will give me pleasures beyond my wildest dreams for your head! He'll never believe I did it!"

"That's because he'll never find out about it," I managed to say as I found a measure of focus to my thoughts. It wasn't complete, but it was adequate for what I needed, though the pain of what I'd planned would be even worse than the injury to my shoulder.

Wasting no time, I drew upon my Jewel as the fiend's marred face stared at me with an egregiously stupid expression.

"Tell me, did your master ever teach you how to divert photons?" I asked as my opponent felt the twist of dimensions that I'd wrought. I watched her eyes focus on the UV emitter that now rested in my hand, saw them widen in helpless alarm as I manipulated forces to adhere it permanently to her clothes. I pressed the button on its surface, and worked the trick I'd planned.

It wasn't a perfect shield, since my mind was still reeling from the blow of the gunshot, but it was adequate to protect me from death. The flare of that deadly wavelength of light burned across my flesh in patches, and my ears were greeted with a sound that never lost its combined horror and satisfaction. The enemy vampire screeched into the empty night as she threw me to the ground. My teeth clenched against the burst of pain from the incomplete shield that my scattered thoughts had commanded from the Jewel. My legs were afire, my arms were afire; my face and scalp were afire with pain as if I'd tripped and landed, rolling like a barrel into a pit of hot coals. I imagined my skin a roadmap of scars like the fiend, whose agonized screams faded into piteous, choking cries, and then silence. My senses were greeted with the scent of burning immortal flesh, giving me hope that my plan succeeded, but my eyelids still burned too much for me to open them. So I curled into a fetal position and waited for my body to repair itself. Sunlight, or at least ultraviolet light was the most destructive to our tissues, and I knew that after healing, I would need to feed badly. I forced my breathing to slow itself as I lay upon the grass, agonizingly aware of every place where the pain licked at my raw flesh. All I could do was wait until it subsided.

The pain in my shoulder was the first to go. As it wasn't caused by the UV emitter, my body could handle it more efficiently. The rest would take even more time than I had to lie here, but I would have time enough to wait for that pain to subside to manageable levels.

Slowly, I opened my still aching eyelids to the sight of the starry sky. I sat up, grimacing at the rawness of my still-injured flesh, and saw what I'd hoped to see: the vampire's charred remains. Flames still licked at some of the ashes of her bones, and I quickly made haste to crush those remains into powder. I drew upon my Jewel to turn the earth where she lay, pausing only once to extract the glittering yellow Jewel from what remained of her ribcage. Satisfied with my work,

I searched with my senses for any other enemy troops who might be lurking about, but found myself alone. I checked my watch before heading back to the encampment, and awakened to a new sense of alarm. The battle and my recuperation had only taken about five minutes total, but I wasn't completely healed. And whoever had shot me hadn't done it for nothing. Certain as death for mortals, he was headed for the camp, and five minutes was more than enough time for whatever assailant that had shot me to reach the baby.

On my approach, I confirmed his identity. Joe's scent became prevalent on the air the moment I came within two hundred feet of the trap zone. Realizing who it was, I seethed with rage in spite of the agony that still fired across my body. The bastard had shot me! And in the middle of a fight to save his sorry arse! He obviously hadn't learned his lesson. I resolved to make a much clearer message to him later.

Then I quickly became aware of another scent: Joe's burning, immortal flesh.

Through my pain, I summoned the will to move at preternatural speed to its source, which I found in the form of a horrifying sight as I came to a stop beside Deb's trailer.

Deb was holding the baby, who was sleeping soundly in her arms. All the while, she hovered above a charred recess in the ground where her victim lay. Joe was barely moving, his clothes charred in multiple places, his flesh blackened in patches. He was alive; I could hear him groaning, and it was all I could do to shield my mind from the full force of his pain. Smoke rose from the torched furrow as the burning scent accosted me. I already felt miserable, and the smell alone was nearly enough to make me vomit. My body was expending enough blood in an attempt to heal my wounds; losing more would place me deeper into a state of starvation, which might prove problematic for the clan. Defiantly, I forced back the nausea and stepped gingerly away from Joe's nearly lifeless form.

For the longest time, I said nothing. My gaze only shifted

from Joe, whose 12-gauge lay three feet away from his charred right arm, then back to Deb, who stared dispassionately at her fellow clan member, and then at me with narrow eyes and unabated disgust. But I was in no condition to demand an explanation of her loathing for me.

"What happened?" I finally asked once I could find my voice. For the moment, I didn't care how she felt about me, but I was, admittedly, a bit miffed about this situation. It appeared that Joe had been the one who shot me, but now here he was, burned nearly to death by Deb's erratic talent. To be honest, I wished I wasn't quite so close to her. Those who had the gift of pyrokinesis tended to be mentally unstable and prone to fits of rage at the drop of a hat. Deb had already made it abundantly clear that she didn't like me, but I wanted to know exactly what had caused her to nearly kill a member of her own clan, and one so close to its leader. To say that Derek was not going to like this would be an understatement to end all.

"He came pounding on my trailer door, waking up the baby," Deb answered. She wrinkled her nose with disgust, which thankfully was not focused on me. "He barged in, and demanded to take the baby away. I protested, but he was like a madman. I threw him out after that, and that's when he made the very stupid decision to aim his gun at me." She tapped her foot against Joe's side, and I heard him make a wheezing groan. "So I taught him a lesson."

"But . . . this?" I protested, gesturing towards his mutilated head and neck. "Look at his throat. He can't even talk to tell us what happened. It takes a long time for injuries like that to heal, even with blood. And what if he doesn't? You may well have killed him!"

"And what business is it of yours?" She snapped, holding the baby away from me as if I had intended to wrench it from her possessive grasp. "You have no love for him; why do you care? He shot you, didn't he? I can see the rip in your blouse; I can smell and see the blood. The hole hasn't completely healed yet either. The way I see it, I was doing you a favor!"

I felt her unreasonable anger, her spite boiling over with her words, but with no logic behind them. I was in pain, and my thirst was growing. I was in no condition to be harassed like this. It was difficult enough keeping the beast at bay, and she made the idea of unleashing it here and now seem very seductive. A dull fury began in my stomach and coursed into my extremities, and I bit down, forcing my fangs not to extend. I could feel them pressing against my clenched jaw. I had done her nothing, and yet she hated me. No matter what I did or said, she would always detest me, but for no reason that I could see. Her mind was unreadable, a storm of rage, a static of maliciousness. This infuriated me in such a way that I very nearly stopped caring about whether or not the baby would be harmed in the altercation that this incomprehensibly cruel woman was trying to provoke.

It was Derek's voice that brought me back to sanity.

"No, Deb. You weren't doing her any favors. Not like this."

Derek appeared by my side. The hunting party was with him, with Grace bounding up beside Lyman to receive a scratch behind her ear. A disembodied head was nestled in her gaping jaws, the blood from the remains of its neck running down the sides of her mouth.

"What fresh hell is going on here?" Lyman said at the sight of Joe, then he shifted his gaze to me. Immediately after, he whispered to Wadih and Pablo to get blood packs. I felt his intent for Joe, as well as for me. I could have kissed him.

"I'd like to know myself," Derek said, kneeling beside Joe's broken body. I felt the anger course through him, but Deb stood hard against the withering gaze he shot her.

"So, you mind explaining yourself?" There was an edge to his voice I hadn't heard before. It was cold and perhaps even dangerous. I knew that he and Joe were close, but until now, I never figured just how close. Derek seemed a hair's breadth from killing Deb where she stood, baby or not.

"He was trying to take the baby," Deb explained, her tone making it sound more like a kind of vehement protest.

"And he shot me," I added, but my voice was flat, carrying far less passion. It was strange that I felt little anger now, despite what had happened. It was like someone had pulled a cork once Derek arrived, and the fury had drained from me like a volatile liquid. I should have especially been furious after realizing what Joe's attack on me entailed. That the wound he'd inflicted on my shoulder almost certainly had to have been revenge for our skirmish inside of Derek's RV, but Joe was currently in no condition to confirm or deny this. Still, he continued to inspect Joe, who, judging by the telltale blank calmness of his mind, had slipped into torpor. I was actually relieved at this. I might not have liked him, but save Lothos, I would never have wished starvation madness upon anyone. Healing must have taken a final toll on his body.

"It was his daughter," Derek said to Deb, not looking at her. I could still feel his suppressed anger mixed with a weariness that had to have been uncommon; I'd never felt anything like it from him before. "You went too far. And no, I don't want to hear any excuses. Joe may be an asshole, but he's the baby's father. And he's definitely not your kindling. You're confined to quarters until further notice."

Deb bristled, but made no sounds of protest. She merely scowled and strode back into her home, baby nestled safely in the crook of her arm.

At the same time, Wadih and Pablo returned with blood packs in their arms. Lyman came to Derek's side and instructed them on how to administer the life-giving fluid while he was in torpor, but changed his mind when Randy and Benjamin suggested taking him back to his trailer and setting him into the bathtub. It was a good idea, I knew. The scent of the blood would rouse him enough to feed, and his body would absorb the rest to heal his wounds. I watched as they carried him off into the encampment, but saw that Derek stayed behind. He turned and looked at me, offering a single blood pack.

"You look like you need it," he said. "You must've been through something awful. You look it."

"Long story," I said. I nodded in the general direction I'd seen Lyman and the others go. "So you caught the guy? I saw Grace had a new plaything."

Derek nodded. "Bastard wasn't hard to kill, but he was fast as the wind. What about you? What's your 'long story'?"

I opened my mouth to speak, but a sudden wave of dizziness stole the words from me. I made a breathy noise as I began to feel very weak. I hadn't bitten into the blood pack yet, so I was thankful that nothing would be spilled as my legs gave out and the world seemed to lurch to the left. Darkness licked at the edges of my vision as I collapsed to the ground.

Or at least I would have, had Derek not caught me, but that was all I remembered of it.

Chapter Eight

I awoke in surroundings that were at first unfamiliar. This was clearly not my pull-out alcove inside the RV. The scents, however, were basically the same, but it smelled like Derek far more strongly than what I was used to.

My vision cleared somewhat as the scales of sleep fell from my eyes. The room was very lived-in, judging from the clutter. Walls were festooned with posters of movies and bands from the past three decades; clothes were strewn about atop wooden dressers and desks; stacks of books were piled at the end of a nightstand and a separate stack of DVDs leaned beside a flat screen TV that rested atop the dresser that lay across from the bed where I found myself. Piles of CDs sat upon an old, dusty stereo and the windows were draped with what looked like strings of Mardi Gras beads. Several used blood packs were scattered across the nightstand and atop a nearby drafting table.

I felt lightheaded, almost euphoric, and the pain was completely gone. Then I noticed the cause of it, which was the IV of blood that was being run into my arm. At my left, I saw Derek seated beside the IV drip, having pulled up a chair next to the bed, which I now understood to be his bed.

So this was what his bedroom looked like from the inside. No wonder my surroundings had left me slightly disoriented. The door to the living room area was open, and I could see the familiar setup beyond. This returned my bearings to me.

Derek was fiddling with his cigarillo again, wanting to light it, and then exercising that usual subconscious restraint. Sometimes he gave into it; sometimes he didn't. The scowl on his face, however, was not because of this piddling issue. I felt the pall of dark thoughts swirling in his mind: anger, worry, anxiety, fear, and a plethora of other emotions that evaded my attempts to single out. Such a mindset was common for him. He was an incessant brooder, and I often wondered if this was simply his default position. Of course, there had certainly been little lately to be happy over.

He heard me when I turned my head to look at him, and stuffed his unlit cigarillo back into the pocket of his hoodie. Despite his emotions, he managed to surprise me by smiling. Even more surprising was that it was genuine.

"Hey, China doll," he said. "Glad you're awake. You feeling better?"

"Significantly better," I said, gesturing with the arm that the IV ran into. "I guess my injuries took more blood out of me than I thought."

"Yeah, you weren't looking too good when I saw you," Derek said. "You were almost skin and bones, and I'd never seen so many scars. You looked like one of those UV lamps got set off in your face."

"It did," I said. "I'm the one who set it off, actually; only I didn't take it directly, or full force. The other one did, though. She looks far worse." I betrayed a smirk. "And by that, I mean dead."

"So there really was another trying to sneak in." I couldn't tell if Derek meant it as a statement or a question, but his interest had been greatly piqued.

"You didn't have your people investigate that area?" I asked

Derek nodded. "We did. Paws and I found ashes, charred earth, and some of your blood, but we weren't sure about what happened. 'Course, if you sunlit the bitch, then there wouldn't be much left to find. Even the scents get erased pretty quickly that way."

"I happened," I said, and then removed the Jewel I'd procured from the fiend from my pocket. I handed it to Derek and watched the look of dismay that expectedly erupted across his face.

"She was a thaumaturgist?"

I nodded, confirming his growing feelings of dread.

"Aw, dammit . . ." Derek seemed to collapse back into the chair. He cradled his head in his hands. He had no idea that this was not the extent of my bad news.

"She spoke of a master. I don't know if it was Lothos, but I believe someone will be missing her. We'll definitely be seeing more of them."

"And the traps won't do us any good then, will they?" He breathed out a long, depressing sigh.

"They're not stupid," I said. "You know that. If the next one or two they send are ignorant, the traps might still work. But eventually, they'll put two and two together, and realize that you've been having far better luck than you should, and the ones after that will start digging a little more deeply before just rushing in."

"God, this is hell," Derek's groan was piteous in a way that made my heart go out to him. "Joe was nearly burned to a crisp after going wild trying to get the baby out of the camp; you say he shot you; wouldn't surprise me if he did, knowing him, but I still don't know what the hell happened there. Then we get flanked by two of the shape-shifters, and now this."

For a long time afterwards, he sat silent, withdrawing so deeply into himself that his presence seemed to almost fade from my senses. Then, when my alarm at his physical and mental silence threatened to lick at the edges of my awareness, he at last spoke.

"How much longer 'til we reach this sanctuary of yours?"

"Too long," I said. "We've still got over a week's worth of travel left using the current route I planned. I can cut it down to half a week, though."

"Half a week?" Derek eyed me with nearly the same incredulity as the fiend I had fought with. "How? And why didn't you do that in the first place?"

"I was at first trying to take a long, circuitous route to throw off anyone who might be following us," I explained, "but tonight showed that plan to be shit on toast, so I'll need to change the route to take us there as directly as possible."

"You should have done that in the first place," Derek snapped.

"I wouldn't be so hasty," I replied, maintaining my calm in the face of Derek's incredulity. "There's a problem with that plan that you're unaware of. If Lothos or anyone in his clan is familiar with that route, we're going to have some problems that even I might run out of options for."

I noticed that Derek's concern had diminished significantly in spite of this worst-case scenario. But I had a good idea as to why he once fixed me with that shrewd gaze. It was easy to forget that he could read others' thoughts, the same as me, since he rarely pried or spoke aloud of anything I had been thinking. Of course, I knew he could pick some things up. Even with training, some thoughts easily rose to the surface, as I often felt from his mind.

"From the way you put it," he said, crossing his legs and arms, "I gather you've got at least some kind of starting option for this case."

"Of a sort," I said, betraying the smug grin that desired to spread across the side of my face.

"You're scary sometimes; do you know that?"

"You're not the first to say that, and you won't be the last."

"Cheeky too."

"I've heard that one as well."

"God only knows how you can stand me." Derek propped his feet at the edge of the bed. His big toe accidentally struck the pole from which the blood pack hung, and I steadied it.

"Well, you're surprisingly easy to like," I said, and felt that same tangle of incoherent emotions well up from his heart. Again, like when we sat together outside in the starlight before things went to hell, he delayed suppressing it.

"As are you," Derek said. And like a fisherman waiting for the right moment to spear a particularly evasive eel, I took advantage of the situation. I would probably never get a better chance.

"Is that why you nearly kissed me?" I asked.

Abruptly and unceremoniously, Derek fell out of his chair.

***

To fall as Derek had done is a rare thing for our kind, as we normally have reflexes and balance that are as superhuman as our strength. So my question must have been especially unnerving. I was sorry for it, and I admit that I'd asked it for a purely selfish reason. But I wanted this selfish moment. The kiss he never gave me had vexed my mind, even during our hunt and my battle against the fiend, and that vexation tore at my heart once again with his reappearance during my altercation with Deb. During the kiss that never happened, my mind had been attuned to his in a way I had never allowed it to be before. His remark about finding me easy to like had betrayed far more than he realized, and so I grasped that opportunity with all the desperation of a drowning victim.

"Derek?" I crawled to the edge of the bed to see him scramble awkwardly to his feet, skittering with his back to the wall into a bow-legged stance. It would have been amusing, had I not felt the howling torrent of indecipherable emotions that burst forth from his heart. But this time, he did not force them back down. It was as if my need for answers or perhaps the sound of my voice had laid bare something he'd desperately hoped would stay hidden.

"Elisa, can't this . . . I mean, we don't have time for . . ." Derek's stammering words came out in halting bursts, creating a lame attempt at evasion that worried me terribly. I had never seen him so disconcerted. His mind was a positive war. I grasped my forehead as the strength of his internal conflict sent me reeling.

At last, Derek straightened himself up to a more dignified stance. His eyes, however, were still wild and his fangs were extended and quite visible. He was panting, and his mind was awash with contrasting emotions: so much of a torrent that the most basic natures I could discern from them were attraction and revulsion.

"Derek, calm down, please!" I reached out for him, but he backed away, hitting the wall again. He had been panting heavily when he suddenly stopped. With eerie calmness, he seemed to relax and then breathe in deeply, though his fangs remained extended. He was stock still and propped against the wall. Despite his calm outward appearance, the storm in his mind raged on. Two tears formed at the edges of his eyes, and streamed down the sides of his pale cheeks.

"I can't do this," he at last murmured. And then to my utter, horrified dismay, he began to walk away. Resolutely, he headed for the door, and I felt as if the floor was giving out from beneath me.

"Derek, wait." My breaths came in short bursts; I felt as perhaps a human does when deprived of the oxygen she needs. Without control, my desire for his thoughts became desperation as I felt him drift farther from me. He was gathering his tangled emotions, splayed out for my talent to readily detect, as one gathers his personal belongings for storage in preparation for a long trip, making them forever out of reach. I felt as if I would die from it. "Derek, please!"

I suppose I was desperate enough to even be a little bit cruel, but to me, this was immeasurably important. Derek was a private person, opening up to me only on his terms, like when he discussed the history between himself and Joe, or when we sat under the stars at the remnants of that farmhouse. Here, I tried to open him up, and he was at first receptive. But now, there was utter terror, and he was withdrawing from me, the only one who could set him at ease. And I knew where that fear had come from.

"Derek, do you hate me that much?" I pleaded, crawling towards the edge of the bed. I felt the IV lose its slack, heard the rattle of the pole that supported the blood pack that still fed into my arm as it squeaked along the floor on its wheeled base. My vision blurred as the tears at last came, Derek's back being the last thing that I could see clearly.

"Do you really hate me?" I groaned weakly as I tucked my legs beneath me. Unable to help it, I released a miserable sob, and collapsed into the bedspread, wailing piteously into it and letting my tears dampen the thick cotton spun cloth that smelled so strongly of Derek. I gave up trying to reach his mind, to grasp those last threads of thought as I had earlier tonight. I believe I knew on some fundamental level that he could no more hate me than I hated him, but I also knew that I'd pushed him too far.

Then I felt it. A wave of grueling frustration, anguish, and a burst of that incomprehensible tangle of emotions, all flowing back out of his mind in a deluge. Lifting my head from the bedspread, I wiped my eyes to see that he had not left as I had assumed. He was still there, leaning in the open doorway, bearing his fangs in a pained grimace, his mind wresting with those convoluted emotions.

"I'm such a fucking coward," I heard him whisper, the fang lisp evident in his self-deprecating words. He then turned his head towards me, and I saw the saddest look I had ever seen in his eyes. "But I can't make it stop."

I pushed deeper into Derek's mind with my own will, knowing that he would be aware of this, but I felt no resistance from him. I began to unravel the threads of his emotions, singling out the individual strands in the tangle, and in the process, at long last, finding exactly what I thought would be there.

"I know," I said, speaking gently. And I did know. I knew everything. I believed he knew as well. I sat up and held out my hands to him, my mind calm and without accusation or judgment. "And you're not a coward. Please, come back."

Slowly, very slowly, Derek stepped away from the door. There was a look of defeat and uncertainty on his face as he closed it behind him, leaving us truly alone together. He didn't immediately come to me, but instead, he stared at the floor. Again, he hesitated to speak before gathering his courage.

"You know, I even promised myself that if you pushed me, I would do this," he said, swallowing so hard that the sound actually was loud in my hearing. "I didn't really want to run away, but . . ."

"I know," I said. "Come here."

Slowly, he came to my side. He placed his hand on the bed, and I rested my hand atop his, relishing the closeness of our minds that came from the contact. When he sat next to me, I reached up and touched his cheek. His sad eyes were looking steadily at me, and though I'd laid those strands of his emotions bare, they snapped back into the familiar tangle as I became aware of his heart pounding. This was the same as I would hear from a human whom I had chosen for "grazing" upon when the need compelled me, but then I realized that my heart began beating with the same rhythm and strength within me.

"I could never hate you, you know," Derek said.

"I know."

I caressed his jaw line, smiling with complete acceptance. I let my fingers trace their way down the smoothness of his skin until it reached the wisps of hair at his chin. "It must have been so hard for you," I said. "You held all that in for so long while you ate nothing but duty for breakfast, lunch, and dinner."

"You know damn well it wasn't about duty," Derek said.

I nodded. "But you let down your guard earlier, when we sat outside."

"It was a moment of-"

He and I knew what he had been about to say. "Weakness" constituted a false way of thinking. He knew who I was better than anyone in this clan, aside from perhaps Lyman. And most important, he knew that I was not what I appeared to be.

"A moment of clarity?" I interjected with a mischievous

smile.

"Frightening clarity, I think."

"Like now?"

"I . . ."

"You know how you are reacting," I said, my words having developed a fang slur of their own. "And I felt it. How you can stand it is unbelievable. Even Father couldn't do it when he first met Amelia."

I saw the question in his eyes, and I explained. "Father is married. He met her about fifteen years ago"

Derek nodded with understanding. "You know how I could resist," he said, and I noticed his free hand moving with almost imperceptible slowness to my face. His fangs were so long now that they seemed to reach past the bottom of his lip. I had never seen them so extended, even when he fed from those disgusting blood packs after a particularly stressful night. With a rush of courage, he thrust his hand out to touch my cheek. His touch was soft in a way one handles a quivering, frightened, newly-rescued bird. He then moved the touch to my eyelids, nose, and lips as I explored his face in likewise manner. I had always felt so comfortable around him, despite his brooding and occasional grumpiness, and never more so than now, despite what I was aware of within him.

His free hand touched the small of my back. He was smaller than the adult size members of his clan, but still large enough so that his hand covered almost half of the diameter of my waist.

"Is it keeping you away now?" I asked.

He didn't answer. Like when he stood against the wall, two tears rolled down his cheek. He was frozen, trembling, and my mind was aware of the coldness of the sudden re-assertion of his fear, but this fueled the opposite effect within me. At last, with a boldness that I had heretofore not known, I pushed myself forward, firmly, yet softly closing the gap between our lips.

DOUBLE-CROSS MY HEART

I felt a beautiful warmth ignite my insides and spread like water in a pool at the base of a heated cascade. It moved from the tips of my fingers, down my spine and to my toenails, as powerful as if I'd just imbibed fresh blood from a particularly delectable host. But then it became awkward, as I felt no response from Derek. I was in contact with him, intimate contact, and his mind had all but blanked, with the exception of an incomprehensible static ringing in the farthest reaches of his subconscious like a mad crescendo. I waited, feeling time pass by indeterminately, my lips still pressed against his, dreading that I would have to stop and stammer out an apology for my temerity. In fact, I had been about to do just that when I felt his hand move swiftly to the back of my head and felt his other hand guide me forward by my waist. My eyes were closed, but by instinct I reached out and touched my hands to his chest as his lips at long last reciprocated. I felt his cool breath as he heaved a groaning sigh and his thoughts gained a focus I had never experienced from him before. The tangle of emotions had evaporated, and in its stead was the thing I saw when I had sorted those emotions out. It was the thing that he tried to bury from me and even from himself between duty and a sometimes gruff exterior. It coursed from him and through me, entwining with my own emotions, and dredging to the surface something that had lain subconscious within me. I instantly recognized it as the source of my comfort and subsequent desperate curiosity. It was a resonance of desire, a compatibility of body and soul. It was the mark of that coveted bond that every individual of our kind sought for decades, centuries, and even millennia: those who would be a consummate host.

This usually happened between a human and vampire, and I supposed that had either Derek or I been the human, one of us would have been bonded forever to the other. Whether it would have been Derek for me, or me for Derek, I don't know; I doubt even he did, but our minds knew that drawing, that pull by way of instinct. That bond between us was at long last, brought to light, and would be affirmed tonight.

I felt Derek press me closer to him, though not painfully so. I swung my arm around his neck and shifted my weight to bring him down onto the mattress. Only then did his lips part from my own, and travel to my cheek, then my ear, then down to my neck, searching for their mark. I gave a lilting sigh, feeling a thrill of expectation in the midst of the pleasure his lips gave. I had fed from countless hosts since the time I had first woken up in the Lair as a newly-turned fledgling with no memory of who I was, but never had anyone fed from me. That act was far too intimate, and was shared only between paramours. Vampire blood provided no nourishment, but I was told that the process of feeding from another of our kind was no less pleasurable than when it was from a human. I had never done this before either, and so my heart thrummed within me, as I became nervous, yet trembled with anticipation.

I then wanted to scream in frustration when I felt Derek hesitate, felt his tremors of confusion, perhaps because of my own apprehensive thoughts, but I was determined and resolute, and so I quickly rectified this with a single whisper as I pressed my hand against the back of his neck.

"Do it."

I felt him bite. I heard the muffled liquid pop of my skin as his fangs pierced it, and I shrieked with ecstasy. His toxins coursed through me like a controlled inferno; the world went into a white out, and I felt like I was climbing into a blinding sky, where agonizing bliss pulsed its indescribable cadence into every vein and neuron. Distantly, I heard myself cry out again, and in response, I heard Derek groan in a similar swoon. I felt his pleasure mix with my own, like threads interweaving in a loom of love and desire. I felt his right hand free itself from my back and seek out my left hand, then felt his fingers entwine with my own. In that contact, I became once again aware of the world around me, and I opened my eyes to the sight of Derek's neck, his skin more fragrant than before, having absorbed my blood. It gave off a scent that called to me, as sweet in its masculinity as mine had been to him in its own uniqueness. I did not resist the call. To Derek's initial surprise, I sank my teeth into his flesh, and imbibed the unleashed fount of his own crimson fluid. I loosed my hand from his and locked it as far across his broad back as it would go, anchoring my grip with the fabric of his hoodie. I pulled in a great gout of blood that sent me reeling with absolute delight. I felt Derek groan loudly -it was almost a grunt- as he stiffened against me, but did not let go of my own neck. I swallowed and pulled in again, sighing vocally as he tightened his grip upon me. This went on until we lost track of the time in each other's taste, the pleasure of the drink, and the weaving of our minds, the threads entwining tighter and tighter, and the taste of our blood, useless for food as it was, bringing us higher and ever farther towards the pinnacle of bliss, letting our voices and thoughts guide us to ever higher plateaus until we reached a golden crescendo that seemed to bloom in an electric symphony of taste, scent, thought, and sensation.

This was the crux of it all, the heart of what transpired between Derek and me. I had been taught about it; I had seen it as well, but had never, until this moment, truly known. That moment of that special, most intimate drink, shared between two of our kind, and when that mutual compatibility that Derek and I shared exists, it is the defining, sublime moment of our lives: a time one would beg to last forever . . . when everything comes into place . . . when everything makes sense.

We shook and shuddered, our senses overwhelmed and inundated with our mutual fading bliss. At last, we let go, one from the other, heaving tremulous breaths. We licked over the wounds to heal them, and then lay still, perhaps neither of us fully realizing what had just happened between us. It did not feel at all the same as when I fed from a human. There was no satiation of hunger, but it was all-consuming satisfaction of a different kind.

At last, I felt Derek stir, and he hefted himself upon his palms to look down on me. His eyes were half-lidded, and he was panting a little. He then collapsed onto his side to lie face to face with me. He said nothing, only caressed my cheek, and I returned the favor. I smiled, though he didn't return the expression. But when I moved forward to kiss him, he reciprocated with absolutely no hesitation.

He was exhausted. I could feel it in his thoughts. It wasn't because of the blood he lost; it was an infinitesimal amount compared to my own. I looked at the blood pack connected to the IV and noticed that it was empty. I disconnected the tube from my arm, and I think that Derek saw its condition as well. I was a bit concerned, but he seemed to not be. He still caressed my cheek, his large eyes fluttering closed. Our minds were still entwined enough for us to share sensations, and so I allowed his sleepiness to claim me. After all, we deserved this nap. I was happier than I ever thought I could be, because at that amazing and wonderful moment, I knew that after nearly two hundred years of searching, I truly, finally, had found love.

***

I heard Derek's voice speaking to me the second I opened my eyes.

"You've only been asleep for about an hour."

He sounded slightly farther away than I'd expected. I figured I'd slept for such a short time as our kind doesn't sleep long during the night . . . if we even sleep at all. What had first surprised me was how Derek had known to tell me this. It was only a passing notion. In fact, I had been about to reach into my pocket to check the clock on my cell phone (which was currently useless for calls, as per Derek's phone silence mandate). This intuition of my thoughts was unmistakable proof that he and I had bonded, and our minds were entwined as one. We took each other's blood and laid our hearts bare to each other. From that process, we now belonged to one another, body and soul. His knowing my thoughts was merely the most obvious sign.

"You were still recovering. I've been awake for most of that time."

I sat up and detected a very pungent and familiar aroma of strawberries and tobacco. It was not something I had experienced often, and especially not inside of his RV. Derek was not lying beside me; rather, he was sitting atop the desk beside his window, which was open to the silvery moonlight that flooded the room, more illuminating than any human eyes could detect. What I saw amazed me. Gone was the clutter of clothes, personal effects, and trash scattered about his room. The only out-of-place thing that I could see was Derek, who was hugging his knees to his chest with one arm, and holding a cigarillo in his opposite hand, which hovered over a clear glass ashtray. I was aware of the pall of melancholy that was upon him. He wasn't depressed, I surmised, after peering closer into his heart, and I was thankful for that. It was more akin to being darkly pensive. I had hoped that our time together would have eased his mind and allayed his fears, but I knew that Derek's emotions, his doubts and apprehensions, especially, were notoriously tenacious.

It was then that I noticed that not only had his clothes been removed from their haphazard piles across the bedroom, but his usual jeans were conspicuously absent from his person.

"What the hell happened to your pants?" I asked, stifling what would have been a surprised giggle.

"You happened, China doll," Derek said. His gaze shifted towards me without him moving his head. "I didn't expect your blood to affect me the way it did." He shook his head and breathed out a sultry plume of cherry smoke. "Not gonna lie; it should be a crime for blood like yours to taste that good. After we were done, my pants were completely useless for wearing, if you know what I mean."

A flash of our intimacy came unbidden into my mind, a memory from Derek's point of view gleaned from his thoughts: a sensual torrent, a moment of sight, sound, scent, and sensation. It was powerful, raw, and ferocious in its intensity: my scent, the taste of my blood, and the sound of my voice, all experienced as he experienced them, and what had resulted from it. At once, in the rapid assault of the alien sensations, I experienced what had happened to Derek at that delicious pinnacle we reached in the drink. I blushed deeply in spite of myself, and Derek, whose amusement I felt like a spark in the midst of his dark musings, was not oblivious to how I looked.

"I . . . ah . . . guess I had a profound effect on you, then?" I asked, feeling oddly self-conscious after that flash of memory.

"No need to be obtuse," Derek said with another drag from his cigarillo. "You know you did. And it's not like we didn't enjoy it. Besides, I think you knew your affect on me would be far more powerful than even I would've expected."

"Then why are you still so gloomy?" I asked as I crawled out of the bed. He had been right of course, but with our bond, there was no need to acknowledge it verbally. I noticed a large bin on the night stand which contained three blood packs in warm water. I grabbed one, not looking forward to the repast, and climbed onto the opposite side of the desk. I propped myself against the window and curled my legs up the same way that Derek had.

"I'm not gloomy," Derek said, crushing out the remnants of his cigarillo. The ghost of a smile played at the sides of his mouth as a sultry plume of smoke billowed out. "I'm in love."

"With me?"

I was neither a fool nor was I being obtuse. That was impossible with our bond. I suppose I had asked this simply for Derek to confirm it. I felt electric and lighter than air when he confessed this to me, knowing that I truly was loved by him . . . that our joining hadn't been imaginary, and I hadn't just dreamed it all. I smiled more broadly than I ever had before. I wanted him to say it again, a second time, a third time, and a million times more, for I believed that perhaps those words would have the same effect on me as his drink. When I saw him roll his eyes and felt his consternation and amusement, I had to laugh in spite of myself.

"Of course with you, silly," Derek said, betraying a warble of laughter that I felt relieved to hear from him. "I'd be a real shitty boyfriend if I went off and fed from someone else behind your back. Besides, I don't think I could do that if I wanted to. To tell the truth, it's going to be damn hard to drink any other kind of blood except for yours."

"It's a cruel irony that we can't nourish each other that way," I said. "Had I been human, or vice versa, though, the setup might have been more equitable." My heart ached for us both, because I knew what he said to be true. It would be true for me as well as him. No matter how delicious the blood of another would be, it would now pale in comparison to ours for either of us. Becoming the consummate host of another always resulted in this. And unlike the bond between our kind and a human who was blessed to become such a host during their ephemeral lives, ours would last forever, barring any misfortunes in the war or accidents with daylight.

Derek reached out and took my chin gently between his thumb and forefinger, taking care to lightly run his thumb across my lower lip. At this simple touch, my fangs extended and I shivered inside, wanting him connected to me in that deep embrace once again.

"I'm sure we'll adjust," he said. "You don't hear me complaining, do you?"

"No, but you're still troubled," I closed my eyes as his hand travelled to my cheek. I reached up and took his hand in my own grip and kissed his palm before returning it to where it had previously lain. "And I know why. We've no more secrets from each other. We're bonded."

"I overdid it when we fed," Derek confessed, his

expression darkening. "Elisa, you don't know how hard it was for me to stop."

"Actually, I do know," I said, correcting him.

"Well, yeah, now you do," Derek rolled his eyes in mock annoyance. "But what I'm saying is that I kept my feelings locked down, suppressed, and compressed under God knows how many barriers until tonight." He then leaned back against the wall and sighed.

"I think you deserve to know the full truth. When I first met you . . . and then smelled you, I thought I would freaking lose it. I only had my sense of duty to save you from myself. I wanted to avoid you; I wanted to send you back for another, but I couldn't do it. I knew I'd live in anguish if I did that; hell, the very thought of doing something like that scared the crap out of me. I tried to keep you at arm's length, and keep my feelings bottled up. Of course, tonight, I knew I slipped up bad out at that farmhouse. I hoped you'd forget about it when Paws interrupted us, and after the fiasco with the shape-shifters and Joe, but you didn't. And I knew I couldn't hide it anymore."

Derek slumped forward and his eyes glazed over with a faraway look. "And even though it was . . . well, I'll be honest . . . an indescribable relief to finally do what I longed to do, and then to have you return those feelings . . . when we finally . . ."

His fangs extended with the memories in his head, and I watched as a shudder of his own rippled through him.

"God, when you said 'do it,' something inside me broke. I almost lost control. And then I saw the empty blood pack afterwards. I was terrified. I realized that if you hadn't had that pack connected to you, things might've turned out for the worse."

"Derek, that's something that is easily fixed," I assured him. "You've just never had anyone teach you discipline when feeding. You can give me an IV next time we're intimate, and I can teach you how to master your thirst." I placed the as of yet unused blood pack on the windowsill and moved forward to kneel before Derek, looking him earnestly in the eyes. "But I think you know that this isn't the biggest problem."

"No," he whispered, and averted his gaze. "It isn't."

"It's me, isn't it?"

Derek was silent for a long time. And then, suddenly, he began to shake with laughter. His thoughts slipped into a memory he'd shared with me not too long after I'd arrived, but expanded into something I had heretofore not known. But once I saw it in his mind's eye, I understood.

"Did I ever tell you that that Sarah girl, the one who told me to contact your clan, gave me a prophecy along with her advice? A personal one?" Derek asked.

"No," I said. "But it's not surprising that she would. She does that from time to time."

"She told me that when I sent for help, that help would be the completion of me," Derek's voice was still trembling from his gentle laughter. "I kinda figured what she meant by that, and I was actually hopeful, despite my doubts. But when I saw you, I thought I'd been had. I figured she was just some mental kook who'd managed to get away from Lothos after being turned, and who'd gone one too many nights without a drink. 'Course I didn't think that for long. I could smell you from the bottom of that ledge. And to tell the truth, it scared the living hell out of me, even after I learned about how old you really were. I couldn't bring myself to act on what my most basic instincts wanted to do. I wanted to give you a separate trailer to live in, or even a tent, but I let you share my RV. Like you felt so comfortable around me, I felt that way around you. I couldn't explain it. I trusted you implicitly, and my friends tell me that I'm not easily won over with talk. I can't afford to be naive. But I followed your directions despite some of my people, Joe especially, thinking I was losing it."

His voice softened as he brought his tale to a close.

"Somewhere along the way, I came to realize that your happiness was the most important thing in the world to me. I knew I wasn't being manipulated; I learned how to screen out stuff like that. I thought for a time that it was just fascination, since I'd never seen anyone else turned at anywhere near the age I was, and you'd been turned far younger. But I believe that even though you were interesting on some subconscious level, I rejected that. It took awhile, but soon a bolt of clarity hit me, and it was utterly horrifying. I'd run out of theories, and had to bite the bullet. I was forced to admit to myself that I loved you. And despite everything I could possibly do to try and deny it, I wanted you. Hell, I wanted you badly. You wouldn't believe just how badly! Of course, some part of me kept saying, 'this is crazy! She's a kid! Are you some kind of pervert?' I knew I had never had these feelings before, and especially not like this. But the nagging feeling of . . . I don't know . . . wrongness . . . It wasn't something I could shake, you know?"

"And you still can't shake it, can you?" I asked.

"I'm trying to," Derek said in a low voice. There was a look of restrained anguish and pain on his face as he sat shaking his head. "God help me; I'm trying to."

I reached out, and cupped his face in my hands. I ran my hands softly across the edges of his ears and through his silken brown hair.

"Derek . . ." I whispered his name as if his name were a benediction. Then I leaned forward and pressed my lips against his. The taste of his cigarillo was only faintly on his breath, as his body had been busy flushing out its effects. His gentle hands drew me close to him, and I let my arms snake about his neck. We savored the taste of each other's lips for a long time afterwards, forgetting our troubles, cares, and worries. And yet, in Derek's mind, I could sense that uneasiness, like an infuriatingly tenacious ingrown toenail: the source of his pain and confusion. In time, I would help to remove it. .

"Did you fall in love with my body?" I asked, placing my hand to my breast when I saw that Derek was truly seeing me, and not lost in the haze of desire that our kiss had produced.

"Ah . . . well, first of all, no offense," Derek said after eyeing me strangely. I then realized the way I'd phrased my question, and so I didn't blame him for that look or his feelings of discomfort. The question, after all, sounded like a loaded one: the kind a jealous woman would ask that her spouse could never answer correctly without triggering her ire, but Derek understood my intent. "But . . . no, not really. That isn't to say that you're not beautiful, Elisa. You're a perfect China doll."

"Yes, you say that about five or six times a night," I said with a half-grin.

Derek flustered at this, taken aback for a moment, then regained his faculties. His demeanor was more relaxed, more self-assured as he continued. "You're very beautiful, Elisa. But I'm sure you know that's not what attracted me to you. Even if you had been turned as an adult, I'm not a shallow man. I fell in love with you . . . and I mean you as a whole. Your intelligence, your confidence, your wisdom. You came in with a commanding presence, despite the way you looked, and you had a plan. Nothing ever fazed you. You blew away my expectations of what someone from your clan would be like. And yes, I know that Paws was part of your clan, but he was already an established member of mine when I was added, so I'd only known him as part of my people."

"In short, it wasn't your bravery alone, or your intelligence, or your confidence . . . or even simply your blood that attracted me to you. It was you. Everything about you. I guess you could say I fell in love with your soul."

"But my blood was damn attractive too, wasn't it?" I asked, purring those words into his ear. Derek certainly was not without surprises. He could be a right charmer when he wanted to be, and of course, beautifully romantic.

"Yes . . . that too," he said with some small distraction as

I leaned closer and nibbled very lightly on his earlobe, taking special care with my fangs.

"Then when you love me, think of my soul instead of my body," I said and kissed his cheek. I brought his hand up to my lips again, and spread his fingers. I brushed my lips softly against his palm, and Derek, reading my intent, took hold of my other hand with his free hand to bring it to his lips. "Can you do that, love? Can you think about my soul, and not this body, whenever we love each other?"

"I think so," he said. I wanted a phrase that suggested more of a commitment, but I knew that this was as much of one as I would get from him at this moment. So for now, I was somewhat satisfied.

"I love you," he said, touching each of my fingers with his own.

"I love you," I replied, and asserted my fangs into his palm. He did the same for me, and we indulged ourselves in that tiny drink, delighting our senses until I awoke Derek's instincts and he carried me to the bed. He took my unused blood pack and re-fashioned the IV into my arm before his fangs pierced my flesh again. I soon followed suit, and we brought ourselves into euphoria together. I would teach him control soon enough so that the IV would no longer be necessary, but for tonight, I wanted this of him, free of his inhibition. We melded into one in the drink, sealing our neck wounds just enough to slow the flow to a drip, and making our bliss last as long as possible.

Afterwards, enfolded in Derek's arms, I watched the sun shutters on the window close by way of their automated timer, sealing us off from the faint span of blue on the horizon. And together, our hearts and minds as one, we succumbed to the slumber of daylight, savoring that fleeting peace born in a tumultuous night.

Chapter Nine

The next night was a return to the unpleasant, unfinished business that Derek and I could only temporarily forget about. We were both aware that this evolution in our relationship would complicate things somewhat in that business, but of course, this was something we knew would not be without its problems.

I sometimes envy the fact that humans can disguise their dalliances; mere discretion about one's destination and a simple bath after the act, and most of their kind are none the wiser. Of course, we were not embarrassed by what we had done. Even as I woke up to Derek's voice softly wishing me a good evening, followed by his even softer kiss . . . and when we indulged ourselves in that simple act for a bit longer than perhaps we should have, I knew with perfect clarity that he loved me and was not at all ashamed. Of course, there was still that niggling conflict in the far reaches of his mind that I had resolved to weed out with time, but his touch, his smile, and the clarity of his feelings that sang through our conjoined hearts told me all I needed to know. In that respect, there was no way to hide it even if we wanted to. Our scents had radically changed from our mutual feedings; Lyman could read minds just as easily as Derek and I, and though I didn't know the extent of Deb's talents, I surmised that if she was a pyrokinetic, it wasn't too much of a stretch to suppose she possessed some modicum of telepathy. Still, whether or not this was true, our scents were nevertheless a dead giveaway. And at least one person in particular, our first item of business, would not take well to our relationship at all.

"About time you two settled things," Lyman said when we stepped into the living room. It seemed he had invited himself inside, and was seated in the couch waiting for us.

Derek seemed to pay this no mind, but I gave a start at the sight of him, as if he'd caught us both naked. Afterwards, I felt a minor twinge of consternation. Barring distraction, we of my clan usually were aware of the presence of a visitor, but entering another's home uninvited was still considered rude.

"Yeah, we did, but some of the others won't like it," Derek remarked, stepping around me to shake Lyman's hand.

Lyman raised one of his thick eyebrows, and I knew that he was genuinely surprised at Derek's candor. "Do you care about that?"

"Not really."

"Not even Deb? She's going to break a gut, you know. Probably try to do something to hurt the baby."

"She what?" I interjected, fury spiking in me as if someone had set my spine afire. But Derek remained calm. He gestured for silence with a wave of his hand and a feeling of relaxed ease sent my way, coupled with a promise to explain later. I capitulated, but listened on.

"That's crap," Derek said. "She's too attached to that baby to hurt her; even you know that."

"She's unstable," Lyman warned. "Fire-starters are all that way. And you know she's going to take your relationship the hardest."

"She and I don't speak much nowadays." Derek shook his head. "And she hasn't exactly been endearing herself to me. You know I confined her to her trailer after what she did to Joe. She's lucky I don't kick her emo ass out of this clan for it. For now, she's grounded 'til this trip is over. It'll save us all a bunch of trouble."

Lyman shrugged. "You're the boss. But you'll be getting a lot of funny looks, especially when we run into other Vagabonds."

"We're hoping to avoid that until we get to where we're going," Derek said. "Last night was proof that we're still in danger, and we don't want to drag anyone else into this."

"Can't argue with that," Lyman answered, and I felt from him a sense of weariness as his mind perused the memories of last night's events. "So what do you propose we do?"

"That's where Elisa comes in." Derek gave my hand a reassuring squeeze. I felt his acquiescence and spoke.

"We'll be leaving tonight for a new campsite," I explained and used my Jewel to create a holographic map of our route. I pointed out some areas that I felt were relatively secure or off the beaten path that we could use for safe havens during the day. But when Lyman saw our destination, he let out a belly laugh so loud I thought it would shake the walls of the RV.

"It's a logical choice," I said. I understood the source of his amusement, but still felt a bit self-conscious.

"Never said it wasn't, little lady!" Lyman laughed on, though it had died down to an incessant chuckle. Perhaps he found some amusement in my flustered state. I sighed inwardly. I had forgotten how annoyingly cheerful he could be. "It's genius in its simplicity, you want to know the truth." He then stabbed his finger at the red mark of our destination. But do we really have to use that area?"

"Even the abandoned villages are inaccessible by Lothos," I said. "The trick is getting there safely. Location is secondary."

"Some here won't agree," Lyman commented.

"'Some here' can take a wide step on a narrow ledge," I flippantly remarked. "When our lives are in danger, comfort takes a back seat."

"I don't think anyone will argue with that, China doll," Derek said. "But what I think Paws is trying to say is if our problems with Lothos are going to get worse from here on out, your other plan is going to be a bit trickier."

"It was," I said, and produced the fiend's Jewel from my pocket. "But with this, we might have a way to hide ourselves for the better part of the night."

"Wait, is your plan what I think it is?" Lyman asked. Smiling, I opened my mind to him, and after a moment, he nodded approvingly.

"That's a good strategy," he said, sounding reassured. "I just hope it works."

"You and me both," I said.

"Oh, by the way, I don't mean to pry again," Lyman said, assuming a less assertive posture, "But have you two ever considered how you're going to stay in touch after this whole thing blows over?" His gaze switched to Derek, who seemed frozen at this question, "Unless you're planning on leaving us?"

Derek opened his mouth, but nothing came out. And I felt a very distinct, very awkward sense of uncertainty crawl from his insides, as if someone had broken a nest of spiders in his gut. But if he was having misgivings, he'd slipped into his decorum deeply enough not to show them.

"We'll . . . cross that bridge when we come to it," I replied, speaking up for myself and Derek, who seemed to be rendered quite out of tongue. "Besides, it's not like we've discussed every last detail."

"Fair enough," Lyman said, pushing himself up from the couch. "Well, that's my cue to get out of your hair. And I'm sorry about the intrusion. Your private lives are your own, after all."

"Curiosity is nothing to be ashamed of," I said with a polite smile. I took hold of Derek's hand, and I felt his gratitude for the contact. He had obviously not liked being caught so mentally flat-footed.

"Well, it distracted me a bit from the reason I came in. But once I smelled you two, I couldn't resist." He then shifted his gaze to Derek, and his grin vanished. "Joe's awake, by the way."

"I expected as much," Derek said stiffly, but he was grateful for a change of subject. "Who's been keeping guard over him?"

"Pablo took up the shift at the beginning of the night," Lyman said. "It's a good thing Joe doesn't get up 'til late.

An hour after sunset is just too much time in my book to be wasting the night."

"We'll be there shortly," Derek said. "Let Pablo know."

Lyman nodded and started for the door. Before opening it, he paused, and then looked back at me. "Oh, got one more question for you, little lady," he said.

I gazed at him expectantly.

"You happy with this rascal?" His grin, broad and with a mischievous glint in his eyes returned as he gestured towards Derek, who rolled his eyes in mock annoyance. I glanced at Derek, and felt the warmth of his smile and the love that flowed through me as if I were a conduit for its power.

"Yes," I replied softly, but letting my earnestness come through.

"Good, then." Lyman said. "You seem to be. And that means the Master will be happy with your choice as well."

"You talk as if we're about to get married," I replied, stifling a laugh that I believe would have sounded derisive.

"You know how it is with our kind," Lyman said, fixing me and Derek with a knowing look before he slipped outside. "It takes us a long time to fall in love, but when we finally do, we do it quickly, and we do it hard. You've seen it with your own father."

I looked at Derek, who had been speechless for the last part of the conversation. He was a knot of emotions again, but mostly because of what Lyman had said. Father had indeed fallen in love with Amelia with amazing swiftness, despite any of my warnings, or his own misgivings, which led him to agree to do something as rash as allow Amelia to nearly die from purging herself of his toxins in a forced fast from his kiss, just to find out of her feelings for him were true. Of course, anyone besides Father could see that they were, but he came around. In less than a month he turned and married her, and the two had been perfectly happy together ever since. Derek, as far as I could tell, had no intentions to take our relationship to that level quite so soon, but it seemed as though my long lost friend had left a profound effect upon him.

"Small steps, love," I said, touching his arm. This and the touch from my mind awakened him from his reverie.

"I should've expected that from him," Derek said. I watched him release a good-natured sigh while trying not to smile. "Unlike me, he exploits the hell out of his telepathy, but he doesn't usually spread things around, unless it's about relationships." He snickered as an amusing image came into his mind. "He's like the nosy neighbor from across the street in one of those old sitcoms."

I laughed, and Derek was quick to join me.

And we were soon to discover that we would need this laugh before what awaited us.

***

Joe's RV was smaller than the one I shared with Derek, but it seemed large enough to have a bathtub, as I heard the others talk about last night. The place was more cluttered than Derek's home, perhaps reflecting the way it looked before he made preparations to take me in. The scent of blood suffused the air, coming strongest from the bathroom and Joe, who was brooding in a couch in the living room area. He still sported traces of blood beneath his fingernails and toenails. All traces of burns and scarring on his body were gone, and his skin was ruddy with the overabundance of blood he must have consumed during his time in the tub.

Pablo, having entered the RV with us, stood guard with a loaded M-16. I appreciated the gesture, but with my Jewel, we were in no real danger . . . not that I expected Joe to lose his temper around his closest friend and the leader of his clan. But then again, I didn't know him.

The scowl on his face deepened when his eyes settled on me, and I felt his hatred and impotent rage like the closeness of a furnace.

"Feeling better?" Derek asked his friend as he approached the side of the couch. As if nothing had happened, he leaned casually upon its arm. "You had better nights than last night."

"Well, I was feeling better-" Joe's voice was a low growl, and his speech possessed a slow cadence. Not once did he avert his eyes from me. "- until you came in with that."

Derek's hurt at Joe's demeanor struck my heart, but not a trace of his true emotions showed on his face. I did, however, become aware of a small welling of anger beginning to seethe at the remote edges of his consciousness.

"Well . . . speaking of 'that,'" he nodded my way, "you mind telling me why you shot her?"

Joe looked away for the first time, his gaze shifting towards Derek, then to Pablo, and finally to his feet. Even in the blood scent-filled RV, I could detect the odor of his sweat. But as for words, he said nothing.

"Deb heard it from you when you went ranting and raving at her trailer last night," Derek said, pressing on. "She told Lyman after it all went down, and he told me. Said you were trying to distract the other vampire with Elisa's scent to keep it away from the baby? Is that true?"

"Well, looks like you got it all figured out, don't you?" Joe said with a venomous sneer. "You and your little pet there are both mind-readers, so why don't you just pry the story out of me?"

"You know why," Derek said.

"Yeah, she's got a nice little code of conduct, and you're just too chicken to do it," Joe ended his sentence with laughter whose derision awakened my own kind of fury.

"Let me tell you something, sunshine." I stalked forward, and Joe, his last encounter with me fresh in his rage-filled mind, seemed to shrink into his couch. "If I judged the information I needed to be important enough, don't think for a moment that I wouldn't hesitate to pry it out of your mind with a flaming crowbar, and leave you a bloody vegetable!"

I stopped when I felt Derek's hand on my shoulder, and

with it, the sensation of calm easing its way into my heart. How he could be so serene about this, I didn't know, but his ability to lock himself in step with decorum had never ceased to amaze me, even before we fell in love.

"Elisa's part of our clan, Joe," Derek said, maintaining his composure, but betraying his true emotions in the low, threatening tone of his voice. "And she's not expendable. How could you have thought the ends justified the means here?"

"Look, I spotted the shape-shifter while I was out taking a walk, okay?" Joe snapped. "Excuse me if I didn't trust the girl's traps, but I wanted to be sure nothing was coming after us. When I saw the monster, she was headed straight for the camp. She was going to take my kid!"

"Oh, so now she's 'your kid,' when you didn't give a fuck about her before?" Derek said. "I'm not buying it. Why the change of heart? And besides, you knew Deb would be able to protect her better than you. What is it you're not you telling me?"

Joe once again retreated into silence. Anger and hatred seethed within him: anger at Derek, hatred, as I expected, at me. And from Derek, I felt a churning disgust that grew from his bowels and moved to his lips. I felt only nervousness from Pablo, having been dragged into this encounter, and none too thrilled about the direction in which this conversation seemed to be headed.

"Fine, then," Derek said coldly. "You can stay in here until you're more disposed to talk."

"You can't do that!" Joe shot to his feet, but remained where he stood. I felt fear and helplessness roiling in his thoughts, combined with the usual malice towards me.

"Watch me," Derek said flatly.

And then Joe snapped.

Perhaps he had been unaware of our scents before, but when Derek took my hand, I felt a spike of realization in Joe's mind. Clues he had been ignorant of had come to sudden light, falling into place, and creating a horrifying realization. I heard him groan as this revelation sank in, and felt his cold, appalled disgust.

"Oh . . . my . . . god . . ."

We turned back towards Joe just as he rushed forward at preternatural speed. His motion was fueled by such rage and icy revulsion that even I had not seen him move. He now stood, holding Derek up by his shoulders, squeezing them with his inhuman strength. Derek gasped, wide eyed, and gave a choked cry.

"Are you out of your fucking mind?" Joe spoke through a rictus of bared teeth and elongated fangs. The crimson of his eyes seemed to deepen and glow with his rage. "First you invite this mind-reader into our clan, and now you've bonded with her? Were you that horny and desperate? Couldn't keep your fangs in your mouth, so you've gone off rutting with a damned kid?" Are you some kind of sick per-"

He never got to finish his sentence. I drew upon my Jewel and reversed forces in two directions, prying Joe off of Derek with the ease of slapping a table tennis ball. The effect I conjured sent Joe flying through -and out of- the far wall while Derek collapsed onto the floor.

I watched the cloud of dust billowing from Joe's none-too-gentle landing through the hole. Fortunately for him, there had been no other trailers or vehicles parked beside the RV, and he landed, tumbling, in a nearby field. I wanted to investigate the damage I'd done, but I first tended to Derek.

Both of his upper arms were broken. I wasn't certain how extensive the damage was, but he cried out when I tried to touch them. I could clearly see the bruising, already healing, albeit slowly. Without a word from me, Pablo had hurried off to find some blood packs.

"I'm so sorry," I said to Derek. "I just wanted to get him off of you."

"S'okay, China doll . . ." Despite his pain, Derek fixed me with a reassuring smile that seemed more like a grimace. "I'll be . . . okay in a few. Guess it just . . . escalated a bit more quickly than I . . . expected."

"Did you know he was going to do that?" I asked. Derek shook his head.

"No . . . but I'm not surprised. He's . . . always been a spitfire. Got him into . . . plenty of trouble . . . in the past."

I touched his cheek and sent as many calming thoughts of comfort as I could his way. I was many things with my Jewel, but I was a mediocre healer. This was what separated me from Aiko, who had been extensively trained in just about every known field of thaumaturgy. But of course, she had over a thousand years on my near two centuries. "Try not to speak. I know it hurts. I'd give you my toxins, but I don't want to run the risk of your losing any blood. You'll need as much of it as you can to heal."

Derek's eyes went suddenly wide, and I felt fear spike within him. The emotion flashed from him like a knife, set to impale me through the heart.

"Elisa!" He whispered tensely. But he needed no more words, as I caught the glimpse of Joe in his mind's eye. I turned towards the hole, drawing upon my Jewel, but a split-second too late to stop the impact.

I was slammed across the RV, into the kitchen area as Joe appeared, moving like a ghost through the dust of his outside landing. Everything became a blur of images, the force of the blow, the shards of wood, glass, metal and porcelain, and of course, the pain of it all. But I wasn't knocked unconscious as I suppose Joe had hoped. And that became his undoing.

For alterations that require more finesse or precision, such as blocking photons the way I had in my fight against the fiend, a certain amount of concentration is needed, but in enhancing my strength to take on a larger opponent, only broad strokes are needed. This comes almost as second nature, even to a novice in Jewel training. I deflected a few blows from Joe's fists when we landed in the remains of a kitchen cabinet, and before he could land anything that would have been significantly damaging, I locked into the vast well of energy that was my Jewel and caught his fist in its course. Despite having attacked me before, like most adult-size vampires, he was again unprepared for the "unnatural" amount of strength I displayed. I easily took him off guard, catching his other fist, which he hurled at me after being unable to pry the other from my grip. I then used the momentum of the attempted blow to shove him to the side. With the force I could muster from my Jewel, I threw him like a rag doll above me, and across the kitchen floor.

With preternatural speed, I leaped to my feet. Joe, not yet out of the fight and blinded with rage, righted himself in midair and into a crouching position with like swiftness.

"Not again, bitch," he said in a harsh, guttural voice. It transformed into a resounding snarl as he hurled himself at me. His hands were grasping claws aimed at my throat. Had they found their mark, I would have most likely been decapitated: one of the few ways we can die and stay that way.

Of course, his hands never got anywhere close to my throat. And with my Jewel, I was by far the quicker in the fray, twisting my body to slam my leg into his crotch. It wasn't my intent to cause him pain in that manner -that was merely a bonus-, but instead, I allowed the force of my kick to hurl him upwards for my intended blow.

I shattered his femur.

In retrospect, I should have braced myself for the torrential psychic backlash of pain, or perhaps at least sent a quick warning to Derek, but the agony I brought upon Joe with my Jewel-enhanced fist was nothing that either I or Derek could have fully prepared for. The echo of pain would have sent any halfway sensitive telepath into spasms, but Joe's vocal scream was something utterly unearthly, and would probably be heard across the encampment.

I watched, partly stunned by the burst of agony that rippled across my mind as Joe landed, nearly breaking the kitchen floor, his leg at a frightening angle. He writhed and screamed as if Deb had set him on fire anew. A part of me wished that she would show up now and finish him off with the deed. But he was alive, and his femur was now so many bone shards in his leg. This would take far more than a soak in a tub of blood to repair, and the healing process would take a much longer time to finish.

Pablo arrived within a minute, followed by Lyman, Wadih, Wilson, Randy, and Benjamin -who perhaps let out the loudest expletive of the group when they saw the aftermath of what had happened. Lyman, who most likely understood best what had transpired, was cradling his head and swaying slightly, but that didn't stop him from barking orders. Pablo fed the blood pack to Derek; meanwhile, the others started to transport Joe onto a makeshift stretcher made out of the bed sheet from his room. Joe groaned in agony with every movement, despite how careful they were with his ruined leg.

Once Joe was in his bed, I overheard Derek and his clan discussing whether or not simply amputating it would be an option. I'd secretly hoped that they would do it, as amputations took over a month to grow back, but in the end, Derek, his wounds having healed sufficiently, interceded on Joe's behalf.

"Either way, Joe's stupidity has made us a man short," he said, "but we don't need to keep him laid up for over a month. We'll put the leg into a splint and allow it to heal on its own. It'll be quicker."

"He'll be in a hell of a lot of pain while that leg knits back," Lyman said, followed by a chorus of assent from the others. "For four or five days, to be exact. Maybe even longer, seeing the kind of work the girl did on him."

"That is not my problem," Derek said, looking back on the ruin of the RV with a scowl. "Maybe that'll teach him to stop acting on his every damn feeling."

The entire time this was discussed, Joe was sullen and could only stare numbly at his leg and his friend. For the first time, he avoided eye contact with me, and I was thankful for that. As expected, no one objected to Derek's decision, and Joe was left with several blood packs for the time being. Derek was by now, of course, fed up with Joe and ended the discussion with a particularly ominous word for his friend. I had never heard him sound so cold, or so adult.

"Use the time you have to reflect on your actions," he said to him. "Because during that time, I'll be deciding whether or not you'll still have a home here."

And that was only the beginning of the night.

Chapter Ten

As Lyman had done earlier, Derek began expediting orders to the assembly once we stepped outside of Joe's RV. We broke camp and Derek threw himself into his work, hauling trailers to their hitches and helping Marie-Laure disconnect power cables. Throughout the business, neither he nor his comrades made mention of what had happened in Joe's trailer. I was actually relieved for this respite from the continuing storm of incident as I first set to work retrieving the traps from the surrounding area, while keeping a Jewel-enhanced eye out for any more of Lothos' clan. Fortunately, the breakdown went without incident, and within the hour, we were all packed and ready to move on to our next destination. Perhaps it was because of a remnant of my formerly prejudicial view of Vagabonds, but it amazed me how such a ragtag bunch worked together with such efficiency, despite being two men short.

Joe was moved to a spare trailer and Lyman patched the hole in Joe's old RV with a tarp and duct tape before hitching it to Randy's refitted bus. With reflective paint, he marked its rear with the words "IN TOW" while I, having finished my retrieval work, cleaned up the mess inside.

Being two men short meant that Deb's confinement extended to even group labor. Rather than being a frustration, this suited me just fine. Besides, her primary responsibility was taking care of the baby, and it was easy enough to latch her small trailer to Wilson's truck with her still inside. I caught only a glimpse of her scowling face looking through the window as Pablo pulled the trailer towards the truck's tailgate hitch, moving slowly, as not to wake the child.

We ran through last minute preparations to move to the next camping site and prepared to leave. But before we could set off on our way, it seemed that the curiosity of the clan had gotten the better of them. Only Deb, for obvious reasons, and Marie-Laure, who had retired to her camper to wait for us, were not present outside of Joe's RV, having cornered me, Derek, and Lyman. When the questions began, it wasn't a storm of accusations or a cacophony of inquisition as I thought it might be; rather, Lyman spearheaded it, and it became rather orderly.

"I don't think you'll be able to hide it now, boss," Lyman said to Derek with a hopeless shrug.

"Wait, hide what?" Wilson asked. He fixed us with a suspicious gaze. "And you were in on it too?"

"Derek, what the hell's going on?" Randy asked. He brushed his hand back through his hair, just as thick and dark as Derek's, but longer. "Pablo says Elisa was the one who busted Joe's leg?"

"Yeah, that's crazy!" Benjamin interjected. "Unless she has a Jewel, or something. And only the mind-readers have that."

All eyes, save those of Lyman and Wadih, who were, of course, already in the know, settled on me, and at once, I felt almost as uncomfortable as Derek when Lyman had alluded to marriage. But this time, it was Derek who had come to my rescue, speaking on my behalf.

"I can tell you first of all that I'm well aware of your suspicions," Derek said, "And your suspicions are right."

"So she is a mind-reader?" Pablo said, and gestured vaguely towards Lyman "Like you and Paws?"

Derek forced all unnecessary emotions away into a deep corner of his mind, again making me wish I could do that with the same ease. Without expression, he nodded.

"So what's she doing with us?" Benjamin asked. "She a defector too?"

"Actually, I've come to help you," I said. "I'm sure you know that those attacks by Lothos' followers aren't just him marking you for sport. You're being exterminated. And I've been sent to help you stay alive."

"So you got a Jewel after all?" Pablo nodded his head as if coming to an agreement within his own internal committee. "That's how you were able to fuck up Joe's leg?"

"He attacked her first," Derek assured him.

"It all makes sense now," Randy said. "I'd heard you guys had it out a few days ago."

"Yeah, and after that fight was when you gave all these crazy new orders," Wilson added. "And what's all this about Pablo saying you're sucking red out of her?"

"I wasn't just saying, man," Pablo interjected. "Couldn't you smell him? They smell like each other. You know the only way that happens."

"Jeez!" Wilson gave a small shudder when he met my eyes again. I felt no hate from him, but he was certainly, and not surprisingly, uncomfortable with this. "Derek, just how old is she?"

"Older than you," Derek replied, his voice having turned suddenly cold. Wordlessly, he sent an idea into my mind, and I realized that Wilson was over ninety-three. I sent a comforting thought to Derek, assuring him that Wilson meant nothing by his question. "And who I sleep with, or feed from shouldn't matter to you anyway. She may look like a kid, but she's not. That's all you need to know."

"Look, boss, we've been cool with you leading us," Randy said. "And I don't think you're gonna find anyone here who really has a problem with how she looks. That'd be stupid, considering how you look and all." There was a murmur of assent from the rest of those assembled. "The problem we have is where her loyalties lie. Is she one of us? Or is she still part of the mind readers?"

"She rescued you guys from a sneak attack that could've left this place in ashes last night," Derek said. "Lyman didn't tell you the whole story, and neither did I, because I didn't want to scare you."

"Scare us?" Wadih had finally spoken up. "Derek, we're

already scared here. Everyone's been on edge with all these attacks. We're scared as all hell! You got more bad news, you may as well just spill it!"

A roar of agreement came from the others, and so Derek told them about the thaumaturgist. His story silenced everyone present.

"If we've taken one out, then there will be others," Derek said, then gestured to me. "And she's the only one standing between us and being wiped out. I can't even guarantee the safety of the others in our clan who've been in hiding. But for now, it seems they're safe. That's all we know for now. I silenced our cell phones because I thought we were being traced somehow, but the attacks still keep coming. Now that they're sending their Jewel users after us, we need her."

"Does she have a Jewel?" Randy asked.

"A Jewel isn't gonna keep us safe," Wilson retorted. "Those things are only as good as their users."

This time, I was the one who spoke up. Though I rarely ever used my position for leverage, I knew that now was a time where such a move would most likely be necessary.

"I am the adopted daughter of Talante, the father of my clan," I announced. "I am Lieutenant Chief thaumaturgist under Chief thaumaturgist Aiko."

There was a long silence in the crowd. Then Benjamin spoke.

"The witch? You're her?"

"She's not a witch," Lyman's admonishing voice came on top of Benjamin's words. "But you did get someone who'll definitely save your collective asses."

Another period of silence followed, and I could feel the roiling emotions of the crowd: awe, fear, distrust, shock, discomfort, and even a small bit of hope. Despite the latter emotion, it was altogether a mix that was most unpleasant, and I longed to be away from this, driving with Derek in the RV, just him and me.

"Okay, guys, enough of the 'Q&A,' okay?" Lyman began

to herd the assembly away from us. "Let all this soak in on the way to the next camp. We've got a long drive ahead of us."

His voice faded in the din of hushed conversation and cacophony of stress from both the crowd and Derek. Blindly, I reached for his hand, and once we made contact, I felt him calm down. I wrapped my heart around his and leaned into his side, sighing.

"That could have gone far worse," I said finally as I listened to the rolling cough and subsequent roar of the engines of the assembly of trucks, campers, and RVs.

"Could've gone better too, if Joe had kept his damn cool," Derek muttered. There was no anger in this, only a weary frustration I detected as I held on to his hand as he led me inside the RV. I only separated from him when he sat in the driver's seat. I took my place in the passenger seat and readied myself for the long journey.

"They'll come around," I assured him as he started the engine.

***

They didn't exactly come around as I expected, so much as settle into a slow simmer. And though I was willing to bide the time and see what would happen, this situation put Derek somewhat on edge for the next two days. No one mistreated me or was disrespectful; in fact, they seemed a bit more personable, and even welcomed my assistance when I offered it. Even Marie-Laure, who no doubt had learned what happened through the rest of the clan, was not quite so abrasive. Still, she tended to avoid me. Derek assured me that her coldness was nothing personal, that she was a recluse by nature, but I always felt somewhat unnerved by her behavior, which was a pity. I had never lacked for female friends and acquaintances among my clan, especially Aiko, at least before her ordeal, and more recently, Amelia, who had become like a sister to me. Being here, among so many males, and with females who were taciturn at best, and outright hostile at worst, was somewhat difficult to manage. Had it not been for Derek, I think I would have become somewhat bitter, and certainly much more homesick by now. But I could easily forget about it in his arms.

I used the Jewel I'd retrieved from the dead thaumaturgist to enact a plan that was at once risky, elegant, and positively devious in its simplicity. Though the device had suffered a hairline crack in its surface from the destruction of its former wielder's body, it was still useful for bringing things into that pocket space between dimensions. I first had my doubts about using this particular Jewel for such a thing, especially a task as large as concealing the entire encampment, but my fears were somewhat allayed after I could detect no elements of tracking in its energies, even under my own Jewel's most thorough scans. When I activated it, the process of transition seemed to place no strain upon the Jewel.

Nevertheless, I had to be very specific about how out of dimensional sync I had placed us. Derek insisted that Marie-Laure be able to keep track of the clan's wandering brethren, and so I had to place us in a pocket space that was dangerously close to the reality line. It seemed to be just removed from reality enough, however, as for two days, our camp was undisturbed in that silent, bluish in-between space, with no trace of Lothos or his ilk. My cover having been blown, Derek revealed the plan to his clan, with the exception of our final destination. They did not like it, as expected, and they liked the remaining secrecy of it even less, but they did understand. Also as expected, they doubted my assurances that we would be safe at our new sanctuary. But this I could only prove once we arrived.

So this was the way we traveled. We spent the majority of the night on the road, keeping a wary eye for pursuers or attackers, and spent the final three hours safely in between space setting up camp. This left barely three hours to ourselves before sunrise.

The lack of interference from Lothos should have been as great a relief to me as it was for the clan, but nearly two hundred years of life in a constant war breeds a sort of pathological state of constant wariness that borders between vigilance and paranoia. It is a peculiar state that few of my kind can master, and I feel that if I hadn't come into Derek's life, he would have quickly fallen into his own version of it, had his clan survived this long. However, this quiet time was affecting him in a different manner, as he sometimes slipped into more moments of dark pensiveness that unnerved me. He had gone from worrying about his clan's survival to more practical concerns, chiefly, ones that he and I shared.

"How was Lothos keeping track of us?" he asked during the second night. I sat between his legs, resting my back against his bare chest as he reclined against the headboard of his bed. Having lost his reticence to smoke in my presence, he was puffing on one of his cigarillos while I flipped through a simple book of motivational phrases: one of the few books previously owned by Syd, their former leader. Derek owned one picture of him, kept on his nightstand. He was a gaunt figure, but very handsome, and I found myself wishing that I had met him. He sported shoulder-length, inky black hair and an elongated, smiling face. He wore a black leather jacket with silver spikes on the shoulder which made him resemble a member of a biker gang, but with a surprisingly less threatening visage. Derek, in the picture as well, compared height-wise to Syd in the same manner that I stood compared to him.

We had not drunk from each other yet, but I knew that Derek was preparing himself. My presence alone was slowly awakening his desire for my blood, and my scent would soon set his mind towards that. He liked allowing those instincts to be slowly aroused and increase to their peak, until he could no longer stand not having me. I allowed myself to do this as well, feeding off of the anticipation. We were in little else but our underwear, allowing the physical contact of our bodies to keep our minds in the deepest union. Derek had only recently overcome his reticence to do this, and I was glad when he first allowed this intimate closeness between us. It was a sign that we were making progress in putting his reservations to rest. I was the woman he loved, and he was the man I loved. We were consummate mates, bonded by blood, and we were immortal, no longer defined by our physical appearances. And little by little, he was learning that. Of course, it didn't hurt that I enjoyed the feel of the muscles on his chest. They were naturally less defined, less pronounced than any adult, but were solid in spite of their retention of nearly feminine leanness, and the feel of them nevertheless comforted me just as much as his presence.

Our feedings had become both a pleasant diversion, as well as a time of learning. As I'd promised, I had been teaching him self-control . . . as well as other things. Driven by the desire to not take too much from me in his feedings, he turned out to be an apt pupil, as it took only one evening to wean us from the need for a blood pack and IV. A mutual favorite activity evolved between us when I taught him something that only those with our talents could do. With our bond it was frighteningly easy to perform, and I relished that touch he gave to my mind: a probing that was beyond subtle as he reached inside and induced pleasurable sensations into my nerves. This was something that could easily go awry or be abused by the wrong kinds of people, and so it took absolute trust to do. I, of course, knew that Derek would never hurt me. We quickly found many avenues of intimacy in the bargain as we learned what pleased each other in a prelude to imbibing each other's intoxicating blood. Even now, I felt him tentatively reaching in and activating those sensations, gently distracting me from my reading despite his casual nursing of his perfumed cigarillo.

"As worried as you are about the Others tracking us, you're still cheeky enough to tease me?" I asked, both curious and playful at the same time.

"Just passing the time, my China doll," Derek said, equally flirtatious, but with his thoughts weaving in and out of the issue. "But I am serious about it. I can't help but wonder about how he was able to track us everywhere we went like that."

"He could do it if you had Jewels," I mused. "But you don't have any."

"Could he track yours?"

I shook my head -then nearly bit my lower lip as Derek caused a surge of delight to fire down my spine. I gasped as my back arched on reflex. I almost swore at him, but it had felt too good for me to stay angry.

"You know, that's hardly conducive to my concentration," I managed to say, attempting to sound stern, but betraying a giggle as I felt his amusement. I would certainly make him pay for it later. "But as I was trying to say, you know he'd been tracking you before I even arrived, so it couldn't have been me."

"Yeah, you're right," Derek said, covering his chagrined expression with the breadth of his hand. "I don't know what I was thinking. I guess all this stress has made me a little frazzled."

"It happens to the best of us, love," I said. "Besides, it wouldn't have been my Jewel he would be keeping track of. And he couldn't track mine if he wanted to. It's attuned to my body, and so no one else can use it without my permission. We all have unique brain waves; there's no way to disguise it, and my Jewel recognizes mine. Second, it must only be an active Jewel. Neutralized or inactive ones away from their wielders can't be used."

"But what about the Jewel you got off of the thaumaturgist?" Derek said. "How'd you get it to work?"

"Because it felt its user's death," I explained. "Don't get me wrong; Jewels aren't self-aware like we are, but they are attuned to the life force of their masters. When I killed her, it detected her death as something like a severed connection, like if you pull the plug on an internet router. And so it went into something akin to a standby mode. Plus it was damaged, so it was easy to take over. It can be done if you know how, and I made sure no one was monitoring us through it before I deigned to use it. But I still have my doubts. Still, it was the best plan I could think of on such short notice."

"I see."

I felt Derek's hands wrap about my waist. Like water in a sieve, most of his worries, save the most pervasive ones, slipped away as he fell into a more relaxed demeanor.

"I guess it's back to guessing if we have a mole or not," he said on the edge of a sigh.

"I know it's unpleasant," I replied. "But you may well have one."

"Yeah, I figured as much. And I'd prefer not to think about that right now."

Derek's heart released a flutter of unease that was like an unexpected souring of a sweet candy in our connection. "We've got too much suspicion in this clan already, and the one person I most suspect I don't want to suspect."

"Joe?" I asked, knowing very well what the answer would be.

"I wish I could count him out," Derek said, taking a final drag on his cigarillo before crushing it in the ashtray beside him. He then placed the ashtray atop his nightstand, away from us. "But he shot you. And he tried to kill you."

I felt a knot in my stomach at his words. I had hoped that Derek hadn't seen everything in the fight; I thought he might have been too blinded by pain to notice how Joe had come after me with the intent of separating my head from my body.

"You saw that." I made the question sound more like a statement. I then turned sideways to see his crimson eyes set intently upon me. "Is that what's bothering you?"

"A lot of things are bothering me, truth be told," Derek replied. I knew he was right. Again, there was his decorum, compartmentalizing and storing his worries and concerns for later use, and being damn effective with it. "But I can't let them all get the better of me, now can I? One thing at a time, and all that."

"Yes, but I know how you feel about him," I replied.

"And I know how you feel about him," Derek said.

"Don't do what you think you must do on account of me," I said. "He's your friend, though I honestly don't know how you can stand him."

"He's gotten me through more than you'll ever know," Derek said, "especially after we left Lothos. He knew all the hiding spots . . . and he looked like an adult, so he could get us things more easily. Feeding wasn't a problem, but I was too scared to use my talents, so the lion's share of the work was on Joe. I only kept him sane. He's got a fuse shorter than a two year old firecracker. But of course, you already know that."

"So what makes you think he's the mole?"

There was a long pause. Derek's gaze seemed to drift off into another galaxy before he spoke.

"You know, come to think of it, I don't think he is."

I felt the confusion overwhelm his thoughts for a moment, and then pass over him like clouds that threatened a storm, but failed to follow through.

"And yet it seems like the definite answer, doesn't it?" I asked.

"Read my mind, sweetie," Derek said, holding me more closely to him. "Truth is, there's more than enough suspicion to go around. Marie-Laure's a shut in, and the only one with electronic access to the outside world; who knows what she does all alone in her trailer? Randy, Ben, Pablo . . . they've been running errands most of the time; they might've sold us out, but there's no way to tell. And Deb . . ."

His thoughts seemed to fall into a pit with the mention of her name. It was then that I recalled what was mentioned in the conversation with Lyman two days ago. Derek had hoped

I'd forgotten. I had completely forgotten, actually, with the hustle and bustle of that night, and so had he, but this slip in his thoughts had jogged both our memories.

"Dammit . . ." I heard him mutter.

"You two were a couple, weren't you?" I asked. I wasn't jealous, but I was certainly curious.

"For a brief time," Derek said. "It wasn't too long after I joined up with the clan. I still had yet to shake off some of my . . . shall we say, less than endearing traits from hanging around Lothos' flunkies. I thought I was a badass; I kept others at arm's length, even Syd, who was trying to reach out to me. He's the only one who made me feel welcome . . . . well, him and Deb, at least in the beginning. She didn't see me as some little brat, which I was. She was a lot like me back then. Hell, she still is. I think that's why she and I broke up. Syd's influence on me had an effect. I grew up; she didn't. Maybe she'd always hoped I'd come around, or something. Still, she's always been pretty astute. She can judge relationships. I'll bet she knew I was attracted to you the moment she saw us together."

"Well, that would explain a lot," I said. "But she still agreed to take care of the baby. Was this before or after you two broke up?"

"Oh, long after," Derek answered. "I was only twenty when Joe and I escaped the shape-shifters, and when Deb and I met. We only dated for about a year. Things fell apart pretty quick after that. Syd started making a man out of me . . . . so to speak. Gave me more responsibilities, started teaching me stuff . . . Deb just couldn't handle the new me he was building."

"Yet she still agreed to take care of the baby?"

"She's got a soft spot for kids, believe it or not. And we couldn't have asked for a better protector. You saw what she did to Joe. Yeah, it was overkill and it pissed me off, but she was doing her job. Also, she's loyal to the clan, far as anyone can tell. No matter what her personal feelings are about you or me, I'm the boss. She'll do what I say."

"Heavy is the head that wears the crown," I said, resting my face against his chest. I could smell the blood beneath his cool flesh. I longed to sink my fangs into him right now, to once again obliterate our troubles, if at least for a time by our drawing from each other's crimson well. I would let his fangs find their mark, wherever they may be, so that we could drown ourselves in the drink's amnesiac bliss. But I resisted that urge. Its satisfaction would come in good time, when Derek and I were both ready. "And are you certain it would not be her?"

"Now who sounds worried?" I heard Derek ask with a laughing edge to his voice. I felt his hands press upon my back, his fingers squeezing and kneading gently against my smaller frame, as if trying to massage those apprehensions away like aches in a mortal's muscles.

"Not about the situation," I said. "I was just making sure you were certain. And I worry about you."

"You always seem to do that."

"You have so much on your plate. And all because of me."

I ran my hands upon his chest. I reached into his nerves and induced pleasure as he had done before, and I felt him shudder gently from within.

"Worrying about me," he said in a distant, quiet voice." You're such an old lady."

With a flash of annoyance, I changed my caress against his stomach into a poke with my claws, feeling the abruptness of the pain startle him.

"And you're going to be such a eunuch if you call me that again," I warned, bringing my fingers dangerously close to the waistline of his dark blue boxer briefs.

"Ouch! Okay, sorry!" Derek pleaded, but hearing his voice shaking with a laugh, it was obvious that my pinch was not painful enough to take all the cheekiness out of him. So I made a mental note to pinch harder if he called me by that name again. "And yes, I'm pretty certain Deb's not the one.

She's had plenty of opportunities to sell us out if she wanted."

"One could say that she's just biding her time," I said.

"True, but if that's the case, then we have no idea for what," Derek replied. "So I'd rather not go grasping at straws if I can help it."

"And so, that leaves us back where we started."

Derek hummed affirmatively. "And it bugs the hell out of me."

But before I could talk, Derek stroked a finger down my spine, inducing more pleasure into my nerves, the sensation silencing any comments in me in a choked gasp.

"Okay, enough of that," he said. "We keep our eyes open; it's all we can do, right?"

I nodded silently, the fading remnants of that sensation having put me in a near-dreamlike state, and greatly reducing my vocabulary.

"Good idea," was all I could say as I felt him slouch backwards into the pillow that supported his back, now letting the support go to his head. He fixed me with a broad, half-lidded grin.

"You liked that, didn't you?" He said. "Doesn't take much to fuzzy your thoughts when we're like this."

"As if you don't react the same way," I said, moving my face closer to his, to where our noses touched. "Remember when I first taught you? You were like a kitten in a basket of fresh catnip."

"You had me at a disadvantage then," Derek protested, gently caressing my cheeks and planting feather-soft kisses on my lips that made me shudder. "I've gotten wise to you."

"I like your confidence," I whispered, and reached into his nerves to spread pleasure through his lips at their light touches to my own. For other talents, I perhaps could have said that I'd had nearly two centuries on him, but this was something we were both new at. I was merely book-smart about it, but otherwise just as inexperienced as he was.

"And I like yours," he purred, and kissed me more

vehemently. My head swam. I involuntarily released a spasm of pleasure into his lips, and felt him stiffen, heard his heart pound faster with his sudden intake of air, then felt him relax, submerging himself back into the kiss. But where, like our first time, he would have given in to the drawing of my blood and fed with abandon, I felt him reign in the beast as he took me into his arms, cradling my back and head as he turned over in the bed, placing me atop the pillow beside him. As he hovered over me, his subconscious mind began to chant that mantra I had bestowed upon him from the beginning of his training.

I am not my thirst.

I smiled, wordlessly praising him as his lips met my neck and began to travel downwards. I shuddered as his deft fingers induced delightful sensations into my nerves. I touched him as he moved, inducing my own sensations into him and feeling him shudder at each pulse of delight.

I am not my thirst.

Derek arched his back as his lips fluttered down to my thigh, which he lifted as he rose to a sitting position. I giggled as his lips tickled my toes, then began their descent back down, coming to rest at the beginnings of my inner right thigh, where I began to pick up on his ever clearer intent. Anticipation flared through me as bright as the pleasure of his soft touch. I'd heard that this was an especially pleasurable way to feed, but of course, had never experienced it.

My mind echoed with his drum-like cadence of I am not my thirst. And this was the last coherent thought I had received . . . and perhaps its processing was the last coherent function my brain had made before his bite. The rest was in flashes, like a series of camera freeze frames being shuffled through my mind's eye on fast forward. I knew that Derek maintained control through it all, stanching the flow from my femoral artery to small, languorous drips that his lips pulled at, but the sheer force of the pleasure that coursed through me from that drink was as if he had taken it directly from my carotid artery at full flow. This was incredible. I was certain I cried out innumerable times, and he brought me to ecstasy again and again. Anyone's guess would be as good as mine as to exactly how many times this happened. Just how often did he cause me to tremble and wail in complete bliss as my blood coursed a constant river of euphoria in his own body? I only recall, as if in a dream, sending a pleading impression - the only semblance to a thought I could muster - to him for his blood, which he satiated by handing me his wrist.

At some point, we were again literally at each other's throats, and my thoughts had returned to something akin to comprehensible. This was not as intense as what Derek had done to my thigh (or what I certainly planned to do to his thigh at a later time), but it was no less pleasant. And it was a welcome change from fast to slow as we let our minds and bodies entwine in its fulfilling bliss, and allowed our talents to find new places to induce pleasure. My flesh tingled at the point in my thigh where his fangs had asserted themselves though I knew the wound was long healed. But this was not the remnant of pain. There never was pain from our kiss. Rather, it was an echo of that rapture, and my heart swelled with love for my bonded mate.

My China doll . . . Derek's mind whispered to me with a flare of love that made tears erupt from my eyes.

My Derek . . . I sent back, speaking directly through thought with him for the first time, my love riding on each word.

Through the haze of pleasure, I became aware of the movements of Derek's hands, which at first had been clasped with my own. Though our lips never left each other's necks, I followed the intent of his mind and let my awareness drift to his actions. His fingers slid down my forearms to the crook of my elbows, and down my arms and my sides, to where they rested at last at the waistband of my underwear. I pulled at the wound at his artery in wordless encouragement, and felt his fingers wrap about the waistband.

I froze with curiosity and no small amount of anticipation. He was breaching another one of his many walls of reservation, possibly the last. I could feel his powerful need that had awakened in the part of him that was human. He wanted this, and I wanted him to do it.

But then I felt his boldness falter. Something inaudible pulsed in the farthest reaches of his consciousness, but left a scar that jarred both him and me from our passions. I knew that he would not be following through with his intent tonight. As if my thoughts had been prophetic, I felt his fingers slip out of my waistband and drop to the sides of the bed. He licked over the wound, and I did as well, as frustration, fear, and anger soured the sweet resonance of our minds. We pulled away from each other as quickly as our bond would allow, and Derek sat upright, leaning against the headboard. I crawled up to my knees and looked at him, watching as he averted his eyes from me, as if he were ashamed of the sight of me.

"I'm sorry," He finally said, and I felt another upwelling of anger and shame erupt from his heart. "I really am sorry, Elisa. I guess I wasn't as ready as I thought I'd be."

Before I could assure him that everything was all right, the words again skirted the edge of his mind, and I could read them this time. It was more familiar than I had wanted, as they echoed in Joe's mocking voice, repeating a phrase that he had tried to say during our altercation, but I had stopped.

Couldn't keep your fangs in your mouth, so you've gone off rutting with a damned kid? Are you some kind of sick per-

As if that memory had been booby trapped, Derek yanked it away as far as it could be taken. It wasn't painful, but the experience was most unpleasant, similar to someone pulling a rug out from under your feet. Stunned, I stumbled back but caught myself, reeling from the combined cessation of our feeding and Derek's reaction. His knees were drawn up to his chest, and he appeared as fragile as gossamer. His mind was silent, but I could feel his pain and shame. That was the blessing and curse of a bond such as ours. No matter how deeply he buried those feelings, I would know. I could sense them, and it went both ways. I told him this without words.

"Aw, dammit!" He shouted, pressing the palms of his hands into his eyes. He keened in abject misery, drawing himself deeper into that fetal position as Joe's sneering voice vexed his thoughts. "I can't hide this even from you, can I?"

"Hide what?" I asked, becoming frightened for him for perhaps the first time. "Derek, please, talk to me! What's the matter? I know it was difficult for you to accept me at first; why is this memory tormenting you now?"

This was worse than alarming, the amount of vexation this memory was causing, and for a moment, I felt utterly helpless, and at a loss to explain, let alone do anything about what was happening to him. But then it dawned on me. And at that moment of revelation, I realized that his memory was dredging up something far deeper than I'd known, pressed to the innermost recesses of his mind that even I had not seen fit to go. And its connection with Joe's words could only mean one thing.

"Who did it to you, love?" I moved closer to him, facing him, and then lifted his face to where he could see me directly. My voice was gentle and as neutral as possible as I asked again. "Derek . . . who did it?"

Two large tears streamed from Derek's eyes as he shuddered. He inhaled a shuddering breath.

"Lothos."

I could barely hear his voice. Red rimmed his crimson eyes, but the second he spoke that dreaded name, its floodgates were breached. Two tears became a stream. My heart broke at the revelation of the horrors to which this door in his heart opened, and more than anything, I wanted to stop him, to take him into my arms, to resume the bliss of our drink, and just make him forget it all. But that would be neither right nor healthy. Those demons needed to be banished. But I knew what this would entail, and it slowed any response from me.

My reticence, however, came from a different source, yet eerily similar. And it was because of this that I was just as afraid for myself as I was for him. I knew that in casting light into this dark place, some of my own demons would need an exorcism as well.

Chapter Eleven

"You don't have to talk about it if you don't want to," I said, though I knew immediately that Derek would read the disingenuousness of my words in spite of my kindness. I felt his hand touch the top of my head and move down to my chin. Gently, he tilted my head upwards to where our eyes locked. He smiled, but it was not happy.

"The bond really is a curse, isn't it?" He said. "You know what I know, and you know that I know you want to know. And I need to tell you this. It's been eating at me since that fight with Joe. It just wasn't so bad until I tried to-"

"I know, love," I said. I tried with all my strength to soothe his troubled soul, though I knew that he was determined to dredge up this inner turmoil despite my words. I reached out and glided my hand down his cheeks, which were soft with what little had been left of the baby fat from his human days, keeping in contact with him, feeling the words that were at the cusp of his lips, but waiting patiently for him to form them.

"I guess the beginning's the best place to start." Derek pressed his palm to the edges of his eyes to wipe away the small pools of tears that had collected there. He managed something of a silly grin. "I didn't exactly have the best of childhoods, but you probably figured that out from my charming personality. Mom held two jobs; so did dad. Mom did a lot of cocaine just to keep up, and dad drank a lot to forget about the daily grind. Can't say that I blamed them. It was a typical dysfunctional American home, you know. I stayed away as much as I could. Most of the time, they were away at work, of course, but when they were home, they always wanted me there. But I only ever managed to piss them off. They'd yell at me about never being around to take care of Robin -she was my little sister. It was pretty stupid, really. Robin was just a year younger than me. And by the time I was the age I was when I was turned, she was already running the streets.

"Maybe I could've done a better job of trying to stop her. God knows I've thought more than once about why I didn't. The world isn't kind to a thirteen year-old, our world, even less so. She also looked a lot older than her age. I knew all it'd take would be one guy who was smarter than the rest to find out the truth, and we'd probably never hear the end of it. So, yeah, I probably should've said something. 'Course, it would probably have been useless. She never gave two craps about what I said. Would you believe that I used to cook for her, waiting until she got home? That was back when I was trying to be a little goody-two-shoes and do what mom and dad told me, but it didn't take long for me to realize that it didn't amount to much. Robin would come back home when mom and dad weren't around, already having eaten with her boyfriend du jour. And by 'eaten,' I mean food and other things. Not only was she older-looking than she was; she was also more mature, if you know what I mean.

"We used to be really close, Robin and me. I'd take her to the park after school, back when the gangs hadn't moved into our part of town; I'd play with her when her friends weren't around. When dad started drinking, I shielded her from his drunken fits. That's when she started getting distant and cold, and I started staying away."

I felt the pain before it choked his voice. I felt his muscles stiffen, felt his heart beat faster, and his mind become inundated with deep emotions that he'd long repressed, and never shared with another.

"I . . ."

He inhaled with shuddering breaths, and I gave my love as an anchor for him.

"I sometimes think that if I'd stuck it out more with her, tried to make her understand, then maybe she wouldn't have

. . ."

Derek's voice quavered, then broke, but he caught himself. He swallowed hard before he continued, his heart breaking in the throes of his misery.

"Cops found her in a hotel room. She'd been raped; little surprise there. All the money in her purse was gone, but whoever did it was sloppy. Fingerprints were traced back to a local ex-con, who spilled the beans about some local pimps running a prostitution ring in town. They got rounded up, but that was little comfort to me."

"I imagine there wouldn't be," I whispered, and prompted him nonverbally to continue.

"You don't understand," he said. It's far worse than you think."

"But I do now," I replied. And indeed, I had gleaned the contents of the ever darkening pages of his memory before he narrated them.

"But you know what the worst thing was, China doll? Mom and dad were too stoned and drunk to even realize that she was dead. It took three days for them to learn it. And all that time, I was the one who mourned. Me! And mom and dad were in a damned stupor for three fucking days! And then when they learned about it, they hit the white pony and the bottle even harder than before. They had to be walked into and out of the funeral home. Dad was kinda coherent, but mom was on her own little vacation. I hated them for that . . . hated them a lot more than I should have. God, I hated my life, my family, the fact that my sister was gone . . . I thought I'd just go and get my dad's gun from under his bed and end it all . . ."

"And that was when the Others found you?" I asked, then became somewhat chagrined afterwards for jumping ahead of him.

"That was when Lothos found me."

It was as if the temperature of his soul had dropped three degrees.

"'Course I had no idea how rare this was: him going out and about to pick up new recruits. He offered it to me, gave me the entire spiel about the powers, eternal life, and leaving my old world behind. I was a kid, and I was in pain. He knew this. He knew I'd be easy pickings. So I let him turn me right there. I was in my sister's room; no one had been in there but me; no one disturbed me there. The garbage can was full of beer cans. I was well on my way to becoming like dad. But then, Lothos turned me and set me to my first meal."

"Dear God . . ." I whispered as I witnessed the memories, again before he could tell the tale. I could have retched with horror, but I managed enough control to subdue my reaction to a shudder and cringe. The memories came fragmented by the madness that was all too dreaded and familiar: the dementia of blood starvation . . . the look on his parents' faces . . . the ecstasy of satiation . . . and the consuming of what remained of their bodies. There was little more I could say, faced with the sheer horror of it.

"He stuck me in an in-between place, a sub-dimension, he said, same as where you put us when we rest during the day," Derek explained as his memories raked me across every searing detail of the gruesome tale. "It looked like my sister's room, but it was quiet -too quiet. And dim. And he'd sealed the doors somehow. He left me there for days. At first the weird ringing silence started wearing on my nerves, but then the thirst came. It was tolerable at first, but after three days, the pain just kept growing . . . and then . . . God, it . . . everything became some kind of a hazy nightmare. I couldn't think. There was only pain. And when I finally woke up . . . when it finally went away, the first thing I remembered was the taste of blood. I didn't even recognize the bodies. I was too drunk and stoned; their blood was so tainted with cocaine and alcohol that I only realized what happened after the comedown. They were only skeletons by then, picked clean. I didn't even realize who they were until I saw what remained of their clothing. And then I saw Lothos."

In his memories, I heard his scream. In his mind, a spectral spectator to his memories, I was trapped behind something akin to an impenetrable mirror, helplessly witnessing this horrifying scene, and all I could do was let my tears flow as Derek moved me from frame to frame in his private gallery of horrors.

"Lothos took me away from my old home, and brought me to one of his hideouts. Like your clan, they call them Lairs, but they're not hidden. The outside world thinks of them as weird-but-harmless cult houses. But trust me when I say what I did to my parents was the least of what I was to see there. Lothos, I couldn't get away from. He was obsessed with me. He showed me off to his underlings, his vassals, his slaves for their appreciation, as if I were some sort of pet or plaything. I never knew why."

"Because of your age," I explained, at last managing to pry myself away from the whirlwind in Derek's mind. Derek paused, frowning, his question forming without words.

"They must have never told you this," I said. "There's a reason we don't turn others at my physical age, or yours. We don't take well to the change. I'm sort of a case in point, though with a far less unfortunate result. The process damaged me: brain damage, the result of which was amnesia. It's why I can't remember who I was before my turning, or any of my human life. In my case, the damage was very minor. Still, because of what the change makes us into, any damage is irreparable. I've read stories of ancient times, before the practice was abandoned; the results were horrifying. Maimed and crippled children doomed to eternity as half-wits or neurologically damaged into semi-vegetables, or sometimes fully catatonic, only good for being mercifully euthanized. At the age you were, the risk of damage is greatly reduced, but at the very least, we wait until a candidate is in his or her early or mid twenties before we even consider turning them. Even Lothos' clan does that." I paused and eyed him with specificity. "Or so we thought."

"So you're saying he was showing me off as if to say that the process worked with me?" Derek asked.

"I'm almost certain of it," I replied. "Modesty isn't exactly a trait that defines Lothos."

"But why do it at all?"

"I don't know that," I answered with a frown. "And come to think of it, I really don't think I'd want to know. His clan has avoided doing this for thousands of years, the same as us."

"You've got a point," Derek said, and with a sigh, sank back into his story.

"This part is the hardest to tell. You have no idea the kinds of demons I have to let back out to do this, so if I can't go on . . ."

I nodded, and sent comfort to his heart for what it was worth. I slipped my hand into his, waiting with rapt attention, and bracing my mind for the horrors yet to come.

"I don't think I'm telling you anything your clan doesn't already know. Lothos isn't picky about those who join his fold. As far as I knew, he's had the numerical advantage in your war, but you guys were better at strategy. But he's never been without recruits: the infirm, mentally ill, homeless, thugs with something to prove . . . they come flocking to him; all he needs to give is the opportunity. But if he chooses to turn you himself, it makes you a cut above the rest, as far as his clan is concerned, so you're not just sent out as cannon fodder, or need to work your way up the pecking order if you survive long enough. And that was how it was with me. I didn't realize it until after the endless showcase tours was over. But by that time, I'd already learned his true nature."

I felt Derek tremble as I leaned upon his breast. I heard his rapid intakes of breath, and I knew he felt my tears rolling down his chest as the flashes of memory rained upon my mind like drops of acid.

"I thought that making me kill my parents was bad enough, but . . ."

His words sank in to a gaping tunnel of memories, which engulfed me with all the suddenness of a whale from the abyss: Memories of Lothos . . . Memories of fear, helplessness, fighting against the pleasures of the drink, and the pain such resistance produced . . . Violations of the blood, violations of the flesh . . . Lothos as himself, ebon-skinned and white-haired, his fangs exposed at full length in an inhuman grin as he took his pleasures, as both a male, and then in the form of a female. And finally, the darkest, most horrific recounts: memories of waking up in the finale of battle, soaked with the blood of countless victims, human and vampire, with no memories of what had happened.

With inescapable horror, I recognized some of the faces of those massacred.

I screamed.

When I was better able to sort out these memories later, I realized that the reaction had come from a combination of my own anguish, and the horror I felt through Derek. He had been used. Lothos did not possess the gift of telepathy; it was introduced into his clan by those who had defected from ours as well as the handful of humans who possessed this gift, albeit in a latent state, but amplified when they were turned. Jewels could amplify the mind as well, even in non-telepaths like Lothos. Derek's memories conveyed a horrifying truth about this. He had been an assassin, but a puppet, if he did not remember his crimes.

But this nightmare was not over, as the shock of these memories dredged up my own musings of years ago, and the reality and vividness intermingled with Derek's mind, creating a horrendous effect that was like being forced to stare into lightning, with all the pain and agony it would entail, but with all of it burned forever into your psyche. I squeezed his hand, perhaps to where it nearly broke, but I was past knowing this. I wailed in the pain in which his soul had voluntarily flooded itself, mixed with my own, engulfed and inundated in the burst of memory.

I heard Derek say my name, but it sounded as if he spoke from across a great chasm. It repeated like an echo, but in reverse, growing in volume and in vehemence. Distantly, I became aware of a rattling sensation, which it took several moments for me to realize was my body being shaken in Derek's hands.

"Elisa! China doll! Snap out of it, please!"

I awoke, realizing that I'd wrapped my arms as far around Derek's midsection as they would go, and was anchoring them with my claws in his flesh. I could feel the warmth of his blood on my fingers. As if the reality of it had finally sunk in, I gasped and let go. For several moments, I sat wordlessly and stared at the fragrant, glistening fluid that coated my fingers and dripped down my hand in ruby-colored rivulets. And then I finally awoke to the realization that I'd hurt Derek.

"I'm . . . I'm sorry!" I at last stammered, looking up into Derek's pained expression. I then saw it relax somewhat as the wounds began to heal. With preternatural speed, I went to his bathroom, washed my hands, and removed some napkins from the dispenser below the sink to wipe the remaining blood from his back.

"I'm so sorry, love," I whispered, gently cleaning the streams that flowed down to the waistline of his underwear. "Those memories, they . . ."

"It's okay." Derek looked over his shoulder and smiled at me. "I've never told the story to a fellow mind-reader. It wasn't pleasant for me, either. But I had no idea that it would affect you that way."

"It's because I have dark pages of my own," I admitted.

You want to talk about them?" Derek asked. He turned around when I was done. I felt his hand brush back the stray curls from my face. Despite my feelings, I did want to share my memories. It was only fair. I should have known that his story would raise these particular demons from my past, and I was prepared to relieve my soul of its own respective burden. But there was a part of me that desperately desired to put it off, and raged against what I intended to do. Derek knew this. As I gave comfort to him from the ravages of his own tale, I felt his heart embrace my own.

"I'd like you to finish your tale first," I said at last, though I had no idea why I was attempting to stall for time.

"Fair enough. But there's not much more to tell." Derek slipped into another moment of dark pensiveness before he spoke again. "But before I start again, I think I've come to understand something, looking back on it all. I believe I know why Lothos gave me such special attention. Not the 'attention' you saw in my mind, but the reason why he kept me so close. Mind-readers in his clan are rare. I got the blood from him when I was turned, but even though he couldn't read minds without a Jewel, I became one. That means I was latent as a human, right?"

"Not necessarily," I said. "Lothos could have fed from others of his kind in bed." I wrinkled my nose at the thought of even musing over the kinds of sexual proclivities he enjoyed behind closed doors; to see them visited on Derek had been more than enough. "Our blood doesn't nourish us, but it can incorporate some traits from one clan to another, like a virus from a carrier. He wouldn't be 'affected' by the trait himself, but can give the condition to another. Theoretically speaking, since you have the blood of his clan, and I've fed from you, if I were to turn another, that person might become a shape-shifter, or even have both gifts, though the latter is very rare. So Lothos may have passed that gift to you through his blood. There are a few shape-shifters in our clan, but we tend to shy away from that gift. It can often twist the mind of its recipient as easily as they twist their bodies. But as for the rarity of the gift and why he kept you so close, you might be right."

"I figured as much," Derek said with a nod. "But of course, I digress.

You know my memories. You know what he did to me. You know what I had to endure. You've only gotten a glimpse at some of the things I've seen. It was like I was living in an opposite world where everything I knew to be wrong was right . . . encouraged, even. We were taught that humans were our cattle. At best, I'd seen them as privileged slaves with hopes of being turned; at worst, they were treated like meat on the rack or toys. The misery I'd seen when the shape-shifters satisfied their own sick lusts on them: men, women, children . . . it made me want to puke. And even worse, all those perversions were not only let loose on humans, but even on the lower ranks of our own kind . . . and even me when Lothos wasn't around to do it himself. I thought I'd be safe when he started giving me less attention and more time to myself, but I was wrong. They found me, chased me, caught me, had their way with me as I struggled and fought, which made them want to do it more. But in time, I bought my freedom through making them regret what they did. Lothos hadn't just left me a babe in the woods, so to speak. He'd been having some of his thaumaturgists train me, and though he still kept a tight leash on me and what I could do with my Jewel, I learned enough skills to soon keep the more insistent perverts away - some permanently - and have a few moments' peace. And with Lothos less a part of my life, such as it was, I could get away with a lot more than I'd used to. Because I was a mind-reader, I could build up mental defenses better than most, so it was more difficult for him to know what I was thinking, even with a Jewel. I met Joe during that time. He was a grunt who'd managed to survive the lower ranks and had had enough of Lothos and his bullshit. One night, we made a run for it. After Lothos was done with me for the evening, I took off as soon as I figured he wasn't paying attention. He tried to hunt me down, but we managed to either outsmart the mooks he sent after us or kill them ourselves if we got backed into a corner. After awhile, the attacks stopped. I guess he got bored with me. And then Joe and I were taken in by Syd and his clan.

"You know the rest, China doll. And you also know what's bugging me. When I first started to fall in love with you, it reminded me of that time . . . of all those times . . . and the things I'd been through. I thought I'd been with the clan so long that it rubbed off on me. Your words about loving you for your soul settled me somewhat, but what Joe said the other day brought it back. And it's been bothering me ever since."

He squeezed his eyes shut, and I saw the tears begin anew.

"God, I love you. And you know just how much I do. It's not just your blood. I feel like I'd die without you. You're all I can think about lately, and I want you in every way. But whenever I do, my mind goes back to Joe. And then it goes back to my time with Lothos, and what I went through with him and his bastards. And despite all my feelings, I go back to wondering if I've become just as much the pervert as Joe said I was."

I slipped my arms around Derek's slender, but strong neck, rising to my knees to nuzzle against it. I could smell the blood so close beneath his skin. My desire for it threatened to distract me once more, but I restrained myself, biting against the lengthening of my fangs, which were more honest about my feelings than my actions.

"Derek, never say that about yourself," I sharply whispered. "You're not like that at all. I can tell you right now that you're not like those perverted monsters. Because I've had to deal with those monsters, both in Lothos' clan, and in the outside world."

I slid off of his neck and composed myself after the assault on my senses that his blood produced. I swallowed hard and breathed in deeply, allowing my fangs to retract. Still, I kept a hand on his chest to retain our physical contact. Understanding that underlying need, Derek encircled my waist with his arms. He had finished baring his soul. Now it was my turn.

***

"I know this because of something I went through long ago," I said. "It was at the end of the Nineteenth Century, not too long after Father and I had begun the move with our inner circle to the New World, where Lothos was busy amassing a new power base. We spent long nights scouring back alleys, brothels, insane asylums, and monitoring hideouts for organized crime syndicates in order to catch Lothos and his people before they could seduce any humans to his cause.

"At that time, I'd just finished my training under Aiko. I was her star pupil, and had bested some of the enemy's most skilled thaumaturgists, making me more of a celebrity than I already was among my clan, despite the fact that I was nearing fifty."

"Wait," Derek said. "You were almost fifty at the time?"

"I wouldn't make an "old lady" joke if I were you," I warned, "not with my hands so close to your jibblies."

"No, no! It's not that," Derek shook his head, but chuckled in spite of himself, "I was just wondering how long you'd been in training; that's all."

"Oh." I smiled and relaxed, feeling somewhat chagrined at my overzealousness. "I'd actually been training for about ten years at the time. That was when I decided to become a thaumaturgist. Before that time, I trained under Justin in combat, and usually ran errands from one village to another. I wanted to get more involved in the war, despite Father's misgivings. But he eventually gave in when Roland told him he couldn't be the protective parent forever."

"Not to mention your size afforded you some advantages?" Derek teased.

"That too," I admitted, and sank back into my tale.

"One night, I got word of one of Lothos' subordinates meeting with a certain man of interest: a human who had a knack for getting children to do his dirty work. He ran a bunch of crime rings in Southern California. The name of the city escapes me right at the moment; we were sifting through so many at the time, and it wasn't one of the major ones.

Lothos tended to stay away from those unless the pickings became especially slim in other places. But to make a long story short, I ferreted them out. Looking the way I did, it was easy to play the homeless waif, and I was taken in by some kids who said they belonged to my target. They called themselves a family, but it was obvious that they were all afraid of their so-called 'daddy,' and for good reason.

I expected, just as you're envisioning, that he was some overweight slob of a man, but he was actually quite handsome. But even without having touched him, I knew his true nature. He was violent, selfish, manipulative, and his sexual predilections fell towards his charges, the female ones particularly, and those who were about my physical age. It wasn't something he did often, as the children told me, but it was a moment they all feared, as he bottled up his lust for as long as he could, then expended it all on one unfortunate victim who, normally, did not survive the night.

I ran odd jobs fencing stolen goods for the group during the night, all the while, distracting the other children's thoughts from asking questions about where I went during the day or why I never ate with them. But as time passed, I began to notice a growing sense of disquiet. Little by little, the children were becoming ever more unnerved. At first, they wouldn't talk about why, but one child, a thin blond-haired girl named Lilly, at last confided in me the whole story . . . and that their 'daddy' had been holding out on his 'playtime' for much longer than normal. Needless to say, I was horrified to learn this, but it caused me to take a more proactive approach.

'Daddy' usually stopped by the abandoned warehouse where the children lived in the evening in order to hand out food and clothes bought from the thrift stores and places that paid insurance to the gangs he was connected with. As I slept elsewhere for obvious reasons, I was able to follow him one night after I was told the truth. I already knew by scent that he had connections to Lothos' clan, but I'd been working with the children to see if I could find out where they were gathering, rather than follow him on a wild chase. It turned out he tended to conduct his business in a separate city in order to throw off the police, as well as to prevent his vampire benefactor from learning where most of his business came from. I gleaned most of the information from his mind, which made it easier to trail him as he took a roundabout route to get to his home. There, after watching him play host to the visiting vampire dignitary, I knew what I had to do.

I surmised that this representative of Lothos was rather low on the totem pole, but I took a couple of nights to make certain. At last, when I was satisfied there would be no retaliations, I killed the fiend as he neared his hideout, leaving his remains in a place where I knew his colleagues would find them and interpret my clear message. Sure enough, once I did this, the town was cleared of enemy activity overnight. But this had an unfortunate effect to the human client. 'Daddy' was understandably confused and distraught after the mysterious disappearance of the one who probably had become his sole financial backer. I learned that he'd blown off his previous bosses for this one, and had to go crawling back on his hands and knees to get them to help him. This kind of humiliation stressed him to the point where his will broke. Upon his next visit to the warehouse, I could sense the full floodgate of his lust opened. While he entertained the children, I was distracted by several rather insistent members of the rabble over a matter of clothes that they'd procured from the newest pile that had been given to them. I bowed out as quickly as I could, but by then, it was too late. I realized that 'daddy' was gone, and so was Lilly."

I felt Derek pull me tighter to him, and it was at that time that I realized that I had been shaking. I'd shelved the memory so deeply within me, and it had been so very long, but the experiences of those last few hours were still there, fresh as if it happened yesterday.

"As quickly as I dared, I left the warehouse, then hurried

at preternatural speed back to 'daddy's' home, but only to find that he wasn't there. At first, I figured that I had arrived before he did, and so I waited. After nearly twenty minutes had passed, I realized that he'd most likely gone elsewhere to do his deeds. Then it struck me, and the anguish I felt at the simplicity of my mistake was enough to nearly kill me. If he was to do what I dreaded, it would be better to do it someplace more discreet than his own house. I had to make my way back to the warehouse to begin the search anew using my Jewel. But my skills with it were not what they are now, and I didn't know exactly how to use it for tracking. It took me an extra fifteen minutes to get a solid lead on his whereabouts by examining traces of the wheels of his coach on the road. After several dead ends, I found the old apartment where he and his would-be 'playmate' had retreated to.

I was too late. I knew it before I even climbed to the window. I could smell death leaking through, along with smells that are associated with things you're all too familiar with, and would be best left unsaid.

But do you know what the worst part was, Derek? The most absolutely horrifying part of this sight? That filthy beast of a man had never even realized yet that he'd killed that poor girl in his lust. When I arrived, and knew that she was dead, he was still in the throes of sating his own desires with a broken corpse.

I screamed on the inside, only able to imagine the horrible way this poor, innocent girl had left this world. I tried to cry, but my throat was in paralysis. I wanted to scream in a manner that would cause any humans to lose their fear of banshees. But instead, I summoned Justin's training into my heart and steeled myself to do what needed to be done. I swallowed my emotions completely, then broke through the window just as the pig had finished. I hoped that that last bit of pleasure he'd had would be his greatest torment in hell . . . and I sent him there slowly. I can still recall how he stood, for a moment, staring at me as one stares at a ghost, dumbfounded and disbelieving at both my presence and my silence. But he soon switched gears, becoming emboldened by how helpless I seemed. He came charging my way, but it took very little time to show him that I was anything but helpless. After I repaired the glass and soundproofed the room with my Jewel, I broke his arms and legs, crushing bones one by one, limb by limb. His screams would have been deafening to human ears, had anyone save me heard them, but at this point, I merely existed. I performed my gruesome deeds as dispassionately as a saw blade cuts through wood: methodically, and blind to any pain that my strength inflicted. I had become a dismembering machine, and stopped only after I'd crushed all of his non-vital organs.

I should have been disgusted as I grabbed the outer organ with which he'd performed his own twisted deeds, but it might have been another limb for the casualness with which I'd removed it from his body. By then, his screams and pleas for death seemed merely a curiosity. And I felt nothing as I finally obliged his pleas, again slowly as I ripped open his throat inch by inch. There was not even the desire for blood, which, by the end of it all, had pooled in a hot, dark spot in the carpet.

"I took Lilly's body and buried it outside of the warehouse afterwards, then went home to the Lair, where I informed Father of what I'd found, and confessed to what I'd done. I didn't know what to expect then; I knew that I'd gone too far, but I could dredge up nothing when I contemplated my actions. There was no regret. No pain, no rage, not even a spark of anger. It was like staring into the proverbial abyss. I had steeled myself to do the deed that night, but it was like I couldn't undo what I did and unleashed the fount of anguish, grief, and guilt that by all rights should have been there. Even worse was the fact that no one, not Roland, not Aiko, not Justin, nor even Father, could tell me why this was so. And after learning what had happened, Father said that perhaps this void was the punishment, and he could not, in good conscience, admonish me for my actions.

During the years after, later missions brought me face to face with more people of that nature, but I'd lost my stomach for meting out justice on their ilk. So rather than kill them myself, I left that duty to others. Still, some good came out of that first incident, and I was grateful. It eased my troubled soul somewhat. My clan rescued the children, and gave them new homes, some among our clan, after slowly introducing them, and others with normal human families outside of our world."

I stared into Derek's eyes, at his rapt expression as he listened to my every word.

"Even to this day, love, on the rare occasions when I think back to that night and the scenes of that theater play back in my mind, I still feel absolutely nothing. But I've come to believe that perhaps it was meant to be. Still, I need you to understand this. This man - and I use that term in its absolute loosest sense - lusted most powerfully after children and satiated a perverse desire that nothing else could satisfy. It was solely because they were children that he was attracted to them. And he was ruled by his lusts as he expended it, purely because they were what they were, losing himself so deeply in what he did that he could not distinguish between their being alive or dead until after it was done. But I assure you by our very love that you are nothing like him. His attraction was not born of love. And you did not love me because I was in this form. And consider me. You're younger than me. And I could view your body as quite young myself. But ours is a deeper love, and you know this. We spoke of this. And we affirm it every time we kiss, and when you feed from me, and I from you. And you know that I'm not what I appear to be. I haven't been a child in over a hundred sixty years, Derek. So try, I ask. Try with all your might to forget about what has befallen you in your past, and I will try to forget this dark page in my life. Forget what Joe has told you, and remember who you love."

I ran my fingers gently across his smooth chest and to his neck, but my eyes never left his. "Can you do that, love? Can you do that for us?"

Derek exhaled softly, and the faintest hint of a smile lifted the corners of his mouth.

"I'm gonna have to, aren't I, China doll?"

"It wasn't an ultimatum," I replied, but gently, as to assure him that I wasn't offended.

"I know," Derek said. And then I felt a welter of mild confusion within him. "It's just that . . . I don't even know why I wanted that kind of intimacy with you in the first place. It's not like I'm a virgin or anything, but feeding, and from you especially, is worlds better than the human way."

"It's because you're still grounded to your human side," I answered, and before I felt his confusion grow, began to explain. "You've only been what you are since you were fourteen. You're still grounded in many human predilections: the desire for food, and the need for sex being chief among them. Now, I myself am a virgin, as those things go; I only remember being a vampire, and since I was turned so young, I guess that perhaps my body never matured enough to have those desires. The drink satisfies me completely, and especially feeding from you. The human way has simply never been attractive to me."

"It hasn't?" Derek asked with even greater confusion. "Then why did you want me to do it? You encouraged me."

"Because I was curious," I said. "And I knew you wanted it. So I welcomed it."

"Even though you've never experienced it, or wanted it before?"

I nodded. "I'd never fed from another of my kind before you," I said teasingly. "And you wanted me. But I knew your conflicts. And just like before we first fed from each other, I wasn't going to pressure you. But you want it more than I do. And when you do want it again, and have the courage to do it, I won't stop you."

"It may be awhile," Derek said.

"I am nearly two hundred years old, love," I said with a lopsided grin. "Having lived that long, if it's one thing you learn over anything else, it's patience. When you practically have eternity, then why be hasty?"

"Good point," Derek said. And suddenly, with a rather wicked expression, he fired a stream of pleasure into the nerves where his arms and hands touched my back. I gasped from the suddenness of it, and he laughed. He then smothered my consternation with a kiss. And I, glad to have been done with revealing such dark pages in both of our lives, reciprocated with eagerness. Although his hands never strayed anywhere near where they had before this interlude began, we satiated ourselves in satisfactory ways, melting away the darkness of our mutual memories.

Lyman brought in a new storm when we awoke the next night to the sight of him barging into our bedroom. He gathered our clothes into his hand and tossed them onto the bed as Derek and I stared back groggily, and somewhat indignant.

"Hate to ruin your fun, you two," he said as Derek reached clumsily for his pants, "but I've got bad news. Joe's missing."

Chapter Twelve

Lyman took his leave as quickly as he arrived, knowing that we would not be far behind. I, however, had been left quite shaken from the suddenness of events. Derek and I had been in physical contact all of the previous evening and throughout the day as we slept, and with the exception of the time we'd shared our mutual dark pages of the past, I had never seen him so calm as now. So serene were his thoughts, in fact, that I believe that if I had asked him to finish what he'd intended to begin with me before his courage felled, he would have done so in spite of his discomfort just to make me happy. But the second we heard Lyman's words, it shattered our admittedly fragile peace as if it were no more substantial than a pane of thin glass-spun sugar. It was a small touch of agony for us both; though he maintained his outward decorum, Derek's heart was now anything but calm. At Lyman's devastating words, my mind swallowed a torrent of memories along with his burst of near-paralyzing fear, and it was all that I could do not to cry out at this. I felt the depths of his love for Joe, and I felt a glimmer of shame for hating him.

It passed. But I still cared for Derek, and what this situation did to his mind. His wash of emotions was so strong that it was as if I'd never broken that intimate contact we'd shared in his bed. Outwardly, he maintained a perfect poker face, but inside, he was a mess.

"Derek, it will be all right," I said. He could not even concentrate enough to achieve preternatural speed, and so I finished slipping back into my discarded clothes long before he did. Once dressed, I sat at the edge of the bed, watching him swiftly finish his routine, but as distracted as a child who had just been witness to something horrible outside the classroom window during a lesson. Of course, I hadn't believed that my words would be of any comfort. I was, in fact, completely unsure if my assurances would even be true, but any words at all, I felt, would be better than helpless silence. Plagued by his negative emotions, I retreated into myself, waiting, both afraid and eager for something to happen. Derek would go and search for Joe; that was obvious, but I worried over what his emotions would do to him in that search. Even I ran the gamut of questions in my own mind, and I sat there with a mix of fear and impatience, feeling the seconds tick by until he roused my attention with a touch of his hand to mine.

I heard him speak my name, and I looked up to see him standing before me.

"Last night, in my memories, you saw what I did to your clan," he said.

"What Lothos made you do," I corrected, nodding.

"I . . ."

He paused with a blank expression that, in another circumstance, would have been quite hilarious. Feelings of initial surprise burst from his heart, which were followed by understanding mixed with chagrin. His face then softened into a wan smile. "So that's why you didn't hate me."

"I could never hate you, love," I assured him as if I needed to. I was almost stricken by his words, but understood the misunderstanding they had come from. I rose to my feet, standing precariously at the edge of the mattress. I steadied myself against his chest, and, in spite of his raging emotions, kissed him with perhaps more passion than I'd ever mustered before. To my surprise, in spite of the situation, in spite of his boil of emotions, despite everything, he reciprocated in kind, careful, as he always was, to not smother me with his larger mouth. We kissed as if it would be our last time, our arms about each other, and our minds woven together in those fleeting moments.

"Fucking unbelievable, the way things keep on happening around here," he whispered when it ended, and we were pulled back into ourselves. "But now, you've seen it, China

Doll. You've seen me." His voice was near to breaking. "And I have to ask . . . do you still want me?"

At first, I could say nothing, only send him my assent without words through our bond. But when I could finally find words to speak at this, I chided him.

"Why would you ask such a silly question?" I touched my forehead to his, with my fangs extended for satiation that would have to be postponed. "Of course I want you. I'll always want you."

"I guess I wanted to be sure that at least something was right with my life," Derek answered in a soft voice that was almost a murmur. I felt his fingers move through my hair, and then down my arms to my hands, which he grasped loosely in his much bigger set. He was in such pain, and my insides wrenched at the way our mutual peace had been so cruelly ripped away.

"I hope to always be what is right with your life," I pledged as his hands slipped away, followed by his forehead. I felt the expected diminishing of the strength of our bond, but in such close quarters, it still remained very strong.

"We need to go," he said. Feeling him steel his courage and wrapping his emotions in his usual decorum, I followed him without a word out of the RV and into the night that awaited us.

***

I half expected the clan to be surrounding Joe's RV like police at a crime scene when Derek and I arrived, and was somewhat surprised as we approached to see only Lyman, Wadih, and Pablo standing guard. The rest of the clan was about their business in the camp proper, as if nothing had happened.

"They're guarding it," Derek explained, noticing my confusion as Lyman met us halfway. "Better than having any evidence disturbed."

"Ah . . . yes," I said, now feeling a bit silly for not having realized this.

"Very little of that's happened," Lyman told us as he caught up to where we were, "practically nothing's been taken or violated, in fact. We've been over it from top to bottom."

"There's no sign of breaking in, or anything tampered with," Pablo said as we arrived at the trailer's entrance door. "Tarp's the same way we left it, no shifting of it or the tape. Joe's just . . . gone."

"No signs of a struggle, either," Wadih added.

"Like he just got up and walked away." Lyman stopped and leaned beside the door. I knew he was more frustrated than the other two; gleaning his memories, I discovered that he'd had Grace investigate the site, but to no avail.

"That's impossible," Derek said as he stepped into the RV with me. Lyman and Wadih followed close behind, along with Pablo.

We made our way across the cleaned, but still-ruined interior to Joe's bedroom. Its accommodations were simple: only a sitting and sleeping area, a small washroom, and a tiny refrigerator between the bed and sofa. The place stank of whiskey and old blood, and there were several bottles on the floor as well as a small pile of used blood packs, giving a clue as to how Joe had whiled away his hours while his leg healed, but none as to what had happened to him. We were unable to get drunk through alcohol alone, but mixing it with blood would get a mild version of the effect, as well as a deadening of pain. Of course, we normally did not stay in pain very long, unless, like in Joe's case, our injuries were especially grievous. The sheer number of bottles and blood packs suggested how much pain he had been in, though I didn't feel an ounce of sympathy for him. A shotgun lay half assembled on the sofa, and the rumpled bed sheets still retained the imprint of a person. I saw all this just as I had finished investigating the sitting room where the tarp still covered the hole from last night's altercation, just as it had been left. There was no recent scent indication that Joe had been anywhere near it. Indeed, it was as if Joe's leg had miraculously healed, and he'd just walked away.

After a moment of consideration, as well as a bit more scenting, which, as expected, turned up nothing, Derek and I came to the only logical conclusion. We spoke that conclusion almost in unison.

"Someone used a Jewel."

All eyes, save Lyman's, instantly went to me.

"Elisa was with me all night," Derek said to them, reading their naked suspicions. "So don't get any ideas."

"She could've hypnotized you," Pablo said, but not with much confidence.

"We're both mind-readers," Derek said, intent on, and perhaps somewhat desperate to crush any suspicions, "and we're bonded. She couldn't control me like that if she wanted to."

"But she's the only one here with a Jewel," Pablo protested.

"Or someone else here isn't who he or she seems to be," Wadih chimed in. I watched him throw a scowling glance back towards the camp.

"You know something we don't?" Lyman asked him, "'Cause we've been down that road before. Otherwise, you're just wasting our time."

Perhaps the stress was cracking through Wadih's facade of nonchalance, or he merely had a bone to pick, but some of his cool demeanor had melted away. "Come on!" He said, his voice straining, "It's gotta be Deb, or maybe Marie-Laure."

"Like Paws just said, you got proof?" Derek asked coolly.

"Deb's the one who started it, didn't she? Beat the lovin' man-shit out of Joe the other night? And she's in charge of the baby, right? And she's always been a loose cannon." Wadih's movements were nervous, furtive, almost as if he himself were the guilty party. "Freaking firebugs. I never could trust them."

"Then last night would've been the perfect night to take the baby from us if that were the case," Derek remarked. "So most likely, she isn't the one."

"What about Marie-Laure? She's such a shut-in and a hacker . . . and she's the only one who has the power to communicate with the outside world since you had us shut off our cell phones . . ."

". . . for all the good that did," Pablo said. I could feel the resentment seething off of him; he must have been someone who lived on his phone, perhaps with more than a few lady friends-cum-blood banks whom he kept in touch with.

"Who knows who she's talking to in her trailer?" Wadih continued.

"Oh, come on, you guys both know she can't walk and chew gum at the same time away from a computer," Lyman said. "And this is hopeless anyway. At this rate, we're just going to end up killing each other out of distrust. We need to figure out how we can find Joe, instead of playing the blame game again. Maybe then, we'll figure out who took him."

"I rather doubt that," I said at last, and I did not relish the bad news I would have to give. "Lothos' clan may be a motley band of savages, but they're not stupid. If they don't want you to find out who took him, I doubt you'll be able to find out exactly who did." I glanced back towards Derek, who was clearly crestfallen at this. "So you can call off the witch hunt before it begins."

"No surprise there," Lyman commented. There was a shrewd grin on his face, and I knew that'd anticipated what I would say next. "But tell 'em the good news."

"The good news," I said, "is that I may be able to find out where he was taken."

"Your Jewel can do that?" Wadih asked.

"If a Jewel was used to take him, which I'm certain it was, I might be able to lock onto its resonance," I said. "As they bend the laws of physics momentarily, they cause a ripple effect in space-time, like a wake in a pond when you drop a stone in it. If not too much time has passed, I can track it down, especially if the Jewel was in continuous use. More than likely it was, since offsetting Joe's weight would be helpful for someone who needed to get out fast, especially if the sun were to come up soon. This is only conjecture, but I believe we'll find that our kidnapper was trying to get him far away in a short period of time. So that would mean teleport, if he or she knew how to do it. That would leave a significant ripple to track."

"But if you can track Joe, then why can't you track down who took him?" Pablo asked.

"Because I'm not counting on whoever took Joe to be so stupid as to keep the Jewel active all the way back to the camp," I said. "Maybe we'll get lucky, but I doubt it. Still, it's rather iffy to say that I'll even be able to track Joe down, but I plan to try."

"See if you can, then," Derek said. I nodded and had been about to set my mind to link with my Jewel when a distant sense of worry, fear, and anger shook me from my concentration. Another member of the clan was approaching quickly, running at a full sprint, as if resisting the urge to move at preternatural speed. The scent that came from downwind was that of Marie-Laure. But there was something that set off a sense of foreboding in the back of my mind.

"Hey, boss, we got more bad news," she said, skidding to a halt from her run from across the camp. "I went to the cooler to get a snack and found these."

"Shit," Lyman said. His word echoed all our sentiments as we saw the heartbreaking sight of her findings. The smell alone was enough to make the grim conclusion.

"They're all like this," Marie-Laure said as she came to Lyman's side, "All over the floor, ripped through and busted."

Disgust and despair emanated from Derek's heart like a sickness as he dropped the empty blood pack to the ground. There were no fang punctures in the medical-grade plastic bag; it just appeared to be sliced through with a knife, or perhaps a set of claws.

"All that was left of our blood supply is now gone." Marie-Laure kicked at the empty blood pack. "It's all over the floor, a big pool of it. There's nothing left. All that we have of our supply is whatever we've got stashed in our homes."

"Damn, I don't have any," Pablo murmured.

"Ditto for me," Wadih said. "I just go for the cooler whenever I'm hungry."

"I have a few," Lyman added, "but they're all for Grace; I can't spare any. You know what happens when a turned dog doesn't feed."

"What about the others?" Derek asked.

Lyman shrugged. "We'll have to find out. Deb's bound to have the most for the baby; otherwise, I'm pretty sure we won't have enough to make the remainder of the trip, even if we pool it all together."

"You gotta admire the strategy at least," Marie-Laure said, staring pensively at the spent blood packs. "Joe's missing, so we add more time to this trip to track him down, which will increase our need for blood, which we don't have."

"So we split up?" Pablo suggested. "One part looks for Joe; the other goes to get more blood?"

"That's what they want us to do," Marie-Laure said. "Don't you see?"

"Doesn't look like we have much of a choice," Pablo replied, "not unless we can find out who did this. We could squeeze a confession out of him . . ." He made a quick glance towards Marie-Laure, ". . . or her."

"I don't like what you're implying," Marie-Laure's tone deepened into a warning growl, and her fangs lengthened just enough to be noticeable.

"Well, it's not like we can tell who it is," Pablo protested.

"We have three mind-readers in our midst," Marie-Laure thrust an accusatory finger towards me and Derek, and then to Lyman. "You care to tell me why you can't just pry into our heads to find it out?"

"Because none of us have that skill." Lyman spoke before I could, and he was absolutely right. "We could try, and we might get lucky, but it's also dangerous, especially if you have other secrets to hide. And Lothos has mind-readers of his own. They make sleeper agents out of their own clan members all the time. They could hide their true personas so deep that even if we pried into everyone's mind here, we might never dig up the alternate one."

"We'd more easily hurt you than find something out," I explained further. "There are some in my clan who might be able to do it more safely, but I've maintained phone silence along with you all. I don't want to risk exposing us."

"We're already exposed, dammit!" Marie Laure practically screamed, and her anxiety rose to the top with the same frightening clarity as her voice. "Look what happened to us, Derek! I told you this girl was bad juju. We're all going to die here!"

"Enough!" Derek snapped, and his voice had a finality that put Marie-Laure's tirade to a sullen, but definitive end. "We're not exposed. This was an inside job; you know this. You've been monitoring all communications and movements of our other clan members, right? You're the only one who knows where they all are, so when this thing blows over, we can get the others back. Have there been any outgoing cell phone signals? Any unauthorized movements outside the camp? Any communication of any kind?"

Marie-Laure scowled, but was somewhat placated. "No. But if whomever did this used a Jewel, even I wouldn't be able to pick it up."

"Then if Lothos wanted us all dead right now, and had the means to do it, we'd all be either ash or six feet under without our heads," Derek said.

"Either that, or he's taking his own sweet time," Lyman remarked.

"Which might very well be true," I added, and shuddered

inwardly at how grim that sounded alongside Lyman's morose comment. "But we're all still here now. And I, for one, will not let this clan fall on my watch."

"And just what do you plan to do about it?" Marie-Laure asked with unbridled skepticism, and more than a little hostility.

To tell the truth, even I was not feeling terribly confident, and it did not take a mind-reader to see through my guise.

"Do you have blood packs waiting for us at this sanctuary of yours? Or are there willing human hosts there, waiting to slake our thirst? We're going after Joe, aren't we? Who knows how long that search will take? And we won't be able to go and feed in any nearby cities; that will expose us for sure if we're being followed. Damned if we do, damned if we don't. So I apologize if I'm the only one who seems to be aware of how royally screwed we are!"

"Look, I'm just as aware as you all that this move had a multi-tiered purpose," Derek said with a thoughtfulness which, in light of the moment, surprised me. "It served to confuse us, cripple us, and demoralize us. Marie . . . you're letting the enemy win. Calm down or you'll be of no use to us. And dammit, we need you." With narrow eyes, he scanned the clan members present, and I loved how he seemed to radiate that confidence which came so easy for him. "That goes for all of you."

He cast his gaze towards Lyman, who shifted to attention. "Paws, I need you to have the guys stop unpacking for the night. Have everyone break camp and re-pack the trucks and trailers. Marie-Laure, Google us a good spot nearby to procure some donors. Prepare to move out for a blood drive when I tell you."

"You have a plan, love?" I asked, buoyed by his unexpected burst of confidence. "I just might." Derek pursed his lips. "And it's one that may save all our asses, if we can be calm about it."

Chapter Thirteen

I might have known that things wouldn't be quite so easy, even after Derek outlined his plan. Some of the clan's concerns were assuaged; he and I could both feel this in the crowd, but there were some whom I supposed were career pessimists, or as Lyman so eloquently put, "equal opportunity bitchers," like Marie-Laure. Once she realized that she couldn't turn the crowd against me, she began to complain about the very object of my assignment.

"We should have left the baby at a church, or near a police station. Humans would've been able to take care of her for a little while, and she'd be out of our hair."

But Derek had been quick to shut her down. "So you'd prefer to be responsible for abandoning one of our own," he said with no shortage of impassioned indignation, "running the potential risk of humans finding out about us, and pissing off both the mind-readers and shape-shifters? And let's not forget human curiosity; they'd subject even that baby to God-knows-how-much poking and probing! And then, worst of all, the fact that she'd be fair game for the shape-shifters? Can you live with the corruption of her innocence on your conscience? Or are you just thinking, 'better her than me'? Are you really that heartless?"

It was a brief, but impressive lecture: one that cowed Marie-Laure quickly, but left her fuming all the way to her trailer.

Despite her anger, Marie-Laure was not derelict in her duties as she had produced a map less than half an hour later, with a planned route into a nearby town. How they would procure blood unknowingly from humans was not a thought I enjoyed contemplating, even less so by the time Lyman had found me while I was helping Pablo and Wadih with the remainder of the packing.

"Boss wants to see you, little lady," he said, but with a practiced nonchalance that betrayed something more that he wanted to say. "He's in his RV doing last-minute stuff."

I had both expected and not expected this. Derek never did tell me which part I would have to play in this plan; all I knew from his first announcement was that he was going to split the clan into two groups: one to fetch the blood, the other to rescue Joe or avenge him. But since I knew how to find Joe, and the trail was fast growing colder by the moment, I figured, though I wasn't fully certain, that I knew where I'd fit in this endeavor.

"By the way, you might not see me again," Lyman said as I started off.

His words caused a coldness in my stomach that made me pause in my tracks. I did not have Sarah's unique gift of future sight, but as unreal as they first sounded, there was something almost portentous about Lyman's statement. The words came out with the sober, determined timbre of a man who well knew that he was walking to his own death. It was not the first time I'd heard it. Too many other members of my clan spoke this way before going into battle or situations where there would most likely be combat. Traditionally, such things were done before a hopeless battle, and the battle that ensued usually was.

"It might not be so bad, you know," I said, trying to sound cross, but Lyman only gave me a knowing grin and shook his head.

"Call it a sixth sense . . . A gift of my own, aside from my skill with animals, set off when I'm about to face my long-ignored mortality."

"Sounds suspiciously like something you can only do once," I said."

"Maybe," Lyman answered with a guffaw that understandably sported less humor than it ought to have, "but don't you worry. I'll make sure Derek gets back to you safe and sound."

"Can't I have you both back?" I pleaded. I was grimly aware of the absolute certainty that was in his heart. God, how could he could be so calm about this?

"That's not up to me," Lyman answered with a sad smile. "And I can't make any promises." In a manner that reminded me achingly of father, whom I was beginning to realize I missed terribly, he touched his finger to my chin and smiled. "It was good to see you again, you know. You were one of the folks I missed the most."

I stepped forward, and wrapped my arms around his wide midsection. I didn't want to believe it, but I felt his certainty bleed into me. This released a stream of reluctant tears, which I let flow onto his shirt as I felt his arms wrap about me.

"I just wish we'd met again under better circumstances," I said.

"So do I, little lady," Lyman murmured and patted me on the shoulder. "So do I."

I wiped my face of the tears after I gave Lyman one last kiss on his scruffy cheek. I then gave a final plea for him to return safely, to which he did not answer. As I made my way to the RV, I realized with some chagrin that Derek would know about my feelings at seeing our mutual friend for what might be for the last time. Surely, I'd be going with them on the rescue mission. And I'd be damned if I allowed the enemy to take down Lyman, especially with such a prodigious guardian as Grace by his side.

"I'm in the bedroom," I heard Derek say once I stepped inside.

I saw him as I passed through the narrow, short hallway. He was dressing in a black ensemble of long-sleeved T-shirt with padded elbow guards, cargo pants, utility belt and a pair of combat boots I never realized he owned. He was facing away from me, securing a combat knife in a leather scabbard at his back that was looped into the belt.

I walked inside. Though we'd shared this room for

several nights to the point where it was like home to me, I made a tiny cough to announce myself. Derek turned around, and immediately, I felt his mind lock onto my memory of the conversation with Lyman.

"The fatalistic bastard had better not die on me," he said, giving the scabbard a firm tug as he approached me. Even now, going into what was almost certainly a trap, he radiated a calm that was almost Zen-like.

"You didn't tell me we'd have to dress for the occasion," I said as I held the hand that he caressed my cheek with. But no sooner had I said it than I felt his twinge of dismay, like an unwelcome bitterness in an otherwise delectable meal. I did have some expectation of this, so I tried to not let my face reflect my own welter of mixed emotions, even though I knew he would feel it. Derek, after all, was calling the proverbial shots with this plan.

"Please don't be angry," he said.

"I'm not angry," I said. "I just don't understand. Won't you and Lyman need me to track Joe down? I've already gotten a bead on his scent, and we need to hurry."

"Can you show me how to do it?"

Now there was a question I hadn't at all expected.

"Not unless you have a Jewel," I said, biting back a noise of incredulity that threatened to intrude upon my words.

"Ah . . . Yeah," Derek drawled, looking somewhat chagrined and feeling as if he were about to reveal some sort of betrayal, which the ramifications of his actions almost seemed to do. "About that . . ."

"Wait. You're telling me you have a Jewel?" I asked. "All this time, you've had one?"

"Had to have an ace in the hole, China doll," Derek said. "I'm sorry I kept that from you."

"Wait. Just how did you keep that from me?" I was more astonished than angry, even though I felt I should have been far more the latter. "You and I shared everything!"

"Not exactly everything," Derek said, reaching onto the

bed and removing a 9 mm. He then chambered a bullet from the clip and holstered the gun. "You're a badass to be sure, but I knew you weren't invincible. And if bad came to worse, I wanted to be able to do you a solid and keep you safe in case the shape-shifters tried to capture you. They couldn't interrogate you for something you didn't know."

"I wouldn't have broken for those monsters," was what I wanted to say. But of course, there was no way I could say such a thing with any honesty. My thoughts had immediately spun back to Aiko. She was one of the strongest of us, and Lothos had broken her. Reanon was still counseling her, and it was slow going due to my sensei's obstinate nature. Only Father knew what had happened, and neither of them was talking. God, what could have shattered that indomitable will that made my clan practically worship her?

I should have been angry with Derek. I should have bitten his head off for withholding such an important thing from me. I had shared the other Jewel that I'd filched from that enemy thaumaturgist, had I not? Of course, Lothos hadn't been looking for me at the time as far as I knew. Derek had perhaps been keeping that secret since long before I came into his life anyway, so in hindsight, it really was none of my business.

I frowned, and accepted defeat. "I guess you're right," I said, and Derek gestured to his dresser.

"Top shelf on the left, tucked into the back left corner."

"Now that you mention it, you did say that you were being trained as a thaumaturgist for Lothos," I said, going to where he indicated. "You managed to escape with your Jewel?"

"Not exactly," Derek replied as I fished through the unsorted socks that composed the contents of the drawer. Reaching the spot that he mentioned, my hand touched the small, fuzzy, and vaguely cubical surface of what could only be a ring case.

"I got it off of a thaumaturgist," Derek explained as I removed the black velvet case from its resting place. He reached out, and it was dislodged from my hand. I watched it float into his waiting grip.

"How'd you best a thaumaturgist without a Jewel of your own?" I asked. Such a feat was not unheard of, but it usually required more luck than skill.

"Snuck up on him in a crowd one night," Derek said as he sat down on the edge of his bed. He flipped open the box. It was facing him, so I didn't see its contents, but I felt a surge of power that was indicative of a Jewel as he reached into it. The fact that I had felt nothing before meant that the box was specially designed by our kind, meant for concealment and containment of the Jewel's energies, rather than just a decorative placement for ordinary baubles.

A light emanated from the box as Derek spoke. "Did the deed so fast no one even saw it. Joe and I grabbed the body and took off before anyone noticed. Lothos' cronies don't usually travel alone; we must've scared the piss out of them. They don't expect anyone to be so ballsy, especially a couple of Vagabonds in a crowd. He never saw it coming."

At last, he removed the ring: flawless in every way, but hardly structured for a man's hand, though it was the proper size.

"I changed it somewhat from the way it looked when I first retrieved it," Derek explained. He set the box to his side, and took the ring in the index finger and thumb of both his hands. "It turned out a bit girly for my taste."

"Wait. What do you mean you changed . . . ?"

The last word of my sentence died upon my lips as I sensed what Derek was doing. The amount of power he drew from the Jewel inset into the ring was so immense that it felt as if I were being drawn into it from an invisible hand that grasped my chest from the inside.

The room seemed to grow very warm as the ring and its Jewel began to glow from a soft red to a white heat, and then flare as blindingly bright as a welder's torch. I averted my gaze from the dazzling light. Suddenly, I heard a loud crack that echoed as if it were a thunderclap. I winced from the shock of the noise and final flash from the light . . . and could not believe what I saw.

Two rings were there now, instead of one.

"You . . . you're a replicator!" I whispered, partly unable to believe that I'd said it myself. Replication was one of the rarest of rare gifts among our kind. Even rarer than Amelia's gift of psychometry. There were only three known members of my clan who could do it, and those were never allowed out of their villages without specialized guard. Their existence was such a well-kept secret that I doubted even Lothos's spies knew who they were. Only they could replicate Jewels, which, using conventional means, were extremely difficult to make, even in the best of circumstances. Even reconstituting matter properly into a Jewel was inhumanly tricky when re-structuring their indescribably complex energy matrices. Replicators, however, could make perfect copies of that highly specialized matter with ease.

"I haven't done that in awhile," Derek said. Though he sounded only slightly winded, I noticed how his voice trembled, and I saw him shaking and with a thin sheen of sweat covering his brow. I removed a tissue from a dispenser on his dresser, and went to him to wipe the sweat away. While doing so, I caught a first glimpse of the rings. They were perfect copies of each other: pure gold and pink diamonds.

"Now you know why I had to keep this from you," Derek said. "What I know -and what you now know- could get you killed."

"We didn't even think that Lothos had any replicators," I said. "Do you have any idea what this could mean to my clan?"

"Are you going to take me in, then?" I noticed that Derek's expression had hardened somewhat. "Will you sequester me like the others with that talent?"

"No!" I protested, doubly embarrassed at having allowed my memories of the condition of replicators in my clan to be so easily accessible to his mind. "Never, love! Derek, we would never make you do anything you wouldn't be willing to do. Your clan is your own."

"Good, then." Derek spoke less tersely than before, and I felt the twinge of regret within him for his previous tone. His thoughts then sank into his former haze of Zen-like nothingness with only an impression of fear as his gaze remained fixed upon the two rings he held in his hand. At last, he produced a delicate chain from the gold of one of the rings, threaded it through its finger hole and clasped it about his neck. Afterwards, his gaze fell upon me so intently that it was as if he'd never seen me before.

"Will it take you a long time to teach me how to track Joe down?" He asked.

"No," I said. "It's actually very simple, but I thought you'd have me go with you and Lyman?"

Derek shook his head. "You'll be going with the caravan."

"But wouldn't I be more help with you tracking Joe down?" I asked, trying not to sound crestfallen at this.

"China Doll . . ."

Derek had slipped the ring back into his box. He then slid out of the bed and descended to my level, kneeling.

"You came here to protect the baby. And I'm keeping you to that."

"You have Deb -"

"Look, you didn't hear this from me, but I don't trust her," Derek said. "She's too clingy with that kid, and she capitulated way too quickly when I confined her to her trailer. I expected her to raise the stink of a million roadkills when I did that, but she didn't make a peep. That was weird. Not to mention the fact that our separation is something Lothos is probably expecting. But I don't think he expects you. You're my ace in the hole."

"And the woman who loves you," I added with a gentle smile.

"That too," Derek cracked a grin of his own, and I felt

some of the gravity of the situation lessen.

"They don't like me," I said.

"Pablo does. Randy and Ben don't mind you either, though they're wary, especially since you and I confessed our relationship to the clan. But can you really blame them?"

"Not really, I guess."

"And Wadih respects you, at least. They're my family, all of them. Even Deb and Marie-Laure. Even the baby. Wasn't she your mission?"

"I see what you're getting at," I remarked with a frown, "but I don't like it. I don't like your means for procuring blood."

"I expected you wouldn't," Derek said, "but I'm sure it's not the reason you don't want this assignment."

I wanted to sulk, but Derek was right. I couldn't follow his coat tails into battle the way I wanted, and I knew that though I didn't relish his clan's methods of blood procurement, this was, in truth, all because I was more worried about his survival.

"I'll do what you say," I finally said, nearly mumbling the distasteful words. "The baby is my main charge; you're right about that."

"One more thing."

Derek's fingers touched my chin and guided my gaze up to him. He was smiling, and I felt his love for me burst from his heart, shattering through his Zen-calm. I could have melted into his arms right there, but I maintained my composure.

"I notice you never asked me why I replicated the ring." His voice had turned as soft and silken as it was wont to do when we were in bed together.

"I . . . I was going to get to that." I felt my face begin to heat up. "I just thought you were making a spare."

"I was, after a fashion," Derek said, taking my hand into his own.

"Derek . . . ?" I whispered tentatively. Again, there was that tiny flash of fear.

"Lyman was right," he said.

"About what?"

I saw it in his free hand. The ring box, which he presented to me. He opened it one-handed, and presented its contents to me. It was the same as the ring he wore threaded in the chain around his neck, but he had changed it even more since he made the duplicate. It was now much smaller.

Small enough for my finger.

"We vampires do fall in love quickly," Derek said, and let go of my trembling hand only long enough to remove the tiny ring from its resting place. "So, China Doll . . . now you know I have a ring. And I also have a question."

I didn't even wait for the question. My response was a quaver so faint, even I could barely understand it.

"Beg pardon?" Derek asked.

"Yes," I whispered as my vision blurred. I felt my heart pounding so loudly in my chest that I was certain that Derek could hear it as well. My head swam as I let him slip the ring onto my finger.

"Yes!" My words came out shakily, but at last loud enough for him to hear me clearly. I think I might have hurt him a little when I kissed him. No sooner had he finished fitting the ring onto my finger, I slipped my arms around him and pressed my face to his. He let out a tiny cry; my impact was almost like a punch.

Yes . . . was all my thoughts could repeat as he recovered and we remained this way, our lips locked together, our thoughts refracting into each other's as they would do whenever we fed. Yes . . . yes . . . yes . . .

I love you, China Doll, I heard his heart send amidst the patterns of love our souls created in our bond. I blended my confession of love with his, letting our words overlap and entwine as our lips remained in sweet conjunction. When we at last separated, I inhaled his scent and smiled, touching my nose to his, relishing our touch. I felt his arms enfold me and I was gladder than I'd ever been before. He loved me. He wanted me.

He wanted me forever.

"You'd better come back to me alive," I whispered.

"Wouldn't dream of any other way," Derek said. He was giddy with his own happiness, as well as feeling quite smug that he could hide his intentions from me, even in physical contact. He was high on joy, and felt ready to take on all of Lothos' clan for me. "You know I'll come back for you."

"I'm holding you to that," I said. "And I want you to promise me something else."

"Anything."

"That you will lose all your fear with me." I made the intent of my words clear in my heart so there were no questions about what I meant.

"I promise," Derek replied.

Indeed, Lyman was right, I thought as we kissed again, and then one last time for good measure. Our kind does fall in love quickly. Of course, there was still that issue of what would happen to us after this blew over, but for the time being, we were happy.

Chapter Fourteen

Derek and I managed to hew out a serious moment in the midst of our elation as I taught him how to use his Jewel for tracking. I thought he would be a bit rusty with his skills, but clearly I had been wrong. He caught on quickly to my instructions, and was soon able to flawlessly lock on to Joe's fading trail.

He kissed me one last time before leaving with Lyman in his truck, and Grace hunkered down in its spacious bed. Wadih took command of Derek's RV and I rode shotgun with him as our team soon departed for their blood hunt. But for the first hour, and perhaps for the first time not around Derek, my mind was anywhere but the mission.

I was still there, in Derek's room, in his RV. It was only Derek and me, locked in our kiss, keeping our lips pressed to each other's for as long as time would allow, losing ourselves in each other's thoughts. I felt his hands wrap around my waist, smelled his comforting scent, and drowned in his thoughts as they left their indelible imprint on and within me. I felt coated with his love, and more a part of him than even when we fed. My lips tingled as much as my thigh had from that night when I'd nearly blacked out with the bliss of his feeding from my femoral artery. He wanted me. He gave me a promise, sealed in a ring. Such a promise means everything to our kind, as we literally promise each other eternity . . . or as long as the war will allow us to live. Why he wanted me so much, I perhaps would never know, despite the fact that we'd bonded in soul as well as blood. Knowing Derek's thoughts was not always a perfectly clear mirror into his heart. He was his own person, with his own will. And I, for all my understanding of him, for all our understanding of each other, could not be him.

I bit my lower lip, and clutched my arms about my chest to stop myself from shivering. I wanted to talk about this with someone, but Derek and I had agreed to withhold the information of our engagement from the clan until everyone was brought to safety. But as I sat there in the passenger seat, staring out at the vibrancy of the night that only our kind could see, I felt that I would explode if I didn't confide in someone.

"Penny for your thoughts." Wadih's question removed me from my reverie.

"Would that I could," I said with a sigh.

"You two are in love, I know," Wadih said. "To be honest, I'm happy about it. The boss needed it, you know. Before you came, he was a good leader . . . at least when he chose to be, but he was grumpy most of the time, even before that baby came along and the shape-shifters started giving us grief."

I couldn't help but manage a guffaw at this. It was certainly news to me, though I should have guessed it by Derek's memories. His past had indeed been as dark as that of nearly all defectors whose minds I chanced to glimpse into.

"I'm not kidding," Wadih assured me, "I swear. You made a brand new man out of him. If we survive all this, I wouldn't be surprised if he begs you to come along with us when we can get back on the road without worrying about getting killed in our sleep."

"If he survives . . ." I murmured.

"You're really worried about him, aren't you?" Wadih spoke more softly, and I felt his sense of alarm, as well as his swift attempt at suppressing it.

"You're worried too," I said, forcing him to tip his hand. Tact was sweet, but it also annoyed me, since it was often based on dishonesty.

I'd never turned to face Wadih as I talked, but I saw his reflection in the glass. He was ready to protest with the way he opened his mouth, but then seemed to change his mind as he closed it slowly and frowned.

"Damn mind-readers," he said at last. "Am I that transparent?"

"You're no different than the rest of your clan," I replied with a smile. "You're all worried. Except for maybe Deb."

"She hates him?" Wadih asked, immediately suspicious.

"I don't rightly know," I admitted. "Her mind is one of the most difficult to read that I've encountered in a long time. Anger comes off of her easily, as well as affection for the baby, but that's about it."

"She lords over that pipsqueak like it's hers," Wadih grumbled.

"She may as well be," I reminded him. "From what I've been told, Joe didn't seem to want her until that last attack. And everyone else was more than happy to leave Deb to the task."

"Yeah, well, I guess that we never thought we'd be saddled with a kid," Wadih said with noticeable discomfort. "That's supposed to be nigh on impossible anyway, isn't it?"

"Not really," I said. "You ought to live among my clan for awhile. Babies are a fairly common sight."

"Human babies, yeah," Wadih countered. "I've run into more than a few of your clan. Vampires with human girlfriends or boyfriends, or married human couples who are hosts . . . that smell's unmistakable. But the babies have all been human."

"I never said it wasn't rare."

"So you say," Wadih said, pursing his lips. "But of course, that's the only reason Lothos would be on our asses like this, isn't it? He must want that baby pretty damn badly. If it were just greens from the shape-shifters trying to carve out a reputation, they'd have given up by now. I've met a few other clans -Vagabonds like us, mind you- who've been in Lothos' crosshairs like that. The abuse usually lasts for about a week or so, then they move on to greener pastures."

I wanted to plead a case for their joining our clan. God knew I could have made it a convincing one. There were only a few of them still braving the road while the rest, according to Derek and Marie-Laure, laid low. They weren't fighters, despite Lyman's training and Derek's leadership skills. With the exception of our human hosts, who could travel in the daylight in relative safety, our clan members rarely left our villages alone. We were all trained in some form of combat from turning; humans were trained as well, and often taught thaumaturgy in order to protect our interests during the daytime. Among our clan, one had a fighting chance, but Vagabonds were a notoriously proud and stubborn lot. And I had no intention of allowing a clash of ideals ruin the understanding I'd managed to cultivate with the greater portion of this group. Even those who didn't like me seemed to tolerate me for Derek's sake, but I would perhaps never be seen as one of them. Even now, they were on their way to procure blood. They harvested humans: lured them away from the safety of numbers, subdued them, siphoned them of their prize, and moved on. And without our mental abilities, when traveling without Derek, this had to be done with drugs that blurred their memory. At least while I was with them, I could mitigate the damage, and erase their memories in a less harmful way.

"All the more reason to get you to safety," I said. "However, this business complicates things."

"I know. Trust me; you're not the only one who's pissed."

I let things fall into a long, semi-comfortable silence between us. All the while, I kept my gaze focused on the road ahead and to our sides. I expected an ambush. I had no precognition like Sarah, but there were things that you just knew would happen: things you couldn't explain you knew, but could predict nonetheless. But no matter how wary I tried to remain, try as I might, my thoughts could not help but return to Derek. If I'd had any doubts as to whether he and I were bonded mates, this time on the road certainly allayed them. As certain as I was that we were driving into some kind of trap, I was just as sure that Derek and Lyman were headed into something similar, perhaps even worse. And there I was, on a lonely stretch of road, separated from him and unable to do anything about it, fearing to even think it, but nonetheless terrified that he would be lost to me. If I could have taken over Wadih's mind, have him break from the group, and head back in Derek's direction, knowing that the rest of the clan would be all right, I would have done it instantly. Of course, that was only wishful thinking. I had to trust in the skills of the one I loved, wherever he was, as his clan would have to trust in mine.

"So what's your story, if you don't mind my asking?" I asked at some point. About an hour had passed, and Wadih had remained as silent as I had been, guessing correctly that I wanted the time alone with my thoughts. I asked this more out of boredom and to break the silence than anything else. I knew many of our kind had tragic histories, and those who were not forthcoming with them would prefer to not be asked. Others, however, were silent simply because no one had ever asked, and they weren't the talkative types. I'd heard Randy once mention something vaguely about Pablo's past, but Pablo didn't react well to it, and so I refrained from asking. Wilson was stolid and spoke little, preferring to let his actions speak for him, and Randy and Benjamin, though affable enough, were consummate busybodies, more concerned with working to keep the clan on its feet than being social. They were always busy tinkering with the generators and vehicles, making sure everything was in running order, and so I left them to their passion. Heaven forbid anything would break down if we ever needed to break camp in a hurry, which we'd already had to do once. They seemed invaluable to the clan.

And that was where it hit me. Each member of the clan still present was performing a vital task. Randy and Benjamin trafficked goods and maintained machinery; Marie-Laure kept them in communication with the outside world; I saw little of Wilson, but he, like Wadih, Joe, Pablo, and Lyman, served as security, and Deb took care of the baby. With everyone else lying low, basically, the clan was running on a skeleton crew. I was with only the ones best trained to fight -and Lothos had been slowly picking them off since before I had even arrived. And now Joe was missing. Regardless of my feelings about him, he was necessary for the survival of the group. We were in a sad state of affairs indeed.

"Well, it's kind of a long story," Wadih began . . . but got no farther. His fear spiked so high that it nearly caused a backlash inside my own mind. My head was spinning as he slammed on the brakes, and I felt my body lurch violently forward like I unknowingly had taken a seat inside the mitt of a giant pitcher. Thankfully I was wearing my seat belt.

"Shit!" He exclaimed as I reeled from his emotional flare and the assault of Newton's First Law. Quickly, I managed to shake it off and concentrate on what he'd seen.

The flashing lights were unmistakable. We were at the top of what seemed to be a hill or large overpass, and in full view of a roadblock of some kind not but a hundred feet ahead and below, at the foot of the incline. That, however, was not the reason for Wadih's sudden stop. A lone cop stood directly ahead of us.

"What the hell is this?" Wadih whispered as he put the RV into neutral. I rolled the side window down and looked behind us to see the rest of the clan stopped in a neat little row. There had been no traffic on this stretch of road, and it seemed that we were the first unfortunate few that this roadblock had stopped. And that, to say nothing of the fact that it was practically the middle of nowhere, made things instantly suspicious.

The CB radio attached below the dashboard, crackled to life with Deb's voice. "What's going on up there? Why have we stopped?"

Wadih grabbed the microphone, but kept his gaze trained on the cop who stood unmoving ahead of us. "There's a roadblock," he said. "I don't like the look of it. Stay frosty, and keep the baby quiet. Everyone, stay in your vehicles. I'm gonna go check this out."

"Might be a good fat supply come to us," I heard Pablo say.

"Bad idea, genius," Wadih replied. "We don't need that kind of attention. You want the mind-readers after us as well as the shape-shifters for drawing too much attention to ourselves? 'Sides, the boss left me in charge, so I say keep your butts where they are."

There was a pause long enough for me to begin to wonder if they were seriously considering rounding up a squad of policemen for their illicit "blood drive." Wadih was right; despite their resistance to siding in the war, Vagabonds were just as beholden to the few mutually-accepted rules of our world, which even Lothos held to. Making ourselves known to humans was a taboo that was close to the top of the list. Were they to find out, both Father and Lothos would have punished them for making such a high-profile mistake as waylaying a squad of cops for their blood. Even though I would be able to erase their memories, I wouldn't be able to help the clan if the leaders of either my people or our enemy took umbrage.

Thankfully, it seemed that I had nothing to worry about, as one by one, everyone in the clan replied with a brusque, "Ten-four." Satisfied, Wadih opened the door and slid out onto the road. I heard the beginnings of him speaking in an overtly friendly tone before he shut the door behind him.

"What seems to be the problem, officer?" I heard him say as he stepped around the RV towards the policeman.

Then, as humans are so fond of saying, the shit hit the fan.

The gunshot sounded like a distant pop through the RV's interior, but the crunching of Wadih's internal organs was horrifyingly clear. The police officer had drawn his gun quicker than Wadih could react. I felt his pain in one sickening wave and he was on the ground. Gunshot wounds, though just as painful as they were for any human, were nothing to us, but it took several moments before our bodies could expel the bullet. We stood to lose a lot of blood if there was an exit wound and we didn't heal fast enough.

The officer's eyes were cold, empty. I reached out, caught the timbre of his mind . . . and gasped. I flew over the driver's seat, taking cover as I watched the officer's cold gaze shift, and then saw him take aim for me. I fumbled for the CB's microphone, nearly yanking it out of its moorings with the radio set.

"It's a trap!" I practically screamed as a volley of bullets pierced the windshield. "Lothos knows we're here; the cop is a bloody puppet! Wadih's been shot!"

"We're coming out," I heard Wilson say.

"No, stay where you are," I said. "I can see multiple police lights ahead. There are too many of them, even for you. I have a Jewel; I'll handle them."

Three more shots rang out, and the windshield's shatterproof glass cracked ever more into a tangle of intersecting webs with the holes they produced. My size allowed me to duck into the leg area below the dashboard to avoid the round. I could only hope that the clan had chosen to listen to me. They had no means to deal with what was hunting them now.

Once there was a sufficient space of silence, I moved with preternatural speed, scrambling into the relative safety of the RV's interior, and then moving to the side entrance door. Forcing down my momentary torrent of combined shock and adrenaline, I focused my mind, linking myself with the energies of my Jewel before I slipped outside. Knowing what we were dealing with gave me a potential advantage, such as it was. I had a plan, but one that would only work if my guess was correct.

I leaped out onto the road, and several shots joined in with the lone officer's. I looked ahead, siphoning time into a bleed that made reality seem as if it were made of jelly. The squad further ahead was running forward to join in the fray. There were twenty in all, and at the sight of their clothes, I swore in dismay.

"Bloody hell!"

They were in full riot gear: helmets, boots, and Kevlar vests, but no shields. They all sported SMGs and rifles. A few had opened fire from the distance, but none of them had hit me or the vehicles just yet. I aimed to make sure each shot missed as I ran my fingers along the RV's surface, compressing an electromagnetic field and casting it about the vehicles of the caravan with my mind's eye, forming a contoured shield. As long as the clan remained inside their respective RVs, trailers and buses, an anti-tank round wouldn't penetrate it. Satisfied with its completion, I shifted my attention to the approaching squad.

The lone cop had taken notice of me and aimed. My natural reflexes could already keep pace with a bullet, but were still beholden to physics, assuring some kind of injury if it struck me, due to Newton's Second Law. But with a Jewel, all bets were off.

"Entropy bleed is your best friend if you are being shot at," Aiko had once taught me. And she had been right. The first round was aimed for my chest, but got no further than the length of my arm as I swatted it away . . . and then each successive shot. One, two, three, four, five . . . all sent flying in acute angles to my right and left as if I'd been swatting mosquitoes, with the impact of my hand being of no greater force than that. The air cracked with the compressed heat of the bleed from each strike. The squad closed ranks, and tore the air with their shotgun shells and submachine rounds. I repelled these as well, raining lead into the terrain beyond the road from whichever angle it came. The ease with which I did this awakened an amusing memory of a demonstration by Bruce Lee that I once saw, where he played a game of table tennis with only a pair of nunchucks.

Such a feat that I displayed before the attacking police

squad would have demoralized any normal human, but these were puppets. All their eyes were vacant and passive as they went through the motions of attack and blindly stood their ground. They fired, reloaded, and fired again like machines. Their real selves had been pushed aside by a greater will.

Derek used to be one of a handful of telepaths that Lothos kept in his ranks. My clan knew little about what Lothos taught them, but we did know that they were trained to use their talents in perverse ways that we tended to avoid. One of the most horrid violations was possession. Some in Lothos' cadre of mind-readers -puppeteers, we called them- could take over the thoughts of anyone with a weaker will than theirs. I'd heard that they could control multiple hosts, but this was the first time I was a witness to it.

I wanted to subdue the squad, knock them out safely so that I wouldn't need to hurt any of them, but I knew that even with time slowed down, the way they kept me busy with their gunshots was going to be problematic. I also wanted to check on Wadih. I couldn't see him where I'd thought he'd fallen, though I could smell his blood. The scent, however, was faint. That might have been a good sign that he didn't bleed much before the wound sealed. Perhaps he even made it back into the safety of the RV; the EM field would let him back inside, still repelling any ammo. A quick glimpse into the sky made me thankful that there had been no helicopters brought onto the scene; of course it stood to reason that Lothos had had just as much incentive to keep this as low profile as possible.

At last, there was an opening in the fray, and I reached out mentally to the first cop, the one who had shot Wadih. I hit a wall as solid as the one surrounding Deb's mind. It shoved me out with an almost painful force. I reeled back, and dodged a semiautomatic round that barely missed my shoulder. Damn, this puppeteer was powerful! Trying to undo what she did would be difficult. But of course, she didn't know the ace up my sleeve.

I then proceeded to delegate functions to the shield about

the caravan to the Jewel I'd won off of the dead thaumaturgist. Though it was damaged, it would hold out well enough for this purpose. Several more shots distracted me, but to my good fortune, there was another lull in the fire. Seizing the opportunity yet again, I reached into the power reserves of my Jewel as deeply as I could, and siphoned it into my nervous system.

The world became aglow with light even brighter than what I supposed true daylight was like. Every object seemed to shine with its own vibrant patterns of color as my mind, buoyed on the energies of the Jewel, prepared itself. Time stood as still as a painting, and I lurched forward, my mind moving at its own preternatural speed.

There was no wall. The barrier was like paper as I plowed my way inside . . . and into what resembled an empty room that stretched for eternity. Rarely did other's minds manifest themselves as any kind of landscape, unless the owner of that mind was either unconscious or setting a trap.

Alertness spiked within me so severe it hurt. The mindscape shifted and became like glass revealing an infinite sea with about twenty nearby glass baubles. Each was a separate mind, and each, including this mindscape, was enveloped by a crimson mist that thinned out into a thread that passed through the infinite sea to a singular point. This point was a distinctive, powerful presence: one that cast a baleful awareness upon me and bled malice like an open wound.

The puppeteer.

Out of that mist, threads shot out, seemingly soft and pliable as silly string, but their ends were sharp as daggers as they struck, and then pierced me. Agony crackled through me as I felt pulled every which way, sensed claws reaching into my thoughts. No sooner than the pain struck, however, I felt it give way to a growing, insidious numbness. By degrees, my thoughts were overwhelmed with a growing lethargy, the temptation . . . the urge . . . to not think.

How sweet it would feel to just let go . . . to just surrender . . .

I shook myself violently, delving into the strength of my Jewel. I gasped with the power surge, the ensuing euphoria so much like feeding from Derek in our most sublime moments of love that my heart wrenched with longing as much as it swelled with elation. The threads shattered, and crimson oozed out of me like befouled blood, impotent and void.

I reached out into the substance of the mist, and made contact with the presence behind it. My senses were overwhelmed with a burst of indignant rage from the puppeteer, then cold terror, which was quickly suppressed by a shifting, obfuscating slyness. I felt my body smile. I had quite unnerved this one, and the mindscape rippled with a voice.

You . . . are a powerful thing.

The voice was oily, filled with cold malice, and distinctively female. While I sized her up, I was certain she received a brief enough glimpse into the timbre of my own mind to know what I was, and where I'd come from. My cover would be blown if I couldn't do anything about this fiend, and so I had to act quickly. In another's mind however, "quickly" tended to mean "dangerously." But what choice did I have?

Didn't peg you for a talker, I casually remarked. I had to distract the fiend just long enough to do what I needed to do.

You won't win, witch, the puppeteer said. My master will know who has upset his plans.

If you're revealing some grand design, it leaves a lot to be desired, I replied. The flash of rage I felt from the puppeteer at my words amused me to no end.

You think this is a game? The voice thundered high and shrill with furious indignation. It nearly disrupted my concentration. Time flows even in here, and you only have so much of it. Do quickly whatever insignificant thing you came here to do. These humans are mine.

Oh . . . Not anymore, love.

Before the puppeteer could ask, the threads dissolved. Placing a suggestion in one's mind is a fairly easy and subtle trick. And such a thing easily carries over through a link. Some of us choose to link our minds to a human mate, and things like suggestions carry over that bridge. And this puppeteer had multiple bridges. Each mind had been asleep, forced that way by their enslaver. I woke them up, and the feedback from such a mass shift to consciousness sent a scream across the mindscape that still rang in my ears when I returned to my body . . . and echoed into eerie silence.

The entire squad was on the ground, unconscious.

I was puzzled at this at first; my command should have snapped them back into their normal minds. But then I realized that the feedback might have rendered them unconscious again. In fact, I realized that the backlash had gone much farther than expected. It had rendered them comatose. They would be out for a very long time, and this was fine by me.

The fight was over, but the puppeteer was still at large. I figured she had to be in a reasonable range to have placed those officers under her control. But my senses were still on high alert with the uncertainty I felt. Had she fled, or was she merely waiting to seek retribution?

"Hey, kiddo, do we have the 'all clear'?"

Wadih's voice gave me such a sharp fright that I nearly distended part of the caravan's protective force field to smash him in the face. I spun around and saw him leaning out the RV's side window. His gaze was amused, but surprised by what he'd just seen. I must have indeed been a sight: a little girl taking on a squad of armored police, and causing them all to drop like flies at once in only a matter of seconds. I was, however, relieved that he was all right after all that had happened, but with how keyed up I was from my ordeal, his scare was enough to nearly give me permanent death. I resolved to give him a suitable punishment somehow, were we to survive the night.

"Get back inside the RV!" My order came out as a harsh whisper as I gestured emphatically. I needed to concentrate. I was trying to detect any vestige of a foreign mind. I was certain the puppeteer was still out there, and I needed as few distractions as possible. If the mind of any member of this clan were weak enough, he or she could easily be possessed. That was a complication I didn't need.

Wadih began to sink back down into the RV when the baby began to cry. Nearly as surprised as I was, he shifted his gaze towards Deb's trailer at the rear of the caravan. I hissed with exasperation. I felt that this was proof positive that God, for whatever reason, hated me at the moment.

"Bugger all!" I fumed at the noise that I knew would further disrupt my concentration. "Wadih, get on the CB and tell the others that we're not out of the woods yet. And for the love of God, tell Deb to stop that baby from . . ."

I went stark still, listening as the baby's wails echoed down the empty road from the caravan's rear. It had been over ten seconds since she had started crying, and Deb had never allowed her to carry on for any longer than that. Even pyrokinetics had some telepathy, and it was a godsend when dealing with infants. She knew exactly what that child needed, and since she had been confined to quarters, we'd hardly heard the baby cry at all. By now, she would have been changing, feeding, or doing whatever it took to mollify her. But instead, the crying and screaming went on, unheeded and untended to.

It wasn't difficult to sense the clan's disconcertment about their situation, but it was then that I noticed that all but one member was awake to feel this way. The timbres of the minds of Wadih, Wilson, Pablo, Randy, Benjamin, and Marie-Laure were all awake and accounted for . . . but Deb's mind was silent.

"Oh no."

"What's wrong?" Wadih asked. "You went still as a statue, and then-"

"Something's wrong," I said with a newfound urgency. "Go check on Deb; she's either unconscious, or something's happened to her."

"What about the others? Don't you still want me to-?"

"Now!"

I felt a touch of regret for my harshness, but Wadih did have a slight tendency towards indecisiveness. I watched as he leaped from the RV and moved at preternatural speed to the rear of the convoy.

Then, I found her.

Perhaps it should be more accurate to say that she, the puppeteer, found me.

I didn't hear her land behind me; I didn't expect to. I didn't even have a moment to see her face. But I certainly heard her voice right before she drove my face into the shield-covered chassis of Derek's RV.

"Looking for me, bitch?"

Her words were the same cold oil as lightning crackled across my field of vision. The shield held in spite of our superhuman strength, and our bones do not break as easily as a human's, but that first blow, and every succeeding one served its purpose.

Her hand, nearly as large as my head, grasped me painfully as my senses were rattled blow after blow, each one harder than the next. I lost count of how many times she slammed my head, striking me against that indestructible EM field like a pile driver. It felt like a joy buzzer every time she pressed me into it, and it was an effective strategy. Jewels could only work when we concentrated, and nothing disrupted that like severe concussions. How I managed to not black out, even I didn't understand.

The puppeteer had made a litany of other epithets, and I know I cried out at least twice, but her continuous assault reduced any sound I made to a miserable groan. I was past comprehension by the time she stopped; the world was wreathed with a halo of red and black fog, and I both smelled and tasted blood. My vision was blurred and I couldn't bring things into focus any more than I could change the color of the sky. The puppeteer was silhouetted by the lone streetlight. But the crimson of her eyes seemed to radiate a malicious light of its own as she palmed my face like a basketball and lifted me into the air, my legs and arms hanging as limp as an old towel.

Her other hand slammed against my throat like a hammer. I gasped, but only on reflex. I was too weak and listless to do much else. New pain wracked my body as she began to squeeze. I coughed dryly, and my body twitched. I tried grasping at her hand, but my claws barely made a scratch. The cutting off of my air and circulation ignited a fight-or-flight reflex that gave some strength to my limbs as I kicked and tried to gasp, but she was an iron statue, a death trap slowly winding its gears towards its ultimate goal. I could feel the sick pleasure she derived at this; it was almost sexual, the way she reacted to slowly crushing my neck. She was caught in an orgasmic euphoria as she waited for the eventual severing of my head from my neck. My eyes rolled back as darkness further encroached. At that moment, I simply let go of everything. I prepared to give myself over to what lay beyond. There was no fear, only sorrow and wistful regret that Derek would have to deal with losing me so soon after we'd found each other.

I'm so sorry, I thought, finding that I could mysteriously form my thoughts again. Derek was so clear in my mind's eye now. Goodbye, my Derek. I love you.

Then she dropped me.

A loud noise preceded it all before I hit the ground hard. My throat was free and I gasped for air, my head and my throat wracked with throbbing pain. The blackness and redness began to retreat from my field of vision, but when I tried to focus, my eyes wouldn't obey. I kept gulping in air; we needed less air than humans, but what had been done to me had exhausted my body of even that lesser amount that was needed. I was like a dying fish as I lay on the asphalt. The scent of blood was everywhere. I rolled back and forth, satisfying my starving lungs. Seconds felt like minutes, and I was too preoccupied with my injuries to even think to ask what had happened, or what was now happening. Had the puppeteer not intended to kill me in the way I thought? Had she planned some new torture? Or was I dead, and awaiting the providence of whatever powers that were upon my broken body and truly immortal soul?

I sensed another presence beside me as my vision finally returned to focus. It was accompanied by a familiar scent, but I was still not fully cognizant of my surroundings. I bared my fangs at the sudden touch I felt on my shoulder and spun around, ready to sink my teeth into whoever it was.

"Easy there, girl! It's me, Wilson. You're okay."

His voice was enough to make me pause. My vision was clearing as my body began to heal itself. I shifted my gaze to the figure that knelt beside me and relief flooded through me. It really was Wilson. That lean frame and thick halo of red hair was unmistakable. Though I was still in a considerable amount of pain, my body relaxed. I was healing, slowly but surely. There was bleeding, but it was nearly all internal; my body would easily re-absorb the blood. The pain in my head was ebbing away, and I could feel the tendons in my neck resetting themselves.

"Here, drink this," Wilson said and pressed a blood pack into my hand. "It's my last one."

I would have protested under normal circumstances, since I needed the least amount of blood in the whole clan, but this was the only thing that would allow me to heal faster. I bit into the pack and drained its contents, suppressing my usual gag. Its contents were tepid, stagnant, and nearly tasteless. It made my longing for Derek even more powerful. His blood, though useless for nourishment, at least satisfied a need for flavor where the clan's blood packs could not. Besides, even if the blood in the pack had been fresh, its taste would still pale in comparison to what Derek and I found in each other.

"I think . . ." I coughed and brought my hand to my throat. My voice was almost unrecognizable when I'd spoken, and it still hurt to talk. "I think this is the most I've . . . heard you speak . . . directly to me." I managed to smile, then winced as the muscles in my lower jaw realigned. It was a good thing that despite my injuries, I had no trouble swallowing as the last of the blood made its use in completing my healing.

"I usually speak when I have something to say," Wilson replied, "like when I shot that bitch in the neck." His words shook with a slight chuckle as he spoke. "She said, 'was that supposed to stop me?' And I said, 'No, but this will.' And that's when the delayed explosion round kicked in."

I laughed, and immediately regretted it as I erupted into a fit of coughing. The pain was far from gone, but it was much better. The pain in my head had vanished, however; apparently she'd done more damage to my neck and throat than anywhere else.

"I didn't know you had that kind of firepower," I finally managed to say.

"We had to keep some secrets," Wilson answered, "in case we were being watched. Derek suspected that, as you probably know. Besides, normal rounds don't do much good against us."

I tried standing up. I managed to wobble awkwardly to my feet, once nearly staggering to the ground before Wilson caught me. That was when I saw his grisly handiwork. The corpse wore a black dress: a one-piece, akin to a pinafore. Several yards away, there was a smattering of unrecognizable blackened chunks, which, Wilson mentioned, were all that remained of the head. Blood and viscera, in various stages of charring, were scattered everywhere. The smell, which I'd only just begun to notice, was utterly disgusting.

"Messy, but effective," Wilson observed of his own handiwork, and I was inclined to agree.

I reached into the energies of my Jewel and combusted the

remains. The corpse, blood and all, went up in a plume of fire like a funeral pyre sprinkled with thermite. I watched with grim satisfaction at the brief display, which, at its conclusion, left only a black stain on the road, which I then erased.

"By the way, you have your blood supply," I said, and gestured to the police squad, which still lay motionless on the road. Using my Jewel, I envisioned a bubble of null space about the area, and the surrounding world became encased in the bluish hue and utter silence. "They're comatose from a psychic backlash. Even a mortar round wouldn't wake them up. Just don't drain them dry; they were only pawns, and we only need enough blood to last us 'til we get to the sanctuary."

"I'll have Marie-Laure roll out the equipment," Wilson said as I headed towards the rear of the caravan. "Where are you off to?"

"To check on Deb," I said. "I sent Wadih back there before I was attacked; I haven't heard from him since."

"Don't see why you want to do that girl any favors with the way she's treated you," Wilson said.

"I'm surprised you've been keeping tabs on me." I truly was genuinely surprised at this, as he usually kept to himself even more than Marie-Laure or Deb.

"There's a lot you don't know about me," Wilson said with an odd grin. "And I wouldn't have it any other way."

Chapter Fifteen

Unsure of whether to be amused or offended by what Wilson had said, I moved with preternatural speed to the small trailer at the end of the convoy that I usually gave a wide berth to. The moment I arrived, I was accosted by Pablo's scent in addition to those of Wadih and Deb, whose mind still was disturbingly blank. I could always sense at least a presence, if nothing else, but at the moment, I was getting nothing, as if she were either not there, or dead.

I stepped inside, and was met with very relieved looks from Pablo and Wadih.

"Elisa!" Pablo exclaimed.

"Thank God you're okay," Wadih stepped forward from the entrance to the sleeping area in the rear. "Last I heard, Wilson broke in on the CB and said you were being attacked. I'd called Pablo in here to help me get Deb into her bed. I was going to head out to help, but I didn't just want to drop Deb like a sack of rice. Then Wilson told us all to stay put, and then I heard gunshots."

"Let's just say that the cause of our little roadblock has been dealt with," I said, "And you have Wilson to thank . . . as do I."

Rightfully suspecting that I'd been through an ordeal, Wadih and Pablo exchanged nervous glances before speaking again.

"I think it was because a few of us still didn't trust you completely enough to listen to you when you first told us to stay put," Pablo said in an awkward attempt to inject levity into the situation. He smiled at the baby, who was sound asleep in his arms. "She just needed changing, is all."

"And Deb?" I asked.

"Yeah, about that . . ." Wadih gestured towards Deb's

sleeping area and I followed him inside. The trailer was almost antiseptic clean, but her bed formed the most extreme of contrasts. Dried bloodstains -a result of feeding the baby, I conjectured- freckled the mattress and walls of the alcove in a scattering of running splatters. Deb lay on the soiled mattress, motionless as the cops outside, and barely breathing.

"Wadih found her on the floor next to the baby's crib," Pablo explained. "We haven't been able to wake her up, though."

I touched her forehead and made mental contact so quickly that it left me breathless. Beforehand, Deb's mind had been like a steel vault. All I could receive from her were a cacophony of contrasting phantom emotions, but little else. Though I never had attempted to pry before now, I knew the timbre of a mind that was specifically closed off. But now, I understood everything. The timbre of this mind was completely different from what I'd been exposed to during my sparse encounters with her. She literally hadn't been herself. My thoughts returned to the mental fight with the puppeteer. Those threads that I perceived in that mindscape didn't just lead to the minds of the police squad. There had been others under her control, others I hadn't known about. I'd freed them all, and Deb had been one of them.

"Will she be all right?" I heard Wadih ask.

"She's like the police officers out in front," I said. "She's been hit by the backlash from when I severed the puppeteer's connection."

"Wait, you're saying that she was under some kind of mind control?" Wadih ejected. "How? For how long?"

"I'm hoping she'll be able to tell us that," I said, preparing to reach into her mind. "I can snap her out of it, but I don't know how deep the control went. Her conscious mind might have been so deeply repressed that she might not have any memory of anything that happened."

"Is she even in there, then?" Wadih asked. "I mean, this puppeteer thing didn't just tear her mind apart, right?"

"Oh, she's quite intact," I said. "Puppeteers don't work that way. They only take over. The lucky ones are just put to sleep, but sometimes, if the victim has a strong enough will, he or she will stay awake, all voluntary control of their body having been pushed aside. They're fully aware of what's going on, but unable to do anything about it."

"Shit," Pablo drawled out in a whisper.

"So they were trapped inside their own bodies?" Wadih shuddered, making a sound of combined disgust and horror. "Deb was a bitch sometimes, but even I wouldn't have wished that on her."

"Shoulda figured something was wrong," Pablo remarked, stepping through the doorway. "She was acting worse than normal."

"Derek suspected something as well," I confessed, recalling his words to me before our parting. "It was probably a matter of time before she was found out . . . but then again, I think the Others had expected us all to be dead before we discovered anything."

I reached into Deb's mind and flipped the switch of her consciousness.

Deb's eyes flew open. She gasped, her body giving a convulsive heave before she sprang into an upright position and braced herself against the corner of her sleeping alcove.

"Easy there, Deb!" Wadih reached out his hands reassuringly. "It's us. You're okay. We know you were under the control of something. You're free now."

Deb's eyes shot back and forth from me, to Pablo, and then to Wadih. I was assaulted by a rush of emotions from when I'd awoken her. This was followed by a split second of absolute terror, but that quickly passed, and faded into an almost painfully keen alertness. She was taking stock of her situation but her mind was a jumble. She was confused, and felt empty, for lack of a better word.

At once, when her gaze returned to me, all of the confusion vanished.

"Do you remember any-" I started to ask before she lunged forward and took me into her arms. At first, I wasn't sure what had happened, but then, in contact with her, I felt the upwelling of relief and joy radiate from her through me.

"Thank you," Deb whispered, and her voice broke into a near-sob. "Thank you for freeing me."

As barmy as it sounds, I had to suppress the urge to say, "Who are you, and what did you do with Deb?" Incidentally, I felt the same inclination from Pablo and Wadih, who were certainly staring slack-jawed at us. Now having gleaned from her mind, I had to remind myself that this was the real Deb, and that she had been under the control of one of Lothos' disciples for a long time.

"You were possessed by a puppeteer," I explained after she let me go and I'd reassembled my dignity, "an expert in mind control. She-"

"I know," Deb replied, nodding quickly. "I know everything. I saw everything."

"So you were conscious," I said, confirming my fears. And Deb seemed about to cry again.

"Unfortunately."

Deb got to her feet and went to Pablo. She smiled with endearment as she caressed the baby's cheek. I felt her attachment to the infant, mixed in with an unexplained sense of relief. The baby yawned, then slept on, perhaps contented by the scent of her surrogate mother. Deb then cast a furtive glance outside her trailer before focusing all her senses back upon me.

"Your Jewel can track other thaumaturgists, right?"

"Ah, yes," I answered, uncertain about what she had planned. "Why do you want to…"

"You're being watched. We're all being watched, the whole clan. We've been watched for a long time, in fact. And if you want to know by whom, I can bring you to her. She's still out there, planning."

"So it's another female?" I asked. "You know this?"

"About the only thing I really do know about her," Deb said.

"Wait, how do you even know we're being watched?" Wadih asked.

Deb rolled her eyes and gave an exasperated sigh. "Remember, genius, I was a puppet of theirs. I saw everything they did. Your puppeteer was just a peon, like all the others that were sent after us. They were just cannon fodder to test our defenses. Their boss is still out there, probably thinking of how to kill me."

"So the thaumaturgist I took out by that abandoned farm wasn't directly following Lothos?" I asked.

Deb shrugged. "I'm not sure. My- the puppeteer . . . she wasn't privy to all the info. Lothos' clan isn't stupid. They worked separately, so if one got caught, he or she would only be able to give up so much information. But they all worked through one person, another thaumaturgist." Her gaze fell coldly onto me. "And because you fucked up her plans, little girl, you're on her short list with me, unless you can get to her first."

"Another thaumaturgist . . ." I felt like I needed to go lie down. I'd been given a concussion, and nearly had my throat crushed and my head separated from my neck by one of Lothos' Jewel specialists. I groaned. I did not relish the thought of hunting down another.

"I don't like this. Fighting thaumaturgists is always a risk, no matter how skilled with a Jewel you are."

"But if we have an opportunity to end this, then you just can't pass it up," Pablo said.

"Excuse me, but I'll remind you that it's my arse that's on the line out there if we have to fight a thaumaturgist," I said. "None of you have any training with Jewels, and I'm not too bloody keen to go out there to try to take on one of them again. Some even are competent, and have a very real chance of killing me. I came close enough to that fighting the puppeteer."

"You won't have to go it alone," Deb said. "I can help you. I may not be a thaumaturgist, but I can still hurt her from a distance if she doesn't see me."

"That's a big 'if,' I said. "But can we trust you now? Last time you were out and about, you nearly killed Joe."

A fire seemed to come alive behind Deb's eyes, and for a moment, I was afraid that she would use her gifts on me.

"That wasn't me." she said through gritted teeth. "That was . . ."

"So you were under the control of the puppeteer even then?" I asked.

"For longer than I care to think about," Deb answered. There was unrestrained grief and disgust in her every word. "But we really don't have time for me to give the whole story. The leader may go into hiding, or she may have learned about you and will be trying to get into contact with Lothos. Once she learns that we have a mind-reader working with us, she'll throw everything at us but the kitchen sink."

"Got a point," Wadih remarked.

"Then we'll go," I said and stalked towards the trailer's door. "But you're going to explain to me how you know all this on the way."

"I'd rather not relive all that," Deb said, following me from behind as Wadih and Pablo stepped aside, "but I do believe I owe everyone, especially you, an explanation."

She paused only to make a subtle threat to Pablo that translated to something along the lines of, "guard that baby with your life, if you know what's good for you," before stepping out onto the street. Wilson and Pablo paused at the entrance, noticing that I'd shunted the caravan and the police officers into the between-space.

"Wait, what if you two don't win?" Pablo called after me. "Will we be trapped in this place?"

"It'll last as long as I will it to last," I explained, shaking my head, "or until something happens to me. So if I don't succeed, you'll know it. And you'll need to get the hell out of here as fast as you can."

With the two satisfied, I made sure to let Wadih know about the blood that Wilson and the rest of the clan were procuring out in front. Wadih headed off to assist them while Pablo waited for us with the baby. With all loose ends tied up, I made a way out of the dimension with Deb, and set my concentration on any trails left from any Jewels.

It took practically no time to lock on the trail, which led up a forested hill very close to the caravan. I found this puzzling at first; any trained thaumaturgist could mask the energies of their Jewel. But then I figured that for whatever reason, this leader perhaps didn't want to be hid -either that, or she was still ignorant of my presence and subsequently, my skills.

"How well hidden was this leader?" I asked Deb as we climbed over the guardrail and set on the trail. We didn't dare move at preternatural speed, since I received a vague perception that our quarry was on the move, and we are not completely invisible to our own kind when moving that quickly. Even the puppeteer knew this when she attacked me; only she'd managed to catch me while I was distracted. We would have to do the same with this fiend, but I doubted we could.

"She'd been trailing us the moment word got out that one of our clan had fathered a dhampir," Deb said. "The human woman wasn't exactly quiet about it. But of course, when your baby drinks blood from you instead of milk when you nurse it, it's hard to keep quiet about that among other humans, especially in a hospital. She managed to get out with her baby before they could attract the press, but one of the humans who worked for Lothos somehow learned about it anyway. Didn't take long for the shape-shifters to track her down, but by that time, Derek and Joe had been entrusted with the baby. Lothos sent one of his top thaumaturgists, and her circle of cronies."

"You know a lot about this," I said.

"That happens when the puppeteer not only takes you

over, but melds with you," Deb replied. I could feel a swelling, bitter hatred roiling in the back of her mind.

"I gather it wasn't a pleasant experience?" I asked.

"Not when the puppeteer is your sister."

I paused in my tracks.

"What's the hold up?" Deb said, noticing my momentary pause. "She's not going to kill herself . . . though it would make our job a lot easier."

"Yes, I know but . . ." I was unsure how to go on with what I needed to say. "But she was your sister? I know siblings being separated by clan isn't unheard of, but . . . I guess I have to know."

"Know what?" Deb was more than a little impatient, and this confused me even more.

"Well . . . are you okay with this? I mean, she's dead. She nearly killed me, but Wilson finished her off. I got rid of the remains. I just don't want you looking for retribution . . ."

Deb snorted and turned away, but beckoned me to come along without looking back. "I'm sure we have a good bit of distance to cover, so I'll explain it to you on the way" she said, "just so you know I won't kill you in your sleep or anything."

"Rebbie and I were runaways. Had a bad home life, blah, blah, blah . . . you know the sob story. Same as just about anyone you'll find who gets Lothos' attention. Only when we were turned, they found that Reb had a gift for reading minds, so she got special treatment while I got the shaft. I could read minds too, but nowhere near as well, and so they left me with the peons. Only when a stronger telepath spoke with me, or when thoughts were mixed with strong emotions, could I read them really well, and that wasn't good enough for the big dogs. So I was left with the mooks to climb the social ladder . . . for a little while, at least. Reb found me pretty soon afterwards, frazzled and shell shocked after some close calls with your clan on a few missions. They were culling the herd, of course, but each time, I was one of the few who made it back alive. After Reb found out what happened to me, she protected me, and all was well . . . for a time. Then her bosses found out what she was doing, and they punished her by sticking me in the special corps.

"'You want to rank up, then you'll do it here, or die trying,' they said. Then they put me under the thumb of some asshole who liked to torture us with UV light and live ammo during training runs . . . and sometimes just for fun. But when I got sick of it, his 'fun' cost him sixty-eight percent of his skin in third degree burns, as well as most of his internal organs. The stress of the training made my other gift awaken, and he got a permanent dirt nap out of it.

"I would've been executed for killing a superior officer, but my being a pyro saved my ass. By that time, I was sick of Lothos and his bullshit, and ran away. They tried to chase me down, but after I barbecued several members of the hunting party, I think they got too scared to send more after me. Later on, I found Syd and his clan. Derek and I had a fling not too long after, but it didn't last. I had a good thing going here, though, until Derek and Joe brought in the kid. Then I came face to face with Reb one night. Let's say it wasn't a fun reunion. She took over my mind before I could set off even one little spark. We were sisters, and so the control went deeper than either of us expected. She took on some of my personality, and I took on some of hers. It amplified some of my less endearing traits, hence my general bitchiness around you and, well . . . anyone.

"No one suspected anything because I was never the easiest to get along with. Also, I already was suspicious of you . . . and then jealous when I learned that you and Derek were shacking up. That made it worse. But through her, I learned that she was reporting to one of the higher-ups, and I saw who was working for her. I didn't get all their plans, but I knew that Reb didn't know about you, though she was suspicious. But she didn't think it was important enough to report it to her superior, who, by the way, had been following the clan as well. It was a pain in the ass when you started setting the traps, but being a thaumaturgist has its advantages, as you know. She let her cronies do the dirty work, and most of them were too stupid to realize that there was a mind-reader in our midst. It wasn't until you kicked Joe's ass out his front that Reb was able to put two and two together. That's when they went for the divide-and-conquer strategy. The leader had one of her underlings, another thaumaturgist, kidnap Joe. The plan was to put you out of commission, but then she underestimated you."

"She underestimated us," I corrected. "I guess there was bad blood between you and your sister?"

"'If you're not one of us, you're little people.' That's what they taught us in Lothos' happy family," Deb said. "Looks like Reb took it to heart. I tried to break free myself, but our bond was too deep, and she tortured me with it. She knew I loved that kid, and so she used it to her advantage. I wouldn't stop trying to break her hold until she promised that it didn't matter whether or not Lothos wanted the baby; she'd risk death to kill it if I tried to break free again. I told her she'd pay for that. I only wish it was me who made her pay. I can at least do this. So don't worry, kid. I'm not raw about it. You did me a favor, is what you did."

"You're bloody cold," I said after considering her chilling story.

"I never said I was an angel."

"Duly noted. So, do you still hate me?"

"I said I was jealous. I never really hated you. Reb just brought out that part of me and cranked it up to eleven. Yeah, I was pissed when Derek and I broke up, but that's ancient history now. And he's happier with you anyway."

"Well, at least you're talking to me now," I said.

Deb reluctantly let out a guffaw, and for the first time around her, I felt more relaxed. But our circumstances were not long in rearing their proverbial ugly head. We had made some headway through the thick underbrush of the woods when a chorus of mocking laughter seemed to rain from above us. I paused, and dipped into the well of my Jewel's power, my senses keen and alert.

"Well, so much for sneaking up on her," I heard Deb say.

"Oh, so was that the plan, little prey?" The voice had an accent similar to mine, but more flattened by American speech, where I'd stubbornly held onto my own. "You could have fooled me. Even your whispering was enough noise to wake the dead."

"Playtime's over, bitch!" Deb's words were so loud they left me momentarily shaken. "You don't have any more peons to do your dirty work, so why don't you face us yourself?"

"Deb!" I whispered harshly for all the good it did for our secrecy. "I don't think it's a good idea to piss her off." But I could feel her righteous anger burning as if it were true fire right next to me. Or was that the effects of her suppressing her gift? I decided to take no chances, and set up a psychic filter. Now, any destructive thoughts she would cast in my direction would not be enough to ignite me. Of course, by now, I knew my warnings had fallen on deaf ears, with Deb having a score to settle. Her challenge was returned with more of the fiend's disturbingly pleasant-sounding tittering.

"Oh? And will you be the one to punish me? Just what did I do to you? I thought all your grief was from your dear sister?"

"She's not here. But you are."

Deb was answered by even more of that mocking laughter.

"Well, this will be a sight, now won't it? A piece of defecting Vagabond scum and a pretentious member of Talante's weaklings picking a fight with me? I must say, you've got some exceptionally large nonexistent balls!"

I heard a sound like a thousand birds fluttering from one treetop to another. And the trail from the Jewel scattered into multiple points.

"Shit." I hissed, glancing back and forth.

"What?" Deb said. "What happened?"

"You shouldn't have provoked her," I said. "She's masked herself from me. I can't sense her, and she's doing something . . . big."

From the foliage, several forms emerged, twenty in all, though it was difficult to tell in such subdued light. But one thing was obvious: each of the figures was exactly, disturbingly, alike. They all wore some kind of form-fitting black burka, which made them nearly invisible, and all that could be seen of their faces were a set of sneering ashen lips directly below where their veils ended.

God, but this lot has a barmy sense of style, I thought on some insipid reflex at the sight of this small army. Adrenaline coursed through me with the expectation of a fight, creating a thousand pinpricks on my skin. At first, I thought we'd walked into an ambush until I realized that there was only one scent, though I could not tell from which of the figures it came. This meant that that they were all copies of the same thaumaturgist.

"Tell me, prey . . ." All of the fiends seem to pause and speak in unison. "How will you kill me when you don't even know which one is the real me?"

I saw the one closest to Deb lunge forward with preternatural speed. Deb stumbled to the ground, dazed, but not incapacitated. With the same speed as the thaumaturgist, she scrambled to her feet. She struck full-force at the black-clad figure's head, which tumbled, spinning, to the ground. It rolled to my feet and began laughing a nightmarish, maniacal cackle. All the clones echoed this laughter like some demonic chorus. The beheaded figure collapsed to the ground, the black of its burka flowing in the air like mist, then fading as if it were actually just as substantial. Even Deb had not expected this, and the other copies seemed to take advantage of her stunned state, lunging at her, and leaping into a fight that was blinding in its speed, but one that I could not see to its conclusion as the copies nearest to me pitched themselves my way.

I saw silvery claws glint in the scant moonlight below the canopy from their gloved fingers, but they met only air in their efforts to eviscerate me. I drew from my Jewel and enhanced my speed and strength as I had in my fight with Joe, catching one copy of the fiend by the ankle, and the other by the arm. Buoyed by my new strength, I slammed the one whose ankle I had in my grasp into a nearby tree, easily separating her head from her body while the other I pulled towards me, and with an uppercut, tore her lower jaw loose from the rest of her skull. Black ichor spilled from their grotesque wounds, and became smoke, along with the contents of both my hands. Still, the laughter persisted.

I ducked a swipe at my neck by another bladed set of claws, punched upwards, and broke the arm at the elbow, feeling the sickening crunch through my fingers, and then the melting away of flesh into smoke. A kick in the stomach winded me, and sent me careening into the trunk of another tree, but not before I grabbed the black fabric of the burka and willed it to become strong as steel cables, and shrink like it had been put through the wash on high heat. The clone laughed even as it was being crushed into pulp . . . and then faded into smoke.

I was winded, but not out of the fight. I leapt over two copies that lunged at me, cracking their skulls one against the other with explosive force -which became vapor in seconds. I happened to notice Deb in the midst of the fray holding her own, striking out with decapitating force against clones that closed the gap between themselves and her while other clones on the attack burst into flames before they could even touch her. But there seemed to be no end to the sea of copies as they came literally out of the woodwork. I had my Jewel increase my speed and strength, and they fell like matchsticks in a hurricane, but I knew that Deb didn't have such a luxury, and even the Jewels I had could be taxed to a limit. This fiend was several notches above the rest. She was whittling away at our strength, more and more, and there was no way I could detect the timbre of her mind with her Jewel jamming my telepathy. It was as if she was trying to shut down all subtle tactical approaches.

Then it hit me . . . as I hit the legs out from a would-be clone assailant and transformed her into yet another fading puddle of laughing gas. She was shutting down tactical moves! I knew what she was doing! It came to me in the midst of the fracas; she was using a technique called "shatter." I'd heard of it during my training with Aiko, but had never tried it myself. It was said to be incredibly taxing, though it provided tremendous advantage in battle by way of suppression. It divided your consciousness into multiple pieces for each clone you produced, and dramatically reduced the chances of you becoming a target yourself. It was pretty much a massive, short-lived "kitchen sink" strategy, intended for taking on large groups, though this opponent had found a way to make it last much longer than she ought to have. Perhaps, I figured, this was because of the small number of opponents she had to contend with.

I realized that I had to do what would otherwise be an extremely unwise thing. One of those clones had to be the real one, and the only way to take her out would be through the same strategy. It would be equivalent to a frontal attack. Punching into the spines of two clones that charged me, I sprang into the canopy. I heard the clones pursuing me, some leaping into the branches and giving chase, but with my Jewel, I kept well ahead of them. I swung and clawed my way from branch to branch, searching for the highest tree in the immediate area, until I found it, a massive pine tree nearly eight stories high. I frightened a group of roosting crows once I leapt on and clung to its highest bough, and created an air vacuum compression to force the pursuing clones back into the canopy. I watched from the swaying top as they struck thick branches and were reduced to splotches of mist. I then delved into my Jewel. Through it, I willed my vision to extend deeper into the EM spectrum. As I'd hoped, the bodies of the clones, the thaumaturgist, and Deb began to burn with the deep indescribable hues of infrared. Though I could tell which of the forms was Deb, as she was the one slowly losing ground to the ever-increasing horde, there was, however, no variation between the signatures of the clones or their creator. Only Deb, exerting herself to the limit, shone in brighter shades of the wordless color. I had to at least give grudging respect for the fiend's skill. She'd planned for even this tactic, cloaking her doppelgangers in a low-level infrared field matching a vampire's in order to throw off any other means of detection. But she didn't count on the fact that I wouldn't need to know which one was her. Her luck had run out.

I launched myself into the air yet again, careening over the tops of the trees, my concentration split between the images of the cackling clones and their twisted master, as well as Deb. I inhaled deeply, and reached as deep into my Jewel as I dared, bringing forth the shatter effect through sheer force of will. I would become a rain of death upon the thaumaturgist and her creations, and finish this fight.

It began . . . and I shattered. Even as I landed, buoyed by the energies of my Jewel, I felt as though I were floating in a sort of nirvana. I was above the forest, yet surrounded by it at the same time. I had a million eyes, and it seemed as if I were facing each and every clone present. I could see Deb, beaten and on the ground, but not deterred, her expression that of unparalleled shock. My body had a million parts, and each was a wound-up spring, ready to strike at each laughing clone with all of its Jewel-enhanced might.

The fight -or rather, fights- lasted barely a minute, for I believe the fiend had not expected this. Few of Lothos' brood ever expected my skill, and that was my ultimate advantage. I was deceptively a "little girl," and the enemy, if they lived, lived only to regret ever tangling with me. Joe knew this, and precious few others did. They didn't call me "witch" for nothing.

They couldn't touch me, and one by one they fell, limbs and heads flying and disintegrating into mist. But one fought back with the same speed. One burka-clad fiend defended herself with ferocious desperation. And the laughter was gone.

I broke the shatter effect, and all my concentration slammed into that moment, where I deflected her blows with strength that was unnatural even for my kind. She swiped at my face, but hit only air, and received my foot in her ribs for her troubles. She snarled, and flailed her fists out for my face. I snatched her wrists from failed punches and threw them back at her. Her mouth, the only thing visible beneath her concealing veil was a rictus, her fangs extended below almost white gums, creating a horrifying sight.

The shatter effect had taken its toll, I began to realize. I could feel my strength nearing its end. I believe the thaumaturgist sensed it. As the well ran dry and the energies of my Jewel began to fade, she grasped my wrists. I leaped forward and kicked her in the midsection, but the blow only landed with a fraction of the force I'd intended. She hissed like an adder rearing to strike, and fell forward, attempting to pin me down with her weight. Her hand grasped my face and forced my head to the side, exposing my neck. She began to laugh again: a cold, soft, mocking thing.

"All for naught, piddling child," I heard her whisper in my ear. I knew what she intended, and I thrashed with futile desperation. She didn't intend to just kill me. She wanted to feast on my blood: the ultimate humiliation before death.

"I wonder what you taste like?" She whispered with cold breath into my ear.

Those were her last words as she burst into flames.

I watched as searing heat radiated from her body and she leaped off of me, shrieking that nightmarish dying scream of our kind as flames consumed her. Flames usually take a long time to kill us, but as I scrambled back, thanking God that the psychic diffusion effect still worked, I saw Deb standing there, clothes torn, her arm outstretched, turning the flames higher, albeit slowly. I could sense her intent, and I knew that she was making this last intentionally. The hatred and malice burned just as the fiend, shrieking like a demon, did. I could have begged her to stop, but I knew it would be useless. Her intent had been clear even before we were ambushed. I knew what she wanted to do, and I didn't stop her. And yet she had saved my life, the same as Wilson. I just didn't want it to be like this. But I had no choice. I hated that creature as well, but not as much as Deb. She gave the order to make her life a living hell; she'd pursued the clan and had her minions pick them off one by one. Perhaps Derek would have done no different. I hoped better of him, but like Deb, he did not live under Father's rules. No doubt vagabonds did things differently. Even now, Wilson and the rest were procuring illicit blood from unwitting vessels - something we'd never do, except in the most dire of circumstances. But to them, it was merely Tuesday.

I felt tired all over. I was in no pain, but I was thoroughly exhausted. I just wanted this mission to be over, to be back at home in my village, in our Lair, where my coffin and bed awaited in my own quarters. I cradled my head in my hand as the screams of the thaumaturgist died away into hacking squeals, and then nothing. I let the dying flames' light lick behind my eyelids, and longed for Derek with me in more peaceful times.

"You okay, kid?" I heard Deb say.

"I'm not a 'kid,'" I retorted. Then I sighed. "Sorry. I shouldn't be snapping at the one who saved my life."

I opened my eyes to see the ashes of the fiend crumble into dust in a blackened pile. I noticed the glint of a Jewel and reached into the ashes to retrieve it. It was a piece of obsidian, blacker than the sunless abyss of a yawning cavern. I thought of making it into a trophy along with the Jewel from the other lesser thaumaturgist, but thought better of it. A cunning mind like hers would have certainly booby-trapped it. So I crushed it in my palm, feeling it crumble into black powder, just as the fiend's bones had.

"You think we got her before she could get in touch with Lothos?" I asked Deb. I led the way back to the caravan and she followed.

"I hope so," Deb said. "But the way she fought . . . I don't know. She was too cocky, too busy with us. But then again, she didn't have a long time between your killing Rebbie and us finding her."

"More like she found us," I said. "Well, I choose to be more cautiously optimistic. After all, if we did succeed, we oughtn't expect more disruptions on our trip."

"Not if she wasn't a favorite of Lothos," Deb said. "But if she was, we're in deep shit."

"Was she?" I asked. "Did you- I mean, did your sister know?"

Deb shook her head. "Very little is shared with peons. Privileged though she was, my sister was still one. She wouldn't have known. So it's anyone's guess. Sorry, ki- I mean Elisa. But I don't know if we're out of the woods yet."

"Damn . . . tonight's just getting better and better," I muttered, feeling my confidence waver somewhat. And this served only to add to my exhaustion.

Chapter Sixteen

In spite of how tired I was, I still had to sit through Deb's lengthy, more detailed retelling of her forced involvement in Lothos' machinations, since by the time we arrived back at the caravan, the news of what had transpired in the trailer at the rear was common knowledge. The blood from the officers had been procured and they were now resting in their vehicles to wake up none the wiser. Now we stood as a group listening to Deb spin the untold story.

"And what about the police that tried using us for target practice?" Randy asked after Deb had brought her story to a close.

"Yeah, and who wasted our blood supply?" Benjamin added. "Was it you . . . I mean, the puppeteer chick?"

"She kept control of me only because she was on standby, as far as I could tell," Deb explained. "When she made her move, it was to sabotage the blood supply, so in answer to your question, she's the one who made me do it. But it was another thaumaturgist in the know who'd been keeping an eye on us, and was able to get through Elisa's traps. He laid a false trail with Joe, who was just a . . . lucky accident, I guess. The police were supplied to the puppeteer after we broke camp. I don't know all the details, but their superiors were in Lothos' pockets, so they became deniable assets."

"Bastards," I heard Marie-Laure say behind me.

"She's telling the truth?" Wilson's eyes were fixed on me as he asked this, and both Deb and I knew what he implied. I laid a restraining hand on Deb's midsection as I felt the spike of her anger and outrage. I didn't blame her; I was just as angry with Wilson for this. She was not on trial; with the whole clan aware of my talents, my word had seemed to become better than any lie detector.

"That wasn't necessary," I said, watched as an awkward expression flashed across Wilson's face, and a felt a wash of his self-conscious embarrassment flash across his mind. "She ran most of this by me earlier, and killed the bitch that was responsible for your grief. If I thought she'd been lying then, I wouldn't have let her recount it now."

"All right, all right," Wadih spoke up before any others could join me in protest. I was glad of it; Wilson didn't need to be shamed any further. "If Elisa vouches for her, then I'm cool with it. Besides, they both managed to save our collective asses twice tonight. We owe them big."

He sighed just as deeply as I wanted to. The battle had taken a lot out of me, and we still had a bit of a way to go before we reached the rendezvous point. Even Wadih's normally keen eyes seemed somewhat bleary. Fortunately, Derek and I had factored in being waylaid into our plan's timetable. "Time to get back on the road, people. With any luck, this will be the last of Lothos we'll see until we get to where we're going."

I wished he hadn't said what he did. I don't generally believe in luck, but something in me was fearful he'd jinxed us by those hopeful words. We all began to depart for our respective RVs and vehicles, and I took advantage of the momentary chaos to take Marie-Laure to the side.

She was surprisingly less abrasive than she'd ever been before. And though I knew the story that Deb and I had shared had perhaps changed her demeanor, it still took me aback to hear gently spoken words from her.

"I, ah, owe you an apology, you know," she said before I could speak. She spoke with awkwardness that rivaled Wilson's reaction to my admonishment of a moment ago. "The boss was right to take you in. So what I'm trying to say is . . . I guess you're not bad juju after all."

With flattery added to my surprise at her sudden turn of humility, I smiled. "It's not a problem at all, love," I replied. "I'm not easily offended anyway. But if you don't mind, I do happen to have a favor to ask of you."

"This has to do with the thing Deb said about the cops' bosses, isn't it?"

I'd been about to say something, but then my words were stolen by her question. An amused guffaw escaped my lips. Marie-Laure was more perceptive than I thought. I nodded, and an eager smile spread across her face, the length of her fangs transforming it into something predatory. "I want something that will hang their superiors by their goolies. Can you do that?"

"Girl, it'll be the most fun I've had in weeks!" There was no hesitation from Marie-Laure. No sooner had I asked the question than she gave her enthusiastic reply. And her laugh was one of sinister glee, and infectious in spite of my fatigue.

"Just print me out the headlines when it breaks," I said as I felt the press of time and headed back to Derek's RV to join Wadih. "I know you probably have something big planned."

"Oh, do I ever," Marie-Laure answered. "It'll be like Christmas."

"Well, be as creative as you like, but no killing."

Marie-Laure pursed her lips. "Well, that takes out a little bit of my fun, but as you wish." Despite my restriction, I could practically feel her shiver with delight and anticipation on her way to her trailer, though she took a moment to call back to me, "I feel like I just scored red from a young Chippendale buck!"

"A bit more information than I needed," I muttered with rueful amusement, but I was nevertheless buoyed by her excitement. I personally couldn't wait to see what she had planned. In fact, I avoided looking into her mind in order to keep it a surprise. With preternatural speed, I hurried back to the RV, situated myself, and Wadih gave the signal to move out.

***

The rest of the journey was blissfully without incident.

The rendezvous point was an abandoned motel, nestled deep within a wooded portion of a tall hill. From the outside I knew it would look barely suitable for habitation: water damaged paneling, cobweb-clogged windows, greenery taking over the abandoned parking lot; even one of the rooftops appeared to be sagging. But this was all a ruse. I'd informed the clan beforehand of what it all would look like; nevertheless, as I expected, the complaints began about the buildings' dilapidated appearance . . . until I showed them the rooms. Understanding transformed their grousing into a magnificent chorus of stunned silence.

"It's . . . like a resort," Deb declared.

"Four-star at that," Randy added.

"It's designed to be misleading to humans, and, at least in the beginning, to Lothos' clan," I explained. "I guess his people found it useful sometimes, which is probably why it hasn't been razed to the ground yet."

I gathered the clan about the room's posh furnishings: king size bed, satellite flatscreen TV, and the crowning glory, which was a massive bathroom with a Jacuzzi-style tub inlaid into the floor, as well as a multi-headed shower alcove. The latter prompted Marie-Laure to declare that she'd died and gone to Heaven.

"You'll also find a fully-equipped laundromat adjacent to the office so we can wash our clothes," I explained. "I know some of you have been hurting for that luxury. There should be enough washers and dryers for everyone. Also, the windows to all the rooms are fitted with automatic sun shutters and concealed coffins below the beds in case of a daylight emergency. The rooms are also timed to reset -that means they self-clean- in three nights to prevent freeloaders, so we'll all need to be out before that time. But we all should be, if we follow the plan. We give Derek and Lyman two nights to rendezvous with us . . ."

I swallowed back the tinge of fear that threatened to

produce inconvenient tears. I would handle this on my own in due time. ". . . after that, we'll be on the road to the sanctuary, whether they're with us or not."

"Aren't you the least bit worried that some of Lothos' clan might come sniffing around while we're here?" Benjamin asked.

"It's not likely they will," I replied. "I linked my Jewel with the systems that runs this place when we arrived. No one has been here for about fifteen years. For all we know, Lothos may have even forgotten about this place. Besides, it's far enough off the beaten track for the chances of him finding us to be very slim."

"Yeah, that was the point you seemed to make before this trip," Benjamin said with a nod.

"It's what I hope for at least," I replied.

"But just to be on the safe side, why not just stick us in that blue place, like you did on the road?" He said after some thought. "Wouldn't that keep us completely safe?"

I had to shake my head. "That wasn't part of the plan for a reason. Derek and Lyman wouldn't be able to find us if I did that, and we wouldn't be able to see them. But once they arrive, I'll do it. Believe me, I'll feel safer as well, once we can."

We stepped back outside the room, and I doled out the keys that I'd retrieved from the desk in the office when we'd arrived. Only Marie-Laure refrained from making immediate use of her respective room. Her computers were difficult to move, and no doubt a nightmare to set up, and she was more comfortable with "cozy" spaces like her trailer anyway. But I knew that even she would not ignore the allure of such a luxurious bath. I felt her longing for it like the longing for blood that consumes us all.

There was a mixed blessing about the danger, stress, and fear of only a few hours ago, and that was the fact that it served to keep my mind off of Derek. Thoughts of him were a luxury I could ill afford at the time, but now that we had breathing space, he came back to my mind like the addiction to the most intense, seductive drug. I missed his presence in a way I never thought I could. And it hurt . . . God, how it hurt! I wanted his touch the most. The memory of those times that we lay simply wrapped in each other, in nearly full contact, our minds overlapping and flowing into each other, became a torment. Father once told me of this effect of a consummate bond. Our hearts and bodies ache for each other's presence, especially when our future is uncertain. And it was that uncertainty that I could not bear to face. I fought back the anguish and need for him that kept me awake in spite of how tired I was. I had planned to rest in my room alone, plotting a new route that might be less conspicuous in order to get my mind off of Derek, but my mind seemed to have other intentions. And soon after I'd dressed down and laid face down in my bed, someone else made their plans known as well.

I had not yet opened a single map, and was trying desperately not to think about Derek. I knew if I began to cry, I would not be able to stop, and I would dry out my tear ducts. Unlike humans, who don't easily run out of tears, we only have a limited supply due to our bodies' incredibly efficient waste processing, which delegates waste products from the blood we drink into our exhalations, sweat and tears. Once the tears run out, our bodies break a few blood vessels near our tear ducts to replace what is lost, making for a gruesome sight. I wanted to at least look presentable for when . . .

Don't do it, girl, I thought to myself, desperately scrambling for a reason to stop. You'll soil the sheets.

Don't you plan on doing that anyway when Derek comes back?

The intrusion on my thoughts startled me fully upright. The voice was faint and muffled, and the timbre of the mind was Deb's, but the suddenness of it, as well as the inappropriateness of the question, had nearly scared the life out of me. My eyes ached, and when my initial shock subsided, I was back at swallowing against the urge to cry.

Where the hell are you? I sent. Next door?

Oh, please. I may be less sensitive than you, but I learned a long time ago to stay as far away from the love nests of paramours as possible. I'm outside the door to your room.

Chagrined at the fact that I hadn't figured this out sooner, I went to the door and unlocked it. As ever she was, the baby was nestled in Deb's arms, sleeping soundly. Wrapped around her waist was a multicolored patchwork apron that contained an array of fresh-smelling baby supplies.

"She's been sleeping straight through the day lately; thank God," Deb said as I let her in. She ran a finger across the baby's puffy little cheek. "It's been such a relief. I can get a decent amount of sleep now instead of nodding off in the middle of the night. And I can finally set her in her crib while I wash my bedsheets. I know that alcove in my trailer must've looked like a murder scene to you."

"Well, it was a bit off-putting," I admitted, though I didn't want to say that she'd been spot-on in her analogy.

"Babies are going to be babies," Deb said, taking a seat in the chair at the desk beside the TV. "Even dhampirs can be messy eaters. And just like human babies, they spit up sometimes, blood as well as milk. I had to do most of the feedings in my bed after Derek put me under house arrest."

"Ah, so that explains it," I said, thinking back to that appalling sight.

"Well, anyway, it looks like you've gone and made yourself comfortable," Deb observed as I hoisted myself back up to the edge of the bed. I let my legs dangle as I sat. "He's right, by the way. You do look like a China doll."

Hit by a wave of self-consciousness, I tucked my legs underneath me, and Deb laughed. "I meant it as a compliment, you know," she said.

"I guess I'm just so used to Derek saying it."

"It's still a little early for PJs, by the way, isn't it?" Deb gestured to my over-large T-shirt. "It's still about three hours before sunrise."

"It's Derek's," I said. "It was actually a couple of sizes too big for him, so he let me have it. But tonight's the first night I've gotten to wear it."

"I figured they were pretty big for PJs," Deb said and laughed. It seemed that for the first time, I had seen her genuinely relaxed and happy.

"Well . . . we don't really wear PJs," I said, casting a sly look her way. In spite of my expression, I was aware of the flush that began to erupt on my skin's pearlescence.

Deb's eyes nearly bulged out of their sockets, partly due to my frankness, and -as expected- partly due to the thought of intimacy between Derek and me.

"It's not what you think." I shook my head to cut off that avenue from her thoughts. "We're still in our knickers . . . well, the bottom part, anyway."

"Oh, right!" Deb snapped the fingers on her free hand as a memory flitted through her mind, too brief to catch. "Maximum contact for maximum sensitivity."

"Exactly," I said with a grin.

"Derek and I did that a lot, but we never felt open enough with each other, even though we were totally naked. That's probably one of the reasons why it didn't last." She cracked a tiny, self-deprecating laugh, though I caught a ghost of self-consciousness from her mind. "I'm not jealous, though. That was . . . well . . . only anecdotal."

Her words, awkward though they were, made me feel tremendously relieved. For once tonight, my anguish had settled, and I couldn't have been gladder.

"Thank you," I said, and found my grin becoming bigger.

"For what?" Deb asked.

"For talking about Derek in a way that didn't leave me a complete mess," I said, realizing how completely out of left field my remark must have seemed to her. "I didn't think it could be done."

"Well, I felt you needed someone to talk to." Deb shrugged,

and then checked the baby's diaper with a vague sniff. I must have had a very odd look on my face at the time because Deb had to restrain herself from cackling loud enough to wake the baby. Truth be told, it was rather funny. Catching my puzzled look at her actions, she explained. "Sorry; force of habit. Runaway commune I lived at when I was human had a lot of babies."

"And you used to take care of them?" I asked.

"For pretty good reason," Deb replied. "For most of us who couldn't find work, there wasn't much else to do when we weren't scrounging for loose change or taking our chances with the cops and stealing, except fight, do drugs, or fuck each other's brains out. So, there were a lot of unplanned pregnancies, and babies whose moms were too blasted on whatever they could get their hands on to take good care of them. I never did drugs; I had too much self-respect for that. And as for sex . . . let's just say there are a few guys out there who are about an inch shorter because they didn't understand that 'no' means 'no.'"

"They couldn't have all been that bad," I said.

Deb frowned. "They weren't. But trust me, you didn't want to be sneezed on by some of those guys with the stuff they had, let alone go for a sausage ride in some nasty corner with them. So I was usually sober and alone, and I was pretty handy with a knife to keep away the scumbags. So guess who became the unofficial nanny?"

"Had you always been good with kids?" I asked after the momentary surprise at her effusiveness had passed.

"More or less." Deb reclined in her chair, using the nearby ottoman from the chair beside the lamp table. "God, it feels so good to be out of that trailer! I'd have had cut my own head off just to have stopped Rebbie's nagging laugh when she made me burn Joe."

"I think you surprised the whole clan with that spot of information," I remarked. "I can only imagine the hell she put you through."

No sooner than those words had left my lips, I felt a sharp sense of discomfort and reluctance from Deb. "Don't worry; I won't ask you about it," I quickly assured her.

Deb seemed to relax at this. "Sorry; I know you felt me get a little uptight with what you just said. That time just isn't something I want to think about right now."

"It's my fault," I said. "I took the conversation in a dark direction."

"I said not to worry about it." Deb made a dismissive gesture and smiled. "It's in the past now, anyway. And as long as the baby made it through our current shitstorm okay, I'm happy."

"You really love that little munchkin, don't you?"

"She doesn't have anyone." Deb smiled beatifically at the infant's slumbering face. She'd placed a pacifier into her mouth, and she worked on it with gusto. "I kept hoping that Joe would've warmed up to her but it doesn't look like that's ever gonna happen. So where does that leave us? With the way I've been because of . . . well, you know . . . it makes me wonder if Derek will still think she's safe with me."

"Remember, he can read minds too," I said. "He'll be able to tell, just as well as I can, that you've taken good care of her and would never hurt her."

"I hope so," Deb replied, but did not sound terribly convinced. "Plus I hope he'll at least let me, or someone, think of a name for her. It's so impersonal just calling her 'the baby,' you know?"

"I guess that really does mean you've given up on Joe ever gaining some kind of affection for her," I said.

"He's a lost cause." Deb said flatly. She made her thoughts on the issue clear with a loud, derisive snort. "Until that night when he came pounding on my door, he didn't seem to give even part of a crap about her. So it's pretty safe to say that I'm not holding out much hope for him. But Derek hasn't been in any kind of a hurry to pick out any names."

"He's got a lot on his plate right now," I reminded her.

"I know. Maybe he'll cross that bridge once we're all safe."

"Maybe," I said. "What would you name her?"

"Rhonda," Deb said without skipping a beat.

"Why 'Rhonda'?" I asked.

"It means 'noisy,'" Deb explained. "And yes, I know you hardly hear a peep from her; its translation is closer to 'trouble.'"

"Yes, that does seem to suit her," I smiled. "And yet, look at her. Through it all . . . not a care in the world."

"Yeah, we'll have a pretty big story to tell her when she's old enough," Deb said, adjusting the infant's soft pink blanket.

"You know, if you meet a human, you might be able to have a baby of your own," I said, becoming aware of Deb's longing wistfulness. "It's not easy, but with enough time-"

"Humans are too much trouble," she said. "We don't have many rules here, but one is that if you bring a human on board, he or she gets turned. Or you leave."

"You wouldn't have to do that in my clan," I said. "Romantic relationships with humans are somewhat rare; marriages are even rarer, but they happen. And no one is thrown out because of it. And if you're lucky, you can have a baby of your . . . Oh, dear."

The memory had surfaced with no warning; I doubt even Deb knew that my words would have triggered it so quickly. She struck it down with an inner fury that momentarily frightened me, until I realized that those emotions were not aimed at me. Gingerly, she placed her hand across the bridge of her nose. Though I knew that she tried to keep it from me, I did notice the glint of a tear.

"It's okay," she said in a choked voice. "Really; I'm over it. More ancient history, that's all."

But I had to pursue this, even just a bit, after what I saw.

"Still, I thought you said that you-"

"-that I'd never been with any of the other runaways?"

Deb sniffled wetly. "Yeah. That is true. But there was this one guy I met when I was digging through the trash. He wasn't one of us. He and his folks ran a restaurant. That's how he discovered me; it was their trash I was digging through. So he started slipping me food every day. We'd meet in the park and talk after that. I didn't have plans to stay in the place I was, and he had big dreams of his own. It was all kids' stuff, really. Still, he managed to find me and my sister a place to stay in an air-conditioned storage unit for a time. That was like heaven. I guess we got a little too close; one thing led to another, and all that. But we were both happy about it. Then Lothos and his clan found me and Rebbie. Of course, they knew I was pregnant when I only suspected I was; I didn't know vampires could smell that kind of thing. Would've been nice of them to let me know what I was in for, but of course, we're talking about the damn shape-shifters. So they conveniently left out the fact that being turned automatically causes you to miscarry. You think being turned is painful? I had it worse. Not only the pain of expelling it, but the anguish that I endured after it."

Suddenly, as if the whole thing had been little else than some twisted joke, she began to laugh. It was not loud, but rather soft and utterly devoid of humor.

"And they thought it was a joke, the bastards; did you know that? You should have seen how they laughed!"

"It was to break you," I said. "That's how they do it. And they're damn good at their work."

"Didn't work with me, though," Deb remarked, and her laughing fit quickly dried up. "No, I played their game for awhile, then beat it." She rubbed at one eye and sniffled again. "Yeah, just got the hell outta there, and never looked back. But I gotta ask, Elisa. Did you mean what you said about me being able to have kids?"

"If that's what you want," I said. "Some relationships with humans do result in children. But again, it's rare. Even if you're lucky to find love with a human, actually trying to have a baby . . . it's an endurance run for the human. It takes months, sometimes over a year, to conceive, and the couple must try every night, sometimes multiple times a night. Humans just don't have our stamina in bed. I've even heard of a few deaths that resulted from couples trying. And you don't want to have your host die on you. That's an anguish that is nearly crippling. Some of our kind have begged for death afterwards."

"That I know," Deb said. "I've seen it before. That kind of stuff isn't unheard of with the shape-shifters. Once, I saw a fellow grunt get torn away from this human girl. No one knew he'd been seeing her on the sly. She was part of the cattle stocks, and someone wanted her on the menu. What happened after that . . . Well, let's just say there were a lot of new openings in our department after they managed to put him down."

"Are you sure you're all right?" I asked, not fully convinced of her calm demeanor, especially after such a grisly tale. "You went to some dark places just now. I know what that's like."

"We all do it from time to time," Deb said. "You've got your share of them, I'll bet. How old did you say you were, by the way?"

"One hundred seventy-three."

"Then you've definitely got your share," Deb said. And of course, she was right. Derek and I had gone to our worst ones only a few nights ago, but came through stronger for it, and with a deeper connection. I could only nod without saying anything, and she understood.

"Still, it helps to get this stuff out in the open, I guess," Deb said. "And it feels good to be able to share it with another girl. This place has been a sausage fest for too long since Derek ordered the rest of our clan into hiding."

"What about Marie-Laure?"

Deb fixed me with one of those subtle, "you-have-got-to-be-kidding-me" looks.

"No offense, but her best friend is an iMac Pro," she said. "And even when we were 'fully staffed,' I wasn't exactly the kind of person who had lots of friends. I kept people at arms' length, and was pretty insular."

"Not quite a party girl, I'd wager?"

"Hardly. And people talk. So that's why most of the others stayed away from me. That speech I gave after all the static on the road was probably the most I've said to anyone in the entire time I ran with this clan. Only Derek really knew me. That's why the baby ended up in my care. Most of the others thought he was nuts, but I was thankful for the task. I was pretty lonely."

"You did seem to be a bit more personable than I'd expected," I said. "And really, I'm thankful for that. I've been needing a little 'girl talk' myself."

I believe I had not yet seen Deb smile so broadly and genuinely until now. And though she said nothing about it, I believe I felt her begin to seriously consider what I had to offer in my clan.

"Well, taking care of this little drain on my O-negative, I'd say that I'm glad for the company," she said, rocking the baby gently. "But what about you? How are you holding up?"

"I've been bouncing back and forth from indomitable confidence to abject terror," I said, deciding to throw away all pretense of false bravado. "We knew this was a trap from the beginning, and we walked right into it. There's just no way to know whether Derek, Lyman, or Joe came through it like we did, or if something happened. And if he doesn't show up by tomorrow night, we'll probably never know." I inhaled a ragged breath, and swallowed back the tears that once again threatened to pour. "I really hate this, all the waiting and anguish. And I know that it's because we're consummate hosts to each other-"

"Wait. Consummate hosts?" Deb asked, cutting me off. "What's that?"

It was easy to forget that there are some of our kind who

have never known that kind of a joy, and so I paused to explain the consummate bond to Deb.

"Shit . . ." Her eyes were large white and crimson orbs after I was done. "So you're like . . . addicted to each other? Like how a human gets addicted to us if we feed from them one too many times?"

"Something like that, yes," I said. "But when love is involved, it becomes even more of a torment. You want them so badly, and they want you too. After a point, your host becomes all you can think about and vice versa. And when we feed . . ."

"Yeah, you explained that one already." I saw her body give a vague shudder. "And you two have never . . . ?"

I shook my head.

Deb shrugged after a moment of consideration. "Maybe he's afraid of hurting you," she said.

"It goes deeper than that," I said, "but I don't think he'd like me sharing it with everyone else."

"Don't worry; I wasn't going to ask. But I wish I could fully understand what you're going through, girl. And I wish that I could tell you more than not to worry, and that he'll be back soon."

"I hope so," I said, my voice soft and distant. "I really do."

Deb entertained me for about an hour and a half more, though the majority of our time was spent watching movies on the TV. She allowed me to hold the baby, but when she woke up and tried to nurse from me, I quickly handed her back. She didn't hurt me, but of course I did not have nearly as much blood to give as Deb. She assured me that she was going to start the baby off on formula soon in order to acclimate her to human foods as soon as we arrived at the sanctuary. Admittedly, I felt more normal with her around, and it was relieving to have another female to talk to. I was glad that most people's impressions of Deb had been mistaken. She had a hard life, and so I did not fault her for her behavior towards the outside world.

She left about an hour and a half before sunrise, and only because we heard the beginnings of a storm outside. We parted ways, and I hoped that we would have more of an opportunity to talk soon, both tomorrow night, and after the clan was brought to safety.

Again, I was alone with my thoughts, and my fear for Derek.

I sat in the bed with my knees curled up to my chest, not so much watching TV as staring at the pictures, colors, and light while my emotions gnawed at me. At some point, even that gnawing began to remind me of the tiny, exquisite bites that Derek would make on my earlobe, arms, and stomach as we fed. Each time it happened, I shook those memories away, but as certain as the next commercial, they returned.

The clock on the far wall above the TV counted down the minutes until sunrise would bring the blessed lethargy that would cause me to slip into the healing oblivion of slumber.

At last, with nothing left to do, I went into the bathroom and drew a bath in the massive tub. I'd cleaned my body off with my Jewel after the fights and repaired the rips and tears in my clothes, but nothing could quite compare to a nice, warm soak. Perhaps that would relieve me of some of this torment, but I doubted it. As close as it was to sunrise, I was slightly worried that I would fall asleep in the water. That would be an unpleasant way to wake up, but I was not in any mental state to care. I removed the over-size shirt, donned a bath towel, and waited as I watched the water filling the tub, staring at the flow from the faucet to the basin with the same passiveness that I watched the nondescript images on the TV. It was almost hypnotic. I felt myself slipping into an almost-trance where I would forever seek out Derek, and he would forever slip away.

Then my mind locked onto him. I gasped with the suddenness of it, and at first I thought that I was losing my mind, but then I realized that I was awake and alert. The presence was solid and so very, blessedly real.

He was alive!

He was here!

At first, I nearly staggered to my knees with joy. Then I ran with preternatural speed, nearly crashing through the door, nearly ripping all the locks from their moorings . . . and nearly damaging the wall as I threw the door open to bring my dream to life.

Chapter Seventeen

Derek!

My heart shouted the name before I spoke it. I knew his scent before I even opened the door, and I was drawn to him like the planets are drawn to the sun, with a force that I could not resist if I'd wanted to.

I fell into his arms as he stood before me across the threshold. Derek collapsed to his knees, and our fingers touched . . . then our lips. My senses were inundated by his scent and the timbre of his mind, easing my fears and anguish into a forgotten memory. I felt the same happen to him as he ran his fingers through my hair, heard him inhale my own scent, and heard his quaking breaths calm down to a steady rhythm. Perhaps I would have been embarrassed by how much this resembled some scene in a cheesy romance novel or movie, but I was long past self-consciousness.

Elisa . . . His mind whispered to me with love that poured out with the very thought. At last . . .

It's all right, love. You're back. I'm here. We survived. We're all right.

Then he released me, to look me in the eyes.

God, his eyes . . .

His eyes were that of someone older by far more than merely three decades. They were so very sad, and wreathed with so much pain. Like refuse on the tide, I felt his memories wash into the fringes of my mind. I knew what happened before he even said it.

"They're dead, China doll," he quavered. "Lyman . . . Joe . . . they're gone. Oh, God . . . Gone . . . gone . . ."

His voice cracked as he repeated the word over and over, his sorrow and anguish growing each time he said it. His thoughts played back a horrifying scenario at lightning speed, and his eyes flowed over with tears as if he had been holding back a deluge for months. I felt the tremble of his body as he leaned into me and loosed the pain that struck me like a thousand knife points.

"Derek . . ." I gently loosened his grip upon me. "Derek, please, let's talk about it inside."

I slipped out of his arms as gingerly as I dared. Giving him reassuring thoughts, I encouraged him to his feet, and for the first time, took a clear look at him. He was covered with dirt and leaves and his clothes were torn, filthy, and charred, as if he'd been rolling around in hot coals, rocks, and mud. His eyes were the eyes of one nearing blood starvation, bleary and unfocused, with the red of his irises beginning to intrude upon the cornea. I would get him part of his ration as quickly as possible, but first, he would need a bath.

I winced with the pain of his roiling memories as I held his hand. Just touching him was almost like the wail of feedback from a microphone too close to the speaker. The news of the loss of Lyman cut a grievous wound within me and brought forth a myriad of questions that I longed to ask, but I refrained for the sake of Derek's current state. Had he merely been consigned to his own overdue mortality and just given up? Had he fought like a lion, with Derek on one side, and Grace on the other in order to save Joe's life? Had one of the Others just gotten lucky? Nevertheless, I refused to pester Derek. For now, he needed to simply be with me.

He was listless, almost zombie-like as I led him to the bathroom. I sat him at the edge of the walkway that led into the tub, and began to disrobe him.

"Shower . . ." I heard him whisper.

"You'd prefer to use the shower stall?" I asked superfluously. I'd heard him clearly in spite of the lowness of his voice. He nodded, and I felt a twinge of disappointment from out of nowhere.

I opened the door to the shower stall and let the water run and heat itself to a steaming warmth before I returned to Derek. He hadn't moved at all, only sat in contemplative silence at the edge of the tub, still in that paralyzing pain.

I set to continue my task of removing his clothing. Before I started the shower, I'd only taken off his shoes and used my Jewel to destabilize the molecular bonds of all the dirt, mud, and grime they had accrued. I continued to do the same with his shirt, pants, and socks. The damage to them I would deal with later. Through it all, Derek was quietly cooperative, but his heart was an open and still bleeding wound that I longed to heal. His mind had fortunately not been damaged; this I was relieved to discover, but he had certainly been through a horrific ordeal: one that claimed the lives of both his closest friend and someone very dear to me.

"I know how you feel, love." I reached out and touched his face, and his eyes listlessly focused on me. "I see your mind. I feel your pain. And we will talk about it soon. But for now, take a shower. Rid yourself of the physical stains, and then we'll work on the spiritual ones afterwards. You'll feel better afterwards. I promise."

Derek made a barely perceptible nod as he took hold of my hand . . . and I couldn't believe it.

To my unexpected surprise, his pain had actually lessened. It was certainly still there, but now it had diminished to a sort of background noise, if it could be called such a thing. As for how it had happened so quickly, I had no idea. And to even further add to my relief, I saw him smile.

"China doll . . ." he whispered as he leaned forward. His forehead touched my own, and I closed my eyes, feeling his nose gently touch mine. I felt his intent, and tilted my head to softly kiss his lips. I was struck at that moment by an unreasonable fear, since he had, of course, readily kissed me at the door, but as I had been during our very first kiss, I was struck with the fear that he would not reciprocate. But Derek completely erased those fears in seconds, and I felt his love, no less potent, and buoyed by a renewed passion that rose up from the miasma of pain.

My China doll . . . his heart echoed faintly to me.

My Derek . . .

I took hold of his love in our bond and let it soothe our aching hearts as the kiss lasted. In those sweet moments before our lips parted, I felt Derek caress my cheek, and I reached out to feel every contour of his face. Even with his very real presence, I almost supposed that a part of me still had not been completely convinced that he was truly there, and that my longing had produced some kind of fever dream.

Our lips parted only once, and need drove us to the kiss again. I shuddered at the scent of his enticing blood, my mind swimming and threatening to be distracted from the task at hand. And so reluctantly, I brought our sublime moment to an end.

"You don't want the water to get cold," I whispered.

Derek gave only the faintest hint of a smile. He ran his hand through my curls one last time and caressed the back of my neck before he stood up. He made his way without guidance to the shower stall. I turned around as I saw him slip his thumb into the waistband of his briefs to remove them. Under normal circumstances, I believe I would have perhaps peeked, as I'd never before seen him unclothed, but despite our moment, such a thing right now seemed somewhat inappropriate. Of course, as I slipped off my towel and climbed into the tub, I further contemplated on just how inappropriate such a thing would be. Derek was clearly hurting. He'd been through perhaps a worse ordeal than I had.

The bath was nothing short of heaven, and I realized just how badly I missed this luxury once the hot water flowed over my skin. Our muscles might not become sore, but this was one of the most exquisitely relaxing things I'd experienced in several nights. Distantly I heard the rumbling thunder of the approaching storm, and the thrill of expectation this produced a nice contrast to the soothing bath, pushing the adventure of tonight and Derek's sad news to a distant part of my memory.

I heard very little movement in the shower stall, save for

the rush of water. Of course, there was also Derek's ever-comforting scent, which gained a sort of headiness through the thickening fog and condensation. All else was calm for the moment, and though I was still worried for him, I was nevertheless glad for this brief interlude.

I suddenly sat upright, remembering that he needed to eat. Fortunately, I had brought our ration of blood packs into the refrigerator in the main bedroom. I drew upon my Jewel and summoned a single pack from the refrigerator into my hand, and then plopped it into the heated water of the tub, feeling it settle down beside the alcove where I sat. Considering how recently it had been procured, I knew it would have far more flavor than our usual fare, and would be as warm as if it were from a fresh source. I closed my eyes and tried to further enjoy my bath.

That enjoyment came to a swift end when I heard a loud thump coming from the shower stall. Nearly spilling the perfumed soap I had been indulging myself with, I turned to see Derek's blurred image behind the door's frosted glass, slumped down in a kneeling position. Before I could wonder what had happened, I felt the pain surging from him anew, as if he had never calmed down and I'd just thrown him callously into the shower.

Without bothering to dry myself off or don a towel, I scurried out of the tub.

"Derek!" I exclaimed as I threw open the door. I squinted against the spray of the water from the shower heads. "Are you okay?"

He knelt there, hunched over, the water pouring languidly over his body and hair, which hung like limp strands of ink over his face. He was trembling, though the water was extremely hot. His thoughts were as much a jumble as the droplets of heated water that were scattered about. I reached over to the controls and shut the water off as he spoke.

"I'm sorry, China doll . . ." His whisper was so low as to be almost subvocal. "I try not to think about it . . . but it won't stop. It hurts. It hurts so much!"

"Derek . . ." I whispered back. I slipped into the stall, closing the door behind me and knelt beside him. "Oh, Derek . . ."

I laid my hand on his shoulder in spite of the bite of renewed sadness and raw, throbbing pain, all fueled by his flashes of horrifying memory: faces of the enemy, flames, a dark room, amorphous shapes, laughter that seemed even darker and more sinister than that of the thaumaturgist Deb and I had bested. His emotions made my senses interpret it as like hugging a cactus, but I bared my teeth and endured the pain. I was his bonded mate, and he was mine. I would soon be his wife. And he needed me.

As before, when I had prepared him for the shower, I felt the pain begin to ebb away as darkness receding from daylight. And it was then that I came to understand something about our bond that I hadn't realized until now. It was me. My connection with him, my direct connection, was what stopped the pain. His heart touched mine and entwined as solidly as mine did to his. Our hearts supported each other.

"I should never have left you in that stall alone," I said, embracing him as far across his back as my arms would allow. I pressed my head upon his shoulder blade. Slowly, I felt his tremors fade, heard his heartbeat slow down to a normal cadence, and heard his breathing become regular.

"Let me help you, love," I said. "I'll do the work for you. I'll finish bathing you, and when we're done, you can tell me everything."

"I'd . . . rather start telling you now," Derek said.

I turned the water back on and reached for the soap and a towel. I found, instead, a bottle of body wash, and I began to apply it first to his arm. After we were done, I would rinse and dry him off, and he would rest in the bed.

"I should have let you do this first," I said, regretting my rush to get him cleaned. "I thought it would make you feel better."

"No, you were right," Derek protested. "I needed this. I thought it would make me feel better as well."

"But I should have known just how connected we were. I should have stayed by your side since you stepped through that door."

"And would you still have done what you're doing now?" Derek asked. He flashed a tired, but vaguely amused smile. "Both of us naked, you bathing me?"

I felt a small amount of embarrassment from his words, but not as much as I thought I would. Still, I was certain I'd turned quite an interesting shade of red, sensing the flicker of amusement in Derek's mind.

"Well, I'm glad you still have your sense of humor," I said, working the towel over his shoulders and back, "though it seems to have taken a turn for the cheeky."

"Contact with you makes me feel better," Derek said. "I can even laugh again . . . at least a little."

"It makes me feel better too," I confessed, both glad and relieved that he was more talkative. "We support each other, it seems. I ought to have kept you with me in the tub, but . . . well . . . I was . . ." I flustered at my flustering, and for a brief second, felt like I wanted to fall into the drain with the used water. I'd never been shy or self-conscious around Derek before, and it was a most consternating thing. Even more so was the ripple of amusement that I once again felt from him. But when I cast a glare at him, he could only smile serenely at me.

"You were nervous," he said, "the same way I would have been. But here we are. It looks like we've come a long way, if you ask me."

"Are you really happy about that?"

The question was superfluous, of course. This close in contact, we were like two transparent panes of glass, and our emotions flowed so strongly through each other that I could not tell where mine ended and his began.

He took a gentle yet firm hold of my wrist with his right

hand as I passed the towel across his chest, and with his left hand, he touched my chin. It was a soft and gentle thing, this touch. With his thumb, he caressed my bottom lip as he looked at me with eyes that were more tired than sad. Again, there was that ghost of a smile that played at the edges of his pale lips.

"Yes, I am," he said. "You've tried to hide it. I have too, but I know we've been wanting to see more of each other . . . if you know what I mean."

"We practically do already," I said, but in truth, I knew we had been averting our eyes where it counted.

"Yes, but we've never been comfortable about this much . . . exposure before. Not you, and especially not me."

I kissed his palm as I was wont to do before we fed, but I restrained myself. The scent of his blood was not quite enticing me as of yet.

"I'm happy too," I admitted as the water poured over us and washed off the soap I'd applied. I nuzzled his arm as my hands went back to the business of washing him.

"You know, you've been awful quiet about telling me what happened," I said after some time had passed. I had nearly finished the end of my labors, washing where I could, and allowing Derek to finish where I could not yet bring myself to venture. I knew that he had been stalling for time, that he was not yet ready to tell his story. But I had no desire to rush him. Instead, I relied on my presence to heal the wounds in his heart and let things happen as they would.

"I know," Derek said after another longish pause. He sighed as I finished rinsing out his newly-washed hair and helped him to his feet. I had finished washing him, and had begun using the body wash on myself, as I had never finished my bath. To my surprise, he moved the towel out of my hand and began to apply the wash to me. A sigh of delight escaped my lips, to my initial surprise. Thus far I had only been feeling this vicariously through Derek. I, in fact, had no idea how sensual an activity like this could be. Perhaps I was now picking up too strongly on a part of Derek's feelings, but the longer he remained at the task, the more distracted I became. And Derek was becoming equally affected by this distraction as well.

"I guess I just need to prepare myself. Maybe I wasn't as ready as I thought."

"Then I'll tell you what," I said as the motions of the towel on my back nearly put me in a dream state. "I'll tell you what happened to us, and then you tell me your story."

"Just answer me this first. Did everyone come through safely on your end?"

I nodded.

"Then yours is a happier tale than mine," he murmured, and I felt another shard of melancholy sour the current mood. "At least that's a plus."

"I wouldn't be so sure about that," I said before I began my tale.

My ordeal with the bulk of the clan was harrowing and grim enough to bring about his undivided attention. When I turned around to face Derek as he washed me, I noticed for the first time that light had returned to his eyes. Our closeness was definitely healing us, Derek especially. The longer we were together, and in such intimate contact, it kept the melancholy in his heart from becoming crippling.

I paused to run the shower water over my head to prepare it for the shampoo that Derek had retrieved, then continued my story as he lathered it in, and perhaps indulged himself for a bit too long.

The sobriety of my tale washed away all distraction as we finished our shower. I was unsure of whether it was due to how captivating my story was, or if he simply enjoyed the activity of us washing each other -most likely, it was a little bit of both-, but he allowed me to dry him and I let him return the favor after we stepped out of the shower stall. Through it all, I spoke on. I told him about the police controlled by the puppeteer who had held Deb in her thrall since perhaps the start of their adventure with the baby; I recounted my near-brush with death after the defeated puppeteer's surprise attack, then my fight with the wily master thaumaturgist with Deb at my side, then shared what we had learned from her experience in the aftermath.

"Seems I was both right and wrong about Deb," Derek concluded after my tale was done. We were seated at the edge of bed now; I had left a spare set of clothes for us both in the main room, but for the time being, we remained wrapped in our bath towels, which I had to admit were quite a bit more comfortable than I had expected.

"I think you still owe her an apology for the house arrest," I said, leaning into Derek's side. I wrapped my arms around his arm, resting my cheek upon his shoulder, maintaining the contact we both seemed to need.

"Oh, I never said I wouldn't." Derek said. I suppressed a giggle at the flutter of mild frustration he felt when he tried to run his fingers through my drying curls, but was thwarted by the towel I'd wrapped about my head. "But after all you've told me . . . it just makes things even more unnerving. I mean, damn . . . I can't believe we were being followed all that time! If I hadn't been too chicken-shit to have used my Jewel, I could've better protected them all. I could've saved us a lot of heartache . . ."

". . . or you could be dead," I retorted. "Remember, she was a master thaumaturgist. Even she got the better of me in the end. If Deb hadn't been there-"

"Please don't."

Derek's anguish surfaced anew, if only briefly, and I apologized.

"There's nothing for you to be sorry for, China doll." Derek gave a shallow sigh. I felt his finger caress my cheek, and a flash of almost manic possessiveness skipped across our bond. "I just don't even want to contemplate that thought. I'm only glad it didn't happen."

"I'm only putting things into perspective for you," I said. "How much Jewel training did you receive when you were still in Lothos' clan?"

"Some . . ." his words came out sounding awkward. Indeed, that word itself was an understatement. In fact, immediately after his reply came a feeling of resigned defeat. ". . . but not enough. I can only pull a few tricks, and maybe enhance my mental talent here and there, but that's about it." He drew one knee up and leaned forward. His voice became distant as he passed into yet another pall of melancholy. "That was probably the reason why I failed."

"Failed?" I asked as unobtrusively as I dared.

"The whole thing might have gone down differently if I hadn't been so pissed about the whole kidnapping situation, or so gung-ho to find out whomever it was that fubar'd our plans. I would probably even have listened to Paws."

"Wait. You didn't listen to him?" I didn't understand this. Even worse, the ramifications of this had set me ill at ease. Lyman, though having had little experience with Jewels, was a master tracker. He'd even possessed some talent in tracking Jewel energies. Failing to heed his suggestions was rarely a good idea. "Why? Did he say something wrong?"

"I told him that the trail seemed much stronger than it probably should have been," Derek said. "When we started out on it, it was weak, just as you said it would be, but further along, about ten miles out, it became stronger. Paws said this meant that someone had been reinforcing the signature on purpose. I know I should've taken that as a warning to be more wary about it being a trap, but anger and zeal can be a bad combo."

He ran his fingers down my arm, leaving a trail of goosebumps down to my hand, which he slipped into his own gentle grip. "And I had unfinished business, of course. I might have not been focused; I might have been too eager to return; I don't know. I'm too upset to care now."

"How did Lyman take it when you chose not to listen to

him?" I asked.

"He wasn't happy about it. Hell, even Grace growled at me a little. Those two were so connected, it was scary sometimes. But in the end, all he said was, 'you're the boss.' Even though I didn't have anything remotely resembling a plan. And then, our prey turned the tables on us."

Before I could ask, an image of the truck being violently toppled down a ravine exploded into my mind. I gasped and dug my claws into Derek's arm so forcefully that it was only when Derek shouted in pain, and the sensation rebounded across our mental bond that I realized what I had done.

"I'm so sorry!" I squealed when I saw the wounds. I jerked my claws back from their purchase, and took Derek's arm gingerly into my hands. To his initial surprise and subsequent delight, I took a moment to lick the blood away from the swiftly-healing wounds. My toxins gave a pleasurable interlude to what would most likely become a dark tale.

"Well, that was probably the nicest apology anyone ever gave me," Derek breathed as his euphoria settled. I giggled at the wide, Cheshire cat grin on his face.

"It only served to interrupt your story," I said. I wrapped myself around his now-healed arm once again.

"Hey, you didn't hear me complaining," Derek protested. "But I guess you're right. I let you stall me on purpose. It's not a pleasant tale."

"Neither was mine, if you recall," I said.

"Yeah, but when you told me your story, you had my undivided attention."

Well, you'll have no more distractions from me, love," I said. "I promise."

It was astounding how much my presence and my touch put him at ease, even after having lost a valued comrade and one of my closest friends. I certainly hurt for his losses, Lyman specifically, and had a time of distracting my own mind from the encroaching wall of grief. Now, there was no doubt in my mind that Derek and I drew our strength from each other in those moments.

"You saw the memory. Someone tossed our vehicle into a nearby ravine. Neither Lyman nor myself could figure out how it happened, but we were soon to have a pretty good idea. Besides, I'm sure that whoever did it didn't intend to kill us. That would come later. Rather, they probably meant to throw us off our game. And it worked, it seemed, because once we got our bearings and retrieved Grace -who somehow managed to bounce back from being thrown out the back of the truck without a scratch-, I realized that the trail had gone cold. Grace picked up the slack, though. She caught on to a scent that even we couldn't detect. We knew it had to be from Lothos' clan, the way it set her off.

"We followed her some distance through an overgrown pasture until we caught the scent again. Paws stopped Grace before she could attack, and we hid ourselves. It looked like the vampire we spotted was all alone, and he was standing about a quarter mile outside of an abandoned building in the distance. Paws and I closed in, flanking him, but Grace took the direct approach. Paws stopped her from eviscerating him long enough to get some info. The guy was a giggling idiot, probably one of the crazies that Lothos sometimes finds and picks up for cannon fodder. Interrogating him wasn't much effort; he basically sang like a bird, letting us know that his boss was inside the house with another vampire with a busted leg, but that was all he knew. So we gave him a little mercy and made his death a quick one . . . or about as quick as a vampiric dog can make it.

"The thing you easily forget about Lothos' goons is that the crazies aren't always all that crazy. Or that there are sometimes plans within plans. It was a little bit of both, this time, and we learned it the hard way. After we gave Mr. pants-on-head a headless dirt nap, we got jumped by the twelve or so vampires that poured out of the house. Of course that could only have happened if someone in that group was another mind reader, keeping track of the one outside. And so, he was kind of a living tripwire, which we tripped by offing. Or that's what I guessed. So this mind-reader knew instantly that someone was knocking on their door and his posse was instantly on our collective asses.

"At first, I thought we were boned, until about a minute or so into the fight. Sure, they came at us with whips, chains, baseball bats and -I shit you not- a board with a nail in it . . . but they had all the skill of a herd of drunken chinchillas on stilts. They were as much grunts as crazy was. The fight ended up being not so much a fight as a rout. A few tried to get away, but I guess they never read the memo about vampiric dogs being able to move faster than they could. They didn't get far.

"Though I now know, because of what you told me, that it was only an elaborate, sadistic trap . . . at the time, I was working hard on figuring out this puzzle. I didn't think the thaumaturgist who was hiding in the house had expected us to find him, or maybe his plans to hamstring us were sloppy, since we survived the tripping of our truck and the gang-up. When we made it inside, it was pitch black. The only thing I could see was Joe propped up against a bare wall with a lamp light shining on him. If I hadn't heard him breathing, I would have guessed that he was dead. I guess keeping him alive, this monster thought it made us less likely to cut loose, but we were about to show him how wrong he was.

"Paws, Grace, and I tore inside, despite the lack of light, aiming to have our proverbial guns blazing, but the thaumaturgist stopped those pretty quickly. I admit that I favored my plan for a frontal attack over Paws's suggestion that we confuse him by coming in one at a time. I didn't consider that the clusterfuck with the other vamps outside the house had been to buy him some time, which we gave to him in spades.

"Joe had been treated pretty rough. He'd lost a lot of blood; his fangs looked like they were sticking out of a skeleton's mouth, and his bad leg had been sliced off at the knee, with the stump cauterized."

Derek drew in a trembling breath, but I knew what had happened. I saw it in his thoughts before his lips could speak. I cried with him, gripping his hand, but said nothing. I only maintained my wordless reassurances as he faced the demons of his guilt while bringing his story to a close.

"I started thinking of a way of getting him out of there," he said, "but it all happened so fast after that. Grace bought it first. Paws and I, we . . . God, I'd never heard an animal scream like that! I knew the thaumaturgist was waiting in that room to ambush us, but neither of us expected what happened. She just went up in flames. It was like she exploded, but all upwards, like a pillar of fire. Looking back, I think she suffered the least.

"Joe was next to go . . . but not before he could warn me. I could barely hear him over Grace's screams, but I remember clearly him saying "UV," and telling me to get the hell out of there. Of course, I kind of figured it out when the flames lit up the place for a few seconds and felt the burning sensation that could have only come from a UV light. I saw the thaumaturgist for the first time . . . or at least the black blob of the UV shielding that surrounded him. Can't say he wasn't a clever sonofabitch.

"He had to have picked up on what Joe had been trying to tell me, so he lit him up, right in front of my face. I think he intended to fry me too, but he didn't count on me having a Jewel, let alone being able to block UV rays myself. He still managed to burn part of my shoulder and arm, but I was able to work through the pain and bring up the shield. It was too late for Joe, though. But he went down like a warrior. He didn't make a sound; guess he didn't want to give the bastard anything to gloat over. Quietly was never the way I expected him to go out, but I have to admit, it was a hell of a way of giving the shape-shifters the finger.

"Paws, however, went totally ape shit after he saw what happened to Grace. After watching Joe go up in flames, I got busy trying to take out the thaumaturgist, but only had scent to guide me in a room where I couldn't see my hand in front of my face. Paws was doing the same thing, but with the aid of a shotgun and no common sense. Paws can move real fast when motivated, and I think he managed to fool the bastard a couple of times, but the thaumaturgist was good at disguising his footfalls, and with no reference but scent to tell us which way he went, we couldn't really get a bead on him. And with Paws's mental state, there was no coordination between us. Twice, his shots almost nailed me. I screamed at him mentally, but he was beyond reach. The whole fight was like a game of cat and mouse, but with all of us trying to be the cat. I couldn't find the thaumaturgist and I couldn't keep up with all the moving around. Something would have to give. So I tried another approach.

"You know how being able to read minds can give us some pretty big advantages? Well, with me, I can manipulate minds like play-doh. That's why I don't use my talents much when around my clan. Even that power scares me. I can even alter my own mind if I have a Jewel to make sure it's reflected back on me. So I used my talent on him by shutting off his mastery of the Jewel. It turns out that didn't end like I hoped it would. When you lose mastery of something, you lose fine control, and this guy lost it all. You can't actually see UV light, and I didn't know he was trying to hit Paws with one of his blasts at that very moment. He lost control of all focus and intensity. I think it expanded and filled the whole house. Paws was fried like an egg. I didn't even realize how intense it was until I noticed the shielding around me start to crack. So I didn't have a choice but to haul ass out of the house.

"What happened afterwards was something I didn't see, but sure as hell felt. Though I guess if I could have seen it, it would have been something like a laser exploding. I can only guess it tore the bastard's shielding apart like paper, and he was vaporized while I went flying along with pieces of the house. I blacked out when I hit ground and woke up with some of those same house pieces lodged in my body. I had several still-healing burns from when my shield broke and I got a taste of the tail end of that UV blast and I was a couple of miles away from the house, but I was still alive. When I made it back to where the house had been, there was nothing left but a giant crater and a broken well of gushing water.

"I was so dazed at that point that I didn't realize that I was alone, that Paws and Grace were dead, until I pulled the truck out of the ravine. Only the chassis was damaged, so it started, but when I got inside, it hit me. I was just . . . overcome with this feeling of horror and loneliness. It was so bad that I just ran on automatic. I got here safely after that, but I barely remember the drive. I was lucky that I managed to make it without a traffic accident. All I could think about was how it all went belly-up, and how it was all my fault. If only I'd listened to Paws; if only I'd been a little less cocky; If only I'd been a little more cautious . . ."

Even my presence and touch wasn't enough to calm his troubled heart at this point. But to my surprise, Derek neither broke down nor did he bawl. He was never shy about displaying his emotions to me, and I had seen him openly weep by my side for fallen comrades whom I'd never known. So in silence, I watched as the tears streamed down his cheeks, and I wiped them away, never condemning his actions.

"And do you know what the worst thing about it all was?" He said. "It was the fact that I knew we were walking into a damn trap. We all were! And you were on the other end with the rest of my clan ... the only family I had, facing some other threat . . . and I could arrive at the rendezvous point alone and waiting in vain for the woman I love . . . and come face-to-face-with the possibility that not only had Lothos wiped out the bulk of my clan, but that I would never see you again!"

"Derek . . ."

I brought my legs up into the bed and scooted across his lap. I didn't intend to stay there; I was smaller than him, but only by about a head, so I knew that I was too heavy to remain there comfortably. Also, though my presence was a comfort in spite of his grief, I could feel that it was becoming something of a distraction for him.

"We survived, love. And we're here. I'm here. You're here. And I'm with you now. I wish it had gone the same for you, Joe, Lyman, and even poor Grace, but all isn't lost. We're here; the baby is safe, and Deb is herself again. And best of all, we may have even stopped Lothos from tracking us. According to Deb, we may have killed the mastermind. That all has to count for something good."

Derek leaned forward and wrapped his arms about me. I felt his pain recede somewhat as his heart succumbed to my love and the soothing words I gave. But his doubts were still far from allayed. I had never before seen him so unsure of himself.

"Remember that Sarah herself came to you," I said, cupping his face in my hands. My heart reached out for his, wanting desperately to give him some hope, some reason not to drown in his own despair. "She had to know that there was a future where your clan would survive and prosper, and that the baby would be safe. And thus far, we are surviving! The baby is safe! We've gotten through this thus far, and I swear on my life that I will fight to make sure we get through the rest, whatever it may be. But Derek . . . love . . . If you remember anything of what I say, remember this. Sarah never said that we'd all arrive there in the end."

"But that's just it, China doll!" As if my words had the opposite effect, a crackle of renewed pain seemed to pass across Derek's formerly passive features. "We may have to look forward to the loss of even more. I don't know if I could stand it. And if I lost you . . ."

"Shh . . ." I pressed against him and touched a finger to his lips. "Don't talk that way. Never talk that way. I know you have your doubts; we all do. I worry just as much as you do, if not more. You should have seen me before you came back. Deb can tell you; I was a complete wreck. But even if the worst had happened, I would still have needed to complete my mission, the same as you need to complete it as your clan's leader."

I rested my forehead against his chest, and my voice fell to a whisper as a welter of unexpected passion burst from me. "I love you, Derek. It frightens me how much I love you, and how much you love me. But please, don't make me your Achilles' Heel."

"Elisa . . ."

His own whisper was so faint, it was almost inaudible. But his emotions spoke volumes worth a scream. Such love poured from his heart at that moment that I thought that I would drown in it. It made me momentarily lightheaded, in fact, and the smile that I returned his way was perhaps wider than one any sober person would have worn.

"I won't make you my Achilles' heel," he said. "I promise."

"I don't believe we ever did fully understand what we're getting into with each other," I said. Derek shook his head.

"Probably not. But tonight, I know I learned."

"And . . . do you still want me?" I asked.

"Forever."

There was no hesitation in his response, or his lips as they found mine. He repositioned me to where I straddled his legs rather than across, as I had been doing. I would have protested, knowing this would most likely provoke a response that perhaps he was not yet ready for, but his kiss never once broke, and neither did I want it to. We had survived the enemy once again, and were, for now, still together. And though the losses hurt us both, we would deal with them in our own ways in due time.

There was another thunderclap, much closer than before. This was coupled by the soft whirring of the sun shutters over the window. Strange, how neither Derek nor I felt tired, even after such anguish.

"It will be dawn soon," I said, reluctantly parting my

lips from his. I ached from my lingering want as well as Derek's as I slipped off of his lap. I located the over-large shirt I had worn before my bath on the floor near the entrance to the bathroom where I had discarded it, and summoned it into my hands along with the still-warm blood pack that lay undisturbed in the tub.

"Yes, I know," Derek said with confusion, "but . . . why are you-? Are you going somewhere?"

"I'll be sleeping in the RV today," I said as I placed the blood pack on the nightstand.

"Why?"

"Derek . . ." I rested my hand atop his knee. "I know my presence is comforting. But it's also becoming a distraction. I've been feeling it since you arrived, and especially after you finished telling your story. I just don't want to . . ." I became aware of a warmth creep outwards from the center of my chest to my face, and I sensed Derek's reaction to the scent of my blood. He reached for the blood pack with his left hand while his right hand rested in his lap, strategically disguising another reaction that I was already aware of. Quickly, I averted my gaze, though I knew that he knew about it. And when I spoke, I found that my voice sounded far less forceful than I'd intended. "I . . . don't want to be a distraction to you."

At my words, Derek removed his hand from the blood pack and instead, brought it to his knee. Again, he laced his fingers with those of my hand that rested there. At his discreet touch, the clarity of the emotions from this contact sent a shudder through me like the crack of a whip. I felt a warmth within me grow, as if some vessel inside had spilled over.

"Maybe . . . I want you to be a distraction,"

Derek's words came out husky, almost a purr. Gently, he pulled me back to him. I did not resist as he hefted me back into the bed and to his side. His gaze was fixed as steadily upon me as a pair of camera lenses. "Maybe we both need this distraction."

His fingers brushed against my skin as he swept away a few strands of my hair that escaped my head towel, and I trembled with an ache that surpassed the need for blood, a feeling that pulled at something deeper than anything I knew - something that I had never experienced before. Was this what humans felt during this moment? My fangs lengthened, though it was not his blood that aroused me. That scent was, of course, ubiquitous with his presence, but I'd long since learned to keep my reactions in check. I longed to pursue this new reaction . . . to take it as far as it would go, but the shadow of that night when we shared the dark pages of our pasts became a wall. Now, I dared not even wonder . . .

"I won't force you into anything you're not ready for," I said to Derek, unable to meet the intensity of his gaze or absorb the equivalent intensity of these feelings that had appeared to come from nowhere. I swallowed against my suddenly dry throat. "We agreed not to pursue this until you're ready."

His fingers travelled down my shoulder and arm in a sweet, gentle caress, sending me reeling. At last, I made myself hold his gaze. His fangs were extended with a prominence I hadn't seen since the first time we fed. His face was flushed as if my blood had taken on a new level of irresistibility. And though I could feel the thirst gnawing within him, it was not primed to be satiated by me -not that it ever would be. What I felt was more fundamental: primal in a way that surpassed the immortal things that he and I had become.

"Elisa . . . I am ready," he said. "Are you?"

Again, my thoughts went back to his first attempt, opening my eyes to the contrast of the situation. At that time, I had welcomed whatever it was that Derek had wanted to do, even though he had ended up being unable to follow though. This time, however, there was a genuine desire, a drawing between us both, as compelling as blood. And when he touched me, that drawing, that mutual want, became evidently, powerfully, and inescapably clear in the overlapping of our minds.

"Yes," I at last whispered.

Derek said no more as he turned to face me fully. He took me by the arms, and with unsurpassed gentleness, drew me to him. I leaned forward and before we came together, he loosened the simple tuck that held my towel in place. I felt it slip away as his arms enfolded me, and our lips gently touched.

We were one in mind long before he did anything else but kiss me. And it was only as a distant impression that I knew that his towel had joined mine, slipping off of the bed onto the floor along with the towel that had bound my curls. Words had only become a distraction as I let him guide me into the mattress . . .

. . . And we were ready.

Chapter Eighteen

Exactly how did I feel when I awoke?

The best description I can muster is the sensation from when Derek fed from my femoral artery -which I did return the favor for. But that sensation was now over every inch of me: the lingering, delicious memory of Derek's touch. And through my present contact with Derek, I knew my remembered touch echoed upon him as well. What else could I say about this than it was the most exquisitely wonderful feeling I'd ever known? Even in his slumber, the echoes of our night, which had quickly become our morning, resonated like chimes of bliss upon and within us both.

I smiled wide as the horizon, and my heart sank into Derek's heart, flowing like a river fish in the currents of joy and contentment between us. I rested my head on his bicep and snaked my arms around his forearms. Idly, I compared my arms to his. Both were lean of build, but mine were noticeably smaller and thinner. Had Derek not been turned until adulthood, I imagine he would have been very sizeable and muscular, but as he was, trapped partway in what would have been his passage into adulthood, he still was quite solid, not at all lanky, but still built with boyish leanness. I, however, with the exception of my legs, which I suppose had only been just starting to fill out a little at the point of my turning, was very slender and slight, almost spindly in comparison, as to make me truly like a China doll in his arms.

Perhaps this was why Derek had first been so gentle with me . . . so slow. It was delightful at first, but quickly became frustrating as he was soon unable to match what I needed from him.

"Derek, you're not going to break me," I'd said to him, at last making my frustrations known. Even I didn't know that those were the words that he had needed in order to set him free of the last of his fear. After that, we loved each other with alacritous abandon while the storm raged outside.

My glance passed over the empty blood pack on the dresser. We had shared it intermittently throughout our time together. I inhaled the scent of that same blood beneath the skin of his arm and felt my fangs lengthen. And this sensation roused Derek awake. I suppressed a guffaw at this. Typical male. Give him even the notion of intimacy, and they'll rise to the occasion.

I felt Derek's sides rise and fall as he sighed and stirred, and his thoughts floated to wakefulness and recollection. His love sent ripples of goosebumps across my skin as he pulled me closer to him.

"China doll . . ." he whispered into my ear. His voice was soft with affection, his words husky and slurred with the lengthening of his fangs. The way he held me brought my neck within range of his lips, which touched their mark, giving kisses that traveled slowly towards my ear. He then nibbled at my earlobes, inducing delight that made my every breath catch in my throat. Every part of me wanted him to do it. He would feed from me in the traditional way while my fangs pierced the veins of his arms, and somewhere along the way, we would repeat last night . . .

But alas, my better judgment proved to be the stronger part of me.

"Derek, I want it," I said, but held him back by making the underlying intent behind my words evidently clear. Nevertheless, I was unable to keep the purr out of my voice when I spoke. Derek comprehended, and I could feel the disappointment course through our bond like cold water on white hot steel.

"God knows I do." I spoke with sympathy. "God knows we both do, but you might want to look at the time."

Derek shifted slightly to get a better look at the bright blue digital numbers upon the face of the clock on the dresser. I felt a spike of surprise from him as he noticed the time. The sun had set two hours ago.

I doubt either one of us had slept in that late in a very long time, if ever. But Derek's surprise only lasted a moment, and settled back into the mellow sensuality that permeated his thoughts only moments before.

"We slept in," he observed.

"The others will be waiting for us," I said.

He purred against my ear, settling back down into the pillow and sheets, holding me against him in a manner that was comfortingly possessive. "Let them wait," he said.

I shuddered, and passed my lips upon his arm ever so gently, but refrained from taking his blood despite the excruciating temptation. The little sneak was trying to tempt me! He was hoping to make me forget about what he said just before we fell asleep, and that I would bite first to give him an excuse.

I turned over and kissed him, giving him the impression that the proverbial jig was up. I felt him deflate like a balloon in my arms, and I giggled.

"Nice try, love," I said, running my fingers along the thin wisps of hair at his chin.

"Damn those plans I made last night," he groaned.

"Well, you knew I would hold you to them," I said, sliding out of his arms and feeling his dismay even deeper. But free of our contact, he didn't know of my intent to make it up to him very soon.

"Just a taste?" He pleaded. I felt him run a finger along my spine, the sensation of which made my fangs extend anew, and my eyes roll back as goosebumps erupted along the path his finger had trod.

"Keep that up, and you won't get even a drop," I said. I tried to sound cross, but fell woefully short of the mark. I heard Derek chuckle knowingly as I slipped off of the bed.

"I'll go and draw us a bath," I said as I returned to the bathroom. The tub would easily fit Derek and me, but the water had gone cold. I drained it and started a new bath, and prepared some fresh towels from the nearby linen cabinet. As I did this, I mused with expectation on the mutual bathing that awaited us. That would at least be some consolation.

Suddenly, I felt the familiar faintness of Deb's mind intrude upon my thoughts.

We're up, I sent to her.

About time, Deb's thoughts were laced with a leering shrewdness. I was wondering if I would've had to separate you two with a spray bottle.

You're a few hours late for that, I'm afraid, I sent.

So that explains it, Deb sent back on a chord of combined surprise and wistful satisfaction. Glad you two got it out of your systems, but the others are getting anxious. They see the truck, but are waiting for the other shoe to drop.

I thought they'd be happy for a little extra down time. Derek wants us to leave as soon as we can.

Should I tell them? Deb asked.

I think it would be a good idea, I sent. I didn't take much out of the RV when we got here, and so it won't take Derek and me long to pack up again. I can keep Derek . . . ah . . . busy . . . until you're nearly ready.

Well now, Deb's words came at the tail end of another shrewd, knowing mental hum. We've certainly become bold in a short period of time. Care to spill the beans?

I wanted to let her know of what befell Lyman and Joe, but I felt that Derek would want to personally relay this news to the clan as a whole. Besides, I did not want to believe that the catalyst for the long-delayed consummation of our relationship had been merely the deaths of our mutual friends; that seemed almost too morose to contemplate. If it had to be a factor, I believed it was, rather, a synthesis of this combined with the evolution of our love. Perhaps it took the understanding that we'd all faced death for Derek to realize he no longer needed to be afraid. My own brush with death had certainly caused me to awaken to a facet of our attachment that even I hadn't known previously.

Call it . . . 'mutual revelation,' I sent, choosing deliberately to be coy, but not completely lying. The entire story I, of course, kept shut safely away: an easy feat, due to Deb's limited telepathy.

Well, I'm glad you finally got over yourselves, Deb sent, seemingly none the wiser. I had to get over my own hang-ups with Derek when it was him and me, young as he looked. Now he at least knows what it was like for me.

No doubt. I cast a mental laugh.

Have fun with your 'distraction,' then, Deb sent. Just don't be 'distracting' each other all night.

I make no promises, I sent with facetious humor before I broke the connection.

After waiting a few minutes more for the tub to fill, I was struck with a realization. It was, in fact, something that should have been insipidly obvious. Deb would already have known that Joe and Lyman were conspicuously missing, now that Derek was back. In fact the entire clan would most likely know by now. Lyman's truck was certainly in the parking lot, but neither Lyman nor Joe's scents would be about the hotel. Why, then, if she'd inferred what had happened, would she not mention it?

"Perhaps it was out of respect," I thought aloud as I shut off the water in the now full tub. After all, Deb was no fool, no matter how I tried to obfuscate in our brief mental rapport. Derek and I had indeed received a mutual revelation of each other before that voluptuous night and morning, but as much as I hated to at last admit it, the most important affair that brought us together at long last was almost certainly the impact of the losses of Lyman and Joe. Our union was, in part, a confirmation of life, consummated, however ironically, by creatures that were, according to legend (and most incorrectly), supposed to be "undead."

"What was out of respect?" Derek said from directly behind me. His voice startled me from the depths of my reverie.

"I scared you?" Derek said on the edge of a laugh as I turned around.

"Not really, no," I said, maintaining my grace. "Deb was talking to me. The bath's ready, by the way. I was just about to call you."

I took him by the hand and led him to the tub's inviting entrance. Smiling, I brought him in with me, walking carefully backwards in upon its steps, watching as the paleness of Derek's skin flushed to an almost human tone with the warmth of the water, the same as it did for me. His face was an amusing sight as he allowed himself to be guided. No doubt he'd caught on to my intent, and that improved his temperament greatly.

"She wants us to hurry up, I bet?" He asked with undisguised slyness in his voice.

"More like she wanted to tease me," I said, leaning back into the water so that my hair could once again become limp strands from my former curls. After all that Derek and I had indulged in, it had most certainly developed copious tangles by now. "And she was understandably curious."

"You didn't . . ." Derek said with mild dismay. In response, I sent a sting of reproach across our bond.

"You know I'd never do such a thing," I said. "She'd already figured it out. But she really just wanted to know when we'd make our -ahem- grand entrance."

"Did you tell her to be patient?" Derek asked, "And not to be jealous?"

"Oh, she was hardly jealous," I replied.

We don't attract enough odor with our sweat for humans to detect, and so all Derek and I really needed was a good soaking. I'd added a neutral fragrance to the water, and we did the rest to make the bath a pleasant experience in its own right.

"Deb is actually happy about us," I said, allowing the water to warm my skin and my blood. I scooted closer to

Derek's side and sat in his lap, leaning back against his chest, doing as we normally did to allow our mutual thirst to grow. Settled against him as I was, and in full contact, my every desire bled into him and became his own.

"Not jealous at all?" Derek asked. "You're sure?"

"Love, you're talking as if you want her to be jealous!" I giggled, partly due to the humor, and in part due to the tickling motion of his fingers folded together above my navel.

"No, that's not it. I'm just a little surprised, is all," Derek said. "As possessive of me as she used to be . . . I guess she changed a bit more than I thought. I never noticed."

"She said that you changed her, actually," I said, "that she had to put away preconceived notions when you two started seeing each other."

"Yeah, that she did," Derek replied. "Funny how I had to get over some things with you, when I was always getting on her case about the same stuff with me. I don't exactly look like a grown-up myself, after all."

"Deb mentioned something like that," I said, stretching my legs in the warm water. "You know, appearance-wise, you and I are actually closer in age than you are to Deb."

"I guess it makes for a sort of symmetry when you compare relationships," Derek mused, and again I laughed.

"Again I assure you, my very insecure love, that Deb is nothing but happy for us," I said, reassuring Derek for the final time. I lowered my voice to a whisper as I turned to face him and crossed my arms over his chest. I rested my head against that solid, lean chest, staring into his eyes, adoring the slight flush that came to his face as I smiled. "So enough about the ghosts of the past, right? Let's talk about the future."

"And which future would we talk about, exactly?" Derek asked, calming himself from my recent assertiveness. I felt a new tickle as he ran his finger along my spine just below my hip.

"The clan . . ." I said, shivering somewhat from his touch, "the baby -we need to figure out a name for her, by the way-, and of course, us."

"Well, there's not much to talk about with the clan, is there?" Derek said. "I mean, we'll be at the sanctuary soon. We'll be under your clan's protection and all that, right?"

I nodded. "With any luck, yes."

"I do have a question, though."

He paused, and I waited expectantly.

"Of all places, why Louisiana?"

I doubled over with a peal of laughter at this, and then felt his slight chagrin at my reaction.

"I'm so sorry, love," I quickly said, attempting to settle down. "I'm not laughing at you; I'm just surprised you're asking this question only now."

"It hasn't been heavy on my mind, or anything," Derek protested. "It's just that . . . well, I remember Paws asked about it once. And I just now realized he had a point. I haven't known of any other vampires going there for a long time."

"That's because there aren't any other vampires there," I said matter-of-factly.

"You're serious?" Derek's expression drained into blankness. "None at all?"

"Now you know why I chose it," I said. "Most of us avoid it since novels and TV shows popularized and romanticized the bloody hell out of the place. So both clans abandoned the region. We got tired of posers and attention whores; too many of us were accurately spotted, and so it became a danger to us. So, for the last few decades, the entire state has 'gone fallow,' I guess you could say. But our old homesteads are still there, still intact, still hidden."

"I've heard of your villages," Derek said. "So you're basically loaning one out to us?"

"It can be your home for as long as you like," I assured him. "And you can recall the rest of your clan from hiding when you get there. But I know you won't want to stay there long."

"Some might," Derek said thoughtfully. "The whole

adventure with this baby got even the ones I sent away spooked. Some of them might not want to come back; others will want to stay with you guys. And I don't doubt some of the ones in the group now will probably even want to join your clan after all they've been through. Either way, my clan isn't going to be the same. I love the freedom of the road, but I have to admit that I feel like I've just been ignoring a very real problem, choosing this life."

"Sounds like you're having a change of heart yourself." I was only half-joking at this point, but I knew better than to get my hopes up.

"It's . . . tempting," Derek said after a palpable moment, which he ended with a sigh that told me all that I needed to know, "but I have responsibilities."

"I know," I whispered at last, closing my eyes. Somewhere between melancholy and desire, I listened as his heartbeat beneath the cords of muscles in his chest. It was too much to ask. Derek's predecessor, Syd, had groomed him for this position and placed all his confidence in him. Even if some members of his clan would choose to stay with us, as I had no doubt they would, it would be selfish for me to take him away from all of that.

"I'll be with you for a little while, at least," he said. "We have to wait for the baby to grow up some. And didn't you say that you'd be training her to survive?"

Those words gave me some comfort. Derek and I would certainly be wed once we reached the sanctuary, but how long would it be until the baby was "old enough"? Ten years? Twenty? Even those lengths of time were an instant in our lifespans. What would we do then? I couldn't leave my clan so easily; I was committed to the war. And as for Derek, the open road was in his blood, and he had a clan to care for. What would happen then?

"Let's take small steps, China doll," Derek said, catching onto my scattered worries and concerns and soothing them as best he could with his love. "We can't keep worrying about everything that might happen."

I smiled, my face still hidden against his chest and the sweet scent of his blood. "And I was telling you the same thing last night, wasn't I?"

"Yeah, that you were," Derek said before going quiet for several minutes. I felt his desire to say something, and so I waited for his courage to gather.

"And . . . we ought to get married in your home."

A thrill of joy fired up my spine as quickly as I shot my gaze into Derek's smiling eyes. I had to have been grinning almost childishly broad. I'd been afraid to ask, afraid that he would not commit to any kind of milieu, and now I felt foolish for even possessing that sort of fear. "Do you really mean it?"

Derek unhooked his hands from my waist and brought his finger up to my chin.

"Elisa, you know I'd do anything for you, right? I'm not big on pomp and ceremony, and all that crap, but I know you have family. You got a dad, after all. Why would I have us elope somewhere and deprive him of seeing his daughter married? Hell, I haven't even met the guy, and I want that for him. And you saved our lives, after all. And we'll be guests of your clan. It's only fair that you'd call the shots for the wedding."

"But I don't want to call all the shots," I protested. "I was hoping that we'd get married among my clan, but it's not like I'll be picking out every bit of the decor. I just wanted us to come to an agreement over where it would be."

"Like I said, let's have it where you live," Derek said with finality. "And yes, I do mean it."

I never thought that I, of all people, would break into tears at such things. But as it had when he'd proposed to me -or rather, attempted to- before my rather enthusiastic and premature acceptance, I felt the orbs of tears begin to pool at the edges of my eyesight and stream down the sides of my face. I supposed I was as prone to the same reactions that I saw on the movies with some things. Better this than anything else, I figured.

"Oh, Derek . . ." I quavered, and, overcome with a wave of self-consciousness, I looked away, only to hear him chuckle.

"For someone as badass as you in the field, you sure get flustered over the strangest things," he said. I knew he wasn't being cross or rude; it was, as Deb had once remarked, merely anecdotal. It was something that perhaps would have started a heated disagreement between normal human couples, and so I was glad of our mental bond.

"We have a chapel in our village," I said.

"Vegas is more my speed," Derek replied, then shrugged. "But whatever you want."

"When do you want the wedding to be?"

"As soon as you're ready."

"I wish we could do it now," I said, my every word dripping with the impatience I felt so keenly.

"I don't think your dad would be too happy about that," Derek quipped.

". . . Or Roland," I said.

"Roland?" Derek's mental sputter of confusion made me realize that I'd never mentioned him before. "I thought your father was-"

"Oh, no, it's nothing at all like that!" I said, hurriedly steering his mind away from the direction it was headed. "Roland is one of Father's lieutenants. He was born in the UK, like me, and was still fairly young when Father took me in. He and I got on best, and so he took to looking after me whenever Father was away. He's like a second father, I guess you could say."

"The fun one, rather than the serious one?" Derek asked, "Like in those old sitcoms?"

"Something like that," I said with some amusement. To be truthful, he was exactly right. "He certainly didn't do Father any favors with some of the bad habits he taught me."

"Bad habits?" I laughed at how much this piqued Derek's

curiosity.

"Roland . . . prefers to hunt," I said, "exclusively."

"So? What's so wrong about that?" Derek asked.

"Nothing directly," I said, and realized that I sounded more evasive than I meant to. "It's like this. In your clan, hunting and perhaps even grazing humans, are all par for the course. But you forget that we -my clan- live alongside humans. They give us their blood willingly. So hunting is something that went out of fashion a long time ago. Unnecessary stress on the human, if we're found out, makes some of the memory wipes we do afterwards go wrong. Nowadays, it's actually taboo, unless we do it for emergencies. Roland does it for . . . ah . . . sport."

"And your clan frowns on that?"

"Mostly, yes," I said. "But on the topside, I became the best at it. I could take a human in perfect stealth, and erase the memory of it before he or she even knew I was there." My mind went back to how I took the park ranger, and I felt something of a perverse thrill. Regardless of what my clan would think, Roland would certainly have been proud of my stealth and precision.

"Doesn't seem like such a bad habit, the way you seem to be so proud of what he taught you," Derek remarked, catching my tangent of thought with a shrewd grin. "In fact, you seem to like it."

"It's a useful skill to have," I said in my defense. "It may not be pleasant, but if we're caught in the field and in need, it's best to know how to streamline your body's instincts in order to do the least damage. Though Roland does it for . . . other conquests . . . as well as food."

"I can imagine."

Derek spoke in a soft voice, and I became aware of his finger brushing just as softly against my forearm. It then dawned on me that my talk of Roland's training me in the hunt had awakened something just as primal within him. He was certainly well aware of what "conquests" I spoke of, since those thoughts were quite close to the surface. And from the reactions of his body, which began to ignite reactions in my own through our touch and through our bond, I knew he was prepared for a conquest of his own . . . though he of course, did not see it as such. His desire, flowing through our bond, was like a drug to me, and I was very much willing to allow it to take control. It was a high that precluded the high of the drink, the high of love, and the high of making love.

God, if Roland discovered that talk of his predilections had set off a chain such as this, I would never hear the end of it from him. And as my lips searched across Derek's skin as his did mine, and I shuddered with the expectation of the sharp, scintillating ecstasy of his "kiss," which would quickly be answered by my own, I resolved to never let him know.

The drink is a high without parallel. But both Derek and I had, since last night, learned that combining it with other activities gave it depths that made the experience into something that was, for lack of a better word, transcendent. And it was certainly, for a dramatic understatement, a distraction that had been exactly what Deb and the clan had needed . . . not that I did it solely for them.

Chapter Nineteen

Counting our protracted bath -It is was good thing that our skin does not prune from prolonged immersion-, it took Derek and I a full hour and a half after Deb's communiqué to exit the hotel room.

To be more specific, I was the one who first emerged in that time frame. I was met with more than a couple of gazes and emotions that ranged from playfully shrewd to mildly annoyed. Nevertheless, it turned out that my "distraction" had provided more than enough time for the clan to pack up and prepare for a rapid departure, leaving all present with time to occupy themselves with idle chitchat and a few smoking sessions, but with everyone standing conspicuously about Lyman's now derelict trailer.

I also realized, much to my chagrin that I'd forgotten to place the motel into the in-between space as I'd promised. Fortunately, this wasn't a primary concern on anyone's mind, but I planned to apologize for my inattentiveness later.

"The boss gonna be long?" Wadih asked as he came to my side. He sounded understandably anxious; he was just as eager to get back on the road as everyone else. "This place has nice digs and all, but after everything we've gone through, the crew's getting more than a little antsy."

"I completely understand," I assured him. "And Derek's probably not too long in coming."

"Gather you tired him out?" I heard Marie-Laure say as she came up from behind me. I turned and faced her shrewd grin. It was the same expression as what was plastered upon Deb's face some distance away as she glanced briefly our way from her business with the baby. Of course, I had nothing to worry about with her being any kind of a snitch; with a company of vampires whose preternatural senses of hearing and smell were just as acute as each other's, it was impossible to hide what had transpired in our room both last night and tonight. Derek and I had already begun to smell like each other, but even bathing would not completely wash off the particular scent that we now shared.

"No, I just dressed more quickly," I said with nonchalance that belied my selfish amusement. Derek had never learned many nuanced tricks with his Jewel such as dressing. I had dried myself off, hair and all, and slipped into my waiting clothes freshly removed from my satchel while he was still toweling off. He was noticeably jealous of this, but I promised that I would one day teach him.

"Wow, didn't even blink," Marie-Laure said on the edge of a chuckle. "You two must've gotten used to each other rather quickly."

"You might say that," I said, and changed the subject. "By the way, did you manage to get anything on what we discussed last night?"

"Sure did."

I'm not certain how I hadn't previously noticed her holding several leafs of paper, stapled together and rolled up in her hand, or missed her intent to give them to me. Perhaps her amusement at my telling scent overshadowed those thoughts. Nevertheless, she brightened and presented the papers to me for my perusal. It was a hard copy of a news article from a website that I figured was local to the area. Apparently, late last night, the news received an anonymous tip and a large cache of data presumably retrieved from the hard drive on the police chief's computer, citing multiple admissions of fraud, extortion, corruption, and, as Marie-Laure described as the "icing on the cake," a very generous stash of child pornography. This quickly had become an issue that involved the mayor and commissioner, which resulted in the police chief's swift arrest. What was most particularly amusing was how the writer used the phrase "a real bloodsucker" to describe the police chief.

"Oh this is absolutely precious!" I exclaimed as I handed the paper back to Marie-Laure, more pleased with her skills than I thought I'd ever be. "It's exemplary, in fact. I don't think that even Reanon could have been so artful!"

"Reanon?" Marie-Laure asked, and I realized how casually I'd been throwing around the names of my clan members as if these Vagabonds were part of it.

"She's my clan's resident scientist and medic," I explained. "She's also a hacker when the situation demands it."

"I don't think I've heard of her," Marie-Laure said with a thoughtful frown. "She go by any other kind of name online?"

"If she does, I don't know it," I said. "But she keeps to herself when she's not needed. And I doubt she'd be visible to anyone online anyway. The computers she works with are . . ." I grimaced, trying to think of a way to explain her work that wouldn't sound offensive. "Ah, well, please don't think that I'm patronizing your work, but the computers we use in my clan are quite a bit more advanced than what you've been using. And besides, Reanon doesn't really care much for the Internet. She's not terribly social, as I said."

"So she never goes online?" Marie-Laure asked.

"Oh, no. She goes online when she must. But what I'm saying is that the system she uses is unassailable. It's built by Father, and he's had about ten thousand years on most of human civilization."

Marie-Laure was anything but offended; rather she seemed quite impressed, even intrigued. I felt from her a strong desire to see Reanon and her setup that went beyond mere curiosity. It was something similar to the drawing a human host has to us when their bodies begin to feel the effects of deprivation of the drink.

"Wow. Heavy stuff," she said at last, and licked at what appeared to be the beginnings of drool. "Sounds like her setup is something I'd like to see one day."

"Oh, it's quite impressive," I said. "You know, you could become a trainee under her, if you wanted. Reanon's been looking for people with skill."

Marie-Laure frowned, and I felt my suggestion left a sour feeling in her thoughts. "That would mean joining the mind-readers, thought, wouldn't it?"

"Only if you wanted," I replied in an attempt to mitigate what my suggestion had entailed. I wasn't sure if Marie-Laure was merely not easily offended, or that I'd given away how much her reaction had troubled me, but her demeanor quickly shifted to something that was surprisingly pleasant. I saw her shrug, and then shake with a soundless chuckle.

"Well, I can't say that it's not a tempting offer," she said, "but really, I've got too many responsibilities here. And I think my leaving would piss off Derek. He needs me more than he knows."

"That he does," I said in agreement and at the same time, relief at her lack of resentment.

"What about you?" She asked. "What will you and Derek be doing?

"We . . . haven't quite crossed that bridge yet," I admitted. "But we'll figure something out."

"I'm sure you will," Marie-Laure said with a grin. "It's not as if you'll need to decide it right now, after all. As for me, I'm glad you gave me that job. I can't tell you how much I was itching to give some kind of payback to Lothos and his assholes. You know, as far as the police chief is concerned, my little info dump has made him, shall we say, a bad risk to Lothos and his clan."

"Did he really have that kind of porn on his computer?" I asked, more than a little troubled at the prospect. My thoughts briefly returned to that faraway time when I had done away with that pig of a human, but I quickly shook myself free of that dark memory.

"I wish," Marie-Laure said, pursing her lips with disgust that was just as strongly felt as seen. "That was just about the only thing that I had to 'embellish' for the coup de gras. Believe me, it wasn't pleasant digging that shit up, let alone planting it."

I nodded, again feigning nonchalance, but inside, I was a bit uncomfortable with this particular liberty Marie-Laure had taken. But whether she had gone too far, I guess I would never know, as I didn't inquire any deeper.

"Well, as I said, you did a lovely job," I said with a smile as I took my leave. The questionable nature of her planting evidence of that kind aside, she had indeed given that police chief a fair dose of karma. Whether or not it would all come up as admissible in court didn't bother me, as long as we left a sizeable thorn in Lothos' side in the bargain.

I'd packed extremely light before I had begun this mission, keeping my clothes and personal effects mostly in my satchel, and Derek had come into the hotel with little else but the tattered clothes on his back, which I had cleaned and repaired with my Jewel; so with little else to do, I busied myself by taking my satchel, which I had slung over my shoulder, as well as the cooler of blood packs that I'd carried out of the room and set beside the door, into Derek's RV. All the while, I overheard several of the clan talking about the conspicuous lack of animals inside Lyman's trailer. This struck me with some surprise, and even a stab of consternation before grief softened my mood. Hadn't he told me that it was only him and Grace? Had he actually kept other animals in his trailer? His scent was always so animal-like to begin with that I never would have been able to tell if he did have other pets. Knowing Lyman, he probably did. But if he'd set them free, did this mean that he had truly given up on any hope that he'd return alive? Regardless, the tones and thoughts of the clan made it clear that they suspected his fate, as well as Joe's. Even Wadih hadn't bothered to ask me about him, and I knew that it hadn't been from anything Deb had mentioned. Of course, Derek would confirm it.

I stepped outside of the RV to see Derek finally making his appearance. I felt a tinge of uncertainty from him, but that was to be expected. One thing he'd confided in me before I went outside was something about our night and subsequent morning together that had still left him somewhat troubled. Though he had no real regrets about us, he could not shake off a conflicting feeling that our interlude was something of an insult to the memories of Joe and Lyman.

"I think it's just lingering regrets," he'd told me, attempting, however weakly, to brush away his misgivings. I assured him that there was no reason to believe that Lyman would have felt the least bit offended by what we did. Needless to say, Joe would have certainly been adverse to it, but of course, that still had not made the consummation of our relationship regrettable, at least not to me. Derek, of course, knew how I felt about Joe, and ironically, it was that which made him feel somewhat better.

I afforded the moment to kiss him, and when our lips made contact, I caught a glimmer of something . . . alien, perhaps even horrible. It faded away before I could grasp onto it. Its caginess, though, was not an act of Derek's volition, but rather, it was more like a scary dream that had finished fading from his mind in a haze of forgetfulness.

I made it a point to try to recover this elusive . . . thing . . . later, but no sooner than we ended the kiss to a chorus of enthusiastic hoots by the male members of the clan, I felt Derek slip into "leader mode," sweeping away the thoughts of me into an ordered place so that he could do what was necessary. Nevertheless, he afforded me an affectionate smile.

"It's good to see everyone on Elisa's end back here safely," Derek began. He cast a relieved smile at Deb, who smiled back. "She told me everything. And I'm even gladder we finally seemed to shake off Lothos and get one of our own back." He then turned to Wadih, who came front and center. "We got everything packed and ready?"

"Ready and waiting, boss." Wadih then gestured to the two trailers that had belonged to Lyman and Joe. "I . . . ah, well . . ."

"They didn't make it," Derek's voice was small. And for the first time since we'd met, he seemed every bit the young boy his body's deceptive age seemed to suggest. The silence that fell upon the assembly was like a lead curtain, and I could feel the air become heavy with their combined grief and anger at Lothos and his clan. Derek frowned and looked away, swallowing hard, and I sensed the floodgates of his sorrow reopen from a wound not fully healed. He allowed the force of his clan's emotions to strike his heart as solidly as it struck mine. "I'm sorry, guys. I . . . I did everything I could. It was a trap. And . . ."

"We know, Derek." Wadih touched his shoulder and nodded, and the entire clan, knowing Joe in a way I wish I had, and knowing Lyman just as well as me, stood in sympathetic sorrow, but cast no blame his way. "We all knew this was just a gigantic trap. And we also knew we probably wouldn't all make it through it alive. But we gotta count our blessings, you know. At least you came back to us. And Elisa, here, saved all our asses. But remember, we're not out of it yet."

Derek nodded, having now heard the same thing twice, both from me and now from Wadih. His feelings of sorrow and anger both at Lothos and at himself had not changed, nor would they, I imagined, for a very long time. God knew I would try to help him to heal. But at least for now, he was able to be their leader once again.

"We'll mourn once we're safe," Derek said after a weighty pause. He spoke decisively and with his usual maturity that belied his appearance. "I know you all probably want to hear the story; I promise I'll fill you in when we're finally out of this nightmare. For now, all of Joe and Paws' former belongings that are salvageable need to be put in the storage trailer."

"Done and done already," Wadih said.

"Leave their trailers behind, then," Derek ordered. "We don't need any extra weight if we have to make a run for it."

He then cast a questioning gaze to the clan. "Unless someone wants to lay a claim?"

No one spoke but Wadih.

"About that . . ." He placed a folded envelope into Derek's hand. "Lyman left a will."

"That's . . . rare," Derek said with visible surprise. Even in my clan, such things were rare, though we lost people in the war all the time. It was tradition that all our worldly possessions were passed to, or divided among our closest friends, spouse, or if there was one, our consummate host by way of a mediator: usually the Lieutenant in charge of the village or head of the homestead for those of us who lived outside the safety of our cloisters.

"We'll look at it when we get to where we're going," Derek said, tucking the note into the pocket of his hoodie. "For now, as I said, we'll still leave the trailers here. Is there anything else we need to do?"

"That's it, I think," Wadih said and cast a glance back towards the assembly. "Anyone else got questions for the boss?"

When no one answered, Derek smiled. It was a relieved, but weary expression: one that truly displayed how much he and the clan had been through. I was glad to have gotten them through this. In a few hours, God willing, they would be safe, and my mission would be complete. No doubt Father would find a way to guide the remainder of the clan in hiding to the sanctuary. Even with my skill with my Jewel, I couldn't bring the main body instantly there, but one by one, our clan members could fetch those in hiding and bring them safely along after all was said and done.

"Saddle up, then," Derek said, and the clan dispersed to their respective RVs, buses, trucks, and trailers . . . all except Wadih, whom Derek stopped and pulled over to a discreet corner beside Lyman's old home. I'd begun to follow them, but then he then tossed the keys my way. "Warm it up for us, will you, sweetie?" He said with a playful wink.

I was curious to know what the two needed to discuss, but I knew better than to pry. I climbed into the RV and slipped into the driver's seat. I heard everyone else start their engines outside through the windshields, and I turned the key in the ignition to join the chorus. I then scurried back over to the passenger seat and waited for Derek, curling up my knees to my chest. With the long, light blue summer dress I wore, along with leather and cork sandals, I looked just about as young as my appearance suggested.

It wasn't long before I first sensed, then saw Derek as he entered through the side door and came up behind me. His steps were slow, but far from quiet. Of course, there was no way he would have been able to startle me like this. His intent, however, was not to scare me. Rather, he was in good spirits, and his thoughts were edged with a sensuality that surprised me, yet left me giddy with expectation.

"Ready to go, China doll?" He asked.

"Quite ready." I felt my skin tingle as he touched my arm with a gentleness that I had not expected.

"You know, I wanted to say, it's the first time I've seen you in a dress," Derek remarked in the soft voice that we shared in our more intimate moments. He reached out and took the hem of my summer dress in between his fingers, as if appraising its blue fabric. "I was beginning to think you didn't wear them."

"I had one in my satchel," I replied as he sank to one knee by my side. "I wasn't sure why I packed it; it's not something I wear often. When I'm in the field, I find pants or shorts to be more serviceable."

"It looks good on you."

Derek's voice was as gentle as his touch. And from him, I felt a faint echo of the feelings that had germinated when we bathed only briefly before. He smiled, half lidded, and his fingers ran through my curls.

"Did I ever tell you before how beautiful you are?" He asked, his question setting a prickling blaze across my face.

"Only . . . once before," I stammered. "When we first fed."

"I haven't said it often enough, then," Derek said, still gently tangling the fingers of one hand in my hair and brushing the tips of his other hand's fingers against my cheek.

"What girl doesn't want to feel beautiful?" I asked, smiling. I wasn't certain about what had caused this sudden shift in mood, but it certainly was not unwelcomed.

"I'll be sure to rectify that," he whispered, and stole a kiss.

Perhaps "stole a kiss" is too light a term, I believe, as this was more like grand theft lips. That very moment of sensual touch ignited a blaze across my entire being. Had it been the anticipation of our impending safety? Was it his joy at finding freedom to love me as he ought to have? Was it simply a whim? I was not able to tell as his emotions poured into me in that kiss. It was perhaps a bit of all these things. I sank myself into the act completely, reaching out to grasp Derek's arms, and opening my mind to absorb all that was bursting from his heart.

It was Wilson's voice on the CB that finally stopped us.

"This is the PDA police citing our boss for a first degree face-sucking violation." Wilson's tone was the exact mix of casualness and sternness of a police officer giving a ticket to make it positively hilarious. I snickered in the middle of our kiss, at last breaking it, and Derek laughed with me.

"The committee politely requests that our fearless leader and his girlfriend get their asses in lead position so we can get to where they'll have all the time in the world for that kind of stuff," Wilson continued, and was met by a chorus of muffled laughter over the radio.

"The committee has apparently spoken," Derek said in mock disappointment. He gave an over-dramatic sigh as he stood and resettled himself into the driver's seat. "Looks like we're going to have to wait 'til later."

"Unfortunately," I said on the edge of a titter.

"How'd they even know?" Derek asked as he shifted the

RV into drive and rolled us into what would be the lead of the caravan. Despite his size, he was a very competent driver and was able to fuddle the mind of any highway patrol officer who might take notice of his appearance. However, he tended to play by the rules as a driver, and nighttime made a good cover for his looks.

"Deb probably sensed it," I guessed, shrugging with a combination of indifference and amusement. "Or maybe someone snuck a peek while heading to their vehicles and decided to pass it along to the caravan."

"Killjoys," Derek muttered in a flat voice and spun the steering wheel in the direction of the parking lot's exit. He pushed down on the accelerator and we were off.

"Did I ever tell you that I love you?" He asked, casting a soft, sincere smile my way.

"Now that you do far more often," I replied, feeling the heat make a brief return to my face.

He reached over to briefly caress my cheek as we gained speed down the road, with the clan following close behind.

"I love you," He said.

"I love you," I answered. And our thoughts met in the kiss that our lips couldn't make.

***

We listened to the radio for the first three hours or so as we drove, until we got bored of it and decided instead to talk.

"You know, I almost forgot," Derek said, reaching out to switch the radio off. "I meant to ask you about your family. The whole time you were with us, you rarely spoke about your home. I know your dad's the leader, and back at the hotel, you mentioned Roland. He's the guy who took care of you when you were . . . well, little? I mean really, little, like a kid?"

I shook with suppressed laughter at his awkwardness in

describing the years that I was truly as much a child in mind as in body. Derek was right. Though I learned quite a bit about his clan, which had served as his surrogate family, I'd been arguably tight-lipped about my home life, though I had nothing to hide about it. I supposed it was time to be more forthcoming. A tiny bit of my suppressed laughter managed to trickle into the beginnings of my speech when I explained.

"Yes, he was. Both he and Father raised me."

"So no mother?"

"Not really. Father married Amelia only recently. We get on well, though. She's a good listener, but really can't give me much advice, since I've got over a century on her few decades. I'm the one who usually ends up educating her, in fact. Before Amelia, the only female I was truly close to was Aiko, but she's always been more of a teacher to me. She taught me all I know about thaumaturgy. She and I are fairly close. Or, at least we used to be."

"Something went sour between you?" Derek asked.

"It was something that happened to her, actually," I answered. "She was captured on a mission and went missing for months until a spy finally dug up her location. He died for his information, but we were able to extract Aiko before Lothos could have her relocated."

I saw a shudder ripple through Derek, and sensed a flurry of unpleasant images flash across the theater of his mind. He had firsthand experience of the unpleasantness Lothos' clan inflicted upon its captives.

"They . . . did something to her," I explained, recalling Aiko's now seemingly perpetual depression, punctuated by periods of bloodlust and sexual ravenousness that she expended upon Roland. "She now rarely comes out of her room, except to find Roland."

"They were an item once, I take it?" Derek asked, and I nodded.

"It was on-again, off-again, even before her capture," I said. "But now, she hunts him down, and no one sees or hears from either of them for about a week or longer. Then Roland shows up again, painfully thin and often walking bow-legged. And pretty much everyone knows what's been going on then."

"Damn."

"Fortunately, that's the extent of drama in my inner circle," I said, glad to be off of that subject. "Aiko aside, the others in my family I've truly seen as more teachers, like Justin and Reanon, or at least doting 'aunties' who come around once in a blue moon, like Nandi. Justin trained me in combat like all new recruits, since he's the weapons master. But since Aiko and I were closer, I prefer just to use my Jewel. I'm more proficient at it than anything else."

"And your size makes using certain weapons a bit problematic, I'll bet." Derek added.

"You have no idea," I said with a rueful grin. I yawned, feeling suddenly tired. It was probably the monotony of the highway, as Derek and I had not tired each other out back in the bathtub as we'd had in bed. In fact, I felt more alive than I ever had afterwards. "Reanon is . . . well, she's not cold, but she's not terribly social either. And Nandi is about the closest thing to an actual mother I've had. But she lives on her own, and visits our village infrequently. She and Father have a history, and she still holds a candle for him, so she keeps her distance. But she's never without stories, and she's always welcomed me with open arms."

"So you've never been short on people who loved you," Derek said, and I could feel a puff of jealousy arise like a very brief, but nevertheless foul odor.

I yawned again and stretched, but this did not seem to offset the unexpected lethargy spreading into my limbs.

"It's okay, love. I know you haven't had the life I've had, but you'll get to know my family soon enough, and they'll be yours. You and Roland, I think will get on especially-"

This time, my yawn was loud and full.

"Oh, do excuse me," I said, suddenly abashed. "I don't

know why I'm so tired, especially at night."

"Could be that you're excited for finally getting out of this mess?" Derek said. By this time, my eyelids were beginning to feel ever more weighted, and I knew that keeping them open was fast becoming a losing battle.

"Maybe it is," I admitted, my words hollowing out with another yawn. "All the adventure we've had, and this sudden cautious optimism can't be a good combo. Perhaps a quick nap couldn't hurt." I struggled against sleep for just a moment more in order to be assured that everything was well in hand. "Have you memorized the way?"

"We went over it several times when we planned it," Derek said, and gestured to the map curled up in the drink holder. It was our only key to finding our way, without a GPS that Lothos' clan could track. "And I'm not above asking for directions if I have to."

"Good, then."

By this time, his words and mine sounded distant and muffled, as if through a paper towel tube lined with cotton. I was falling fast asleep, and I leaned back in my chair, settling against my seatbelt and closing my eyes.

"Wake me if you need anything," I murmured with sleep-slurred words. I felt the RV give a gentle lean as Derek turned down a curve in the road, and I allowed the rocking motion to lull me into even deeper rest.

I floated there on the thread between sleep and wakefulness, aware of everything around me, yet of nothing. I heard Derek's voice in my ear. It whispered something to me with an urgency that I'd never heard before. And even in the state that I was in, I could sense something in his tone. The tone and words were tense, carrying an accompanying sensation that was stridently suppressed, lest it pull me along and fully out of sleep.

How I wish I could remember what it was . . .

Chapter Twenty

I awoke disoriented by the near total darkness, yet fully aware of two things. The first was that I'd slept for far too long for it to have been merely a nap, and the second was the keen throb at the edges of my awareness that caused the nauseating pit in my stomach. It was the clear and terrifying sense that I was in terrible danger.

That second notion went beyond instinct. It was buoyed by the background static of minds that surrounded me, though they were subdued, blurred, as if they were all inebriated or cloaked by way of a Jewel. Yet I could sense one quality that stood out and spoke volumes above their subdued timbre. They were all evil.

Vile, corrupt minds, though their thoughts were not directed my way, tormented me in the darkness. The scents in the immediate area, however, were familiar. I was still in the RV, still curled in the passenger seat; there was the familiar leather and carpeting and Derek's scent, but only prevalent as a background odor, as if he hadn't been present for hours.

I was driven by the desire to be away from the RV as quickly as possible, though in hindsight, I came to believe that perhaps it was the safest place I could have been. As quietly as I dared, I slipped out of the passenger seat and tiptoed through the living area.

It was when I tried to summon a weak infrared light to more quickly find out if the RV had been ransacked that I realized the next horrifying thing. My Jewel no longer functioned. This meant two things: First was that the Others knew I was here; second was that they had attuned an anti-Jewel to my Jewel somewhere in the vicinity. They were a thaumaturgist's bane, these anti-Jewels. As long as one was active, my Jewel would be nothing more than a pretty, but powerless gemstone, fused with the inside of my body.

Fighting down a distant feeling of growing panic, I searched for my satchel. I found it where I'd left it, on our bed and untouched. Within its disproportionately vast interior, I kept a belt of small throwing knives. In spite of their size, the blades were long enough to pierce the heart. Such an injury would not kill our kind, but it would cause an egregious enough wound to slow us down significantly as we healed. Justin had trained me extensively with these, and so I felt somewhat safer as I quietly opened the door to the outside. There was a line of running lights along the floor, marking its intersection with a sheer stone wall, but no one seemed to be nearby. I'd expected some guards beside the door, but I neither received the impression of any other nearby presence, nor had I seen any.

My insides burned with a pang of anguish and barely-suppressed fear as I thought about Derek. Where was he? If he had been taken, why hadn't I? As it was when he and Lyman had driven off to parts unknown to find Joe, I couldn't even sense him. It was as if someone had cut a mental rope that set me adrift in blackest space. And though I tried not to let my mind wander to such musings, I could not help but go back to the fear of the worst fate for him.

This already unsettling worry was accompanied by another persistent, nagging feeling that I had to remember something. It had been with me from the moment I awoke, and through my search of the RV. Even now, it was on the edge of my memory, a fly in the corridors of my mind, dancing maddeningly out of reach, evading all my attempts at capture. It would have been merely annoying had it not been for the urgency to know what it was that I felt. For all I knew, it could have been a matter of life and death, for me, Derek, or the clan.

I leaned forward and cradled my forehead in the palm of my hand as the weight of my fears and worries threatened to cave in upon me. I felt as if my insides would spill upon the ground from press of internal and external emotions that suddenly accosted me. There were minds nearby; that was certain, but all of them belonged to the enemy. I doubled over trembling as the questions overpowered my thoughts, and the muffled droning of the minds of the Others buzzed about me. God, where was Derek? And what happened to the Vagabonds? Had they been captured as well, and taken elsewhere? And the baby! That poor, innocent thing . . . was she now subject to Lothos' tender mercies?

With willpower that I did not understand, I pulled myself together, willing myself free of that consuming miasma of melancholy and misery. This would not do at all. I couldn't continue like this, not in this much danger. I had to prioritize. The first order of business was simply to get the hell out of wherever I was, and that was what I set myself to do.

Nowhere smelled like outside, not even the direction opposite the RV. In fact, I backtracked to find the tunnel stopping at a sheer drop, the opposite end of which I could not see. But I did smell running water from somewhere deep below the chasm. The lack of an outside scent was not unexpected if the place was deep underground or hermetically sealed; knowing Lothos' clan and their love of the shadows, I supposed the former. Nevertheless, the RV had been moved here somehow. I supposed someone had used a Jewel for the job.

At the thought of Jewels, I felt a relapse of my frustration from discovering that mine did not work, along with the sensation of near-recollection, which was fast becoming infuriating. I was lost in what most likely would be a maze of tunnels with the enemy who were, equally likely, playing some elaborate game. I could get by without my Jewel; Justin's training had left me quite capable of fending for myself in other ways, but the thought of squaring off against adult-sized vampires with little else but my bare hands and blades, could not help but diminish my confidence just a little.

Fighting back against the stifling fear and worries, I picked my way through the corridors ahead of the RV, turning through its twists, and keeping as much of a mental record of my path as possible -not that it would do any good; the RV was the last place I wanted to be. I'd kept a spare belt of throwing knives in my satchel, which I used to mark the direction opposite of which I had gone, but these soon ran out, and I was left with little else but my wits to remember the path I'd trod.

Soon, despite my best efforts, I was completely lost.

The minds, however, were certainly closer.

Had there been any cover, I would have relied on my small form for stealth, but aside from the darkness, I was out in the open: a fact that made me feel worse than naked.

The tunnels were almost like sewage systems: bare floor and sheer walls, but with no flow of water, no pipes, service corridors, or ladders leading to the surface. It was all an endless, monotonous, unlit labyrinth.

Then came the Minotaur.

More accurately, it was a lone vampire carrying a flashlight. Its brightness caught me by surprise. At first, I was afraid that he would spot me; he was certainly close enough to have caught my scent. But it turned out that he was distracted by his own joviality. I watched as he ambled down the corridor perpendicular to mine, singing "Monster Mash" loudly, and -though I never thought such a thing was possible- worse than the original version. Or perhaps it was my particular dislike for our kind affecting Bela Lugosi's "Dracula" accent.

With preternatural speed, I caught him from behind and pulled him to the ground. He was, of course bigger than me, despite his lankiness, but I managed to topple him by sheer momentum and pin his wrists beneath my knees. God, did he smell horrid! Lothos' clan always had an unpleasant reek, but his was worse than normal. But it was his strength that worried me the most. With my size, and with no access to my Jewel, I was little more effective than a child trying to subdue an adult. Fortunately, I allowed my throwing knives to do the talking.

"Where is the way out?" I whispered harshly, pressing the blade to his neck. His flashlight, which he'd dropped when I attacked, spun on the ground, and its beam finally rested on my face and his, casting our images in stark brightness and inky shadow. "Tell me now!"

The vampire laughed. It was a dry, rasping noise like sandpaper being swiped loosely over plywood. His eyes, tiny crimson beads in an ocean of white, spun around eerily independent of one another. I suppressed the chill that this evoked; Lothos' clan always loved to show off with their shape-shifting talents, drawing of the human revulsion of body horror to intimidate their prey. I was, however, not one whose gut was so easily turned by such things. I scowled, and pressed the blade deeper into his flesh to silence him. But instead of drawing blood, it merely pressed his skin deeper inward. It created an impossible indentation, as if he'd changed into a substance that was no different from rubber. I pressed deeper, but it gave even more, stretching like softened bubble gum.

"There is . . . no way out!" The fiend's voice came as a halting whisper as his sandpaper laugh continued on. I felt his wrists grow thinner beneath the weight of my knees until they slipped from beneath me. I watched as his entire torso flattened and elongated, and began to slip away from me like an emptied garden hose being wound back into its spool.

"Master . . . wants you to come to dinner . . ." he wheezed. Free from my futile grip, he reared upwards, thin and gangly, with a flattened torso, like some grotesque cobra. "But he didn't say we couldn't play with the food first!"

The fiend's sandpapery laugh echoed through the labyrinth's walls, and was soon joined by sounds that were not unlike leafs of paper falling from a stack to the ground. The source of that sound, however, turned my insides into ice.

The walls were not walls at all, but rather a mosaic of vampires who had flattened themselves against the true wall and changed their bodies' color and texture to match it. I watched with consuming despair as they rose to their feet: hundreds of paper dolls that inflated into human shapes, hungry for prey. I fought away panic like a lion within, but felt the steel I'd forged inside falling away at the undeniable hopelessness of my situation. The scent of Lothos' clan had been everywhere in the maze, no matter where I went, and so I had no idea that here, they surrounded me. It brought to mind a grotesque exaggeration of a scene from "The Whiz," where the munchkins had detached themselves from the wall in the playground upon Dorothy's arrival in the New York style Oz. The movie had actually contained quite a fair bit of nightmarish things, far more than just this, but now I was standing in the midst of the true nightmare. I watched on as more flat human shapes peeled off of the walls and ceiling, fell to the ground, and regained their human shapes to advance upon me and join the elongated cobra fiend.

My training funneled all my burgeoning fear into adrenaline until I felt a readiness that keyed me up in a way I hadn't felt since I'd unknowingly fed from a man who had an amphetamine addiction. The cobra fiend, I decided, would be the first to fall. A mental attack was rarely lethal on our kind, but it would incapacitate for a long while if done right. The cobra didn't know what hit him.

Brave though I was, and fearless, if at least for the moment, I was still outnumbered and outclassed. The cobra fiend did die. I saw his head fall unceremoniously to the ground, his flattening useless to the speed and force of the sharp edge of my blade after my mental attack had stunned him. Several more fiends either fell to my blades or were incapacitated by my talents, but they were replaced by five, seven, and ten more, all advancing inexorably. My blades mowed down my share of them, but in spite of my martial skills and mental gift, without my Jewel, I was only a child. I shut off the minds of a few others and exhausted my ammunition, and then the press of the remaining fiends who jumped into the fray quickly brought me to my limit.

The blows continued even as I went down, and, with a sharp crack, faded quickly to black.

***

It is always the same question, ever since I was brought here, unconscious, beaten and bruised. They know when I regain consciousness each and every time. And that is when the questioning begins, always the same, always repeated until I answer. It doesn't matter if I reply with a curse, or a lie, and it both terrifies and comforts me.

"Where are they?"

That question, asked in that flat, creaking voice, means that Derek's clan is safe. Of course, they are. They would have reached the sanctuary by now. Nearly all of my clan's land holdings are locked away from the rest of the world in pocket dimensions of their own, but mirror worlds instead of empty lands, refractions of Earth, with life and livable land, access given only to a trusted few. The clan might be worried about Derek and me, but at least they are safe. That is all that matters.

"Where are they?"

The voice grows insistent and cruel, as if it is supposed to terrify me. And again, I laugh. I hang by manacles which dig into my wrists, naked and in a dank cell that is surprisingly free of cockroaches. Funny, that.

"WHERE ARE THEY?"

I smile, as I am wont to do, despite the pain of thirst. I can neither see, nor sense my interrogator; I have seen no others since I arrived here, neither human nor of my kind, so I have no idea if this is another intimidation tactic, or he is truly furious.

And then, I choose to speak.

"Go to hell."

I never see who speaks, or who does what happens next, but I always know what to expect. But this time, I know it will be worse. Much, much worse. I was at my limit the last time; my body feels light and is wracked with pain that has been growing from the first time the torment began. My fangs stand out without aid of blood or want of sex, and I know I'll be brought over to it this time.

I hear the sound, like two small stones grinding against each other. There is no light, but I know that a hole has opened in the dark end of the room. I hear the sound of metal sliding into place. I brace myself as well as I can, expecting the worst . . .

. . . And it comes.

It is a loud pop, and followed immediately by a sickening blow to my gut. But the pain does not ebb. It remains as the feeling of needles digs into my flesh, followed by an awful pulling sensation. I don't want to look down again; I don't wish to see the horrifying reality, and what it means. But like a train wreck, I am compelled to witness it, and once again see the ring of the thimble-sized funnel that was shot into my stomach, three inches above and to the right of my navel. I watch as the blood begins to pour out of the wound and onto the floor. I feel the pulling sensation agonize me from the inside. I twist in misery and agony, the pain flaring, ebbing, and flaring again, as if machines are inside of me, searching for every last drop that was missed the last time. I know there isn't much left. I am unsure of how much time has passed since I came here, but I know that this pain will increase until it becomes unbearable and unending . . . until I see nothing but red, and only blood will bring me back to safety.

At last, the funnel slips out. I hear it clatter to the ground, ringing in my aching ears.

The pain does not abate. It flares through every vein, every pore, and every centimeter of my exposed body. Even the faint breeze is like needles. My stomach, my veins pulse in agony, crying out for what my kind must have. My mouth is like sandpaper; my throat is like an open wound, but I hear and feel the moan that erupts from me.

Time passes, as it does: slow, interminable, unknowable. The pain remains, hovering about that place that would send me into blessed unconsciousness, but never quite bringing me there. My every breath is agony, and my heart beats a starving staccato cadence that pulses pain through me.

And then, I smell it.

Food.

Blood.

Fresh and strong is the smell, and everything goes black. But what I hear before the oblivion is the inhuman screech that forces its way out of my lungs.

Somehow I wrest myself from the blackness. And instantly, I wish I had stayed there. The thirst is my tormentor now. There is no voice, no scrape of stone, no placement of the barrel, no thimble lodged into my gut. But once again, after indeterminate, maddening time, is the scent.

The blood.
The madness.
The darkness.
And it happens again.
And again.
And again.

Each time, I am pure will. Each time, I pull, drag, wrest myself free of the hunger, and crawl back to sanity . . . back to pain.

But this time, something is different. Through the pain, I realize what has happened. I'm no longer suspended. The chain is on the floor, its links lying like a lifeless snake behind me while cold, stony ground supports my body. But even as the feel of that stone sets off more agony, I don't gasp or spasm. I can't. I barely understand or recognize the pain. It is merely a part of me now, and the beast: that lust, that hunger that resides within all of my kind is right on the other side of the door of my fevered mind, unfettered as I am.

And then, at last, I hear it. The question, denied me time and time again, while I was allowed to wallow in pain and madness.

"Where are they?"

It sounds calm, almost polite this time, and I barely recognize it as words. But the small part of me that is still aware, still sane, still Elisa, understands. And holding on to the vestiges of loyalty, and to the barely-remembered mission, she answers, though I barely recognize the whispering voice.

"Fuck you."

For the longest time, there is little else but the rapid cadence of my starving, immortal heart, firing ever present pain into every cell. There is silence, and there is agony.

And then, there is the sound of stone against stone. Much larger than what precluded the draining funnel. The entire wall across from me is being moved aside.

The scent of blood sets me afire, and the pain explodes as light from the other side of the moving wall highlights a human form.

The beast breaks through the door.

It howls within, and becomes me.

And fade to black.

***

I felt satisfied.

For once, the red was not from the pain, but from the blood.

I began to feel again, and care again. The agony, the pain, the horrifying excrucation were laid to rest. All this I realized as my clarity and sanity returned to me like a kidnapped loved one.

I wished almost immediately that it hadn't.

I saw the limbs, or at least their remnants, scattered haphazardly across the corner. A bit of shoulder, two fingers, part of the forearm. Half of a foot lay across from me less than a yard away. The torso was masticated and eviscerated in a way that made it seem like a wild animal had abandoned it as a meal partway. One leg remained intact. Fragments of bone and viscera were strewn about splatters of blood. Everywhere, there was the scent of old, useless blood.

And then, I saw the head.

I knew that head. I would know it until the day I died . . . if I ever would die.

It was the park ranger: the very same one I'd hunted that night in the woods.

Despair grabbed me like a horror from the deep and dragged me below the reach of any light. It was joined by its sister, horror, which reached inside and tore my heart from my chest. I scrambled away from the remains, kicking at whatever pieces were in my way, putting nearly three yards' distance between myself and my ill-gotten meal. I grasped at the bricks of the floor, threatening to crack my claws with my strength as my vision blurred with newly-formed tears that I'd run out of in my madness.

"No . . ." I whispered, barely mouthing the words, the sound barely making it out of my throat. "No, no, no, no, no . . ."

I gasped and wailed. Lothos' disciples must have seen me that night! It was the only way. Deb had said we were being watched. I had no idea at the time. Sick demons that they were, they must have decided to keep him for sport, perhaps to torment me with later. My sorrow and self-hatred spilled over at the sight of the carnage that I'd wrought. I wanted to vomit up all that I had taken from him, and restore his body, would that I could. I knew that I couldn't help myself, but this violation to myself and my own morals tore at me worse than that damnable thimble funnel. I would have gladly returned to the madness of hunger if it would have saved him, but it was all useless. He was dead, and by my hands. And all I could do now was weep.

Some time had passed before I heard him.

"Poor child . . ."

The voice came from directly behind me. It was a voice that I knew . . . could never forget.

I froze and turned slowly around.

"Lothos!"

Chapter Twenty-One

Lothos' choices of form were as mercurial as his temperament. Father had explained much of his former colleague's nature to me, often leaving me wishing that he hadn't. Among those things he described was his true form. Where our skin was usually a pearlescent white on those of us of European, Mediterranean, or Asian descent, Lothos was onyx black. No one of his clan shared such a color, but according to our histories, his first lieutenants in the beginning of the war had such skin. But as the bloodlines diluted, the blackness faded to the same whiteness that nearly all our kind now shared, save those of African stock. Like Father, Lothos' hair, which fell below his shoulder blades, was white as to be almost luminous, but worn long and straight in comparison to Father's shorter, feathery crown. He was bare-chested and bare footed, wearing only a pair of tan cargo pants. An ornate silver bracelet of very ancient design hung upon his left wrist and a decorative, silver claw ring clasped the middle finger of his right hand. His crimson stare fell upon me like a vulture from sharp, clear eyes.

He smiled inhumanly wide with a near-lipless mouth, revealing a maw with fangs upon the canines of his upper and lower jaw. I forced back a shudder as I recalled a time when Father had told me that this form was a thing that he used only for special occasions. Now I was here as his reluctant guest, and the recipient of this dubious honor. That could mean nothing good.

"Your clan tends to take the fun out of this, you know that?" He leaned forward upon the metal chair that had been placed about three yards away from me, at the opposite end of the cell where I'd hung for God only knew how long. "Normally, I like to toy with my victims you know … usually my own children who have, shall we say, fallen out of favor with their superiors. Most of them are deaf to the thoughts of others, and so few see me nowadays that they have no way of knowing if it's really me, or one of my other children who is just toying with their minds." He shook with a whispering, nightmarish laugh. "It's really funny to watch, actually."

It was then that I noticed the glass. It had been so clear as to be nearly invisible: a single pane, bolted into the brickwork at both ends that stretched from one wall to the left of me to the one on the right. This entire cell must have been quite versatile, rigged with various tools for restraint and holding one against his or her will. My scattered memories of however long I had been in thirst-starved madness, along with the ranger's remains were at least clear on the fact that there had been nothing between me and the human when I began my frenzy. So I was trapped again, though without manacles, and accompanied by the scent of quickly putrefying blood.

"Why feed me?" I asked. The blood had regenerated me, yet I spoke in a voice that surprised me by its hoarseness. "I thought you'd just want me dead."

"Maybe I want to enjoy it," Lothos said. "I know you all too well, little witch. And you've caused me a lot of trouble over the years. You're a special fish I've wanted to get my hooks into for a very, very long time."

"You could've sent an invitation," I said, finding that my ordeal had not drained me of all my salt. It filled me with a singular pleasure, allowing the snark to drip from my words. "It's not like my address is a secret."

"Too bad you've been away on business, though." Again, there was that dry, crackling laugh. And Lothos' grin nearly circumvented half his head. "God, I love it when they're this feisty. Your sensei was exactly the same, you know, when we captured her. How is she these days, by the way? Still broken? Still rocking back and forth from hiding in her room to shagging her boyfriend raw in whatever place is most convenient?"

"You bastard!"

It was like his words had shaken a bottle of pure carbonated rage inside of me. I launched myself forward with preternatural speed. He was the one who did it to Aiko, changed her into the shell that she was. I wanted nothing more than to make him a match for the body in my corner of the cell, but the glass easily rebuffed my movements, knocking me backwards onto my unprotected bottom upon the blood-soaked floor. I scrambled to my feet and pressed my bloodied hands and forehead against the inflexible partition, as if to will my strength to shatter it. "What did you do to her?"

"The same thing I'll be doing to you, my dear," Lothos said with cruel matter-of-factness. "I'm afraid you don't have quite her spirit, though. You eviscerated the very first meal that was sent your way when we drained you to a feral state. Your sensei held on to her sanity for over two weeks before she finally took her first human. But she bounced back from even this. She had spirit that I've seldom seen in your clan; it was truly commendable. But do you want to know what finally broke her?"

"You'll tell me, whether I want to or not," I said.

"Yes, you're right," Lothos replied. "You know me just as well, it seems. You see, she started tearing through her meals pretty regularly after she stopped resisting. But then, after the first three or four drainings, she started restraining herself again. This poor human had to have stayed in that cage for three days, and she stayed in the corner as if he was a wild lion, and she were the helpless human. After the third day, she calmed down, but they never spoke. She did feed from him, though. And normally. No frenzy, no screaming, no gory mess. But the real shocker is how they even went at it like bunnies afterwards! Didn't even seem to matter that someone might be watching; they were just running on automatic. It was, of course, confusing at first. She had us all baffled until we realized what was happening."

I knew what it was. And my rage melted away into anguish for what had been done to her. There was no need for Lothos to say more; the ordeal played itself clearly in my mind's eye, and his description matched it word for gruesome word.

"God . . . she'd found her consummate host . . ." I murmured. There was no need to look into the horrid recesses of Lothos' mind to glean this information, and I wouldn't have dared even if I needed to. Though the passage lingered there like an open sewage pipe, searching his thoughts might be a tantalizing, if disturbing affair for any of our kind who could stomach it. But, as Father taught me, they would be foolish to try, as his Jewel left this seemingly open path as a deadly trap for any telepath with far less sense.

"Indeed." Lothos threw back his coldly lustrous falls of hair, and his facial features shifted into something less grotesque, almost human, in fact, had it not been for his skin's ebon sheen. "She fought us even harder afterwards. No matter how long we let her starve, she always seemed to control herself when that human was brought back. So we decided to see just how far we could stretch the beast."

I could not hold back the tears from my burning eyes as the monster king prattled on. All this time, never knowing what had changed Aiko, my teacher and closest friend, into such a hollow shell of herself . . . all this time, wishing she would share her pain with me, but respecting her silence . . . and now I sat here, covered in blood and viscera, sharing her horrible circumstances and bemoaning the loss of my ignorance.

"Days, weeks, and then nearly a month. Then, my dear, she finally broke. That quaint thing your little clan calls a 'consummate host,' the choice brisket you long for in your human cattle, the thing you write stories and songs about . . . made into what they truly are." Lothos' glee had reached a fever pitch, buzzing in my mind and infecting me with nausea. "It was a truly glorious accomplishment; I made sure to get plenty of pictures."

"I think I'd just prefer for you to kill me now," I said in a grim monotone.

"All in good time," Lothos punctuated each word in the sentence as its own individual syllable, speaking in a mock-fatherly tone. Then with a great sigh, he slouched in his chair, examining me as if I were a prize turkey nearing Thanksgiving.

"You know . . . seeing you there, amidst the blood and entrails, and all that talk of consummate hosts and whatnot has made me a bit peckish."

He shifted his gaze to what I'd first taken to be a grate in the wall, and snapped his fingers. No sooner than he did this, the bricks sectioned away into a doorway or passage.

I had not known that it was possible for my spirits to rise and sink at the same time as I saw who stepped through.

"Derek!"

My voice cracked with such emotion as to make it sound like a squeal. He appeared through the passage, leading a woman close behind. She was human, judging by her complexion and scent, and had been used by other vampires before, both for blood and sex. She was a beautiful specimen: mid-twenties, perhaps, young, lithe, large-breasted, and with blonde hair cut into a fairy style. I don't know why I expected her to be naked; perhaps some of Lothos's more lewd thoughts bled haplessly across the gulf between our minds, but she was. It was, however, a state of affairs many of our hosts found themselves in with us all too often, for "easy access," as we liked to say.

Derek was clothed . . . marginally. His apparel was little more than a loincloth and sandals, giving him the appearance of a slave of ancient times who catered to the desires of his liege lord. But no sooner than I saw him, I knew that something was very, very wrong.

His mind and the woman's were both exactly alike . . . in that I felt nothing from either: no thoughts, no emotions. Had it not been for the presence of their mental timbre, I would have supposed they weren't even really there. The look in both their eyes was distant and blank, and my heart wrenched with hopeless grief.

Desperately, like a drowning woman gasping to stay afloat, I tried to press my way into Derek's mind, hoping to grasp some thread of the familiar mental landscape of the man I loved, but a stab of pain hit me like a three-second migraine. It tore sharply into my body and down to my extremities. My legs weakened, and again I collapsed to the bloody ground.

"If you tried to touch his mind, I recommend against it," Lothos said. His voice was different, softer -an exact replica of a female timbre. I watched as he completed the transformation that he was in the midst of. It was like something out of a cartoon, but disturbing where it should have been funny. His formerly solid chest softened and his pectorals ballooned into very female-looking breasts while his build became sleeker and angles became curves. "You'll run into my 'keep out' sign, courtesy of my thaumaturgists."

Lothos' voice, though distinctively that of a woman, still contained that same whisper, the same implied menace behind every syllable, which had been evident in his true tone. In the span of seconds, he was completely female: a softer, sleeker version of himself: a creature of terrifying regality and as buxom as the human who stood before him for his appraisal, and, as rumor suggested, as fully female as he was male. This was not exactly substantiated, but because Dhampir births were diminishingly rare in his clan, most were born through Lothos in female form by way of human sires. But despite the shell of gender, whether he allowed himself to become pregnant with the seed of humans, he was still every bit the dark enemy of my clan as he had been for nearly ten millennia.

Derek came to Lothos' side, waiting like a lapdog as the fiend went to caress the woman's doll-like cheek and lips with the tenderness of a lover.

"Ah, yes . . . snack fit for a king . . . or queen."

Without pretense, he clenched the woman's jaw in his strong grip. So swift and ferocious were his movements, that had she been in full control of her faculties, I believe she would have cried out, or even passed out from the pain. Instead, she was utterly compliant as he twisted her neck to expose her carotid artery to his extended fangs. I watched as he drained her before my eyes, her form utterly willing in her own demise. I watched her skin grow pale, heard the slowing of her heart and breathing, listening to it fade and weaken, until there was silence. Lothos emptied her like a human would empty a can of beer. With a loud, satisfied sigh, and a rancid and very unladylike belch, he tossed her corpse to the corner behind him. She landed in a twisted heap that reminded me of a yoga session gone horribly wrong.

"Consummate hosts . . ." Lothos mused aloud, now setting his sights upon Derek. He brushed his hand against his shoulder with the affected affection he'd just lavished upon the nameless human girl, and immediately my rage swelled again with fervor that would have burned this cell to the ground. I wanted to rip his head off. Seeing my reaction, he smiled with ever more wickedness.

"You know something of this, don't you?" His voice had lowered several octaves, and his mind leaked with the subtle but distinct menace behind his words, "You and Derek, as a matter of fact? It's so rare when it happens between two of our kind. But I had him first."

I believe he expected me to be surprised, but Derek's story had given me enough cause to infer this. It was disgusting to think that Lothos had forged such a bond with Derek as ours, but to hear him brag about it this way made me want to eviscerate him as they made me do to that poor ranger.

"And he escaped," I said in an attempt to kick his perceived victory in the balls. And from the look of fury that briefly flashed across his face -a look that was quickly replaced by his normal veneer of smug self-assurance-, I believe I had achieved the desired effect.

"It's amazing how easily the appearance of freedom can be maintained," Lothos said, regaining his composure. "You, my dear, need to understand that he never truly escaped. How could I let him? You know of the pleasure you give each other in feeding; you know of the bond: that irritating thing that enslaves you to your host. I could no more let him go than I could stop being me. He gave me too much pleasure; he was a treat that surpassed even the sweetest human morsel. How could I resist that? And of course, I didn't try. After all, this very form you see here is what I used to make him into a man . . . so to speak. It was certainly one of my more sublime moments."

His words caused him to tremble in a way that reminded me of my reaction from Derek's touch in bed . . . and I nearly retched.

"And of course, you certainly don't just let such a treasure like that walk away, do you?" Lothos said as he ran his hands through Derek's hair like a favored pet. "But I gave him leeway, let him go off to join his little band of Vagabonds and play the leader until I had need for him. Tonight, I did. So I woke up the little voice I planted in his head, and had him come back to me, like a good little boy."

Lothos ran his fingers across Derek's lips as Derek would do to me. I tried to maintain my own decorum through this taunting and chilling revelation, but did a less than admirable job. And my rancor only fueled Lothos' delight.

"It needed to be done, actually," Lothos continued. "I'd have been content to let him alone for a bit longer . . . maybe even join your merry clan if that was his desire. Imagine all the secrets that I could have learned! But circumstances forced my hand. That's what happens when you commit a wholesale slaughter of my people, after all. But I think that my little Derek worked well as an 'ace-in-the-hole,' don't you?"

I felt cold all over. Cold and numb. It was as if someone had torn every vestige of hope from me. I collapsed to my knees. Derek's clan had lost so many even before I came, and after that, we'd braved attacks from thaumaturgists and several more brushes with death by his clan, only to have everything taken apart by Derek himself, who had been made into an unwitting pawn from the beginning.

"Now all I need to do is wait until my mind-readers can work deeply enough into his subconscious to get what I need out." Lothos ran a splayed hand across Derek's slightly narrow chest while Derek gazed out at nothing. "That will unfortunately take more time than I'm currently ready to invest. But then you came along: a happy coincidence . . . or perhaps not, seeing as you have become his . . . mate." He spoke the word in a low, flat voice, laced with such disgust as if it were acid on his tongue. "Of course, you have been a lot more fun than my poor estranged host, who has, unfortunately, not been the most stimulating of conversationalists. But he's serviceable in bed. You, however, my dear . . . these last few evenings were merely a taste of the fun we're going to have!"

He stalked closer to the glass and again gave that inhumanly wide smile, which bled all the former beauty out of his female guise.

"So here it is, little witch. Derek, whom you thought to be yours, was actually the ultimate mole. He was mine, all mine, all along. You've been double-crossed by me, through him. He could no more avoid this than I could undo the bond I made with him."

A sharp, familiar agony hit me in the stomach. I looked down with dismay to see another one of those damned thimble funnels lodged in my gut, its tendrils of pain reaching in and pulling on me as I doubled over. I grasped desperately at its slippery surface and attempted, failing, to rip it out, or hold in the newly-acquired blood it siphoned out of the wound.

"And we're back to square one again," Lothos said. "Unless, of course, you want to tell me the location and access to the sanctuary you brought his clan to? If you do, I promise your death with be swift, painless, and even honorable. I'll even arrange for your remains to be sent back to your father for a proper burial . . . which is more than you gave my children these past few nights."

"Go . . . to hell!" I growled through my teeth as the pain wracked my body, and the thimble mercilessly ejected the blood upon which I had gorged myself. It worked with greater fury than it had before, draining me much more quickly, and I watched with tear-blurred vision as the vital fluid flowed across the floor and merged with the drying substance of the park ranger's remains. It would be awhile yet before thirst madness would set in, but the thirst was indeed coming back, starting as a tiny gnawing sensation in my veins, crying out in counterpoint to the thimble's agonizing pull, and growing by inches. I did not want to die this way, tortured until I was nothing else but a starved husk, a mad dog that could only be put down, but I would not betray Derek's clan.

Derek gazed passively through me, as if my suffering were motes of dust in the air.

Help me, Derek . . . please! I believe I spoke this as well as screamed it to his mind, but it was like an empty tunnel. I felt nothing from him.

"I'm afraid he won't be able to help you," Lothos jeered. "My mind-readers are thorough. He is utterly compliant, and responds only to me. Otherwise, he can only do what he is told or asked. Allow me to demonstrate."

I watched, helpless and despondent as Lothos called Derek to his side, with a voice that was as tender as any words Derek would have spoken to me after feeding or making love.

"Kiss me," he said. And Derek obeyed without question. Lothos, still in his female form, allowed it to linger, clearly excited over the act, and perhaps musing over some unsavory acts later on that night, sighed when it was done and smiled, caressing Derek's cheek and lips.

"This is so much fun!" Lothos remarked with another peal of his papery laugh. "I haven't seen you suffer like this since the night you were turned."

"What . . . do you know of that?" My consuming shock was almost enough to override my pain. Almost.

"Oh, you don't know?"

"Didn't know . . . what?" My irritation flared the pain within me. It was all I could do to stare Lothos' way, boring into him with my eyes, focusing all my hatred, for all the good it did.

"Gods below!" Lothos made a noise that was somewhere between a sigh and a cackle. "Your father never told you? This is . . . so much better than I could have ever hoped!"

With preternatural speed, he crouched down to my level, his fangs at full length from the blood scent that must have permeated this room. "I think I will let you live, my dear."

He snapped his fingers, and with a sickening lurch, the thimble popped out of me, clattering to the ground. I watched as hair-like tendrils retracted on its narrow end, moving independently of one another like insect legs. They retreated into its main body as if it were something living.

"You know, I no longer seem to be all that interested in that baby," Lothos remarked. "You, the witch, second only in skill to the great Aiko herself, utterly loyal to the one whom you call 'Father,' the one who raised you so well . . . and he never told you the circumstances of your turning?"

"He told me that he doesn't know."

Lothos leaned closer until he was practically in my face, the pane of impenetrable glass separating us by inches.

"He lied."

"Bullshit."

"As expected from none other than his 'daughter," Lothos sneered. "You'll get the chance to ask him yourself . . . when I'm done having my fun. And I do hope you ask him. I believe you'll find the answer rather enlightening." He then rose to his feet and stood beside Derek. "And oh, what fun would it be, to see the fireworks after you do ask!"

"What makes you think I will ask him?" I said, groaning as the pain subsided only partly, and was now replaced by the sharp, thrumming ache of thirst returned to me.

"Curiosity." Lothos replied after an unusually long pause.

"We all succumb to it sooner or later. And you will too."

I wanted to deny it, but confusion was taking root in my mind in the areas where the pain of thirst had not taken over. I knew nothing of my human life, and only what Father had told me. But Lothos was a capricious, wily, and vicious manipulator. For all I knew, what he said could have been utter bollocks, but something told me otherwise. He had, after all, relieved me of the siphoning of the thimble funnel in my flesh. Was the wound not closing as it slipped from its gruesome resting place? I watched with grim suspicion as Lothos shifted back into his true form, shrugging his shoulders in a comical manner. "But, if wishes were horses, and all that. For now, though, I still want to have a bit of fun with you."

"I thought you said you would let me go," I replied.

"Eventually, my dear. Eventually. For now, I want to see what can be done about you."

He faced Derek, who, though still seemingly comatose, was different somehow. I felt a flash of it, but it was too quick to catch. If our minds could do such a thing, I would have called it a "hiccup." I was certainly mystified, but the pain prevented me from looking any deeper.

"Now tell, me my love . . ." He gestured towards me as if allowing Derek to ruminate, would that he could, over me in my naked helplessness. ". . . do you have any suggestions for me? Maybe something you wish of me to do to this beautiful creature whose body and blood you indulged in with so little regard for me?"

Derek's face maintained the same listlessness, though his lips did seem to move, forming something like words. But he spoke so softly that even my sensitive ears could not pick it up. Even Lothos, it seemed had had trouble hearing.

"Beg pardon?" He asked, leaning in closer.

The look on Derek's face was like scales falling from the eyes of the blind. I saw him shift his gaze towards me -he actually looked at me- and then saw two single tears fall from his eyes. Across our bond, I felt it. It all came to me clear as day, as if he'd broken through a wall of concrete. He did not intend to survive what he'd planned. But he expected me to. My dear, sweet Derek . . . he had not betrayed me!

Lothos had not noticed this. He could not, since he lacked our talents. He simply leaned in closer, waiting for Derek's answer.

And he gave it.

"I . . . wish you were dead."

***

I knew everything.

And I was free!

Would that I could truly give my Derek his wish. But he gave me exactly what I needed nonetheless: the means to erase Lothos from the equation. The evasive memory opened to me as if someone had unlocked the door from the inside, and I used it to ruin the king of monsters.

My Jewel was not the only one.

It had never been the only one!

I should have known this all along. It was so ludicrously obvious. It was the ring he'd given me, the ring he'd proposed to me with, the ring I'd worn proudly, only he had hidden it in plain sight. Just as things and people could be hidden in our special blue in-between space, it lay there, both resting on my ring finger and not, safe from prying eyes, any and all scans, and especially the anti-Jewel that had rendered me otherwise powerless here.

Lothos didn't know what hit him.

I was more than a child-sized version of our kind when I used my Jewel; strength enhancement gave me the power to be a match even for Justin, the strongest of our clan. The glass was thick and tempered to bulletproof hardness, but it might as well have been paper when I forced my way through it and slammed into Lothos. I bared my fangs with a bloodlust that went beyond sexual. Even here, drained and half-starving, I would never have drained him. That was too good for him. He was the demon responsible for my poor Derek's tale of woe; he would have had him on all fours like a dog again, and these were the newest and least of his ponderous list of sins.

He was frozen with indignation. The emotion bled through with digital clarity into my mind, and I used that one crippling moment to finish it. I had been trained too well to banter like Lothos. His arrogance and talkativeness was one of his few weaknesses. This was no longer part of the equation when I finished my deed. His severed head came to rest beside the remains of my human victim amidst the shards of bloodied glass, and the blood from his headless body pooled at the other side of the cell.

I turned to face Derek. He shrank back from me, but only for a moment. My feelings were almost hurt by this, until I saw myself through his eyes. As I appeared to him, eyes nearly consumed by crimson from starvation, straddled across Lothos' headless trunk, naked as the day of my birth, with my hair and skin caked with blood, I was a horror, far less human than ever I had ever seemed before.

"Derek . . ." I frowned, and reached out to him, willing my fangs to retract. In spite of my ravenous hunger, I calmed the storm of hatred and rage that first boiled over from within me, and let my love for him assert itself across the gulf of our minds. He seemed unsure at first, but in moments, his love won the war within and he took my hand. The touch was like a gust of wind that blew away a dense, unnatural fog in his mind, placed there to lose him in its misty maze. It had already been weak when our hearts touched; either it had been deceptively insubstantial, or Derek had broken his way through on his own.

I slipped out of his mind, tears now in my eyes in spite of my pain. Derek fell to his knees, splashing listlessly in the puddle of blood, and embraced me.

"I'm so sorry, China Doll." he whispered. I'm so, so sorry

. . ."

Should I have been cross? Perhaps I should have wanted his head to join Lothos'. But I believe I realized very early on that should I have done such a thing, my anger would have been misplaced. Lothos had been telling the truth about what had been done to him, as much as I hated to admit it. But his words of supposed betrayal had been bollocks. God -or perhaps Derek- only knew how, but Derek had somehow been stronger, with a will that overthrew the effects of a thaumaturgist's Jewel. Despite seeming to have betrayed me, he saved his clan by preventing them from being found, though it required surrendering himself and me into the maw of the enemy. Somehow, he hid the ring away from prying eyes, and had formulated a plan to save us, or at least, to save me, in spite of whatever leash had been placed on his mind.

"You hid the memory of my Jewel," I said. "You broke free of Lothos' control . . . however you managed to do it. Derek . . . just how strong is your mind?"

"Not strong enough," he said, and I felt a blackness of self-loathing grow in the pit of his stomach like a festering rot.

"Love, you broke free of a thaumaturgist's spell," I said. "Believe me, that is remarkably strong."

"It wasn't strong enough to break free of what Lothos did." His voice was a near-monotone croak. "And it was only luck that Lothos brought me to you. If not, there would have been no way I could have given you the trigger word."

"I recall you whispering something to me back in the RV," I said. "Was that what you did?"

"I made you sleep . . . or rather, Lothos forced me to make you sleep," Derek replied with a shallow nod. "I couldn't fight him."

"He makes it a point to know all the angles," I said.

"Don't you mean, 'made a point'? Derek asked, shifting his gaze indicatively towards Lothos' body. "You killed him."

"I wish I had," I said. "He's not that easy to kill."

"But you just tore his fu-"

As if it had been planned, a noise in the corner where the ranger's remains lay rotting captured Derek's attention. It was a sticky, wet noise, as if someone were crumpling sheets of plastic wrap in a shallow puddle of water.

"Good God!" Derek whispered, and scrambled back as if the abomination he saw forming out of Lothos' discarded head had any interest in him at all.

The long falls of his white hair, now splotched with drying blood, were what supported the head. Like an octopus with millions of legs, they swept upon the floor, as if each strand were infused with muscles and sinew, all transferred into countless single threads. From the look of the head, shrunken, with ebon skin dry and taut over the bones of the skull, one would have figured this to be the case. His eyes were on stalks of shriveled flesh, rising out of their sockets and searching in every direction, like those of a crab or snail, warped into some eldritch abomination.

"Now you know where the legend of the penanggalan comes from."

"The what?" Derek's eyes were riveted to the simultaneously mesmerizing and revolting sight. The hairs from the severed head felt along the floor and walls, moving slowly, methodically, until they came to a section where a ventilation duct lay directly above. Like an octopus folding itself into a hole at the bottom of the sea, the head skittered silently along the facade of bricks and manipulated the aluminum grate that covered the duct, opening it wide enough to squeeze into, hair and all.

"A Malaysian vampire," I explained. "Though in the legend, it carries its stomach and entrails along with the head. Someone must have seen Lothos do that once."

"Wait. Why are you so calm about this? You tore off his head! How is he not dead? And why isn't he trying to kill us?"

"I guess this is one thing he never revealed to you,"

I quipped, though the ache from the thirst cut my sense of humor short. I winced, but was otherwise fine.

"First, I am in a dire amount of pain, so I'm not as calm as I look. Second, I've seen this before. Remember, this isn't the first fight against Lothos I've seen, and this isn't the first time something like this has happened to him. I don't know how he managed to figure out how to survive as a severed head, but he can. We're just thankful that as far as we know, he's the only one of his clan who can do it. And third, if you're starved for blood, the last thing on your mind is killing something that couldn't nourish you. You've been starved before, so you know that vampire blood doesn't smell like anything to us in that state. We go straight for humans. They smell like what we need. Lothos is doing the same thing. He'll find a human, feed, then take the head, reconnecting his own to the body, allowing what's left of his blood to initiate the turning process."

"That . . . sounds very painful," Derek said, seeming to hold back the contents of his stomach: an act I was grateful for. A vampire throwing up is not a pleasant sight.

"I don't doubt it is," I said recalling the pain of my own turning, my first memory. "His body will be rebuilt in about an hour. He's the only one of his clan who has that kind of control."

Lothos' hairs swirled around the grate of the ventilation shaft, and placed it back where it belonged, as if we could squeeze ourselves inside and give chase. Though there were many legends about our kind, our ability to transform into mist was sadly, one of those that were little more than fairy tales. With nary a sound, he vanished, and Derek and I were alone.

"Now, we need to leave," I said, scanning the walls for the exit. "I'm hurting, and need to feed. And once Lothos gets his strength back, we'll need to be as far away from here as we can get. Where's the exit? Can we get back into the labyrinth?"

"The labyrinth is a trap," Derek said, and made his way to the panel where he and the human girl had entered. He touched what appeared to be a crack in the masonry, and the passage sectioned away. "Lothos puts newbies in there, or people who've pissed him off."

So the fiend hadn't been lying when he said that there was no way out. "Then where do we go?" I asked.

"Back to the labyrinth." Derek paused and gave me a sly grin, but I was only confused.

"I thought you said there was no way-"

"I said the Labyrinth was a trap . . . but not a dead end." Derek beckoned me to follow. "There is one way out. But you won't like it."

"The pitfall?"

"You've seen it then?" He nodded brusquely. "Yeah, that's it."

"But that's impossible!" I said. "Surely there has to be another way out. That can't be the only way you get in or out of here."

"Oh, there are other ways," Derek said, leading me not to the exit door, but to one of the cell walls close by where I'd hung for however long I was there. "Only you'd have to fight your way through an army of his clan to get there." This way, we're making a back door- Aah!"

Derek doubled over and clutched at his hip as if something had jumped up and bit him. With an alarmed shout, I came to his side as he collapsed to one knee.

"It's okay, sweetie," he said through gritted teeth. "It's just . . . something that Lothos did to me."

He gestured to his left thigh, and I went to look. It was quite plain to see through the split in his loincloth, though at first, I couldn't believe it myself.

"How can you have a tattoo?" I asked.

"Lothos did it, first thing when I arrived," Derek explained. "Some kind of tiny machines; they're programmed with the design, and renew it when my body starts to absorb the ink."

He snarled as another lance of pain stabbed his thigh and the sensation crossed over into my mind through our bond. "'Course it hurts like a sonovabitch."

I was too numb with what Lothos had done and revealed to me in order to feel any kind of anger or rage. Derek and I needed to escape, and this painful device would have to stay behind.

"Hold still," I said and used my Jewel to magnetize the machines. I felt them being trapped in the EM field, like fish in a net. All that was needed now was to haul them to the surface. I touched the area near his thigh and used my talents to reduce his perception of pain. But with how deep below these machines were, I knew I could only do so much.

"Brace yourself," I said, "because this is really going to hurt."

Before Derek could ask, I pulled.

He probably sucked in half the cell's air with his gasp, and the spray of blood merely added to what already covered me (Had I a set of horns and a fake barbed tail, I would have easily passed for a devil on Halloween, nakedness aside).

"I got them," I said as Derek slowly stood, riding out the residual pain as his leg set to healing. He looked at the swirling motes: grains of black sand, spinning in the magnetic field above the palm of my hand.

"Reanon will have to deactivate them," I said. "I've seen something like this before. The material they're made of is like a Jewel. Our Jewels can't destroy them. They're most likely programmed to target you and only you. If I were to spill them on the ground, they'd seek you out, even if you were a thousand miles away. Someday, days, weeks, months, maybe even years from now, you'd wake up and the tattoo would be back."

I solidified the outer shell of the magnetic field, creating a material that gave like plastic, but was stronger than steel. I then handed it to Derek, who had recovered and was standing straight.

"They took my satchel, so you'll have to hold on to it for now. Don't worry; they can't escape the capsule I put them in."

Derek, at first unsure, collapsed the capsule once he realized that it was harmless. He then secured it with the waistband of his loincloth before leading me through the passage. It was a brief corridor, and the light faded out quickly. Soon, we were enveloped by the darkness of the labyrinth, with our preternatural sight catching only the dimmest of beams.

Derek was sure-footed and stealthy as he brought me through the maze's twists and passages. They appeared empty, but of course, they seemed that way during my first trip here. "There's always someone down here," he explained during our journey. "Mostly yahoos with something to prove. New meat comes down here all the time. Someone screws up, and they get tormented."

Soon, the scent of the water at the bottom of the pit came to my nostrils and I felt more confident in my impending freedom. In a blessedly short time, Derek and I stood at the chasm's edge.

"I can use a gravity bleed to get us down there safely," I said, crawling to the top of the railing. "It will only last ten seconds, so I'm going to have to be sure of how deep it is."

I tossed a nearby pebble into the chasm and counted the seconds. Fifteen passed before I heard the distant splash. "Okay, that means we'll have to fall for five seconds before I can make the bleed."

Derek frowned. "Fun times," he said in a flat voice.

And then something that I admittedly should have expected, happened.

A pair of hands grabbed me from behind. I turned and saw a vampire peeling away from the wall, the same as that army that had subdued me and brought me to the cell. He was a portly bloke, or perhaps, would have been, had he not been so flat in form.

But this time, the playing field was even.

As if on instinct, I enhanced my strength, and gave him a most unexpected toss over the edge. I listened with satisfaction to his fading screams, but stopped just short of the splash when I noticed Derek having a considerably more difficult time with his own assailant. Like a rubber band, the fiend's distorted body was wrapped about Derek's limbs, becoming a living restraint, while Derek struggled like a beast, wresting himself free, only to be restrained by a different limb, or even a finger. The fiend cackled madly at his sport and at Derek's growing anger.

Derek, struggling madly against the tangles of his captor's flesh, cast his gaze to me, and in desperation, strained out two words.

"The . . . machines!"

He then proceeded to strike the fiend against the labyrinth wall at preternatural speed. I noticed that he held the capsule in his still somewhat free right hand.

"Elisa . . . weaken the capsule!"

"But they'll seek you out," I said.

"Take a . . . pretty damn long time to do that from here . . . to the surface," Derek said, biting at the vampire's fingers, which were attempting to immobilize his face. The fiend howled in pain and tried to constrict even more. "Hurry!"

I drew upon my Jewel, and did what he asked, weakening the structural integrity of the capsule to that of the glass of a light bulb.

"Do it," I said.

Immediately, Derek threw his arm back and struck the fiend in his distorted face. A sibilant hiss rose from the particles, reverberating with an otherworldly whine. Instantly, the tendrils of his distended body loosened and Derek leapt free. I saw steam rising from the vampire's head as the machines drilled into his immortal flesh. He screamed and wailed, rolling on the ground and shifting wildly into more shapes than I could count. The entire display was almost cartoonishly grotesque, amusing, even.

"Ready?" Derek said, and scrambled atop the railing. He reached for me, and I took his hand as he hoisted me into his arms.

We jumped.

Chapter Twenty-Two

I was able to make our landing far less unpleasant with the gravity bleed, but the coldness of the water and speed of the current was nothing I could control. Derek and I were jostled, rocked, spun, and slammed against sheer rocky banks as the river carried us with the rest of its detritus. The sharp edges of rocks at its edges cut deeply into me, spilling even more blood that I couldn't afford to lose, and further deepening my raging thirst with every gash.

The current eventually, blessedly slowed, and Derek guided me to a grassy bank where we staggered onto shore, then coughed and retched up the water we'd swallowed and partly inhaled.

Derek came to kneel beside me after expelling his own water and touched my chin. For the first time, I saw genuine fear in his eyes: fear for me.

"You don't look so good, China doll," he said. Though the blood had been completely washed off of me, the pain was now gnawing at every inch of my body. It was like being masticated by a starving wolf. My eyes were almost certainly solid crimson.

"Aren't you the charmer?" I said in mock sarcasm, attempting to get my mind off of my thirst, though it was truly attempting the impossible. I needed to feed, and it hurt to even contemplate it.

"Well, at least the blood is off," Derek said, disregarding my abrasiveness. He smiled wanly, aware of and sympathetic to my pain. He then glanced back the way we'd come. A large hill loomed above the landscape, though the rest seemed to be shrouded by woods. The water from the river, now reduced to a stream, carried an unpleasant smell, as if it had been accumulating sewage or flowing into a stagnant pond somewhere. I didn't want to stay there, and Derek sensed this. "Come on, sweetie. Let's get our bearings and find out where we are."

"I hurt so bad," I croaked, struggling to keep up, but feeling my every step like a torture. My body was a sack of weights and needles.

"I know it hurts." Derek squeezed my hand. "Like you said, it really sucks that we can't get what we need from each other."

"We get what we need, love." I cast him a faint grin, and he understood me. "Just not that."

We traveled on through monotonous woods for about five minutes more, as silent as we dared, since we had no idea how far away from Lothos' clan we'd travelled. Our slow speed was because of my condition, but it was also beneficial for keeping a low profile.

Derek suddenly paused. Just before I asked him why he stopped, I smelled it. And I became possessed.

Derek tried to stop me, but I was too close to the edge. I wish I could describe just how it feels, the enticement of blood to a starved vampire: a temptation sets every last instinct afire and practically crushes your will to resist. It is a desert oasis after hovering at the edge of death due to dehydration, a banquet after a weeks-long fast, an invitation to sex after being teased mercilessly for months. These were some of the things my clan used to describe it, but I was certain that it surpassed even this. As much willpower as the newly-turned must muster in order to overcome their thirst, deprivation made even those efforts useless.

And like my time in that cell, I broke.

Derek's voice was across a gulf between universes, with my senses attuned to the spoor of fresh, inviting human. I moved at preternatural speed, and perhaps broke a few of my victim's bones when I pinned him to the ground and took my sweet, hot prize.

Sustenance.

Life.

Bliss.

Relief!

I was well into the drink when my head cleared. The pain subsided to a dull throb in the background of my thoughts, and I began to think of the one who struggled beneath me as something more than a very crafty beast.

His blood was just what I needed, and I remained latched upon him even after I regained my faculties. I was like a leech, drinking slowly, savoring his blood, fearful that the hunger would return in full force if I ever let go.

Derek made that choice for me, though I nearly bit off his hand for his efforts. But it took merely a moment before I came to my full senses, ethics and all.

Of course, recognizing his scent and the timbre of his mind had a lot to do with it as well.

I saw my victim on the ground beside a grove of trees that hugged a pavement of some sort. He was dressed in black fatigues and seemed paler than he ought to have been. Another body was there beside him, dead. I could tell. The first had a heartbeat, though it was weak; the other did not. I looked around, taking stock of my surroundings. The pavement lined a road, and there was a streetlight in the distance. There was a fence near the wooded area with a sign that read PRIVATE PROPERTY in black letters on a reflective yellow field.

"I'm okay now," I said to Derek, reassuring him with my thoughts. I realized that he was holding me in his arms. "You can put me down."

"I did the other one," Derek said, placing me slowly back down to the ground. I noticed him wiping a sliver of blood from the edge of his mouth.

"Did you have to kill him?" I asked, making no hint of my disappointment despite my knowledge that Derek had very little control over this.

"He was dead anyway," Derek explained. "Lothos doesn't like failure. And he was human." He then gestured to a broken walkie-talkie, shattered into pieces on the pavement.

"Besides, I had to drain him. He would have radioed for backup."

"I didn't realize it a second ago," I said, backing away from, but keeping my vision trained on our former victims, "but they smell like Lothos' clan." A new sense of fear about where we were came over me. "I thought we'd escaped."

"Looks like the river took us near the main entrance," Derek said. "Those guards were in a secluded spot, probably keeping an eye out off the beaten path."

Of course, Lothos would use humans for this job, I recalled. These were hopefuls to be turned, at least those who were still mentally competent. They were always given the most unpleasant or menial tasks, or jobs that only humans could do. Guard duty was a place-filler, but necessary as a first line of defense against any would-be enemies. These were weaklings, but serviceable during the daytime. Stronger guards were given doses of our toxins to enhance their strength, speed and stamina, and were placed further within. The one whom I'd feasted on had never stood a chance against me.

"Then we're not safe here," I said. "We need to go."

"Is he going to die?" Derek seemed to have not heard me. Instead, he gestured towards my victim.

"Probably not," I said after a moment of listening to his heartbeat and breathing, and reluctantly taking in his scent that was so much like the offensive stench of Lothos and his degenerate children. "I took a lot more blood than I normally do, but not enough to kill him."

"You should have," Derek said and gently pushed me aside. He moved purposefully towards the prostrate guard, and his intent was perfectly clear. My first reflex was to try to stop him, but my fears were overridden by a logic that was about as cold as I felt that night I put an end to the pervert who killed poor Lilly. Derek was right; this was better. He was dead anyway; he was merely finishing my deed.

A sharp whine suddenly pierced the relative silence, and

I saw Derek stagger back, clutching his shoulder. I hurried to his side, and detected the scent of something that I'd never expected to find here.

The guard was sitting up, or to be more exact, propping himself in a half-sitting position with his elbow. In his outstretched hand, there was a pistol. There was no scent of gunpowder, though. I darted my eyes back and forth from the guard to Derek and noticed the tiny syringe sticking out of his left shoulder.

And that smell . . .

I saw the guard fumbling for another syringe with fingers that I was certain felt like they were individually made of lead. He was about to load it for me, no doubt, but he underestimated how quickly I recovered from my shock.

I finished what Derek could not. I made it quick and merciful, in spite of what he had done to Derek, who had collapsed to his knees, wheezing, his body convulsing in tiny tremors.

"Easy, love," I whispered, hurrying back to his side after the deed. I removed the syringe. Combined with the chemical he'd been injected with, a faint burning scent wafted from the wound, which was bleeding more profusely than it ought to have been. I brought him to the ground. His mind roiled in a combination of pain and near-panic. "You've been hit with sickspray. It won't kill you, but it'll make you wish it had."

I bent over his chest and bit into the flesh around the wound. Derek yelped, but made no other noise as I began to suck at the wound.

The chemical was like acid. I forcefully spat out the contaminated blood, but the inside of my mouth burned as if I had just finished eating ten raw habanero peppers. This was so wrong; Derek's blood was usually delectable in a way that was almost transcendent, but this chemical, one of the only poisons that could affect our bodies, turned this feeding into a heinous chore. I gagged more than once, and my stomach threatened to heave up its freshly-acquired contents. I was strong enough now for what needed to be done, but I wanted to alleviate Derek of the worst of the sickspray's effects in case we couldn't get an antidote in time.

I heard footsteps in the distance and smelled more of Lothos' clan. Some were human; others were vampire, and their thoughts were on full search mode. I was sweating and in a great deal of pain from the sickspray that I'd siphoned out of the wound, but I did not stop until I was satisfied that I'd removed enough to where Derek would be in far more comfort than he was now.

The voices were audible. They were looking for the two dead guards. Someone had heard the struggle on their walkie-talkies. They were very close and closing in. We couldn't stay any longer.

I hastened to end my labor and licked over the wound to speed healing. The traces of the chemical on his skin made even this act painful, but I endured it and trembled with the wrongness of the sensations after I was done. Fortunately, pain would not stymie my concentration for what I needed to do. Now, with my primary Jewel free of the anti-Jewel's neutralizing power, I could bring us to our destination by folding space. With the amount of blood I'd lost earlier, I couldn't do it safely, let alone with two, and such an act used up so much of the Jewel's energy that to use it with Derek's clan was out of the question. It would have shattered my Jewel, and I wouldn't have dared to do it with a new one that would take months to years to fully synchronize with my mind and body. Even now, this was something of a gambit. But I was not afraid.

Gunshots rang out, and I knew, once I felt one miss me by inches, that these were composed of real bullets that could at least injure us. There was no time left. I drew deeply into my Jewel and concentrated. I had been to the sanctuary once before, when the plan for my mission was drawn up and I'd made last minute preparations with Father and Justin. Having gathered together sufficient power, I envisioned the location and concentrated.

A gun gave off an explosion like a thunderclap, shaking the ground just before I transitioned to preternatural speed. Time slowed down and merged with space, compressing like two ocean waves, bringing two points in space together. Derek and I were caught on the combining waves, and my thoughts guided our bodies. As if from far away, emerging through the darkness of the street, "there" became "here." The last thing I saw of the place we had been was a .50 caliber bullet floating between my eyes.

***

I stood on what felt like a grassy hill when the compression released. I staggered to my knees, waiting for my head to clear. Transition is sometimes a sudden and traumatic thing, and I had been under a great deal of stress before I drew upon my Jewel.

It was warm and humid, and save Derek's heartbeat and shuddering breaths, I was greeted by a moment of perfect silence. My lips and tongue were burning from the sickspray and my head swam horribly. In spite of my fullness with fresh blood, I was too mentally exhausted to go on. I heard nearby voices chatter excitedly, combined with blessedly familiar scents. Perhaps it was a sensory overload; perhaps it was exhaustion from the use of my Jewel for this transition, or the fact that the events since our capture had finally overwhelmed me, but I felt myself slipping away. As the darkness licked the edges of my vision and the sensation of utter fatigue inundated me, I knew that I would have no choice but to deal with any more excitement later.

***

It was quiet when I awoke . . . nearly as quiet as the place where Derek and I had arrived. I was surrounded by softness, pleasant scents, and unfamiliar, though welcomed comfort.

I was so disoriented, however, that it took a moment for me to realize that I was in a bed. The scent of it was nothing that I recognized, save that of Derek who lay beside me, fast asleep.

I still was naked, but I had been cleaned. My hip touched Derek's, and I realized that his clothing had been removed as well. Two IVs were separately hooked up to both our arms. Mine ran to a blood bag while Derek's ran to a blood bag and bag of a fluid that glowed faintly blue. The acrid smell of sickspray was weak, but still present.

I recognized that fluid. I sat up and leaned over Derek, who did not move an inch in spite of my jostling. The writing on the bag's label was unmistakably Reanon's. It was sickspray antidote.

As if in response to my thoughts, the door opened to my right, and I recognized the scents of those who entered.

"Reanon? When did you get here? I settled back into my side of the bed and noticed the chair near the bedside with a change of clothes that was my size. In fact, I recognized the blouse, jeans, shoes, and underwear as my own clothing from the Lair.

"I was here on standby after the Vagabonds arrived," Reanon said as I slipped out of the bed and began to get dressed. I had never spoken much with her, but at the moment, I couldn't have been gladder to see her face. I'd never noticed it before, but she somewhat resembled a softer version of Deb, who had come in behind her with the baby in a sling across her stomach. Reanon's laboratory smock nearly resembled a nun's habit, and unlike her almost-doppelganger, there was less of a predatory gleam in her eyes, as well as far less certainty. No surprise there, since Reanon was notoriously shy, but otherwise a capable physician for both my kind and humans. Deb, on the other hand, came up to me, and after adjusting the baby gently to her side, reached out and embraced me.

"Thank God . . ." she whispered. "I thought you and

Derek were in a shallow pit somewhere without your heads. The whole clan was worried sick."

"Your father was equally worried," Reanon added. "He kept me here when we learned that you didn't arrive with the convoy. We had patrols looking everywhere for you and Derek in the area where you both vanished, shaking down Lothos' people wherever we could find them."

"How long were we gone?" I asked.

"Two weeks," Deb answered. "Wadih said that Derek told him to keep driving to the destination, even if he veered off course. He said something about him having a feeling that we were still being watched, so he'd throw them off the trail by taking an alternate route. We got here safe and sound, and had the mind-readers waiting for us. When you and Derek never arrived, more guards came in." She threw Reanon a surreptitious grimace. "It's been a bit less like freedom here and more like a prison. Wadih refused to believe you two were dead. He and the rest of the guys threatened to leave and go looking for you on their own, but your people asked us to give them more time. Then the night before Wadih was going to set out, you suddenly popped in the middle of the square."

"Serendipity, it seems," I said, slipping on my underwear and blouse.

"Isn't it?" Reanon said with a vague smile. "You must've really been through something."

I paused, and it all came back to me like a nightmare. I twisted my face in pain at everything that happened, and especially Lothos' words. The stress of my escape with Derek had distracted me from the memories, but now, with my mind relatively calm and in peaceful surroundings, it sat there like an obstinate, odious beast.

"You could say that," I whispered. If only they knew. Reanon probably already knew something was wrong, but she would never ask. Of course, I saw the concern etched upon her face.

"How's Derek?" I asked before Deb could say something.

Like Reanon, she detected my emotions, but I wanted to derail her. I needed time to sort this out.

"The sickspray poisoning put him into a coma," Reanon said, "but he'll recover. He may not regain consciousness for a few days, yet. I treated you with antidote; you swallowed some of the blood you tried to siphon out."

"Really?" I said. "I thought I passed out because I overtaxed myself. How long was I out?"

"Only about a day."

"I feel like it was much longer than that," I said as I slipped on my socks and then my jeans. "I felt exhausted the moment we transferred here."

"Understandable," Reanon replied. "It was a side effect of the sickspray. Its effects on you were pretty mild."

"Better than a .50 caliber bullet to the head," I quipped.

"What?" Deb probably got a glimpse of that thought, and I buried my face in my palm at that indiscretion.

"Let's just say, 'skin of the teeth' doesn't even come close to describing our escape," I said. I'd finished dressing, but kept my feet bare, and sat back on the edge of the bed, taking Derek's unfettered hand into my own. Physically, I felt better than I had in perhaps two weeks, but mentally, I would probably take a long while to recover. And with Derek out of commission, I didn't know how well I would hold up. After the revelations during my time in Lothos' clutches, I knew it was far from over.

"Where were you?" Reanon asked.

"Yeah, you look like hell," Deb added

"Later, please," I said, massaging the bridge of my nose. "It's just that I . . . Look, I'll tell you all about it later. You and the whole clan, right?"

Reanon capitulated as I expected, but Deb was far from mollified. She pursed her lips, and I felt little else but worry and concern from her. She was going to hold me to my promise, most certainly.

"Were there enough bungalows for everyone?" I asked,

trying to change the subject. I removed the IV from my arm and clamped it to stanch the blood flow.

"Oh, plenty and to spare," Deb said with uncharacteristic enthusiasm. "We had no idea that this place came fully equipped. With the exception of the officials from your clan hanging around, it was like a big ghost town when we got here. Now that you're back, I'm sure they'll let Marie-Laure recall the rest of our clan. It'll actually feel like this place actually has a population."

I was happy for her and the clan; I genuinely was. And I knew they would have lots of questions for me. I was certain that Reanon wanted to take a few more readings from me; I could see the look of dismay on her face when I removed the IV. But for right now, I couldn't handle it. It was more than just the sickspray. I was still mentally overwhelmed by my experience, and there were only two people I knew who could perhaps understand me. But to do this, I would have to leave Derek alone, and that pained me more than I could stand. We were bonded. Even though our blood would never nourish us, we were as addicted to each other as a human host is addicted to our toxins. It would hurt to leave him, and he would want only me when he recovered. Nevertheless, I had to find answers. And I couldn't stay here in order to do it.

"I'm sorry, Deb, Reanon, I don't know if it's the sickspray, or just the sudden relief of being back, but I'm still feeling a bit poorly," I said at last, reclining to a restful position back on the pillow. "I might need to rest just a bit more before I'm ready to join everyone outside. Can you give me another couple of hours?"

"Oh, of course," Reanon made no complaint, only nodded and headed back the way she entered. Deb, however, was a bit more reluctant. The baby was awake, but quiet, and staring at me wide-eyed, even in the room's subdued light. It was almost eerie, seeing her large, mismatched eyes fixed upon me as she sucked vigorously on her pacifier.

"Are you sure you'll be okay?" She asked as I brought my

knees up to my chest. "You really don't look so good."

"Deb, I'll be honest. If you went through what I did, you wouldn't look so good either." I gazed absently at my arms, and then at Derek's free arm. "You can clean a body, but the scars can still remain."

"I really wish you'd tell me what happened." She said.

"I promise you, I will," I said. "All in good time."

"Well, I'm here if you want to talk about it."

I actually wanted to talk to her more than anything. I wanted to tell her about what Lothos put me and Derek through, the things I was made to see, and the lies he told me . . . as well as the possible truths. But in spite of that raging desire to bear my soul as much as my body was bared during my tribulation, I restrained myself.

"I know you are," I said, and tried to cast a reassuring smile. I wasn't certain how successful I was with it, but I leaned back in the bed and exhaled, somehow feeling even more tired than I was when I woke up just a moment ago.

"I'll be okay," I said, noticing how Deb had not moved. "I promise. And I'll talk with you more about it all later."

"I'm holding you to that, you know," Deb said, fulfilling my own prediction. Her tone was anything but that of a playful warning.

"I know."

I waited until she'd shut the door behind her, then drew from my Jewel to write a note. I was a woman possessed. I did not believe Lothos' words at first, but now I realized one glaring thing that had been painfully obvious in our conversation. He had not been lying. I didn't need to look into his mind to know this. Deceit was easily detected by my clan, even in the minds of our own kind. Even Deb, with her slightly muted telepathy, could detect my evasions. She knew that I was far from fine, and I made no effort to divert her mind about my current state. But she did not insist on me speaking about it out of respect. Even self-deceit, which took a modicum of training to recognize, was detectable if one knew what to look for. And Lothos' surface thoughts had generated none of the telltale signs of even this.

Lothos had not been lying about Father. And I wanted to know why.

Having finished the note, I leaned over and kissed Derek. I longed to stay more than anything. I wanted to be here with him when he awoke, and allow him to take me into his arms and celebrate our victory into the night, but instead I placed my head on his chest, listened to his heartbeat and breathing, and allowed time to slip away for as long as I dared.

I laid there for so long that I lost track of the time. I didn't want to let him go, but I had to.

"I'll be back soon, love," I whispered, finally resigning myself to what I needed to do. "So hold on for me. I have to face something I know will be horrifying, and I'm afraid."

I heard my voice break with the last few words, and felt the tears roll from my eyes and onto Derek's chest. I shuddered, wishing he would come alive and respond just to comfort me for at least a moment. But like I had been in the clutches of Lothos, and like I was before this mission began, I was alone.

I left the note on the bed and slipped into the pair of sandals that waited for me beside the chair. Deb and Reanon wouldn't like this, but I needed to do this. I drew from my Jewel once again . . .

. . . and I was home.

***

I ran with preternatural speed through the familiar streets of the village that was my home as if daylight were approaching. It was, admittedly, bad form to run through the streets of our small village, and especially at preternatural speed, which ran the risk of me running into an unsuspecting human with their general clumsiness. I perhaps caused a bit of confusion among human and vampire alike with my arrival and unceremonious rush to get to the Lair, but I was fueled by determination. I needed to know the truth. I had to know it.

But this burden had a most disobliging side effect. As I neared the hill that towered above my village where sat the mansion that was my home, fears began to creep into my zeal and eat away at it like corrosion to metal.

Did I want to know the answer?

Why did Father hide this?

Did I truly want to know why?

These and other questions gnawed away at my resolve with every passing second, slowing me and piling up as I strode up the worn cobblestone path to the front door of the Lair at a halting, tentative gait. By the time I reached the antechamber, I was aware of my father's mind, open to all of our thoughts, like an omniscient eye. I was already quivering with barely-contained fear by the time I pushed my way through the doorway to the Lair's interior corridors, and this realization eroded the last of my resolve. And so I hid for three days.

Chapter Twenty-Three

This was where my memories ended.

I opened my eyes, and I was back in Father's sitting room. Father was no longer kneeling before me, but instead was seated in his own chair opposite me. I glanced at my goblet to find the blood congealed and long cold. His trek through the experience of my mission must have been lengthy.

My gaze returned to Father, and I was truly frightened by the way he looked. Though his features were the same: graceful, pearlescent, and eternally young, he seemed so very, very old now.

A new revelation nearly floored me.

For the first time in my life, I could sense his thoughts!

This was not the fleeting glimpse I'd received before he had traced back through my memories and shut the door; this was the "full Monty," as it were: the whole of who he was. Completely unprepared for this, I staggered back, only to see that Father had not shut me out. He was inviting me in, and I shuddered with the sudden realization of something that I thought I'd never sense. Such depth and extent of memory, it was like staring into an endless library. But his emotions wrenched me. So much shame and anger . . . but not directed at me. Still, it was all I needed to know. I could have done what he did to me, explore the corridors of his mind, saw the truth for myself, but Father was no doubt a man of secrets even darker than this. I held back any tears, but I stepped back from the precipice that dropped into the depths of the universe that was his mind, as tempting as it would have been to let it draw me in and pull me down. Rather, I stayed out of his mind out of respect. His mind was his own.

"He was telling the truth," I superfluously remarked. Father pressed his head into his palm. I had refused to venture into his mind, but even I could hear the phrase, Damn you,

Lothos, repeated across the void between our souls.

"What did Lothos have to do with this?" I asked. "And why did you do this to me? Did he make you do this? Was it an accident? Father, please, I have to know! It hurts more than when he drained me and . . ."

There was nothing that could hold back the tears now. I had hoped and longed for my Father's embrace, his reassurance that it was all lies, but this horrible truth was a torment worse than my two weeks of captivity.

My feet moved on their own. In a burst of preternatural speed, I was at Father's feet as I was when I had been as much a child in mind as in body.

"Father, please! Tell me what happened! Why did you do this to me?"

I begged even more until my words lost their coherence, but my thoughts were clear. The anguish in me must have broken Father's heart even more than my news had broken it.

"Oh, my child . . ." His voice carried so much pain as I felt his hand rub the top of my head. "I'm so sorry you had to learn this. I feared that Lothos would one day use it against me, but it had been so long, I sometimes forget about how patient we can be."

I looked up into his sad countenance, expecting an answer, which he gave. But it did little else but leave me ill at ease.

"I have the answer you seek. But are you sure you're ready for it? I'm not proud of what happened. And . . . you may hate me afterwards."

"Did you do it on purpose?" I asked. I was so focused on the "why" that at the moment, I ignored the "how." To this, Father sighed. It was neither exasperated nor merely tolerant, but rather, quiet. I felt a sense of solid resignation settle fully into this thoughts.

"It's not as simple as whether I did it on purpose or not," he said. "There's a story behind this. A sad one, and as I said, one that may make you hate me."

"Hate you . . . ?" I shot my gaze to his pained expression

with wide eyes. "Father I'm certain I won't . . ."

He smiled sadly, and it was that wisdom in his gaze, that very knowing, which silenced me. It was chilling. And as he stood up, it was as if he were a prisoner being led by the guard of his own conscience to his execution.

"It was a sin to keep it from you, Elisa," he said. "Perhaps my greatest sin. And you need to know. I won't hide it from you anymore. Come with me. I'll show you."

I got up and followed Father to the far corner of the sitting room, to one of the alcoves between the bookshelves that housed the lamps.

"I wrote this journal long after it happened," he explained as he pressed what looked to be a screw that fastened the lamp to the wall. "But I never forgot. Everything stayed in my mind clear as day. I left instructions in a will to give it to you with a separate letter apologizing for my indiscretion, should anything happen to me."

I would have protested against any possibility of his death; he had been with us for ten thousand years fighting Lothos, after all. But I was more captivated by what his words entailed. To secure this keepsake for such an unlikely event meant that this was one of his most secret possessions: secret within secret.

The lamp swung to the side to reveal a circular hole lined with metal. He reached inside and removed a small leather-bound notebook, about a century old by my reckoning, judging from the smell of the paper. It seemed, though, that its outer cover and binding appeared brand new.

He placed the book in my hands. It was no bigger than the copy of Alice in Wonderland he'd bought me so long ago, which I kept on my nightstand in my suite. Father did not move from where he stood, and I felt his mind diminish to a mere presence as I brought the book to the grand table in the center of the room.

I sat down and began to read.

DOUBLE-CROSS MY HEART

***

My first memory after the thirst had vanished along with the red haze of madness was the fresh taste of blood in my mouth and the feel of its empowering essence pouring rapidly through my starved veins. The anguish of unknowable time spent in starvation and insanity ebbed away like numbness in a limb that had fallen asleep and was shaken back to wakefulness. Vision cleared.

My second memory was of utter horror and dismay at the sight of my victims upon the floor before me.

My third memory was of rage as that well-known laughter came through the fog of voices and memories, dry and quiet, like a rapid fit of coughs.

Damn you, Lothos! Was my first clear thought after I had assessed everything, and the true scope of what I had done had touched the deepest core of my being. Had I not been so foolishly inattentive that night in London, the Others would not have cornered me, let alone been able to overpower me. I was hardly difficult to miss, dazed and staggering from absinthe and the drug-saturated blood the casual hosts who had accompanied me, weeping over the loss of Eric, my chief general and closest friend for nigh on two centuries. The children of my clan's hated enemy had captured him, tied him to a stake in a forest clearing, and exposed his still young immortal flesh to the full rays of the morning sun. But if I had merely despised Lothos for commanding this act, this sealed my determination to find a way to destroy him.

Bound in chains that even my titanic strength could not break, I was brought before Lothos. Unsurprisingly, my former colleague had yet again not seen fit to attempt to accomplish his heart's desire and kill me. His flair for dramatics and thirst for attention always overpowered him. Still, I was tortured in the only way our kind truly could be.

"Drain him," was Lothos' single command, and I felt my hatred melt into cold, helpless fear. It was not long before the horrifying thirst, worse than the sands of a thousand deserts . . . more painful than ten knives to my gut, erased everything that was me. They had been sure to drain me slowly; Lothos supervised it himself, watching wordlessly as his disciples saw to my agony. There was only his grotesque, elongated smile plastered upon his ebon face as I fell deeper and deeper into starvation and my mind drowned in the rising tide of pain. For an interminable time, with no reserves to sustain me, my body writhed in an endless red haze, where even the oblivion of insanity was not free of pain.

The faces of my victims –I guessed that they were husband and wife– were frozen in a look of hopeless horror even as their blood rendered me strong and restored my senses. Still, appalled as I was to see that I had taken human lives to slake my thirst for the first time in millennia, it was not until I turned my head towards the shadows below a small bed that I realized the full extent of my sins.

By my reckoning, the girl had been perhaps ten or eleven years old. As if in peaceful repose, she lay upon the carpeted floor, clutching what appeared to be the torn remnants of a stuffed bear. Stitched upon its bloodied arm in black threads, I could make out the name, "Elisa."

This was the final straw, the trigger that caused my anguish burst from me. My scream was a frightening sound. The deafening roar from the preternatural strength of my vocal chords shattered the windows as if they were no more solid than thought. Still, through all my wrenching anguish, I could hear the laughter of my nemesis.

He began to call my name. He repeated it in a high, singsong voice, a twisted mimicry of a mother calling her child when she is playing hide-and-seek.

I saw his form appear before me, tall and black as the surrounding shadows from which he rose. His smile was strikingly white against his body, his retracted fangs glinting in the moonlight.

"Talante …" he sang unmercifully. "You are an animal!"

Lothos coldly twisted the last two words of his sentence with a cruel sneer as he gestured to two other figures near the dead adults. They were dressed in night clothes, bloodied by my maddened rage. With the blending of their scents by blood that was loosed upon the floor, it was difficult to tell if they were related to anyone present, even by smell.

"See how you have taken a human life... five, actually, an entire household, including –my word! – A child! So much for your desire to rise above the thing that you are, eh? Whatever shall you do?"

"The beast resides within all of us," I said, more to myself than to Lothos. I squeezed my eyes shut as if it would erase the glaring, inescapable reality of my actions.

My coordination was still not quite perfect, and so I stumbled away from the bodies, wiping the ill-gotten blood from my face. Even in my grief, the smell of it was no less intoxicating, no less enticing. And this reawakened the thought of what I had done, sending my heart to its own personal gallows. Defiantly, I fought against the urge to retch, and instead, allowed my rage to lend strength to my limbs. With preternatural force, I launched myself towards Lothos' throat. To my surprise, he did not resist. Grinning that distended rictus, he bent backwards from the force of my blow which sent us into the wall at the room's far end. He did not move as my fingers pressed against his throat, albeit futilely. As much as I had fed, I had still not fully recovered. I was still uncoordinated, and Lothos, at this moment, was titanic compared to me.

"This is your doing, Lothos! Not mine!" I seethed. "If you thought that this pathetic act would turn me to the darkness, then you're a bigger failure than I thought! If you're here to kill me, then have done with it. But you'll return to your disciples with my words in mind, feeding your hollow victory."

"A hollow victory, you say?" Lothos said, still impervious to my grip upon him. There was an almost childlike curiosity in his voice.

I was surprised to find myself laughing, despite the lack of humor, but nevertheless, I found the wit to press the knife of my words in deeper. "To tell the truth," I managed to say in my mad humor, "I'm surprised you had the courage to do it yourself."

Lothos dissolved in my hand, his substance becoming that of water as my fingers slipped through the liquid darkness he had become. I collapsed onto the floor, and like a living shadow, he re-formed beside me. He lowered himself upon all fours until he was level with my undignified position. The blood was beginning to take effect, and I felt my strength returning with astounding rapidity. I could have tried to kill him again, but even as strong as the blood had made me, I knew that I still had nowhere near the strength to gain the upper hand in a fight against him.

Lothos leaned his ebon face towards my ear and whispered.

"She still lives."

"Liar!" I snapped, but only barely did I believe my words. In fact, I could tell that Lothos was speaking the truth. As twisted as he was, he had never learned to discipline his thoughts. Deceit rang from him all too easily, but he was smart enough to know just how devastating the truth could be.

"Lower your voice please." Lothos was on the edge of laughter, his vague form vanishing into mist and then reappearing behind me. He knew that he was safe and completely in control, and he reveled in my position of near-complete vulnerability. "Children are sleeping!"

How I wished, how I prayed that he was lying. But in the ensuing silence, the sound came to my ears. I could hear it: the child's breathing. It was ragged and hollow, but present, the same as her heartbeat, though this was weak, and rapidly fading.

"Monster ..." I wheezed, no longer able to hide my

combined rage and anguish. "Demon!"

"You flatter me," Lothos replied gaily, while deftly evading my swipe at his left leg. I had lost a great deal of my self-control, as well as my concentration, but still, I wished it had connected; I possessed strength enough to dismember him from the shin down. "But we shall see who is the monster here."

Lothos glided back over to where the child lay. He stroked her long locks of auburn hair with his dark hand. His nails sharpened into claws as they passed over the soft curls. "You can feel it, can't you, Talante? The struggle in her soul to survive? It is the primal drive of all mankind, this will to live, as if nothing but oblivion lies beyond the veil of this life." He paused, relishing the ages-old memory.

"Is that not why we became what we are? All was utter logic to us, purely science. There were no gods, no soul, no afterlife, was there ... or so we believed? My, my, we were so utterly confident, even after our passing into glorious immortality! But seeing this child's valiant, yet futile struggle to hold back the night ... it makes me wonder. It's fascinating, isn't it? Brings out the scientist in you, does it not?"

He stepped fully into the dim moonlight, creating a striking contrast upon the features that he allowed to keep in human guise. "What say you, Talante? Will you desire that this child, deprived of a future by our hands, go quietly into that great beyond?" His silver eyes flashed fiercely, as his fist squeezed a handful of the child's hair. "Or will you deprive the so-called gods of their due?"

I went numb as wood. Lothos and his mad games had driven me to this point, but even I could not deny that it would still be by my hand alone that this child would die undeservingly as another piece of collateral damage in this secret, ages-old war. My heart, pulsing with the combined blood of her and her parents, wrenched with grief, and at the same time flared with hatred deeper than anything that I had felt before for my nemesis. This was his game; it had been nothing more than a perverse test of honor, all of it! My clan took the blood of humans only as necessary nourishment, at the human's discretion, and never at the expense of a life, if we could help it. Children were no longer turned, neither by my clan, nor by Lothos' . . . not after the horrible damage that had been done with those insane experiments. So much needless damage had ensued . . . so much needless suffering. Lothos was merely deriving pleasure at what I had done, amused himself as I, despite the circumstance, contemplated violating one of our clan's most sacred laws.

"Her life is ebbing away," Lothos said, inhaling in almost orgasmic delight, "but she is young and strong! If she dies, you are truly the monster. Yet if you share the gift with her, she will forever be in your care, never aging, and unable to fend for herself. She will be your eternal charge ... your eternal servant."

"And possibly maimed for eternity," I said.

"What's the matter, old friend? You're not a gambling man?" Lothos asked.

"Then why do you not do it?" I said.

"It's more fun this way." Lothos answered with another inhuman smile. "Killer monster if she dies, father monster if you save her. Make your choice."

The girl's heartbeat was failing. I could hear it growing ever weaker, her breath becoming shallow, as death crept ever closer upon her immature form. Already, her skin had become sallow and pale, and her lips were turning an alarming shade of blue. The guilt raked horribly at my soul, and my hatred for Lothos burned hotter. Still, there was no denial of the painful truth of his words. I could save her, and yet in doing so, I would damn her to this material hell, or even worse.

Still, for honor's sake, my choice was clear.

Cursing Lothos and myself, I knelt beside the child, took her into my arms, and began the ritual that I had not initiated in centuries. I punctured my index finger with my teeth, and dripped the blood to her lips. It was unnecessary to drain her any further; thanks to the actions committed under my starvation madness, her body was already prepared for the transformation. So little blood remained, and she was near to death.

The girl swallowed reflexively at the blood I dripped into her mouth. Afterwards, I only needed to wait.

I chafed at Lothos' presence as I saw the girl through the initial pains of the transformation. The poor child; she was so weak that she could only groan as her body changed slowly within her. And as always, the worst of it was saved for the last few moments. Her eyes flew open, already the deep crimson that they would forever afterwards be. Like an aftershock, her body convulsed in the painful spasms of the final stages, twitching as her metabolism shifted and viscera reorganized. Her tiny human canines fell from her mouth and were replaced with the much longer and sharper tools of our trade.

Thankfully, it was brief. The final throes of the change always were, though still agonizing beyond description. The girl slumped in my arms as her pain subsided, sweating, and sleeping with utter exhaustion. It was done. Her life was spared, but her humanity was taken. She would forever be a child, trapped just short of her beginnings of womanhood, and yet both inhuman and immortal as I. But the question remained: was there any damage? Would she be whole? Would she be well?

"Forgive me," I said to her, on the verge of tears after the deed was finished. "Forgive me, child, for what I did to you."

A force like an oncoming train struck me in the face. It sent me careening across the room, and indenting my body into a far wall. With a greater speed than human senses could record, the child was swiped from me.

"You fool!" Lothos sneered in triumph as he towered above me. Partly dazed, I gazed upon him with blurred vision. I saw that he now cradled the child.

There was a hideous glow in his burning crimson eyes. He glared hungrily at his captive, as if her small amount of now-transformed blood would satisfy him. "You and your idealistic clan . . . You're all so predictably noble, Talante, and it has proven to be your weakness."

"No!" I gasped. I tried to rise, but was still winded from the force of the blow and my months-long starvation. "She is my charge! You will not…!"

"She was your charge, my old friend," Lothos gloated as he held the girl tighter to him. "Not that it is of any consolation, but rest assured that she would have joined us in due time. It is only natural that she would. Our destiny is to rule, and to her, there would be no profit in spending eternity in hiding, playing the hero with you to protect her and watch her every step. I, however, will offer no limits to the gift that she has been given. And when my clan comes to rule, even she, in this pathetic form, will be feared by all."

I was still too dazed to retaliate. Collapsing again to the floor, I could only look on helplessly as Lothos backed away into the shadows, slowly taking his leave.

"Still, you may see things in a more positive light come tomorrow night," Lothos continued. "I have let you live, although the embarrassment that I have visited upon you and your clan will be long remembered. But it has given you a new reason to fight, has it not? She is young yet, and her mind is malleable. She may not yet be turned to our side. Therefore, I present a challenge to you. Save her, Talante. Save her, and attempt to nobly bring her back to the light!"

Lothos shrank back into the darkness, his laugh echoing from nothingness.

But then abruptly and inexplicably, it stopped.

Lothos froze. I saw into the darkness of the shadows, but Lothos enjoyed blurring and distorting his features, which he did now, and this made it next to impossible to see him clearly.

I watched this bizarre scene, at first not comprehending.

But then I heard the sound begin: a liquid sucking noise that was all too familiar to me. A familiar scent wafted my way, awakening my ravenous hunger quicker than I could suppress it. Shaking myself to my senses, I noticed that this noise was followed by a short-lived, wheezing gasp. After it ended, the sucking continued.

At last regaining my senses in full, I knelt upright, now aware of what was happening. The shadows divulged Lothos' form and he slumped forward, collapsing onto the floor, motionless. The child, a smaller figure in a bloodstained nightgown, was attached to his head.

Her arms, peppered with red, gripped Lothos' shoulders tightly as she was still enthralled in her feeding. Her soiled falls of curly brown hair completely covered her face. I froze, paralyzed with fascination and revulsion at the thing that this child had become, and marveling over how strong she was to drain Lothos to incapacitation in so short a time. Like me, when it first happened all those endless ages ago, she had no knowledge of how to control and manage her hunger. She would not be able to stop herself from feeding at the cost of her host's life.

There was, of course, no danger of being drained to death for Lothos, but strangely, as much as I seethed with hatred for him, I had no wish to see him rendered weak and starved as I had been. This would have only put more human lives at stake. There would be no more death tonight. And this girl, who was now my charge by right and blood, would have to learn to control herself, even now.

"Forgive me, child," I said once more, "but you will have to learn a painful first lesson." I then reared back my right leg and roughly kicked her off.

She tumbled across the floor, and her right shoulder hit the leg of her bed, bending the iron rail. She cringed and cried out in momentary pain, but then paused, most likely marveling over how quickly the pain had subsided. Then, just as quickly as she stopped, the heavy scent of blood in the air wrenched away her control.

As she leaped forward, ready to re-attach herself to Lothos and resume feeding, I countered, and clutched her in my arms as momentum tossed us through the window. To my chagrin, I discovered too late that the room had been on a third floor.

I repositioned myself in our fall to where I would be the one to hit ground first. To my surprise, we hit the surface of water from a very large fountain. This was a fortunate turn of events; the water would cut the scent of the blood, curtailing her youthful lust.

I swam to the surface, keeping a tight grip upon the girl's arm and brought her up with me. The girl choked and coughed the liquid from her lungs as I brought us to the edge. She was still conscious, but our fall had taken the fight out of her.

"Are you okay?" I said to her, wiping the water from my face as she persisted in her fit of coughing. The question was, of course, rhetorical. We were incapable of drowning; her lungs would have expelled the water, regardless of how much they contained.

For the longest time, she coughed, nearly rendering herself sick as I saw tiny droplets of blood soiling the concrete of the pool's edge. These I quickly wiped away into the water as even the smallest scent of it might trigger her bloodlust anew.

After her coughing fit ended, she began to bawl. Immortal or not, she was a child. Though I had no experience with children, all I knew to do was to comfort her. I took her into my arms and held her while she cried knowing that once she discovered the full truth about what she was and what I had done to her, she would cry even more … and perhaps hate me forever. And I would not blame her, if she chose to side with Lothos.

She fell asleep in my arms, and I took her with me to our clan's local village. After having searched for me for what I learned had been four weeks, my children swept me and the child up in a wave of love and relief.

Back home and safe with my clan and our human friends,

it was there that I discovered that there was indeed some damage. The child had been stricken with amnesia. The change was unusually traumatic for those of her age, and so this was not an uncommon side effect. In fact, it could have been far worse. As far as we could tell, she still had all her mental faculties otherwise.

We covered our tracks well at the house where Lothos had tormented and tempted me; my clan destroyed the bodies of the mother and father, and burnt the building to the ground before daybreak. Not surprisingly, Lothos was nowhere to be found when we arrived, having moved on to find prey to replenish himself. But as if to add insult to injury, his clan had gotten to the personal effects of the child's family first. Some had been burned, I noticed, due to the remnants of the bonfire in the house's courtyard when my children had arrived. Documents, pictures, everything that could have given either myself or her a clue as to her identity, were all ash.

So the girl with no past that I could find, became one of us. The house was a country home, far away from any cities, and we could not find any news about the slaughter, or any news of missing families in the local papers. There was no chance of her regaining her memory, so I took responsibility for her care. In essence, I became her father. My clan became her family, and with no official records of her name, I called her Elisa.

Years have become decades now. Elisa is now an adult, though forever trapped in the body of a child. This curse I bestowed upon her, to never be physically a woman, I must bear upon my soul as heavily as she bears it upon her body. Still, I came to realize the one positive outcome of my sin … and this was the fact that Lothos had been wrong. I had not turned another in so long before that night, that I had forgotten how strong my blood rendered my closest generals. And this strength, I discovered, played no favorites with age.

Elisa has acquitted herself in our ranks as well, or better than others, and showed keen adeptness with our technology.

In time, she has rivaled Aiko, one of my chief thaumaturgists, in skill and creativity. In countless campaigns, she has proven herself a capable fighter, despite the disability of her body.

Still, I live haunted by uncertainty as to whether or not I should tell my daughter of her past, or my part in it. Since the day I took her from her dead family, lacking any memory of them, she has called me "Father." And I have accepted that role in her life. With Roland's help, I devoted as much time as possible to her education and discipline. Having had no children of my own in my human days, and never having bedded my scant human paramours long enough to leave them with child, I found it surprising how I was able to do so well. I love her with all the love a father can give, and she returns that love every day. Yet I live with the fear that Elisa's love for me would be turned into hate, when and if she would learn that it was I who had taken her former life away regardless of circumstance or intentions. Still, I feel that the day may well come that I will be forced to tell.

But perhaps this is merely paranoia.

Perhaps in planting such a seed of doubt, Lothos has won; I cannot know.

Nevertheless, every night I ask myself:
Am I the monster for not telling her?
Or will I be the monster, if I do?

***

I closed the book, and felt numb . . . cold.
It was worse than when I killed Lilly's tormentor.
I opened my mouth, but no words came out. I sat still, waiting, but I was like a mute. There was nothing that could come to my throat, nothing that I could think to say. I felt a pressure building in my head, and was stricken with a feeling of sudden claustrophobia. I slipped out of the chair and stood up, knocking the chair back halfway across the room.
I heard Father say my name, but I couldn't look at him.

I felt repulsed by his presence. It wasn't hatred, but rather, such an overwhelming mix of emotions that stirred within me a consuming compulsion to leave.

I couldn't stay here. I couldn't be near him. It was all true; God, my Father . . . the one who taught me to control my thirst, told me bedtime stories, educated me, and devoted so much of his valuable free time to me . . . he hid this . . . and Lothos, that monster, damn him to the tenth circle of Hell!

"I . . . I have to go . . ." I quavered. I waited just long enough for a response, but Father said nothing. I wasn't even sure if this silence was out of fear, or merely acceptance. I staggered once, regained my bearings and flew out of the room.

I ran blindly through the corridors, more literally blind than figuratively, due to the tears in my eyes.

Perhaps this was the reason why I didn't see Roland, who I ran soundly into.

"P . . . Poppet?" He wheezed, winded but unhurt. And I made no response, at least not first. I only embraced him about his waist, releasing my emotions to the only one who would completely understand. My weeping became a dissonant, wailing sob. I knew my words would come out as incomprehensible gibberish, and so I let my memories retell the story, allowed the theater of my mind play out what I'd read.

"Shit," Roland first drawled out, and then I felt his burst of shame.

"Oh, Poppet . . . I'm so, so sorry." Roland murmured as I wept into his bosom. His love and sympathy was like a blanket as he silently embraced me. He sank to his knees and kissed my forehead -something he had not done since I was still mentally a child. I allowed it; actually, I felt comforted by it. I wiped at the tears and noticed that some bleeding had begun, and so I forced back any more sobs, as much of a chore as it was to do.

"I didn't know, Elisa. I swear it," Roland said with

pleading eyes. His heart was always easy to read, though. I'd know whether or not he was telling the truth in my sleep. And Father had been speaking the truth as well when he admitted that he had told no one about this. "I don't know what to say. The Master . . . he's the one who did it?"

I nodded, and swallowed back the urge to cry that rose again in my throat.

"Yes . . ." I said, my words coming out as ungainly as an acrobat with vertigo. "But Roland . . . don't be angry with him. This is between him and me. In fact, it's probably best if you don't bring it up at all."

"I honestly don't know what to do myself," Roland said, sounding more uncertain that I'd ever heard him before. "What will you do, though?"

"I don't really know either." I sniffled and wiped away the tears, taking care to smear off the blood from my skin. "I'm going to need some time to think."

Roland and I said nothing afterwards; he didn't need to, and I preferred it that way. I only wanted to remain this way for awhile longer, embracing me and being the confidant and comforter he always had been. At this point, I felt especially blessed to have a second "father" in him, even though I never called him such. He had always been Roland to me. I had no mother, and I needed family who was sensitive to my plight. Aiko was wounded, and would most likely be for a very long time; Justin was emotionally distant, and Nandi was too far away to reach. Right now, Roland was doing perhaps the best thing for me: being there.

"What about your fiancé?" Roland finally asked.

"That I can handle," I said with slightly more confidence. "I'll need to go back to him for a bit," I said. "He needs me. I've been away from him for three days; that's not good for . . ."

I paused, realizing that I'd never told Roland the entire story.

"Your consummate host," he said, catching the notion

from me. He grinned. "Good to see happy things are still happening in your life, eh?"

"Yes, it is," I said. And I had to admit I did feel a little better after contemplating that.

"Do you want me to walk with you to your room?"

I shook my head. I would survive this. I wasn't about to fall apart. But right now, I was barely certain about anything.

"Well, love, just remember that I'm always here for you. Now, more than ever. You know that, right?"

"Yes. I know." I embraced him, and we remained that way for several minutes more. I don't know if Roland fully realized just how much strength I drew from him in that gesture, but I was absolutely certain that the coincidence of running into him was better for me than I ever could have imagined.

Somewhat calmer, but far from settled, I walked the rest of the way to my suite. It was in a remote part of the Lair, far away from the more inhabited section of the building, giving me a sense of solitude that I craved.

I froze as I saw Amelia standing beside the door. It was rare to see her in the Lair at all during this time of night; she was usually available when it was nearing dawn, when she would return from teaching in the village school grounds. She seemed worried, and as I approached and caught the timbre of her mind, I knew why.

"He never told you, did he?" I said. I bore her no ill will, but then again, neither did I truly bear any towards Father . . . or at least I hoped. I was still very confused.

Amelia was graceful-looking and swan-like compared to me: tall and with short, raven hair. She was clumsy as a human, but when she was turned, she became a butterfly. She was almost queen-like, though she never seemed to notice the deferential treatment my clan gave her as Father's wife. When she looked at me, I could feel her worry from across the hall.

"No, Elisa," she replied. "I asked him once before he

turned me, when I first met you, but he told me to never ask again."

"That . . . must have hurt," I said. I was genuinely surprised to hear this in spite of what Father's story had told me. "You once said that he shares everything with you."

Amelia shook her head. "Everything but that. I should've known the bottom would drop out sooner or later, but, that's neither here nor there." She sank to her knees, and took my hands. "What about you, honey? Will you be all right?"

I swallowed back the burn of returning tears and steeled myself. I knew that Amelia would have taken me into her arms if I'd let her. I was small enough, even though it would be embarrassing for me, and she would regret having done it later. Truth be told, she was the only one I would have allowed to do that . . . but only if no one was looking.

"I don't know." I said.

"Then it's a start."

"Beg pardon?"

Amelia tapped her forehead. "Elisa, Talante just told me the entire thing. Shocked the hell out of me, him being so silent and reluctant about it, and then dumping the whole story into your head in a fit of grief. He's my husband, so how do you think I feel? I mean, I'm sure he hasn't told me every last one of his secrets, but this . . . . ." She frowned and shook her head with a familiar sense of helplessness. "I can only imagine how you feel. But I can give you some advice."

"What advice?" I asked, curious, as I was usually the one who advised her.

"I can tell you this quote that I learned from my mom: The first step to wisdom is admitting you don't know. So not knowing if you'll be all right is a perfect place to start. Think about it from that point and move on from there. That's what I say."

I nodded. She was right. Still, this was hell. I wasn't sure how this would end, but at least I would start here.

"One more thing," Amelia said. You know that book of

yours? That old copy of Alice in Wonderland you say your Father got for you when you were still really a child?"

"Yes," I said.

"Elisa . . . you know I can tell things about objects with just a touch." She then beamed one of the sweetest and most genuine smiles I'd ever seen from her. "I found it on one of the chairs in the antechamber one night, so I returned it to your room. Honey, you wouldn't believe how much love I sensed from that book, from both you, and Talante. However you came to be one of us, for good or for ill . . . his love for you is as real as it gets."

"Thank you," I said and hugged her. I needed what she said more than she would know, and I was grateful. "Why are you by my room, by the way? I then asked, remembering where we were. "That can't just be coincidence; you normally never come this way."

Amelia laughed softly, and gestured towards the door. An image came into her mind, and my heart swelled as if to try with all its might to force out my storm of emotions.

"I met him in the village," Amelia explained as I unlocked the door with my Jewel. "He was looking for you, and Reanon was with him, like a chaperone or something. She said he'd insisted on seeing you, and then I smelled him. Of course, I know that scent, and when I shook his hand . . . well, let's say I got a lot more information about you two than I needed. So Reanon sort of passed the task of tour guide to me." She grinned when her gaze settled more firmly upon me. "Glad to see you can still smile. That's a good start too."

I gave a genuine smile back, and Amelia gave me a quick hug before taking her leave.

"You two try not to have too much fun," I heard her quip before I stepped inside.

The lights were off, but the moon was still out, giving more than enough illumination, despite its waning state. Regardless of my emotions, it felt good to be back in my room, though things were now forever different. Derek was standing in front of the window beside my bed, silhouetted by the still-bright moonlight, and the scents of my room were mixing with his scent, which was more compelling than any blood.

He turned around and said nothing, only caught me as I ran -then fell- into his arms, my blood, body, and mind surging with the need for what only his presence could satisfy. We had been apart for too long. We were both wounded by our mutual traumas and needed to heal.

When we kissed, it nearly erased everything I had learned.

Nearly.

Chapter Twenty-Four

"... and Marie-Laure was almost tempted to join up with Reanon, but I think her shyness kinda turned her off. She respects assertiveness, you know, so she didn't think they'd get along, head scientist or not. But the good news is that Deb is seriously considering staying behind. I don't mean that I'm happy to see her go, of course. But it's a gain for your clan, right? I also know you said the baby would have training to survive with us, so it's probably the best option. And Deb's pretty attached to her. She'd make a good mother, with all she's kept that baby through. That way we can get back on the road much sooner, and the baby can be kept safely with your clan. Oh, and you'll be happy to know that we did decide on a name for her. I let Deb pick it out; it's only fair, after all. So it's Rhonda. And speaking of Deb, she says she wants to talk to you as soon as you can. Something about holding you to a promise?"

As Derek continued to update me on his clan's state of affairs, I could not help but stare with dismay at the wounds my fangs left on his body. They shouldn't have been there. To see them still open as they were was terribly unnerving. Thankfully, though, they weren't bleeding out. He still hadn't fully healed, though; he must really have had quite a row with the sickspray despite my having siphoned out so much of it.

I ran my finger gingerly over the mark that I'd made near his armpit and frowned.

"Don't say you're sorry, China doll."

Derek had paused in his story, and I caught him looking at me with understanding. I felt his chest rise and fall as he sighed. "It wasn't your fault, and you know it." He ran his hand through my curls and down my neck.

"You shouldn't have come all the way here," I said. "You needed more time to heal."

"I'll live," Derek answered with a sideways grin. "'Sides, it kinda tingles. Tingles in a good way, I mean. My metabolism's still a little wonky, so it makes the toxins have a longer effect. And after all those times you fed . . . well, I was knocking on heaven's door, to tell the truth."

"You should have stayed at the bungalow," I said, insistent and immune to his levity. "I was on my way back tonight."

"So you weren't happy to see me?" Derek asked. His voice and thoughts were laced with every bit of the cheekiness I expected from him. "Especially after all you've been through? You sure as hell didn't act unhappy. He glanced at the alarm clock on my night stand and chuckled. "Three hours of unhappy? Could've fooled me."

He was certainly right about that. Right now was about as perfect and as complete as we could ever feel, together, having indulged ourselves in each other's blood, having had our fill of each other in other ways, and with scents and minds merged. I giggled, and searched out the sheets for his hand. He, instead, found mine.

"Of course I was, happy, you silly man." I wrapped my arms about his midsection and let our contact submerge our minds into that comforting, familiar place where we felt like nothing could harm us, where every concern was in a place of oblivion. "I just worry about you. And I left you that note."

"I needed you," he said.

His words re-ignited a vague shadow of the flame that drove us into the bed earlier, and I kissed his chest. I let my lips travel near to his throat, but I dared not take another drink until he was completely well.

"As did I," I replied, whispering with passion. I smiled at the rise of goosebumps I felt in his flesh. "And today, that need was almost unbearable.

"Then you know how I felt," Derek said.

He was right. We were attached to each other, addicted and entwined in an inescapable bond. Our souls fed each other where blood could not, though we needed that component as well. And the consummation of that bond was a heaven that neither of us could deny. So we lay there in full contact, sinking ourselves into that bliss for as long as time allowed, safe for now, from our mutual demons and worries.

"You know, you never did tell me how you managed to break free when Lothos had you," I said after quite some time. "When did he take hold of you, anyway?"

"Oh. That."

I felt Derek cringe inside, felt his reluctance to return to that moment in the past, which I was certain was difficult for him. He was still ashamed of having had to deceive me. But I understood his gambit, and was not angry. I reassured him of this through our hearts, and his courage steeled itself.

"You've probably already guessed it, but I have a very strong mind," he explained, "much stronger than most folks realize. It's why I was able to hide my thoughts from you so well. And it was also how I was able to put you to sleep so easily. It shouldn't have been that easy, am I right?"

"That was the biggest shock," I said. "No one has been able to take over my mind like that before. Even the puppeteer couldn't take me when she tried."

"Now you know," Derek said with some bemusement in his tone. "My mind was much stronger than even Lothos or his mind-readers knew. Lyman said I was something of a prodigy when he started giving me some training. When I escaped Lothos, I knew it had been too easy. Now that you know that he was consummately bonded to me, you can see that he wouldn't have given up on me that quickly. I was relieved when I joined Syd's clan, and met Lyman. Being a mind-reader, he could detect what Lothos did to me. He taught me to put myself in trances and look inwards to dig it out, but whoever Lothos used was damn good at his work. We managed to get most of the programming undone, though. If we hadn't done that much, Lothos would've been able to operate me by remote control, like the puppeteer. Instead, he used long distance with the aid of a Jewel, and reactivated what was left of it."

"When did that happen?" I asked. "His . . . 'reawakening,' or at least his attempt?"

"When I was in the bathroom at the hotel," Derek replied. And it all made sense. "You'd just gone outside, and I felt it. I saw Lothos's reflection in the mirror. He said something to me. I don't remember much of it, but I knew he wanted me back. And because I was in my right mind when it was over, I knew he hadn't gotten to me like he wanted. But I could feel it growing, taking me over little by little. I knew it would activate later, as if I were some kind of sleeper agent. But the slowness of it gave me time. So I made plans, both with Wadih, with my orders, and with you, in the form of my instructions, right before you went to sleep."

"Your instructions," I said. "What you told Lothos in that cell . . . it made me remember."

"Thank God it worked," Derek said, and slipped his arms around me as a distant sense of fear wafted through our souls from his heart. "Lothos took over just as I planted that suggestion in your mind to make you sleep, right after I kissed you. I had just enough time to hide the ring in between space. When Lothos took me over fully, I'd set a part of myself in a trance, where I could work at it from the inside, eroding its foundations until I could break free. It took two weeks, and it was just a coincidence that it happened while I was in the cell with you. I would never have a more perfect moment, so I said the trigger words that I implanted in you."

"I wish you were dead," I murmured, repeating the phrase that awoke that nagging almost-memory, and returned the recollection of my ring to me.

"I like how Marie-Laure put it when I explained it to her," Derek said. "'He hacked me, so I hacked myself back.'"

"It was properly brilliant," I admitted, and smiled. "And it paid off."

"Thankfully," Derek spoke the word in an impassioned whisper as he hoisted me forward and closed the gap between our lips. I should have been satisfied now, but as we separated, a new, vague sense of worry accosted me.

"Did he . . . hurt you while you were under his control?" I asked tentatively. And we both wished instantly that I hadn't. My question triggered a flood of memory unbidden. And the things I saw made me cling onto him more tightly, shuddering.

"It's not pleasant, I know," Derek said, holding me as tightly as I did once the memories faded. "If you weren't here, I'd probably be dealing with some serious PTSD episodes."

"Are you sure you'll be okay?" I asked.

"As long as I'm with you, sweetie," Derek replied, and I felt his smile without even needing to look. "But what about you? Will you be okay?"

I looked into his eyes. I knew the sun would be coming up soon, perhaps in about an hour and a half. The faintest of light that only our kind could see was on the horizon, giving the very first ghosts of illumination to the starry sky. The sun shutters would close, and we would soon fall asleep.

I wanted so badly to say that I would be okay . . . that I would live down the devastating tale that I read in that small journal, and that I would love Father again as I'd always loved him, as if things had never changed between us. But I could not say that with any honesty. Would things ever be the same? That was the maddening part. He did this to me, yet he saved my life. He gave into a perverse test of honor, yet he rescued me . . . yet it cost me the life I knew in every possible way.

"I don't rightly know," I said at last, deflated and more frustrated than I thought I'd ever be. Derek had waited awhile for my response, but he had been patient. Our bond was a blessing in that regard; we both understood each other in a way deeper than any non-telepathic lovers did. "It's . . . he . . . He's my Father, Derek. My Father! And he did this to me."

"Lothos challenged his honor. And you were dying."

"He saved my life by taking it from me!"

"But he was there with you every step of the way with your new life, wasn't he?"

"Yes."

I drew in a shuddering breath, on the edge of tears yet again. But I'd had enough of that. I could not let this reduce me to such a state. Not knowing what to do was a start, but I had to move on from that.

I just didn't know how.

"Elisa, answer me this." Derek pushed himself up to a sitting position against the headboard and I did the same, leaning upon his shoulder. His wounds were now almost completely healed.

"What if the shoe was on the other foot? What if it was your Father who was the one nearly dying, and you could have saved him, risk of damage and all. What would you do?"

And there was the next step for me. Though I was loath to take it. Derek, so insightful, so caring, yet so inconvenient with his truth.

"I . . . would . . . probably . . . have done the same thing." I barely whispered it, but Derek heard me.

"Your father loves you a lot," Derek said. "That was one thing I knew right off the cuff when he came to visit. You didn't need to read his mind to know that. You were all he could talk about. When he learned about us, he was happy . . . ecstatic, I think. I can't imagine how much it hurt him to have to reveal this to you, on what should have been one of the happiest days of your life and his. But he did, because he loves you. You know this. Roland knows this. And I'm going out on a limb here, but because I kind of overheard your conversation outside, I'm pretty sure Amelia knows this. I'm not trying to belittle how devastating this whole deal is to you, and to add to it everything that you and I went through. But I think you know what you'll eventually need to do."

My response came after another lengthy pause.

"I know. I know everything you say is true. But . . . At the very least, I can't stay here, Derek, not after tonight. I need time to sort this all out. I need to heal. I need to . . ." I grasped his arm and pressed my face against his slender bicep. "I just need time for us. Just . . . just us."

"So you've changed your mind about the wedding?"

I could feel Derek's burgeoning disappointment, but I assuaged it when I shook my head.

"No, love. Not at all. Never in a million years! I just need for us to be away for a time. We're pretty much married anyway."

Derek let out a soft chuckle. "I suppose you're right about that."

I sighed, hating myself for appearing this way before him. I'd never felt such conflict in spite of the healing closeness to my consummate host and mate. I turned away from him and scowled.

"I'm a wreck."

Immediately, Derek touched his finger to my chin and turned my gaze back towards him.

"You're beautiful."

"You've seen the worst of me," I retorted.

"You've seen the worst of me . . . And I've also seen the best of you."

"Dammit, Derek!" My words came in a harsh whisper as I rose to my knees and pressed my palms into his cheeks. He gazed at me, surprised, but not offended. "How can you want me?"

He took me by my wrists and removed my hands. He placed them onto his lap and took my face in his hands.

"I'll always want you," he whispered, reaffirming his promise. "Forever."

I kissed him. I let our closeness ease my pain and confusion once again. I felt it disintegrate, like a sand castle caught in the incoming tide.

"You know . . . I know this place," he managed to say between the connections of our lips. "It's kind of lawless, but it's great for just getting away from it all."

"A Vagabond hideout?" I asked, pausing, despite the lengthening of our fangs.

"Sort of. It's like one of your villages, though no one really owns it. Vagabonds go in and out. It was established not too long after the war got carried to the New World. It's in the Atacama Desert, away from prying eyes and most of the fighting."

"I think I've heard of that place," I said, recalling some rumors in a few South American villages. "And yeah, it's pretty lawless, from what I heard."

"But I don't think you have anything to worry about," Derek said. "They give thaumaturgists a wide berth, so you're unlikely to find anyone looking for trouble. Though you may have to kick an ass or two to make a statement."

I laughed. "You make it sound so romantic."

"It's actually the perfect place for our kind who want to escape prying eyes, or just be out of everybody's way. They've got nice underground grottoes that they've converted into hot springs, and lots of fresh blood incoming every day. While my clan cools its heels here, you and I could . . . take a little trip? Get out of everybody's hair for awhile and get our heads straight? What do you say?"

"It sounds better than I'd hoped," I replied. "It's a novel idea, love. I'm glad you could make me feel so much better."

"Well, there are more ways than just this," Derek purred, and ended his sentence with another kiss.

It was then that I realized that the recent events, tragic, confusing, and traumatizing though they were, had served to take my focus from all my blessings, chief among which was the fact that my mission had been an unqualified success. The Vagabonds had made it to safety, and baby Rhonda was safe and with Deb as her surrogate mother, would join our clan. They would both have a potentially happy and productive life ahead of them. Derek was an added bonus, and one that I would treasure for as long as I lived. I just needed time to let the wounds of this mission heal. I was so glad that Derek had understood this even before me.

Later, as the sun shutters closed and Derek and I prepared to sleep, he asked me a question.

"We'll still be married in the village, right, China Doll? Is that still what you want?"

I smiled. The answer had come easily. "Yes."

THE END

ABOUT THE AUTHOR

I am a native of Louisiana and current resident of Lafayette. An avid and frequent reader of science fiction and fantasy, I began writing in the eleventh grade. I am a graduate of McNeese State University in Lake Charles. I am a 'classic nerd' and prolific writer who has had dreams of authorship since childhood. I sketch perhaps even more prolifically than I write, and have drawings of just about every character my warped imagination has come up with. I hope to continue sharing these ideas, characters, and stories with others for years to come.